RISE OF THE EMPRESS

Content Warning

This book contains dark fantasy themes, violence and point-of-view depictions of trauma. Reader discretion is advised.

RISE OF THE EMPRESS

JULIE C. DAO

PENGUIN BOOKS

UK | USA | Canada | Ireland | Australia
India | New Zealand | South Africa | China

Penguin Random House Australia

Penguin Random House Australia is part of the Penguin Random House group of companies whose addresses can be found at global.penguinrandomhouse.com.

First published as *Forest of a Thousand Lanterns* by SPEAK, an imprint of Penguin Random House LLC, in 2017
This edition published by Penguin, an imprint of Penguin Random House Australia Pty Ltd, in 2026

Cover design by Adam Laszczuk © Penguin Random House Australia Pty Ltd
Internal design by Jennifer Chung
Typeset in Fairfield LT Std

Printed and bound in Australia by Griffin Press, an accredited ISO AS/NZS 14001 Environmental Management Systems printer

NATIONAL LIBRARY OF AUSTRALIA
A catalogue record for this book is available from the National Library of Australia

FSC www.fsc.org
MIX
Paper | Supporting responsible forestry
FSC® C018684

ISBN 978 1 76135 926 2 (Paperback)

We at Penguin Random House Australia acknowledge that Aboriginal and Torres Strait Islander peoples are the Traditional Custodians and the first storytellers of the lands on which we live and work. We honour Aboriginal and Torres Strait Islander peoples' continuous connection to Country, waters, skies and communities. We celebrate Aboriginal and Torres Strait Islander stories, traditions and living cultures; and we pay our respects to Elders past and present.

The first one's for you, Mom, for all your love and support

FOREST OF A THOUSAND LANTERNS
CAST OF CHARACTERS

THE VILLAGE

- Xifeng (SHE-fung)
- Guma, *Xifeng's aunt* (GOO-ma)
- Mingzhu, *Xifeng's mother* (ming-JHOO)
- Hou, *Xifeng's family name* (ho)
- Wei, *Xifeng's lover* (way)
- Ning, *Guma and Xifeng's hired girl* (neeng)

TRAVELS

- Shiro, *Ambassador of Kamatsu* (shee-ro)
- Hideki, *Kamatsu soldier* (hee-deh-kee)
- Ken, *Kamatsu soldier* (ken)
- Isao, *Katmatsu soldier* (eeh-sow)
- *Tengaru* Queen (teng-GAR-roo)
- Akira, *Imperial City physician* (ah-kee-rah)

THE PALACE

ROYALS

- Emperor Jun, *Emperor of Feng Lu, Empress Lihua's second husband* (jhoon)
- Empress Lihua, *Empress of Feng Lu* (lee-HWA)

- **Crown Prince**, *Empress Lihua's first son, Commander of the King's Army*
- **Second Prince**, *Empress Lihua's second son, an impulsive warrior*
- **Third Prince**, *Empress Lihua's third son, weak and sickly*

LADIES/CONCUBINES

- **Madam Hong**, *Empress Lihua's head lady-in-waiting* (hoeng; long "o")
- **Lady Sun**, *the Emperor's favorite concubine* (swuhn)
- **Lady Meng**, *a childless concubine* (mung)

EUNUCHS

- **Master Yu**, *chief eunuch of the Imperial Palace* (yuh)
- **Kang**, *Xifeng's faithful eunuch companion* (kong)

OTHER CHARACTERS

- **Bohai**, *the Imperial Physician* (BO-hi)
- **Koichi**, *Shiro's son* (ko-eeh-chee)

THE DRAGON LORDS' WORLD

- **Feng Lu**, *the continent* (fung loo)
- **The Dragon King / Lord of the Forest**

  Dominion: Kingdom of the Great Forest

  Element: Wood
- **Lord of the Sea**

  Kingdom of the Boundless Sea / Kamatsu (kah-maht-soo)

  Element: Water

- **Lord of the Desert**

  Kingdom of the Shifting Sands / Surjalana (SOOR-jah-LAH-nah)

  Element: Fire

- **Lord of the Four Winds**

  Kingdom of the Four Winds / Dagovad (DAH-go-VAHD)

  Element: Metal

- **Lord of the Grasslands**

  Kingdom of the Sacred Grasslands

  Element: Earth

1

The procession stretched down the cobblestone road, a serpent made of men in red and gold, the Emperor's colors. They marched forward, ignoring the slack-jawed townspeople gaping at the banner they carried: a dragon with a forest curled within its talon, the emblem of the royal house. A palanquin draped in scarlet silk appeared, resting on the shoulders of four men. People craned their necks to see the occupant, but caught only a tantalizing glimpse through the swaying curtain: blood-red lips, golden blossoms in shining hair, and robes that cost more than any of them would see in a lifetime.

"Another day, another concubine." A bent old woman bared the three teeth she had left. "It seems he has a taste for pretty village girls. May blessings rain down upon him," she added hastily, in case a soldier heard her criticize their sovereign.

"He must not discriminate by class when it comes to beauty," another woman agreed. She was not as old as the first, but she was just as bent. Most of her weight rested on her good leg, while the other hung crookedly, like a dead branch. Her shrewd gaze moved from the procession to the girl beside her.

She was not the only one looking at this girl. More than one soldier admired her as he marched by.

The girl wore tattered, faded clothing like everyone else. But she had a face like a painting: a perfect oval, with lotus lips blooming beneath a sweet stem of a nose. She appeared docile, virginal, but the eyes she lifted told a different story with their sparkle of intelligence. They were the kind of eyes that flashed from the shadows of a darkened room.

"He must not discriminate," the woman said again. "What do you say to that, Xifeng?"

"I wish the Emperor joy, Guma. She must be special indeed if he chose her for his own," the girl said respectfully, even as her coal-black eyes burned.

At the palace, slaves would bathe the young concubine's feet in orange flower water. Every inch of her would smell like jasmine, and when the Emperor put his lips on her skin, he would know nothing of her hardship and poverty—the same hardship and poverty that coated Xifeng like sweat.

"She is no more special than you." There was no love in Guma's statement, just fact. But they were mere words, ones she had said for years. She shuffled closer and hooked a claw-like hand around Xifeng's elbow. "Come. It may be silks and riches for *her,* but it's back to the needles for us. Tonight, we will read the cards again," she added as gently as she ever could.

Xifeng knew these rare glimpses of kindness from her aunt could be swept away the next minute by a dark mood. So she inclined her head in a show of grateful obedience, picking up the basket containing their meager purchases, and the pair trudged back home.

They lived a short distance from the center of town—rather a grand term for a muddy square. There, ragged farmers and crones with more brains than teeth hawked wares that had seen better days: maggoty vegetables, cracked pottery, dull knives, and cheap hemp fabric.

It had rained the night before, a torrential downpour of early spring that would be good for the rice and crops but had turned all else into a pungent soup of mud and debris. A few scrawny chickens ran by, a trail of droppings streaking behind them, as a woman emerged from a soggy cottage to scream at her brats.

Some days, Xifeng thought she would gladly watch this town burn. She ached to leave it all behind and never look back. To think she was trapped here forever, while the Imperial palanquin carried that other girl straight into the Emperor's swan-feathered bed.

She felt Guma's sharp eyes on her and took care to keep her face neutral. To show discontent was to rebuke her aunt for all the sacrifices she had made. After all, Guma had not been required to raise the bastard daughter of a sister who had shamed their family and killed herself. And despite being eighteen, Xifeng knew any small sign of displeasure would earn her a dozen stripes with the bamboo cane. She flinched inwardly, thinking of the scars on her back that had just begun to heal.

And then there he was, walking toward them, as though her thoughts had conjured him.

Wei. The reason for those scars.

His proud, shaven head was turned away, watching the innkeeper across the street argue with a customer. His features were sharper in profile, brutal and beautiful, and the other men gave him a wide berth as he cut through the crowd. With his shoulders like a bull, bare arms that rippled with muscle, and ferocious storm of a gaze, he was the living embodiment of war. But those large, capable hands, which now carried a stack of rusted swords to be repaired—Xifeng knew how gentle they could be. She remembered how they had felt on her skin and struggled not to shiver at the memory of it, because Guma's clever eyes were still watching to see her reaction.

"What would you like for supper?" Xifeng kept her voice steady, as though she didn't know the man approaching them at all.

Wei faced forward. He had noticed them now; her skin prickled with his awareness. She wondered if he would say something. He had an idea that because he was physically strong and Guma weak, he could overpower her and free Xifeng from her control forever. But there were different kinds of strength, and provoking Guma to release hers was the last thing they would want.

She patted her aunt's tense arm as though there were no one else dearer to her in the world. "I could make a soup of these prawns. Or I could fry the turnips, if you prefer."

And then the moment passed. Wei walked by without a word. Xifeng reserved her sigh of relief to release later when she was in the kitchen, alone.

"Do the prawns," Guma said calmly. "They're already beginning to smell."

A few steps more, and they arrived home.

Xifeng's grandparents had once owned the entire building with its handsome dark oak façade and imposing doors carved with a phoenix rising. They had been successful tailors before the war, and Guma and her younger sister, Mingzhu, had grown up here. Xifeng found it more difficult to imagine Guma as a child than to picture the splendor that had long worn off these faded walls.

Despite the poor condition of the place, they had managed to rent the downstairs to a couple as a teahouse. Guma and Xifeng lived on the drafty upper floors with Ning, the girl they had hired to help them sew and embroider. She was waiting for them by the door, and though she was fifteen and scrawny, the glance she gave Wei's hard, retreating back was that of a woman. It was not the first time Xifeng had caught her gawking at him, but she had never seen the girl's longing so raw and sharp. She could practically feel the waves of lust radiating off her.

Xifeng felt something growl deep inside.

But before she could do or say anything, Guma released her arm and cracked a vicious slap across Ning's face. "What are you doing there? I don't pay you to stand idling and ogling," she snapped as the girl touched her reddened cheek and sniffled. "Get back upstairs."

Ning turned wet eyes to Xifeng before obeying, and though a note of pity rose up inside Xifeng, she remained silent. She knew that slap had been meant for *her,* but she had hidden her emotions so well that Guma had to vent her violence on the hired girl, like a teapot with built-up steam. She watched Ning slouch upstairs, both feeling sorry for her and thinking she deserved it if she thought she could steal Wei for herself.

But Xifeng's relief was short-lived. Guma grasped her arm again, pinching hard enough to leave a bruise. Her face had begun to wrinkle like a rotting pear, making her appear much older than her forty years. "Don't think I don't know you want the same thing from him," she hissed, her sour breath filling Xifeng's nostrils. "Don't think I don't know you still sneak around, no matter how many times I pull out that cane."

Xifeng kept her eyes down, biting the inside of her cheek at the pain of Guma's fingernails, hatred boiling within her. No matter how hard she worked and how obediently she behaved, she received only scorn and beatings in return.

"He's not good enough for you, do you understand? You deserve better." And though one hand still gripped Xifeng's arm, the other gently stroked her cheek.

That simple gesture, one a mother might make toward her daughter, dissolved the hatred in an instant. Xifeng leaned into her touch, forgetting the pain.

"Now help me upstairs, child."

The upper level had always seemed an endless labyrinth to Xifeng, even now as a grown woman. Once, these chambers had been full of purpose. Dried flowers still littered the floor of one room, where years ago they had hung from the rafters above vats of boiling water, ready to be made into fabric dyes. Across the hall, wisps of thread still clung to abandoned looms, unwilling to relinquish the past. The large room at the back had housed an army of hired girls, whose quick, clever hands had embroidered endless lengths of silk for noblewomen.

But those days were long gone. Nowadays, they used only four rooms: two for sleeping, one for cooking, and one for eating and sewing. She led Guma to a stool in this last room, where Ning sulked and hemmed a square of cotton with blue-dyed thread.

"Mind your stitches," Xifeng told her, earning a baleful glare.

Ning had come from one of the coastal villages, reeking of fish and poverty. Guma had hired her when she saw what she could do with a needle. Since then, the girl had become Xifeng's shadow, the irritating younger sister she'd never had. Ning followed her, asking questions and imitating her movements, the way she spoke, and the style in which she arranged her hair. But there was a sense of competition, too, and Xifeng suspected the girl's interests had shifted from trying to impress Guma to making Wei look at her the way he looked at Xifeng.

Ning darted a frightened glance at her, and Xifeng realized she had been staring. She turned away, draping a length of pale pink silk over Guma's lap.

For weeks, they had been embroidering plum blossoms all over the fabric. Her aunt had sneered at the choice of color and design, which belied the humble origins of the lady who had commissioned the tunic for a banquet. Truly well-bred women preferred silks dyed darker colors, which cost more. But Xifeng thought wistfully that she would wear the cheapest of silks if it meant she too could enjoy herself at some festival.

"Go prepare the meal, and don't be long about it," Guma told her crossly. "We need to finish this in two days, and you've wasted too much time gawking at the new concubine."

Xifeng held her tongue at this injustice. It was Guma who had wanted to wait for the procession on this chilly spring morning, so she could compare her niece with the new addition to the Imperial harem.

"Was she beautiful?" Ning asked timidly.

"Of course," Guma snapped, though she hadn't seen any more of the woman than anyone else. "Do you think the Emperor would choose an ugly girl like you to bear his children?"

Xifeng turned to hide her smile and carried the basket down the hall. Guma was right. Wei would *never* look at such a plain, moon-faced girl. Not when he had *her.*

But Ning didn't choose to look the way she does, Xifeng thought, with another twinge of pity. *Any more than I did.* She put a pot of water on to boil, gazing at her own reflection.

She had seen that face every day for eighteen years in the washbasin. She never needed to open her mouth. She never needed to do much. All it took was stepping out with that face, and she would get a wink from the innkeeper, the best cut of meat from the butcher, and a pretty bead or two from the tradesmen in the square. One of them had even given her a pomegranate once. Wei had been furious when she told him, and would have made her throw it away if she hadn't already brought it home to Guma.

"I don't ask for these things," she had protested, comparing it to his natural-born talent for metalworking. The town craftsman had hired him because he could shape a beautiful sword from the ugliest bronze. But still, Wei had been gruff and grim and unwilling to understand.

Perhaps the Emperor's new concubine had been born with a face like hers. Lovelier, even, since it had won her a home in the Imperial Palace.

The water began to boil, and Xifeng turned away bitterly to season the prawns. She sliced the last of the ginger and scallions, hoping their client would be satisfied with the pink silk and pay immediately. They couldn't afford more vegetables until then, and eating plain rice—something they'd had to do many times in the past—always put Guma in a fearsome temper.

Xifeng carried the meal into the front room. They ate in peace, interrupted only once by Guma criticizing how she had cooked the prawns, and then worked until the sun went down.

She recited poetry as she worked, something Guma always required her to do. Her aunt had drummed into her head that poetry, calligraphy, and music marked a well-born lady, and so she had endured many a sleepless night to study. She would have resented it, had it not proven that Guma wanted and *expected* a better life for her.

The moon shines down upon us, beloved

The water a vast and eternal mirror

A voice whispers from every tender branch

Turn your face from the world's apple-blossom fragility

And embrace this boundless night

Guma paused in the midst of stitching a plum blossom petal, her nostrils flaring. "Where did you learn that?" she demanded.

"From one of your volumes." Xifeng gestured to a dusty stack of faded texts in the corner, the meager remnants of her mother's and aunt's school days. She often marveled at the wealth her grandparents had possessed, to have afforded such things for mere daughters.

"Show it to me."

The tone of her aunt's voice made her put down the needle immediately. Xifeng located the volume, one thinner and newer than the rest, and presented it to the older woman. Guma examined it, lips thinning as she ran her fingers over the unembellished back and turned it over to look at the title: *Poems of Love and Devotion.*

She hastily shoved the book back at Xifeng, as though it had burned her fingers. "Ning, isn't it time you went to bed?"

Xifeng kept looking at her aunt as the girl put away her work and lit the red tallow candles. She hadn't realized the sun had set until she felt the candlelight relieve her strained eyes. As soon as Ning was gone, she asked, "Did the poem remind you of something, Guma?"

Her aunt spoke often about the past—mostly to complain about the riches she had then that she didn't have now—but rarely mentioned her sister. All Xifeng knew of her mother was what she had been told only once: that Mingzhu had been beautiful and brainless and had gotten herself pregnant and abandoned by a nobleman. The pinched expression on Guma's face suggested she was thinking of her now, but when she spoke, it had nothing to do with her.

"I know that poem. It was . . . told to me many years ago." She licked her dry lips, her gaze flickering from the text to her niece with something like terror.

Xifeng had seen that fear twice in her life: once, when Guma had hobbled home in a frenzy to shut all of the doors and windows without explanation, and again after she had woken from a nightmare of spiraling black snakes.

There was a long silence.

"It's time to read the cards," Guma said.

2

There was another room on that upper level, one of which they never spoke. It had once stored valuable tools: vats for cooking dyes, bamboo dowels for drying fabric, and boxes of needles, thread, and scissors. Guma had once made a bitter remark that her parents must be rolling in their graves now that she had turned it into a sanctuary for her unspeakable craft.

Not so very long ago, the Hou family had been tailors of rare and cunning skill with clients from across the continent of Feng Lu. Desert dwellers journeyed endless miles, bearing cobweb-thin silks to be woven into veils against the sun. Hunters brought furs down from the mountains for hoods and cloaks, telling tales of beasts the flatland folk had only heard of through legend.

Fanciful stories spread of how the Hou tailors would stitch in luck and goodwill if one paid well; underpay, and they took revenge by weaving in an impossible-to-satisfy itch, a harelip for one's firstborn, or a jealous husband. Guma's parents coyly courted these rumors, which brought in money for feasts and music lessons for their daughters, but took care to dismiss the gossip when asked directly. It would not do to own up to such abilities, not when family members had been executed for less in the past. A streak of magic had plagued the Hou blood for centuries, one that only recent generations had managed to suppress through willpower and discipline.

"Hypocrites," Guma sneered whenever she spoke of her parents, "denying the very gift that brought them their fame." Where the rest of her family had sought to curb and smother their magic, Guma embraced it with religious fervor.

Now, Xifeng followed her into the room, each of them carrying a tallow candle. It was so small, they barely fit inside together, but Guma had managed to squeeze in all she needed for her secret trade. Dried plants dangled from the ceiling, polluting the air with a venomous odor, and carvings and oddly shaped rocks covered the walls. On a crooked shelf lay a collection of rusted knives and bowls stained with vile fluids. And in the center of this dark den was a blood-spattered table, beneath which Guma had hidden her most treasured possessions.

She spread the contents of a small oak box on the table as Xifeng watched: nineteen rectangles of fine yellow wood, depicting images in burgundy-black ink. They showed emperors and empresses, crowned dragons, barren rice fields, and a monk raising a skull above his head. Xifeng could not read them herself, but she knew they concealed depths of meaning, each layer of truth peeling back to reveal an even more convoluted answer. And the messages shifted again when combined with other cards.

As she studied the images, her aunt limped around the room, lighting more candles and a large pot of incense. With the door closed, the poison-sweet fumes wrapped curls of thick, heady fragrance around her. Xifeng hated the smell, which made her light-headed and prone to strange dreams while awake, but Guma insisted on the incense for every reading. Whether it was because she enjoyed Xifeng's discomfort or needed the scent for her art, she never made clear.

The foreign deck of cards had come to Guma many years ago. Since then, she had given up the traditional wooden sticks preferred by most seers, favoring blood truth. She had taught Xifeng that the spirits of magic were reluctant to release answers without a blood sacrifice first.

Guma shuffled the cards and turned them facedown, reaching for a knife. Seizing Xifeng's left hand, she flipped the palm upward and sliced the base of her index finger. Xifeng did not flinch when the blade bit into her flesh, knowing how Guma detested weakness. The incense seemed to help, blurring the pain as a line of blood spilled randomly across several cards.

Guma turned the bloodied rectangles over with a smile. These were the same six images the spirits selected for Xifeng whenever the cards drank her blood. And drink they did, for the droplets had already begun sinking into their grain.

"I told you," her aunt gloated, tapping the first card, which showed a withered field. Beside it, the second card depicted a steed with a sword embedded in its heart. "The barren rice field means hopelessness, unless paired with the horse as it is here. When the spirit is gone, the body nourishes the empty earth. You are resourceful. You will find a way around hopelessness, and create something out of nothing."

More familiar words. More promises of talent, of a greatness Xifeng longed for desperately but could not find inside her, no matter how hard she looked.

She worried her lip between her teeth, bending over the horse card to hide her doubt from Guma. The point at which the blade entered the steed's body seemed to gleam. She imagined its heart bursting upon impact, the lifeblood spilling from its body, and felt the urge to lower her lips and drink before it was wasted.

Lifeblood, the essence of the heart, contained the most powerful magic in the world. Guma had taught her to revere the heart, for even that of an animal was enough to perform complex spells. Depending on the skill of the wielder, one could summon and communicate with others who knew this forbidden magic, or even cast a glamour over oneself to compel and attract.

Xifeng moved on to the next two cards. One showed a lotus opening beneath the moon, and the other displayed a man with a dagger in his back, shreds of flesh clinging to the blade.

"Fate finds you alluring," Guma said, tapping the lotus, "but do not be fooled. It is you who are its slave. Let no one stand in your way. If they face you, your beauty will entrap them. If they turn away, you will stab them in the back."

A scowl creased Guma's face when she saw the fifth card. On it, a handsome warrior rode into battle with a bloodstained chrysanthemum, a keepsake from his lady. The slope of his shoulders was like Wei's, and Guma pushed the image away without comment. This card was the reason she didn't punish Xifeng more severely for seeing Wei, for it foretold that he would play some important role in Xifeng's life, whether her aunt liked it or not. The bamboo cane stung but did not stop them from meeting in secret, and Guma knew it.

Sacrifice.

The word seemed to echo in the darkness as Xifeng studied the warrior's bloody flower. That was the meaning of this card, Guma had explained once. A relinquishing of something—or *someone*—dear, as payment for greatness. Xifeng tore her eyes from it, unwilling to think just now about what or whom she might have to lose.

And there it was again: the sixth card, showing the back of a woman's head, uncrowned, the dark spill of her hair like a stain.

"The Empress," Xifeng said.

Guma watched her through narrow eyes as she took in her future. This card reigned above all others; this sliver of wood showed Xifeng's true destiny. *This* was the greatness for which she would have to pay. An undeniable energy hummed through her fingers when she picked it up, but still she hesitated, searching in the ripples and waves of the woman's hair for some sign of truth.

"You doubt." Guma's voice was flat, displeased.

"No," Xifeng said hastily, feeling faint under her severe gaze. "I don't dare question the spirits of magic. It's just . . . difficult to imagine such a future for myself."

"You question my interpretation of the spirits' message, then?" No one grew angry faster than Guma whenever she suspected Xifeng's skepticism. She snatched the Empress card from her niece's hand, mouth twisted with fury. "Any other girl would kiss my feet if I told her she would be Empress of all Feng Lu one day. But *you* spit in my face with your doubt." She raised her sharp, bony hand to strike her.

Xifeng cringed. "Please, I don't doubt you! If you say I'm to be the Empress, then the Empress I will be." That calmed Guma a bit, though her mouth remained downturned. She straightened the cards in a sullen silence, which Xifeng knew could last for days if her aunt wished to thoroughly punish her. "I've grown used to our way of living. I have trouble imagining myself owning servants and silks I might have once embroidered for finer folk. That's all."

"The cards have always told us your fate lies in the Imperial Palace." Guma clenched her teeth. "Why else would I fill your head with poetry and calligraphy? Why would I bother teaching you the history of our world and the politics of kings? Other women dream of warm houses and sober husbands for their daughters. I dream of life at an Emperor's side for you, and this is how you treat me. With suspicion."

Xifeng kept quiet as her aunt continued ranting at her. Had she been braver, she might have asked Guma to reconsider the meaning of the fortune. Perhaps the card meant she would *serve* the Empress, not *be* the Empress. It would make more sense, not to mention it sounded much less terrifying. And it would explain how Wei could still be a part of her future—perhaps the sacrifice merely referred to giving up her old life, and not him at all.

But the danger of Guma's drawn-out silence kept Xifeng quiet. She felt too unsteady to argue, anyway, surrounded by the caustic stench of the incense. She blinked her blurry eyes and noticed that one other card held a droplet of blood, not yet absorbed.

"Guma, there's a seventh card."

"Don't be foolish. There are only ever six, and that one doesn't have enough blood to be yours." Still, she seemed curious, so Xifeng flipped it over.

The card showed a slight boy on the cusp of adulthood, pale and oddly delicate. He wore peasant garb and carried a traveling pack, and his eyes were fixed on the stars above. So intent was he upon the heavens, he did not notice that his foot hovered over the edge of a cliff.

"What does this mean? This boy?" Xifeng's head swam. She felt herself swaying in her seat, and gripped the edge of the table to steady herself.

Guma's cruel eyes took in the card. She turned it over, silent and intent. The drop of blood was gone, as though it had never been there at all. "This is the Fool, the card of infinite potential. This boy means luck."

Excitement slithered down Xifeng's spine. In the musky haze, anything seemed possible. Only moments ago, she had questioned her aunt's reading of the Empress card. But now, she didn't know why she had doubted. A normal reading only ever consisted of six cards, yet she had been granted seven. Surely, that was a sign from the gods themselves. The woman painted on that sliver of wood was her and no other; that was the shape of her own head. "The spirits favor me completely, then," she said drowsily.

But Guma's harsh voice broke into her revelation. "Not *your* luck . . . someone else's. This card shows a stranger born under a lucky star." As quick as she had been to dismiss the card, she now glared as though it were Xifeng's fault. "Someone plots against you, against everything we strive for."

Xifeng's stomach churned as her eyes refocused on the boy's face. The artist had given him such long lashes. They cast a shadow like the fringe of treetops against his skin. If she pulled off his hat, would she find a waterfall of hair to rival her own? "An enemy disguised," she uttered, and it seemed the words did not come from her lips, but from the card itself. Guma went very still. "A snake in the grass. A dark world in the cave."

The room twisted further, and images swam before Xifeng's eyes: a sea of waving yellow grass, and a snake like a disturbing ink stroke on paper. It glided toward the mouth of a cave with unnatural grace, the movement like dark silk curving around a man's beckoning arm.

"The Serpent God," Xifeng murmured as the snake took the shape of a thin, unnaturally tall man. "The true god of us all."

A voice spoke inside her mind, gentle and familiar, one that had spoken at the edge of her hearing many times before but never so clearly. *The moon shines down upon us, beloved . . .*

The images melted into each other, but Xifeng could still sense Guma there, sinking to her knees with her hands outstretched in prayer . . . or apology.

Something shifted in Xifeng's chest. She had heard its growl of fury earlier when she saw Ning looking at Wei, but this was something else, something new: a lazy, satisfied preening, like basking in sunlight. If she closed her eyes, she might even be able to see the creature's spiraling coils through the cage of her own ribs.

Embrace this boundless night, the voice said tenderly.

"Leave her," Guma hissed from where she still knelt. "Let her be!"

Xifeng felt herself falling, heard the crack of her forehead against the edge of the table. Right before she sank into unconsciousness, she thought she saw the strangest thing of all: her aunt bending over her with tears in her eyes . . . as though she loved her.

Xifeng closed her eyes and let the darkness take her.

3

Xifeng woke the next morning in the room she shared with Ning. She lay still, head aching as she blinked away a disturbing dream in which she'd swallowed a snake whole. She could still feel it writhing down her throat, choking her, and shuddered as Guma limped in and placed a bowl of steaming broth beside her.

She struggled to sit up. "I'm sorry I overslept. What happened last night?"

"You don't recall fainting?"

Xifeng winced at a stabbing pain above her heart and tugged at the neck of her tunic, gasping at the sight of the bright red crisscross on her skin. It had been etched by a sharp blade.

"I had to drain you of some lifeblood. There was too much magic coursing through you." Guma tilted her head. "You truly don't remember what happened?"

"The card you showed me—the Fool, the boy who looked like a girl in disguise—he . . . or *she* is my enemy." It wasn't a question, but still

Guma nodded. "And I'm not to know who she is? Or when I will meet her?"

"The spirits of magic were warning us. We must stay vigilant. Trust no one, understand? Nothing can stand in your way when you earn your place in the Empress's inner circle." She lowered herself painfully onto a stool, examining each of her niece's features in turn.

Xifeng often felt as though her eyes, nose, and mouth were all separate entities instead of parts of a whole—possessions whose worth Guma assessed, like pearls and combs and silks. Who would endure more pain if she broke her nose or scratched her eye—herself, or Guma?

"You'll be safer in the palace." Her aunt's voice held the same fear as when she had seen the volume of poetry.

Xifeng remembered Guma falling to her knees the night before, pleading hands outstretched. "Who was the man I saw in the vision?" Three words appeared in her mind, but she dared not say them aloud: *the Serpent God.* Guma had spoken the phrase once many years ago, when Xifeng had woken from a nightmare and described what she had seen.

"He's someone you would do better to forget." Guma swiftly changed the subject. "The spirits of magic only give hints and instructions through the cards. It is for you to take your destiny in your hands. If the Emperor won't send for you, you must go yourself."

Xifeng sipped her broth. Away from the plumes of incense, the notion of becoming Empress seemed ridiculous once more. *But why should it?* she asked herself. Thanks to Guma, she had better than a lady's education, and she was certainly beautiful enough.

"I will finish the pink silk by myself today. Brush your hair, wash your face, and take some air this morning. You look haggard," Guma said distastefully, shuffling toward the door. "And cover your head from the sun. We can't have you getting as dark as a common farm girl if you're to go to the palace. The Empress and her ladies never have to go out into the sun."

Xifeng rubbed her bruised forehead and rose from her pallet with a wince. The basin of water confirmed that she did look ill, so she scrubbed her face well and pinched her cheeks to make them pink. The problem with her looks was that people expected her to maintain them, Guma most of all. Any careless morning in which she did not wash or brush her hair properly, and she would be deemed lazy or slatternly.

She felt better as soon as she stepped into the cool spring air. The sky shone bright blue, rinsed clean by the rain, and the town bustled with activity.

The couple downstairs had thrown open their teahouse doors, and several customers sat bickering about who owed whom in a misguided bet. Two elderly men squatted outside, smoking, and stopped talking to ogle her. One of them released the contents of his nose onto the cobblestones, and she turned away in disgust, only to see a woman empty her chamber pot in front of her house, forcing her small son to squeal and jump out of the way.

Xifeng strolled toward the square, making a mental list of the things she would never have to see again if she managed to get to the palace. The butcher's assistant, who had a limp and a lazy eye and still dared to lick his lips at her. The apothecary's wife beating their servant again, on the pretext that the girl was inefficient when everyone knew it was because the apothecary had taken a shine to her. The delivery men scratching their private parts before digging their hands into tubs of flour and rice that would be sold to families for their supper.

"Good morning to *you,*" leered a man coming out of the bathhouse. "What, too high and mighty to return a friendly greeting?"

"What's the matter with you?" his friend hissed at him. "Do you want Wei to kill you?"

She kept her eyes forward, not meeting anyone's gaze. Some days, she didn't mind the attention. But today, the card reading still preyed on her mind and she longed to be alone to think, far from the scrutiny of Guma and the townspeople. She turned her steps toward the rolling hills that hugged the edge of the Great Forest, wishing she had a palanquin to hide in like the new concubine.

Soon, the crowd thinned and the only people she came across were women carrying their washing from the river. A fencing demonstration was taking place on the adjacent field, and Xifeng shaded her eyes to see two men parrying with swords that flashed in the sunlight. They stopped, switched weapons, and continued more slowly. She recognized the craftsman for whom Wei worked, perhaps testing a new blade with a customer. Which meant that Wei was nearby . . .

Xifeng caught her breath when she saw him. He was bare chested today, gleaming with sweat from fencing. His tawny arms were etched with black markings, ones he had insisted the blacksmith give him with a blade lit by fire, to match those of soldiers in the fierce southern armies. Any girl would have gladly laid down her virtue for him, but he belonged to *her*.

His fate entangled with hers—only hers.

She stepped onto the field with a pressing need to breathe the same air he did. He turned to respond curtly to someone beside him, and that was when she noticed Ning.

She had seen those movements from the girl too often lately: the flutter of those tilting eyes, head turning coyly over one shoulder, wrists twirling to hide her teeth as she laughed. Wei was dismissive with her, but she behaved as though they were on the brink of courtship.

The ground seemed to tilt beneath Xifeng, and a great rushing sound began in her ears.

Not again, please, she begged, standing stock-still, thinking of what had happened last night that she could not remember—and of the serpent man she *did* recall. There was a twisting deep in the center of her body, like a creature curving around her heart. And then the anger came.

The field flickered in and out of sight, and another image took its place: the swamps on the southern edge of town. If it was a dream, it felt as real as life. She heard the squelching of mud beneath her feet as she walked. She took in the scent of damp earth and felt a veil of gnats brush her face. Ning followed close behind as Xifeng led her into the maze of festering gray water.

The creature inside brandished its fangs with delight. Xifeng felt a flash of lidless eyes like beady jewels. It, too, knew what lay hiding in the reeds and the mists: a frame of rope stretched over sturdy branches of cypress and two rows of deadly wooden teeth. Each spike was the length of Xifeng's arm from elbow to shoulder and had been sharpened to a fine point.

Stop it, Xifeng pleaded. *I don't want to see this.*

But this was a waking vision, not a dream from which she could rouse herself. And some secret part of her rejoiced at the sight of the alligator trap gaping for prey. She bent down as to a lover, stepping aside so Ning could approach, the blanket of grass slicking wet kisses against her skin. And then the girl stepped on the trigger rope and the trap snapped shut, stilling the air around them. Even the birds went silent.

Ning screamed—or was it the creature?—and Xifeng felt horror and anguish and obscene joy at the sight of her collapsing on top of her destroyed legs. She held her shaking hand above the mess of flesh and white bone, feeling the warmth that still radiated from the girl's broken body. From deep within her, the voice spoke.

She will never again look at what belongs to us.

"No," Xifeng moaned aloud.

She will never again want what is ours.

"No!" she shouted, heart surging. When she lifted her head, the swamp was gone. She was kneeling on the field with everyone watching her, the men with their swords limp at their sides, the women open-mouthed, Ning's face stunned and her legs whole and intact.

And Wei himself crouched before her, hands on either side of her head, lips repeating her name. Still Xifeng could not respond, and without another word he scooped her up into his arms and carried her away from the crowd of shocked faces.

4

Xifeng felt better when they entered the sun-dappled shade on the edge of the forest. Her heart slowed as the breeze cooled her feverish face. Wei set her down gently against a tree and knelt before her, concern softening his savage features.

"What happened?" he asked.

She put a hand to her cheek, surprised to find it wet. "I saw something horrible. A vision of death." She bit her trembling lip and felt his eyes go to her mouth immediately. He was so aware of her every movement, even the whisper of her lashes against her cheek. "It happened last night, too, when Guma read the cards for me."

"The cards." Wei shook off the words like gnats. "I thought I smelled her demon-scent on you. She's made you ill again with her sorcery nonsense."

"It's not nonsense," Xifeng protested, though she could hear her own uncertainty. Nightmares of pain and death had tormented her for years, visions woven by the creature inside her. But Guma's incense had always had the curious effect of bringing these terrors into day, blurring her dreams with reality.

"If you want to believe something, believe you should be free of her. Why stay?"

Xifeng felt the truth in his words, but at the same time, she remembered Guma stroking her cheek so tenderly. "She raised me, and I have a duty toward her," she said softly. "She's the only mother I have."

"Mothers may be strict with their children, but they're not cruel to them," Wei argued. "She'll never love you, no matter what you do." He put his arms around her, and she leaned her head against his comforting bulk. "Let me take you away from here. Please."

"Where would we go?"

"Does it matter, as long as we're together?"

She raised her face and pressed her mouth against his hard, unsmiling one. He tasted the same way he smelled, of sweat and smoke and metal. He kissed promises into her lips, gentle at first, then fiercer, wilder. She let his unspoken words roll across her tongue and fit her body against his in tacit agreement. He belonged to her, no matter what anyone else said—no matter what anyone else wanted. The cards knew it. The universe knew it.

"I love you," he said.

One breath. Three simple words.

He had always been there for her—her escape, her sanctuary. He knew her better than her mother ever had and her aunt ever would, and he offered his heart to her freely. But *her* heart only gave a coy silence when she asked it about him. And whenever her own promises of love lingered on her tongue, the voice would come from within: *Remember you are meant for another.*

She had never told him what Guma believed the cards predicted:

that Xifeng would one day be the Empress. And if this destiny came to light—if, one day, she sat on the throne—only one man could sit beside her, and it would not be Wei. No matter how she tried to deny it, she felt surer, each time the warrior card appeared, that the sacrifice the spirits demanded from her was Wei.

But if the prophecy turned out to be wrong, then she would have given up the only light in her dark life . . . for nothing. Which would be the greater sacrifice: the crown, or the person she cherished most in all the world?

She held him tightly and ran her lips over his cheekbone. The taste helped her forget the disturbing thought that plagued her in the dark and quiet: that she might never be free to love as others did.

"I'd cross the sky and bring you the moon, if you wanted me to. I would be a free being if not for you." Wei buried his face in her hair and breathed through the strands, a fish ensnared in a dark net. "I've loved you since the day I first saw you. You were eight and I was nine, and it was the coldest morning we'd ever had. You had a brown scarf on your head to keep out the chill."

Xifeng listened, astonished. "That was ten years ago."

"You were with *her,* and she was pinching and scolding you. You were shivering, but still you took off your scarf and gave it to her, to make amends. You wrapped it around her and tucked the ends in so she'd stay warm. I saw you and I wished it were me you cared for." Wei's kiss seemed to burn her, to smoke out the truth about her awful visions and the *thing* inside her.

"It *is* you I care for," she said, pulling away with a shaky laugh. "But I'm not as good as you think. When I saw Ning with you earlier, I imagined doing something terrible to her."

His eyes crinkled at her. "You were jealous."

"Be serious," she snapped. "I imagined killing her, Wei. I wanted her dead. I saw it happening clearly in my mind." Wei always blamed the incense for her visions, claiming Guma drugged her, and she clung to that pitiful strand of hope. The alternative was too awful to contemplate. "What kind of person am I if I could see myself doing such horrible things?"

"It was only in your mind." He caressed her cheek, now dry. "The bad thoughts you think and the evil dreams you dream . . . those come from Guma. But the tears you shed are your own."

Xifeng clung to his words like a rope in the sea, overwhelmed by the love for him that she couldn't express. "You see only the best in me. You make me believe I could be good."

"You *are* good. I don't need sorcery to know I can give you a better life." Wei rested his chin on top of her head. "We could go to the Imperial City, like you've always talked about. We'd have food, rooms protected from the winter chill, and fat, contented children."

"That sounds heavenly," Xifeng whispered, with a soft laugh at how simple his needs were: a hearth, a home, a wife, a child. His innocence tore at her heart. He was so sure they would always be together. But she masked the truth with a smile, to save him from pain, and wondered if it would only hurt him more someday. "I like the sound of a life away from here, with you."

"Have I talked about running away for so long that I've finally convinced you?" Wei asked, delighted. "I've only mentioned it every year since we were thirteen."

"I haven't forgotten."

With each passing year, he had grown more persuasive, and stronger and angrier, too. Xifeng had watched him practice with the swords he made, picturing Guma's throat laid bare beneath the graceful deadliness of his blade. It had been a comforting thought on those nights when she lay curled on her side because sleeping on her whipped back was too painful.

Wei's fingers ran down her cheek to her collarbone, and she felt him suddenly tense. He was staring at the crisscross wound above her heart, revealed by her tunic shifting. She tried to tug the cloth back over it, but he stopped her. His jaw tightened, eyes sparking as he took in the huge, angry red cut on her skin. In the light of day, the injury looked horrific, grotesque.

"Did Guma do this to you?" he asked, his voice low, taut.

"Wei . . ." Xifeng began desperately. She had always taken care to hide the beatings from him—a simple task, since Guma took care never to mar Xifeng's face. But now he tugged the tunic from her shoulder, revealing countless bruises along her arm and side. He turned her roughly, fingers grazing the jagged scars on her back from Guma's cane. When he looked into her eyes again, the tender lover she knew was gone, replaced by the man who had once beaten the life out of a thieving attacker with his bare hands.

"Why did you never tell me she hit you?" He trembled with fury. "She is dead! I'll kill that witch in her sleep."

"Wei," Xifeng begged, but he shook her off.

"Better yet," he said, with a ferocious smile, "I'll break her good leg and we can watch her crawl away from me. She can live out the rest of her life on the cold, hard ground like she deserves."

Xifeng couldn't help recoiling, despite having fantasized about it often. Picturing Guma hurt and twisted on the floor was different from hearing it spoken in Wei's ruthless voice. She didn't want to imagine what would happen if her aunt survived, and what kind of revenge she might concoct in that room of spells and secrets.

She knew Wei never made idle threats. He wore conviction in the set of his jaw. So she said the only thing that could spare a life—either Guma's or his own. "Take me away from here. I want to go with you." There seemed, to Xifeng's ears, to be an odd echo to the words, as though she had spoken in unison with another. *Yes,* a voice whispered, *set us on the path to destiny . . .*

Wei's eyes refocused. "Do you mean it?"

"No more beatings," she said decisively. "No more blaming and lecturing, no more nights without food and sleep." *And no more rare gestures of kindness,* she added to herself, with quiet sorrow. *No unexpected caresses, no hints of approval.*

But the words could not be unsaid, and Wei had already accepted them.

He helped her to her feet. "Go home and pack a bag. We'll meet here tonight," he told her, his eyes blazing. "And if you are not here by sundown, if she tries to stop you, I will come. And I will destroy her."

5

Xifeng went home after cleaning the grass stains from her legs as best she could, though Guma would still know; she always knew when Xifeng had been with Wei. But Xifeng reminded herself that this might be the last beating she would ever receive. She might have laughed if she hadn't been so frightened.

"I am leaving," she spoke aloud. "I am never coming back. I am free."

The words felt dangerous, like skirting the edge of a cliff. But she had chosen to jump, to truly begin her new life—just as Guma wanted. *If the Emperor won't send for you, you must go yourself.* And, if Xifeng did not go, Wei would follow through on his deadly promise and kill her aunt.

Upstairs, Guma and Ning sewed together in silence. It took Xifeng a moment to understand the girl's fearful, cringing posture: she was afraid Xifeng would tell Guma that she had been on the field flirting with Wei.

"You look better." Guma's eyes cut to a spot above Xifeng's ankle, which Xifeng felt sure she had scrubbed. "Ning tells me she saw you fainting when she was running errands for me."

Ning hunched over her sewing like a cowering rabbit, but Xifeng felt no hint of her earlier anger; the girl was only a child, after all, who didn't know better. "Yes, it happened in the market," she lied, and Ning snagged her thread in surprise.

"Take care, you stupid thing," Guma scolded. "Waste thread and you'll have less to eat."

Ning mumbled an apology, her face bright red as she shot a grateful look at Xifeng.

"The sun was too hot for me," Xifeng added, turning her aunt's attention back on herself. "With your permission, I'll rest a bit before cooking supper."

The woman's nostrils quivered, sniffing for truth and reason. "Ning will cook," she said at last. "Get the rest you need."

Xifeng nodded obediently and padded away. It seemed unusual to return from meeting Wei and not be beaten, but she sat on her thin, worn pallet for a time and Guma did not come. So, as silently as she could, she lifted a corner of the pallet and dislodged the floorboard beneath it.

The rough cloth sack had been hidden there for five years, ever since Wei had first urged her to run away. It contained a thin rolled blanket, extra clothing, and a bronze box she had found many years ago in one of the abandoned rooms of the house. She liked to imagine the objects inside had once belonged to her mother: a jeweled dagger made for sharpening pens, and an amber wood hairpin adorned with a circle of jade as green as the forest.

She would smuggle a little food later, when Guma was asleep.

"I knew you were up to something."

Xifeng whirled around to see her aunt, eyes flashing with rage as she limped into the room, each uneven step filled with menace. The bamboo cane dangled from her fingers. It had been scrubbed clean of blood from the last beating.

"I'm leaving," Xifeng said as steadily as she could, her palms instantly damp at the sight of the cane. "I'm going to the palace like you want. I'll do everything you want, but on my own."

"Will you? How obedient. How dutiful." Guma's mouth stretched in a garish imitation of a smile. She stood over Xifeng, placing the tip of her cane on the ground. A stranger might believe she needed it to support her leg, but Xifeng knew too well that Guma's muscles were poised to bring it down upon her. "I presume you won't be going alone? You'll take that lumbering ox Wei, to have something to rut with?"

"He loves me. And I . . ."

"Yes? Go on." She cackled when Xifeng remained silent. "You can't even say it, can you? You *can't* love him back, after all? I've taught you better than I expected."

"I *do* love him," Xifeng said fiercely, throwing all caution to the wind. "And you could never teach me something you've never felt." There was a long silence, as though in professing her love, she had uttered a vile obscenity.

Guma lifted the cane and ran the end of it gently over her niece's cheek. Xifeng went rigid. A bead of perspiration trickled down her back, but she did not take her eyes off the older woman.

"The palace," Guma said in a pleasant voice, as though they were drinking tea and chatting about the weather. "You've decided to believe me, then? You *shall* be the Empress. I'm pleased you're taking it seriously at last."

"I never meant to doubt you. But I didn't know whether I would have chosen that life for myself, if I could." Xifeng let out a frayed breath. "I still don't know, but I intend to find out."

Guma lowered the cane and leaned upon it. "Women never choose for themselves. It is for their fathers, mothers, and husbands to do so, and since you haven't any of those, you must listen to me. Don't you agree?"

"Yes, Guma."

"Tell me, how will you travel to the Imperial City?"

"I don't know. We'll take his horse, I suppose." Xifeng's eyes flickered to the cane again.

"And where will you find the money for provisions?"

"I don't know."

"How will you enter the city without paperwork? Or the palace?"

Xifeng's face warmed under her aunt's smirk. They seemed such simple matters, ones she and Wei ought to have discussed. She had assumed he would have a plan in mind. *But why should he be the only one planning?* "I have some embroidery I could sell at market," she said. "That will buy us food for a day or two. As for entering the city, we could persuade a merchant to let us join his caravan. Wei can sharpen his tools and weapons as payment."

Guma tutted gently. "You say this boy loves you, but he hasn't helped you plan at all. He knows nothing of caring for you." Her voice grew softer. "Let me go with you, to help you."

In that moment, Xifeng understood what she had been afraid to admit: Guma knew *exactly* how to use her. One kind word, and Xifeng would do whatever she wanted. And it would continue: the scolding, beating, and examining every morsel she ate and every minute she spent. It made no difference whether they were in a forsaken town or the Imperial Palace.

"No," she heard herself say. "My life and my destiny are my own."

The bamboo cane came down with a sickening crack. Xifeng collapsed, gathering the sack to her body as she closed her eyes against the blinding pain in her shoulder. She felt Guma's claws trying to turn her over, the nails pinching and scratching her skin.

"You owe your love to *me*!" her aunt snarled, punctuating each sentence with a vicious poke of the cane. "You owe everything to *me*. Who could love you more than I do? After all I've done for you, and you're ready to abandon me after a tumble with some good-for-nothing." She paused, muttering, "You're just like your mother."

Xifeng felt a sob escape at those words, which hurt more than the cane ever would. This was what Guma thought of her after all: weak, useless, contemptible. "I tried so hard to please you," she wept. "I did everything you asked of me."

"It's a pity Ning wasn't born beautiful. She'd be one hundred times the niece you are."

Rage swept through Xifeng, scorching the edges of her sorrow. It gave her the courage to look her aunt in the eye, and when she did, Guma's cruel smile strengthened her even more. "I wish she were your niece," she spat. "I'd rather be dead than shackled to you my whole life. I don't ever want to be as bitter and withered and poisoned as you are."

The cane whipped upward and knocked Xifeng beneath the chin. Guma placed the tip of the cane on her face and let it rest there delicately, like a kiss. "Careful, child," she whispered. "One movement and I could take out your eye. I could break your nose. And where would you be without that beauty? Would life be as easy? Would men still give you gifts? Would Wei still want you without that face?" Xifeng cried out as Guma applied pressure to the cane. It bit into her smooth, blooming cheek, and something warm trickled along her jaw. "Let me tell you a little secret, lotus flower. Your beauty is all you are, and all you have. Your only weapon."

Xifeng gritted her teeth as Guma leaned forward, hand poised on the head of the cane, ready to drive it through her skull.

"I wonder," her aunt murmured, "what would happen if I took it all away."

The anger surged, taking control of Xifeng's limbs. She twisted her body, feeling the cane cut into her face as she lifted her foot and kicked out into the woman's soft stomach. There was a sound like a fist in a sack of rice, and Guma collapsed, the cane rattling uselessly on the floor as she folded herself in half. Her face contorted with pain and shock.

"Guma," Xifeng gasped, her fury bleeding away as quickly as it had come. "What have I done?" But her aunt was crawling, fingers stretching for the cane, and Xifeng hurried to pick it up. She held it out of reach and stood over the woman who had raised her, tasting the sourness of guilt in her mouth. "You will not beat me any more," she said quietly.

"You . . . are all I have," Guma wheezed. "I have been . . . the best mother I could."

"A true mother would love me. Cherish me." Tears burned the wound on Xifeng's face. "I've never been anything to you but a possession, to be used for your own ends."

"Xifeng . . ."

"I am afraid to be without you. I am afraid to face this Fool without you by my side," she admitted. "But I have to believe I can follow my destiny on my own."

She saw despair in Guma's eyes, but knew better than to hope it came from love. Her aunt only mourned the loss of the riches she might have had at the palace. With one hand, she would push Xifeng toward the Emperor, and with the other, she would reap the rewards for herself.

"I'm sorry for hurting you." Xifeng's hands shook as she snapped the cane in half over her leg.

"We only have each other," Guma pleaded. "You are all I have left . . . daughter."

Xifeng closed her stinging eyes so she wouldn't see her aunt's pleading face. She grabbed her sack and held it close to her body, like a shield.

Guma's cajoling manner shifted instantly at this display of resolve. "You'll always be mine. You'll never be free of me," she spat. Her eyes flickered to the side and Xifeng tensed, knowing wounded animals were always more dangerous. Guma had taught her that, too.

But she was only looking at a basin of water on the floor nearby. Xifeng caught a glimpse of her own reflection: oval face, slanting eyes, raven hair spilling over her shoulders. She saw the way she held herself, chin lifted and shoulders back to display her long neck and small, high breasts. Just as Guma had instructed her. An obedient puppet to the very last.

She turned her head and gasped at the blur of angry scarlet marring her left cheek. "What have you done?" she whispered, holding her trembling fingers over it.

"It's your own fault, making me so angry." The gentle tone had returned. "Come, let me wash the blood away and put some salve on it. You are my child, Xifeng, and I'll always take care of you."

Even flat on her back in pain, Guma had the power to make her want to collapse, to cast the die once more by running into her arms and hoping this time, she would be embraced and not beaten. But the cut on Xifeng's face and the fragments of the cane in her hands told her the truth.

"Goodbye, Guma," Xifeng said, waves of fury and sorrow rippling through her. "I'll give the Serpent God your regards if I see him again."

"I hope it scars, you ungrateful little snake!" her aunt howled after her. "You're nothing but a disappointment . . ."

In the corridor, Xifeng pushed past a wide-eyed Ning, who held out a lumpy cloth sack that she accepted wordlessly. And then she left that house behind forever, holding the memory of Guma's terrified expression like a flame in her black heart.

6

For eighteen years, the dusty, forgotten town had been Xifeng's world. The ramshackle buildings, the swamps with their prowling rock-skinned alligators, and the river on the forest's edge were all she had ever known. But now, from the back of Wei's old horse, it seemed the *true* world lay open to her. She could go anywhere and do anything.

"Wouldn't you like to see the desert?" she asked, her arms wrapped around Wei. She pressed her face into his shoulders, inhaling the familiar scent of forge fire and grass. He smelled like home, and the thought of taking a piece of home with her made leaving a bit less terrifying.

"I'm guessing that's a little farther from here than the Imperial City."

She heard the smile in his voice and felt a rush of giddy happiness. "You don't regret leaving with me, then?"

"I was the one urging you to go," he said, laughing as he closed his fingers over hers. "My home and my life are with you, wherever you are."

"And mine are with you." The words slipped out before she could help it. She breathed him in, closing her eyes against the painful reality of his love. To stand at a distance was to feel its comfort . . . but to come closer would be letting him believe something that could never be, if Guma's prediction came to pass.

Thinking of her aunt made Xifeng lightly touch her cheek, wincing at the sting. Each step took her farther away, and she didn't know whether to feel elated or sad.

"Does your face hurt much?" Wei asked, sensing her movement.

She placed her palm over the wound. "It's fine."

"You'll miss her at first, I'm sure. But with time, it will grow easier."

"I know she never loved me, but she must feel my loss. She has only Ning now." Xifeng suddenly remembered the sack the girl had given her and opened it in wonder. "She packed food for us. A carrot, two plums, some mushrooms, and a handful of chestnuts."

"There's half a supper for one of us," Wei teased, and she hit him playfully.

"She must have stolen what she could. She knew it wouldn't end well with Guma." The fruits were bruised and the mushrooms withered, but Xifeng smiled all the same. Poor little Ning, who had wished to return her kindness. "The desert was her favorite, too, out of all the five kingdoms of Feng Lu. She'd forget to keep sewing whenever I recited a poem about Surjalana. How Guma would scold!"

"Surjalana." Wei rolled the name around in his mouth. "It sounds like a delicious pastry."

Xifeng laughed. She had always been drawn to tales of the fiery kingdom of sand and the spiteful Lord of Surjalana, the god who had once ruled it. "I read all I could about it. I wanted to run away and wander its marble cities. Sleep under the stars with a caravan of goods to sell."

"You were lucky. Your aunt did well to give you an education," Wei admitted gruffly.

He had worked all through childhood, helping his aging parents on their farm, and there had never been time for anything else. He was the last and best of four sons, his brothers vanishing with promises of riches only to return in shrouds, having met not fortune on the road but Death himself in the guise of illness and war. After his parents died, Wei found work in town. His education lay in the blades and arrows he shaped with fire, and in each coat of plates he assembled with his own hands. He had wrapped himself in swordcraft the way Xifeng had in tales of far-off lands, and had found his own comfort there.

"I may not be educated, but it won't be hard to find work in the Imperial City. I'll seek out another craftsman and make a name for myself." Wei paused. "Going there was what Guma wanted you to do, wasn't it? What did she intend for you, anyway?"

"To go to the palace and be . . . a maid or a lady-in-waiting," she lied, grateful he couldn't see her face. "There's money and stability there."

"You don't need to earn your own living. I'll take care of you."

She only hugged him in answer, and turned her eyes to the trees to soothe her heart. The main road curved along the southern edge of the forest. She could already smell wet bark and rich soil, growing nameless things deep in the belly of the woods. The treetops stirred in the light wind and beckoned to them like fingers.

Wei peered at the sky. "We have another hour before sundown. There's an encampment where we can stay the night." He patted a bundle near his leg, which gently clanked with metal. "In a few days, we'll find a trading post and I can sell these swords. That should buy us enough provisions for the rest of the journey."

"You've traded there before."

"Many times. I know this road well," he said confidently. "It's the largest trade route across the continent of Feng Lu. There'll be people from those other lands you've read about."

As he promised, they passed many riders along the way, some with their families in tow. Xifeng surveyed them with eager curiosity, noting the women in particular.

One woman passed in the back of a wagon with two children at her breasts. A brilliant blue scarf fringed with gold covered her hair, brightening her rich, dark brown skin. The eyes staring back at Xifeng were a surprising shade of amber brown, like the tips of the waving grasses, and were ringed with black kohl. They held her gaze steadily—almost insolently, Xifeng thought, hastily sweeping her hair over her damaged cheek. A powerful sensation surged beneath her ribs like raw hunger, then disappeared as soon as the wagon passed out of sight.

The stranger had worn her beauty so comfortably, like it was a mere fact of life. Only one part of her, and not the whole. But did she, too, resent the fact that her beauty spoke for her? And once it did, would nothing else matter because people already knew what they wanted to know?

Wei's voice broke into Xifeng's thoughts. "There's the encampment I spoke of."

They were on the crest of a hill, traveling down to where the land flattened into a clearing ringed with juniper shrubs. The wind carried the scent of roasting meat. Someone had hewn two sturdy branches and positioned them vertically on either side of a cheerful fire, laying a spit in the grooves. A wild boar hung from the spit, lumps of fat sizzling in the flames.

Xifeng's stomach rumbled. She felt relieved when they were met with open, friendly faces. Four men in foreign armor were cooking, and two monks in somber brown robes kept quietly to themselves on the edge of the camp.

"Might there be room for two more by your fire, friends?" Wei asked politely, addressing the nearest soldier, who was tall, bearded, and looked to be in his forties. The man spoke to his companions in a strange, lilting language Xifeng recognized. She had heard it once from merchants staying in her town. They had come from Kamatsu, the kingdom across the sea, looking for cheap lodgings on their way to the Imperial City.

The youngest soldier remained quiet during the discussion. Like Wei, he had a shaven head, but whereas it made Wei look fearsome, it only accentuated this man's boyish face. His bright eyes rested on Xifeng. "Do not think us unwelcoming," he said in the common tongue. "Our leader's merely wondering where we might find two more plates." He spoke the language of the Great Forest, the center of the empire, to perfection. Xifeng wished fleetingly that her education had included other countries' languages as well, but Guma hadn't thought it necessary.

"We have our own," Wei said quickly, "but would not presume . . ."

"You are not presuming," the older, bearded soldier answered. "Come and rest your weary feet by our campfire, friends, and share our meal. It would be our honor."

Xifeng dismounted and returned the boyish soldier's shy smile, making sure her hair still covered her blemished cheek. Up close, she saw that his armor was etched with a strange sea animal, curved and spiny like a fish, but with the head of a horse.

"Please sit," he said, eyes still on Xifeng, "and my friend Hideki there will serve you. And your husband." There was a question in his voice, but she noted Wei's tight-lipped expression, so she moved closer to the fire to thaw her chilled hands in silence.

Except for the bearded soldier named Hideki, who was placing meat on Wei's plates, all of the men were watching her, including the monks. Wei handed her the food and threw a heavy arm over her shoulders. Not to warm her, she knew, but to show his ownership of her, as of a sword or a horse.

When had she gone from being Guma's possession to Wei's?

But the minute she took a bite of the piping-hot meat, the skin golden and crispy, Xifeng forgot everything but the taste. Salty, flavorful, and rich, everything Guma's food had not been. She fought the urge to lick the grease off her hands.

"Don't eat too much," Wei whispered. "Your stomach isn't used to it. It might make you sick." She ignored his command and he shrugged, nettled. "Are you going to the coast, friends?" he asked the group.

"We're coming from the coast," Hideki replied. "We're escorting our ambassador to Emperor Jun on important business." He made a gesture of respect to a man who sat across the fire from him, and Xifeng forgot to eat for a moment as she stared.

She had never seen such a small adult. His arms and legs were the length of a child's, but his face and countenance were those of a grown man. He was rather handsome, she thought. The firelight flickered across a furrowed brow, strong chin, and elegant nose above a fine silk tunic, suggesting wealth. A coat of plates and a sword lay beside him, but perhaps they were merely decorative. She couldn't imagine him fighting men so much larger than himself.

"I consider our journey equal parts business and pleasure. I'm greatly enjoying the beauty of the continent," the dwarf said courteously. He had the calm, deep voice of someone accustomed to being listened to, and indeed everyone quieted as he spoke. Xifeng saw that his men regarded him with the utmost respect. "My name is Shiro, ambassador to the king of Kamatsu." He introduced Ken, the young soldier, and Isao, who wore a silky mustache like the plume of some ridiculous bird. Xifeng thought he likely used the blade of his sword to admire it.

"How long have you been traveling?" Wei asked.

"A month. We came along the western edge of the Dragon Scales. They're glorious mountains indeed, and rightfully named," Shiro said. "I could easily imagine myself walking alongside a Dragon Lord of old. Our island home has no such natural wonders."

"Except for the jade deposits," Hideki said bitterly. "If I didn't trust in your integrity with all my being, Ambassador, I would not accompany you to have this treaty signed."

"But friendship with Emperor Jun would benefit us," Ken said, his childish face hopeful.

"*Emperor* Jun." Hideki snorted. "He only married into that throne. He's just a distant cousin of the Empress, not even a pure-blooded royal like her or her first husband."

Shiro cleared his throat, lifting an eyebrow in warning as he glanced at Wei and Xifeng. "We should be happy the war between our lands has ended."

"But for how long?" Hideki asked. "This peace is but a breath withheld. Soon enough, the games will begin again."

Isao of the elegant mustache grunted. "I'm sick to death of lords and kings and emperors. What do they do but play games and let their people pay the price in blood? *We* have no quarrel with each other," he added, gesturing between himself and Wei. "Only kings are arrogant enough to believe the world too small to hold other men."

Wei leaned forward, drinking in their words. "But it must be an honor to fight for king and country. The Emperor's men came two years ago to find recruits. I would have lied about my age to enlist, but my parents . . ." He trailed off. Xifeng remembered how, at seventeen, he had burned to join the war between Kamatsu and the Great Forest, when two Kamatsu nobles had gone against their king's word, mustering an army against the Emperor in a violent bid for their kingdom's independence from the empire.

"Enough. The treaty of friendship will be signed, and we must be content." Shiro turned his handsome face to Xifeng. "Have you and your companion traveled far, miss?"

"Our town is a few hours' ride from here." She noticed he did not refer to Wei as her husband. The soldiers all turned to her as she spoke, and she sensed the monks listening as well. "We're on our way to the Imperial City."

Ken's face brightened. "We'll be traveling companions."

"You're going by way of the trading post as well?" Wei asked, moving even closer to Xifeng. "My horse can't swim the river, as yours likely can, and that is the quicker path." He looked at the fine black stallions grazing nearby. Even in the dark, they gleamed like living coals, their haunches exuding strength and vitality.

"They were bred in the fields and mountains of Dagovad, so we must take the long road as well," Shiro said.

Wei's eyes widened. "Those are Dagovadian horses?" He got up to stroke one of them, his hands running over the mane as though he touched the purest silk. The horse blinked its large, liquid eyes at Xifeng with an almost human expression.

While Hideki spoke to Wei about the horses and Shiro and Isao talked quietly, Ken took the opportunity to sit by Xifeng.

"I heard much about the Great Forest growing up, but I find myself intimidated by how vast it truly is," he told her. "My grandmother told me stories of people getting lost in the woods. She said the trunks would move and confuse them, and they would perish from hunger."

His eyes twinkled, but Xifeng couldn't help shivering. Even here, on the woodland's outer edge, she sensed an unsleeping vigilance, as though the trees watched them. "I've read a poem about light in the forest tricking the eyes," she said. "It might make a man suppose a stream faces him when in truth, a rushing flood lies in wait instead."

"And there are the *tengaru,* the demon guardians of the forest, who take the form of a horned horse with burning eyes."

They looked at each other for a moment, then burst into laughter.

"I've heard tales of your land, too," Xifeng said. "Of how the sea has a temperamental nature: gentle one moment, violent the next."

Ken winked. "It's said that our king has the power to control the ocean. He ordains storms on purpose so that when ships arrive, Kamatsu is the loveliest sight the weary, weather-beaten passengers have ever seen. I'd love to show it to you." He reddened when he realized the implication of his words. "How long have you been married?"

"If you asked Wei, he would say eight years."

"But you can't be much older than eighteen," he said, astonished.

Xifeng laughed. "He asked me to marry him when I was ten."

She remembered how she had kissed Wei that day—their first kiss, and her only answer to his proposal. It had remained her only answer for years, each time he alluded to marriage. Wei as a man still wanted what Wei as a child had wished for, but Xifeng's heart stayed silent.

Wei turned in their direction, arms crossed, so Ken moved away to sit beside Shiro.

Xifeng closed her eyes, enjoying the warmth of the fire on her face. Guma would have lit the candles at home by now, circles of light pushing back the dark. And despite all Guma had done to her, she couldn't help praying that her aunt would forgive her. She thought she could hear her whispering, if she listened hard enough.

You'll never be free of me.

Her eyes flew open.

One of the monks had turned to face her, but in the shadows she couldn't make out his face—only two eyes. They shone as they caught the fire, beady and lidless, like black jewels.

She gasped, startling a drowsy Wei beside her, and realized then that she had been asleep, possibly for hours. The monks lay motionless on the ground, and the soldiers lay wrapped in rugs and cloaks. She saw Shiro's diminutive form, a dark lump beside the dying fire. "I was dreaming," she said. "How long have I been sleeping?"

"For a good long while." Wei pulled her close to him. "Close your eyes again now."

Safe within the nest of his arms, Xifeng slept again.

And if she saw more unblinking eyes and smoking incense in the dreams that followed, they had vanished with the moon by the time she opened her eyes again.

7

Xifeng woke before the sun. Wei and the soldiers still lay motionless, and the monks had left sometime in the night. She crept over to Wei's slumbering horse for a spare tunic to ward off the chill. Something caught her eye: one of the soldiers' shields, propped up against bags on the ground. The sky had lightened enough that she could see her own image in the polished surface.

She looked tired and dirty, and her hair was a mess. She knelt, distracted, and gasped when she saw her cheek. A huge red welt had blossomed overnight where Guma's cane had bit into her skin, and a bruise bled from its edges. It was as unnatural as a third eye, staring balefully out from her flawless flesh, and the harmony of her whole face suffered from it.

Xifeng touched the injury with a shaky hand, heart drumming a frantic rhythm. Would it scar as Guma hoped? Last evening, she'd had the advantage of nightfall to soften the blemish, but soon it would be broad daylight and there would be no hiding it.

She scrubbed frantically at the welt, willing it to disappear, but it only grew redder and began to bleed. Panic rose as she stanched the weeping wound, cursing Guma. Her aunt's punishments had always been merciless, but she had made a point never to tarnish Xifeng's face.

"Gods," she whispered. There was only one way she could hope to remove this disfigurement, and quickly. She dug into their bags for Wei's dagger, the one he used to hunt small game, and it clanked gently against his sword. She glanced in horror at the sleeping men, but none of them woke, so she hurried off into the forest.

She made certain to leave their range of hearing before beginning her work. Gathering thin, strong twigs, she whittled and assembled them into a simple trap held together by strips of cloth from her tunic. She covered the snare with dead leaves, as Guma had taught her, and found a hiding place. This was the hardest part, the part beyond her control: waiting for prey.

The sun began to rise and beads of sweat formed on Xifeng's upper lip, but she resisted the urge to wipe them away. After what seemed like hours, a cracking noise came. She stilled even more, hearing another sound: pattering feet on a branch above her head. It took all of her strength not to look up. She hadn't gone far from the clearing, but she was hidden well enough that if something tried to hurt her, it might be too late by the time the men heard her screams.

She listened hard, but the sound did not come again. Instead, she heard the shuffling of leaves as two fat gray rabbits appeared. She watched them hop forward, closer to the hidden trap. *Move forward,* she urged them. *Just a bit more.*

The trap snapped shut, caging both rabbits inside, and shook as they pressed against the wooden bars. Xifeng approached with the dagger, dread twisting her gut. There was a part of her she had to fight, even now, not to think about how bright their eyes were or how soft their fur. She tamped down her weakness, so that all she felt was hunger for their meat.

Quickly, before she could lose her resolve, she stabbed them.

The rabbits lay motionless as she pulled them out of the trap, and a memory resurfaced in her mind as she held their lifeless bodies.

She had been twelve, sobbing and clutching a tree squirrel caught in her trap. The poor thing had struggled in her hands, its heart hammering against her fingers.

"Please, Guma," she had begged, "please don't make me kill it."

"You're a fool," Guma had snarled. "Remember what happened last time you let one go."

Xifeng's back had stung at the words, recalling how her aunt had whipped her until she fainted. She hadn't known until that day that scars had a memory.

"Break its neck, or I will break your finger."

Guma never said anything she didn't mean. And so, heart aching, Xifeng had snapped the squirrel's neck as quickly as she could. It had taken a few tries before the animal at last lay limp in her trembling fingers. A life gone from the earth, because of her.

That was the first time she had felt the *thing* inside her ribs . . . the coiling of the creature born from that first kill.

Guma had praised her and handed her a knife. "The heart of an animal, no matter how small, bears the essence of its soul," she had said reverently. "To imbibe the lifeblood of another is to guarantee that *your* essence strengthens. The magic within you grows stronger, more powerful, and you heal inside and out. This power and this knowledge is ours, and ours alone. Our blood completes the spell. It is something that was taught to me long ago, and now I teach it to you."

Xifeng had cried as she obeyed, though the squirrel suffered no more. Its little heart had tasted like iron and rotted meat, slipping down her throat like a hot worm. She had gagged miserably, though her horror had faded when Guma placed a hand on her now-smooth, unscarred back. The squirrel's lifeblood had healed her wounds—every last one of them.

Xifeng stared at the dead rabbits, thinking of that day.

She had killed three times since then, but only on command, for spells and tonics Guma required. Her aunt had forbidden her from doing so to heal herself. The injuries inflicted upon her were meant to serve as a reminder of obedience—but now she was free of Guma, and she might do as she wished.

The stirring within grew more pronounced and she closed her eyes in prayer. *Forgive me, great lords,* she begged. *Forgive me for the lives I have taken.* But there was no answer, and no forgiveness . . . only a rising dread that beaded her skin with slick perspiration.

In the silence, the hunger began—deep and primal and fierce, stronger than anger, more potent than lust. The creature preened, its poison caress sending tingles of need into every fiber of her body. She was helpless in the face of its desire, for its craving was *hers* as well. Satisfying that hunger would cleanse her and restore the perfection of her face as it should be on a journey to her destiny.

Xifeng stabbed into the rabbits, snapping their bones to find their tiny hearts. She slipped both hearts, still beating weakly with the last vestiges of life, between her lips and chewed. The blood scalded her throat as it slid down deep inside her, and she felt a roar of satisfaction echoing from within. A feeling of sated, lazy pleasure filled her being.

She ran her fingers over her face, now as perfect as it had ever been. Her cheek felt raw and clean, like she had simply scrubbed the wound out. If she were to see her reflection again, this time it might be glowing with well-being, inside and out. The knowledge of this power—and of being able to harness it for herself, whenever she wished—was as heady and addicting as wine.

"Miss?"

Xifeng jumped, dropping the carcasses in her surprise.

Shiro stood nearby. He stared at her not with desire or admiration, as other men did, but with the dawning horror she'd felt the first time Guma had forced her to eat the squirrel's heart.

Such a look might have made her quake moments ago. But now she felt strong, flawless. "I trapped these for our morning meal," she said smoothly, with perfect calm. "I wanted to repay you for sharing your boar with us last night."

His eyes remained on her. Xifeng realized she must have blood on her mouth still, and on her cheek where she had touched it. But he said nothing as she wiped her face, as nonchalantly as she would wipe away crumbs after a meal. "May I carry them back for you?" he asked courteously. Whether he had noticed the mutilated rabbits or not, he took them without comment and did not inspect them, as Wei would have done. Wei would not have had his tact.

Xifeng wiped the dagger on her tunic and sheathed it quietly.

"Rabbits are a delicacy, where I come from," Shiro said, as though nothing out of the ordinary had happened. "We don't have many of them on our island."

"But the seafood must be delicious," she replied in the same calm tone, clearing her blood-coated throat. "My Guma and I could never afford very good fish or prawns."

"I grew up in a region famous for its pearl oysters. Divers retrieve them from the depths for hours on end, resurfacing only a few times for air. They are always women. So I'm no stranger to having a lady hunt and provide for me," he added, smiling. His eyes on her now held nothing but friendly admiration. Perhaps he hadn't seen anything odd after all.

The tension eased as they made their way back. "I've read stories about the pearls of Kamatsu," Xifeng said. "Does the queen truly have hundreds of them sewn into her clothing?"

"She does. And the princess used to weave them into her hair."

"Used to? She does so no longer?"

"She's dead," he said shortly, and Xifeng made no further comment.

Back at the encampment, the men had all risen. Hideki was building a fire, all the while cursing and brushing ashes from his beard. Wei and Isao were feeding the horses, and Ken was packing his belongings. Their eyes moved to Xifeng immediately, moths to a flame, faces brightening at the sight of her. Wei frowned at the bloody rabbits in Shiro's hand.

"The young lady has kindly provided our morning meal," Shiro announced, and the men's admiration changed to astonishment.

"Why so shocked? Don't I look like someone who can hunt?" Xifeng asked, both amused and irritated. But she could see it in their eyes: clearly they thought her beauty, or the fact that she traveled with hulking, protective Wei, meant she couldn't do anything for herself. They thanked her politely and returned to their tasks, but as she predicted, Wei wasn't happy.

"You killed those?" he asked in a low voice, the crease between his eyebrows deepening. "You know I don't like it when you kill. Let me do it, or one of the other men."

"When it's so easy? Let me contribute. I'm not useless."

"You used to cry every time Guma made you kill. It upsets you, even when done for food. Doesn't it?" He scanned her face, eyes lingering on her unblemished cheek. His fingers hovered over her skin. "The wound is gone," he said, his tone too close to suspicion for her liking. "How . . . ?"

Xifeng braced her hands on her hips. "I healed it with plants I found in the forest. And killing two small rabbits is certainly nothing to be upset about." Wei glanced behind her at the other men, who were surely listening. "You're determined to think me weak and fragile. I don't need your permission to help if I want to. You're not my husband." She felt a pang of regret as soon as she had said it.

Wei turned away, his voice so quiet she had to lean in to hear. "You used to feel pain whenever you took a life. She's stripped you of *that* as well?"

Xifeng came close and rested her head against him. "I'm still the same person," she whispered. But he moved away without another word.

The rabbits tasted delicious, seasoned with herbs and salt Hideki had brought from Kamatsu. Wei ate in silence, not joining in the conversation, and it hurt Xifeng to see him sad. She crept close to his side, hating herself for the unkind words she had chosen. He loved her so much and believed in her goodness. Every flaw, every mistake she made, was Guma's in his eyes. So she wrapped an arm around him and tried to understand. He shifted beside her, and gruffly handed her the best piece of rabbit meat.

Meanwhile, Ken was raving about the Dragon Scales, his face alight with excitement. "There was no time to go through the mountains, and we aren't properly equipped. But how I would feel if I made it through alive!"

"It's not a game," Shiro told him, chuckling, and Isao added tartly,

"You can go by yourself on the way back, and tell us about the Crimson Army . . . if they let you go alive."

"They don't exist. It's a myth," Hideki told Wei and Xifeng.

"It's one I haven't heard," Xifeng admitted.

"How do you know it's a myth if you refuse to go?" Ken asked indignantly. He turned eagerly to Xifeng. "They live in caverns among the peaks. They serve no king, not even Emperor Jun, and owe their allegiance to no man. But they can be persuaded to fight for you if you have what they want."

Isao snorted. "Like husbands? Marry them all off and they'd stop their nonsense."

"They're women?" Xifeng asked, blinking.

"Every one of them, and they're the deadliest killers on the continent." Ken ignored the others' scoffs and drew a finger across his lips. "It's said that they paint their mouths bright red with blood when they go to war. That's why they're called the Crimson Army."

"Or perhaps they're called that because they're only stirred to anger once a month, when the moon is high and their own blood is flowing," Isao added crudely.

"Enough," Shiro said in a sharp voice. "We must be on our way. We'll arrive at the main gates of the Great Forest in a week's time, and the Imperial City is several more days beyond that."

Wei rose and adjusted the bundles on the old gray horse, then mounted, giving Xifeng his hand. She swung up behind him and held him close, this man who wanted so much to think her perfect—who gazed at her like she was the brightest star in the sky. He had tied himself to her without any hope or promise in return.

Love killed your mother, Guma had always warned her. *Give your heart and you lose your soul.* She believed that to love another was to walk the edge of an abyss, and she had vowed never to let Xifeng fall. Not when the fates had marked her for something much greater.

But how could I help loving Wei? Xifeng thought, with mingled fear and sorrow. Already she could feel him relenting, his body relaxing into her arms.

"Please don't be angry with me anymore," she whispered.

"I'm not angry. Not with you."

And that, Xifeng thought as the horses left the encampment, had to be enough.

8

The week passed by uneventfully, and on the final morning before they reached the gates of the Great Forest, they dismounted to stretch their legs, sore from riding. They walked the horses uphill toward the trading post where they would replenish their supplies.

Wei and Hideki took the lead, and Xifeng found Ken beside her at once. "We'll be in the Imperial City soon enough," he reassured her, seeing her grimace of pain. "By the time we arrive, you'll be a trained horsewoman."

She laughed. "Well, if the Emperor's new concubine can travel this far, so can I . . . though she did ride in a palanquin. I wonder how she's faring."

"Likely better than she did in her old life. Do you envy her?"

"Why do you say that?" she asked, a bit defensively.

"I didn't know whether her position was a desirable one. It seems concubines never have any choice in the matter. The Emperor summons them, and they go."

Xifeng smiled, with a tinge of bitterness. "It's a woman's duty to obey." She and the concubine shared that, except *her* masters were Guma and the spirits of magic. *No, not Guma,* she reminded herself. *Not anymore.*

The trading post proved to be small, but busy and well stocked. There were six or seven stalls and booths, each offering different goods. One merchant sold bolts of rough fabric for sacks and saddle blankets, and another displayed shoes and boots of supple leather. Another booth had wooden troughs boasting every grain imaginable: wild rice, millet, sorghum, broomcorn, and wheat.

I wish Guma could see this, she thought. It pained her that she could still care so much for someone she ought to hate. Wei came up beside her, and she pushed her aunt from her mind.

"I wish we could live here," she said brightly. "We'd have everything we needed."

He chuckled. "You wouldn't like the thieves, though. It's a dangerous place to be after dark, with all of this money and merchandise."

Shiro and Ken went off to look at the leather boots, and Hideki planted himself at the crowded stall selling fragrant roasted meat. Wei stopped at a table displaying beautiful metalwork: pots and pans polished to a high sheen beside weapons of iron, steel, and bronze. One corner of the table even showcased a tiger skin, warm and soft beneath Xifeng's fingers. She had never seen anything more beautiful—like fire and ink together in perfect, variegated stripes.

"Warhorses wear them for protection in battle," Wei explained.

She could easily picture the tiger's heart beating beneath this glorious skin. Had its killer grieved over its death, or had he taken its life without another thought, as she had done to the rabbits days ago?

As Wei began haggling over the price of a blade, Xifeng turned and saw a booth covered with shining metal pieces. She pushed through the crush of sweating bodies to examine them and found a collection of gleaming bronze mirrors. They winked invitingly at her in all shapes and sizes, some with ornate carvings and others simple and functional. A few were large enough to hang on a wall, but most were small enough to hold in her hand.

"May I help you?" The craftsman's leering smile lacked five teeth, and his bloodshot eyes roamed down her body. "With a face like yours, you need an equally beautiful mirror, no? I'll give you anything for half the price. Free of charge, even, if you ask me nicely."

Two women with copper skin approached, chatting in another language, and the craftsman turned grudgingly to them. He seemed to understand what they said, but responded in the common tongue: "No discounts. Everything is full price." The women frowned, muttering, and the man gave Xifeng an obvious, obscene wink to let her know his offer still stood.

She ignored him and examined a small, simple hand mirror with a rounded edge. Her reflection greeted her beneath a thin layer of dust, looking distorted in the polished bronze, like a stranger's face.

Xifeng touched her smooth, blooming cheek, and something in the mirror caught her eye.

Over her shoulder, through the reflection of the teeming crowd, a man watched her. A bald, powerfully built man in plain monk's robes, with flashing eyes like dark gems.

She spun, her pulse racing, but there was no such person behind her. She nearly screamed when she turned back to the mirror, for not only was he still there, but he now stood right behind her, close enough for his breath to stir the hairs around her face.

Her face . . .

The welt on Xifeng's left cheek glared like a hideous sun. It was three times as big as before, stretching from her eye to her jaw, and wept green-tinged blood. She opened her mouth in a silent shriek, her reflection blurring as her hand shook. But the skin beneath her fingers was as perfect and smooth as ever. Behind her, the monk bowed and disappeared into the throng.

"Are you all right, my beauty?" the craftsman asked. He and the two customers were staring at her. "Shall I catch you if you faint?"

Xifeng threw the mirror down and rushed away. Her mind whirled with the memory of the two monks at the encampment who had vanished before daylight. She had dreamed about one of them, but that had only been a nightmare.

What, then, was this? Another evil vision in broad daylight, far away from Guma and her toxic incense?

She might have known Guma would take her revenge somehow. Having a man follow and frighten Xifeng might be her way of staying close, as she had promised.

Xifeng pushed through the crowds, tears blurring her eyes as she put as much distance between the mirror and herself as she could.

9

They traveled through the evening and the next morning without incident. Xifeng touched her face constantly to make sure the wound hadn't returned and glanced back as they rode, half fearing the monk would be lurking just behind. But she neither saw nor dreamed of him again, and tried to put him from her mind, knowing that anything to do with Guma would only worry and anger Wei.

In the afternoon, they arrived at an immense archway carved with flying dragons that towered hundreds of feet above them. Xifeng tipped her head back to take in the gateway. In less than a fortnight, they would arrive at the Imperial City, the jewel of the Kingdom of the Great Forest and the heart of the empire. She had read so much of this center of trade, language, and culture, and of the magnificent palace from which Emperor Jun reigned over all other kings on the continent of Feng Lu. Soon, she would see it all with her own eyes.

Shiro studied the narrow path ahead. "We'll have to go single file.

Hideki and I will lead on our horse, then Ken. Wei, you can ride in front of Isao . . ."

"We'll take up the rear." Wei's firm, proud tone brooked no refusal, and the ambassador nodded in agreement.

They passed through the gate and were immediately swallowed up by the woodlands. The trees breathed chilly shadows of mist upon them, and the musty, ancient smell of earth and dew clung to each branch. Xifeng wondered how long this forest had stood here watching, and what it had seen in all the vast and terrible ages of men.

They rode in the near-silence the Great Forest seemed to command, stopping once to rest the horses. When night fell, it seemed more present in these woods than it did outside, though they were under the same sky. All lay still in a stagnant hush, but every now and then, a vine or a branch would move out of the corner of Xifeng's eye—proof of something very small and quiet. And then there would be a soft rustling, like little feet scuttling across tree bark. It was what she had heard while waiting for the rabbits.

Wei tensed behind her; he heard it, too. In the murky twilight, they saw Isao turn and put a finger to his lips, and Wei gave a short nod.

As she turned around, conscious of being followed, Xifeng thought again of the monk. *Had* Guma sent him? Could her aunt's reach extend all the way into the Great Forest? She wished Wei hadn't insisted they take the rear, damn his pride, for they would have been protected by Isao riding behind. If someone attacked them now, she and Wei would be the first ones dead. She longed for Ken to ride near them instead of Isao; one of his stories might help calm her.

Wei stroked her hand soothingly, and she realized she had balled it into a fist. The little feet were still pattering above, broken by silences in which the creature hopped to the next tree.

"What could it be? Did we do the right thing, traveling at night?"

"Of course," he assured her, and she tried to take comfort in his confidence.

The forest was deep and dark and old, she knew, and the trees were not like others. They had a way of bending light for their own purposes. In a larger party, this would not make a difference—there would always be someone more observant, more present, who could warn the others of an illusion—or the stalking approach of a predator. But for solitary travelers, only in the night could this woodland be trusted.

Well, perhaps *trusted* was the wrong word, Xifeng conceded.

Wei pulled the horse to an abrupt stop. The soldiers had halted on the path ahead. Ken and Isao turned this way and that, scanning the trees, but on the back of Hideki's horse, Shiro had his head lowered, listening intently.

A whistling sound came from behind them, sharp and piercing. In one fluid motion, Wei dismounted and lifted Xifeng off the horse, pushing her into the trees. He signaled for her to stay low and she obeyed, crouching against the rough bark of a spruce. Hideki pulled Shiro from their horse as well and pushed him toward her. The little man knelt, a hand on the dagger at his belt.

Through the trees came a great rushing noise and a smell like hot metal. The whistling grew louder and lights appeared, waving curls of red and orange illuminating a dozen masked warriors on horseback. Several carried torches, bringing into view the weapon their leader spun above his head: a wicked, curved blade that glared in the firelight, as long as a man's torso and sharp as sin, making a high-pitched screeching as it slashed through the air on an ebony rope.

"Great lords above us," Shiro whispered, his eyes on the glinting scythe.

Wei, Ken, and Hideki unsheathed their weapons and faced the

attackers. Xifeng dug her nails into the tree as Isao leapt in front of the other men. She had dismissed him for his vanity, but what he lacked in modesty, he more than made up for in courage.

"Who are you?" he shouted. "What do you want?"

It happened in an instant: the scythe came down quicker than the eye could see, and Isao collapsed. The top half of his body flew one way, and the bottom half the other. Something wet sprayed on the ferns in front of Shiro and Xifeng, steaming in the cool air.

With a roar, Hideki hurtled forward as the bloodstained scythe completed its arc and came down again, meeting his sword with a colossal crash. With both hands on the hilt, Hideki sent it flying back toward its attacker, who barreled off his horse to avoid the incoming blade. A sickening thud sounded as the blade embedded itself into the man behind him. Several of the other assassins dismounted and rushed toward Wei and Ken, who struggled to hold them off.

"I have to help them," Shiro said through gritted teeth. "I can't hide here like a coward."

"You'll be killed," Xifeng hissed, watching a faceless warrior's sword narrowly miss Wei's head. Her eyes kept falling on the halves of Isao's body, now trampled in the brawl. His head twisted at an unnatural angle, and his eyes remained open, staring blankly in her direction. She imagined Wei like that, blind, mute, and utterly lost to her, and clutched Shiro's arm, barely breathing.

Wei narrowly dodged a spear and planted his sword into his opponent's chest, the two men whirling in a lethal dance. He threw his enemy to the ground and forced his weight upon the hilt of the sword, grinding its blade through flesh and bone.

He did not see the man with the scythe approaching, the rope looped around one hand as he lifted the blade above Wei's back.

Shiro swore in his native language and wrenched his arm from Xifeng's grip. He dashed onto the path and stabbed Wei's attacker deep in his left calf. The metallic stench of blood and ruined flesh filled the air as the man screamed, a terrible keening wail that chilled Xifeng to her core. Wei spun around, eyes glittering, and beheaded the man with one powerful swipe of his sword, drenching Shiro in the gore that emerged.

"I'm all right," Shiro growled at Wei, spitting out the man's blood. "See to Ken."

Xifeng cried out in horror when she saw the young soldier's plight. He stood in a circle of blazing branches, cornered by the attackers wielding the torches. At first, one of them appeared to be trying to save Ken, flinging liquid at him from a metal flask.

But it was too thick to be water, and Xifeng realized—when the others applied their torches to Ken's body and the fire raged even more ferociously—that the assassin had been flinging oil.

Hideki and Wei rushed to save him, but it was too late. Within seconds, Ken's body had become an inferno of red-and-orange tongues lapping at his skin. A sob ripped through Xifeng's throat as she watched him writhe in a haze of blood and smoke and bodies, finally collapsing to the ground as the flames consumed him. Ken, with his shy ways and his stories and his boyish love of adventure—gone.

Shiro shouted his name, then turned his anguished face in Xifeng's direction, eyes fixed above her in horror. She heard a great rustling, and this time, she did not resist. She turned her face upward and screamed at what she saw.

Faces, thousands of beastly faces in the treetops. They belonged to no earthly man, for they were red like fire, red like love and death, and hovered between the leaves like bloody fruit. They gazed with equal hatred upon Wei's group and the masked attackers.

Wei and Hideki were still fighting off the remaining assassins, but even the sharp grating of metal upon metal could not hide what came next: a sound in the trees like a collective breath, as though all of the faces inhaled together.

Xifeng crawled backward, away from the tree in which a dozen of them glimmered like demonic stars. She did not want to be close by when they exhaled.

Tears for Ken burned her cheeks as Shiro yelled, "*Tengaru!*"

In the brief interlude that followed, she thought how cruelly ironic it was that the young soldier had died right before he could see the beings he had heard of in his grandmother's stories. A hysterical laugh escaped her, drowned out by a fierce, roaring rush of wind—the exhale she had anticipated—and the *tengaru* leapt from the trees.

The men on the path turned as one. In the firelight, the demons' true faces were revealed in all of their terrifying glory: ancient and wild, not quite horse and not altogether inhuman. Their long, angular heads ended in two narrow nostrils and a slash of a sharp-toothed mouth, and were crowned with two viciously curved horns of ivory. Their eyes flared like night fire, full of life and intelligence . . . and hatred, as their pointed ears swiveled to catch the sound of one of the assassins wetting himself noisily.

Their slim, orange-red bodies smelled like the forest itself, like ancient soil unearthed from the bowels of the world. Xifeng shuddered at the *wrongness* of them, of the horse's head and neck poised on a lithe wildcat's body, with a barbed, serpentine tail of soot-black.

Shiro threw himself in front of Wei and Hideki. "We do not mean any harm," he said in a calm, firm voice. He gripped his dagger, but it was pointed downward toward his feet. "We are only travelers on our way to the Imperial City."

The *tengaru* numbered in the hundreds and were the size of large dogs. Five talons emerged from each of their massive paws. Ferns and shrubs fell apart beneath their lethal points, and Xifeng had no doubt flesh would as well.

The one who appeared to be their leader advanced until its wicked, intelligent face was inches from Shiro's nose. The muscles rippled along its elegant haunches as it flexed its tail menacingly. Then, in a voice as old as the wind, it said, "We are the demon guardians of the forest. We protect it from men like *you,* who set fire to our trees without a second thought."

"We do not mean any harm," Shiro repeated, and the demon's ears flicked at his respectful tone. "We were ambushed and our attackers carry the torches, as you see."

The *tengaru* had formed a tight circle around the masked men, who pressed close together as the demons snarled and snapped at their ankles. Several beasts closed in behind Wei and Hideki, and one of them was even watching Xifeng through the screen of ferns and grass. She shrank back as Wei turned to her, lips forming her name.

"Day by day," the *tengaru* rasped, "we see our trees felled and leaves trampled. The beauty of this world is fading all too fast through the cruelty and thoughtlessness of men."

"These are the men who killed our friends and set fire to your branches," Shiro said adamantly, indicating the attackers with his free hand. "We were merely passing through. We bring important correspondence to Emperor Jun from the king of Kamatsu."

The demons' eyes flickered at the word *Kamatsu,* spoken in Shiro's lilting accent. The leader turned its back, and Xifeng saw with relief that the *tengaru* believed the ambassador. They fixed their stares on the masked assassins, pronouncing judgment, just as one of the panicked men leapt forward and began swinging his sword, felling several demons. A pulse of anger vibrated through the creatures as though they shared one body and their mouths drew back in a collective scream of fury. They leapt onto the attackers, talons slicing clothes and flesh like ribbons.

Shiro, Hideki, and Wei scrambled backward, tripping over branches and Isao's remains. Wei opened his arms and Xifeng ran into them, pressing her face against his chest. She knew she would hear the slashing of sharp talons and the endless screaming long after this night.

But the cries of pain stopped within seconds. Xifeng opened one eye to see the last surviving assassin stab a *tengaru* with his spear. Four of its comrades immediately pinned him against a tree while a fifth smashed its barbed tail against the man's broken body. He collapsed in a lifeless, unmoving heap of flesh and bone.

Slowly, the *tengaru* turned as one to face the survivors and approached in unison, one blood-splattered paw at a time.

10

Wei's knuckles tensed on the hilt of his sword. "Let us go."

"Let you go?" the demon leader sneered. "Let you go, when our fallen lie like crushed poppies?"

The woodland had become a gory burial ground of men and *tengaru*. Their torn bodies made odd, dark shapes across the forest floor. Suddenly, the demons nearest the corpses spun in a blur of red and orange. The whirl of activity removed the corpses and put out the dying embers, and then they vanished, leaving only three *tengaru*, who faced the survivors with suspicious eyes.

"We have done nothing to wrong you, great guardians," Shiro said quietly.

"Haven't you? You lured death and evil into our midst," the demon replied. "Those killers were sent after you to ensure all in your party died. We were summoned to help you."

Xifeng trembled at the truth in those words. Had the *tengaru* not intervened, and with only Hideki and Wei able to fight, they would have been overpowered and slaughtered, one by one. *But who had known they would need aid?*

"We seek to save our forest, not you," the *tengaru* continued. "We'd do better to kill you and be done with the whole affair."

Shiro's brow furrowed. "I assume the blame. I am ambassador to Kamatsu's king. The assassins may have been sent by someone who opposes our treaty with Emperor Jun."

Xifeng stared at his presumption. She felt, deep down, that Guma's cards would tell her the attackers had been sent for her—that this had been the Fool's first move, an enemy defensive launched to keep her from her fate. But that might be presumption on her own part, for her Empress destiny seemed as far away as home in these death-filled woods.

"Whichever one of you is responsible does not matter now," said the *tengaru*. "We have all suffered a great loss tonight. Our queen will wish to speak to you." For a brief moment, its eyes met Xifeng's with all the knowledge of the world in its depths, and she turned her face back to Wei, feeling a deep, enduring chill in her bones.

"Ambassador," Hideki protested, but Shiro held up a hand.

"We will go. If the queen requires our presence, we will appear before her."

"I did not offer you a choice, but that is a wise decision all the same," said the *tengaru*. "Your horses wait over there."

The three Dagovadian horses stood in a circle around Wei's old mare, as though protecting her. Hideki helped Shiro onto one and mounted another. Wei lifted Xifeng onto his gray horse, but the demons hissed in protest when he made to climb up behind her.

"You each ride alone," the leader commanded, and Wei mounted Ken's steed instead.

One of the *tengaru* took the lead beside Hideki, followed by Shiro and then Xifeng. The other two demons prowled on either side of Wei in the rear. Every so often, as they traveled through the dark woodland, Xifeng heard the swish of their barbed tails. She knew it was a warning; they could be silent when they chose.

A faint light kissed the forest as the sun began to rise. Surrounded by trees as they were, Xifeng could not tell which direction the light came from. It made her feel unsteady and disoriented, which only intensified as the rays danced off dewy leaves and waxy trunks of spruce, adding blinding reflections to the air.

Wei murmured her name and she nodded wearily to show she was all right. She wished she were home again, sleeping in her old room beside Ning. Her bones and head ached, and her whole body trembled at the end that might befall her. It seemed all of Guma's teachings would go to waste now, if the *tengaru* intended to kill them all. She would be dead at eighteen, lost to the world before she had even seen it—before she had even lived. Perhaps this destiny was only what Guma wished for and not what she truly foresaw; perhaps it had been a terrible mistake for Xifeng to leave her.

"Empress, indeed," she whispered. The *tengaru* in front turned to peer at her, though it couldn't possibly have heard. She fell silent, trying not to imagine what manner of death it might soon give her.

An hour later, they passed a massive granite formation cutting through the underbrush. Xifeng saw crevices high in the rock wall, irregularly placed, and curiosity overcame her fear. "Please, what are those holes?" she called to the *tengaru* in front.

In full daylight, the demon was less menacing—rather like a small, strange horse. But its eyes were still disturbing, and the preternatural awareness in them made her skin crawl.

"Tombs," it told her. "The resting places of men long forgotten. This was the site of a great battle many ages ago."

Xifeng's hands shook, imagining the carnage she had witnessed last night, only magnified: destroyed bodies littering the ground and trees lacquered with fresh blood. "My Guma used to be angry with me for being reluctant to hunt. I think I can see why now."

"Can you?"

"Taking one small life is nothing compared with the violence of the world." She turned away from the *tengaru*'s knowing eyes, suspecting that it judged her poorly for such a conclusion. She rubbed a hand over her left cheek, wishing she hadn't said anything.

They traveled all afternoon and evening, and when night fell once more, the sky through the trees deepened from gold to midnight blue, like a stain of ink on paper. The glaring play of light off leaf and tree disappeared, and Xifeng sighed with relief when they stopped to rest beneath the trees and the *tengaru*'s watchful eyes.

Several long days passed in a haze of exhaustion. They rested only at the demons' discretion and rode without speaking more than a few words, for the *tengaru*—like the trees of the forest—seemed to command silence. Finally, on their tenth evening in the woodlands, the trees began to grow farther apart and the grass became softer under the horses' hooves. In front, Hideki and Shiro sat erect and vigilant on their horses.

"Have we arrived?" Shiro asked, and the demon gave him a curt nod.

An enormous clearing greeted them as soon as they were free of the trees. Sweetly fragrant grass blanketed the space, and in the center lay an immense pond as calm and bright as the stars it reflected. Willows bent their graceful heads into the water, their branches humming with gentle birdsong. A breeze carried the scent of the moon-white lotuses resting on the pond's surface like sleeping maidens.

An island stood on the pond, sheltered by four curving oaks adorned with garlands of white flowers. The whole structure resembled a pagoda created by nature itself, reposing in a secret kingdom of peace. Its beauty filled Xifeng with a deep longing for tranquility, and a strange, foreboding sorrow that she might never find it.

"What is this place?" Hideki murmured.

"This is the sanctuary of our queen," spoke the *tengaru*. "She is the oldest and wisest of our kind, and has lived on Feng Lu since before the time of the Dragon Lords."

Xifeng slid from her horse, landing on the lush grass. She longed to take off her shoes to cool her feet, but didn't dare do so before the *tengaru*'s stern eyes. The demons led them past a wide wooden platform on which four lanterns shone. The platform held a low table piled with food, as well as a few sleeping pallets.

"They were expecting us," she murmured to Wei, who nodded warily.

They crossed a bridge curving over the pond, and the scent of flowers grew stronger as they approached the figure stirring within the pagoda of trees.

The queen of the *tengaru* regarded them with eyes like twin moons, glowing against the ancient night sky of her face. She resembled the younger demons with her long, elegant horse head and sleek limbs, but her horns twisted like antlers, and her coat darkened to onyx around her nose and mouth. A bed of creamy blossoms supported her frail body like the tenderest of clouds.

"You have brought death and destruction with you. Fear and hatred." Her voice held surprising strength for such an old, fragile body. Her moon-eyes seemed to see straight through Xifeng, who forced herself to meet the gaze, and the queen gave a slight, pleased smile.

"We destroyed the assassins they lured into the Great Forest, O

Gentle One," the *tengaru* leader told her. "One carried a deadly blade, and the others damaged many trees with their torch fire. Many of our own have been killed. A tragic waste, but one we could not avoid."

The queen spoke in a grave, sorrowful voice. "We do not condone men's wars and violence in the sanctity of the Great Forest."

"We have the deepest respect for the Great Forest, Your Majesty," Shiro said. "I believe the men came for me. I am a servant of the Boundless Sea, sent on a mission on behalf of our king."

Xifeng felt a surge of irritation. Surely, with a destiny like hers, *she* just as likely had been the killers' target. But as quickly as it had come, her annoyance subsided into shame at her own conjecture. She sensed the queen's attention returning to her at once.

"We should execute them all to appease the gods," one of the *tengaru* declared.

Wei went rigid, but the queen only shook her elegant head. "I do not intend to execute any of them. My time on this earth is almost ended, but theirs has only begun. They each have a part to play in the story that will unfold."

She rose with difficulty. She was larger than the others, her head at the level of Xifeng's elbow, but she was weak as a kitten. Each step she took seemed to pain her.

"The war has ended between the forest and the sea, but the tension grows," she continued. "There will be no peace on Feng Lu. I have seen how humans adapt to a cruel world. I have watched this continent of peace and plenty become the grasping, violent place it is now."

Hideki's eyes flashed. "You speak truly, Your Majesty. Our treaty with Emperor Jun would seem to be fair and put him on an even footing with our king, allowing us to keep the jade on our shores. But we've been bullied into sharing a percentage. It's a theft of our resources and a mockery of friendship, and the people are not fooled." Shiro shook his head, but the soldier barreled on, beard quivering. "Kamatsu and the Great Forest have always been separate entities, though Jun may be Emperor of us all in name. His expectation that we accept unfair terms without question warrants a battle greater than the one we had."

"Warriors." The queen's voice held a note of amusement. "Desiring bloodshed where there is none, and wishing for more where there has already been enough. Make no mistake: my *tengaru* were summoned forth on your behalf, but they did so only to protect our forest."

"Who called for our aid?" Wei asked, but the queen shook her head with an enigmatic smile.

"How do you know of these things, great queen? Of the ways of the world?" Shiro gestured to the surroundings, and Xifeng understood what he meant. The *tengaru* sanctuary seemed a world apart, removed from the troubles of mankind.

"My sons and daughters bring me the news. And I have other ways of acquiring my knowledge." The queen turned to the pond, which reflected the sky's glittering beauty, and Xifeng saw the slightest tremor on its surface. She did not need Guma's skill to sense that the most profound magic lay within its strange, solemn depths.

"War after war has come to this continent for all the ages of mankind. Since the Dragon Lords abandoned Feng Lu and their human children, they have left only strife and hatred behind." A deep despair rang in the queen's words, recalling a greener world full of song and joy, when the gods had walked the earth like men. "Still, there is a thread of hope for peace among its five kingdoms. Do you know the shrine in the Mountains of Enlightenment?"

"It was a symbol of the alliance between the Dragon Lords," Xifeng spoke, with another pang for Ken, who would have loved to hear this tale again. "They were ancient sons of the skies, and each ruled one of the five kingdoms of Feng Lu. They created the continent by bringing together the elements of the world: the wood of the Great Forest; the earth of the Sacred Grasslands; fire from the Everlasting Sands of Surjalana; metal from Dagovad, land of the Four Winds; and water from Kamatsu, the Kingdom of the Boundless Sea."

"They each contributed a treasure to the shrine, as a vow of friendship," Hideki added. "But it didn't last, and they stripped it of its relics."

"Why?" Wei asked, and for the first time, Xifeng felt ashamed of his ignorance.

"Jealousy," she said quickly, to take the *tengaru*'s scornful attention off him. But she saw the queen tilt her magnificent horned head, missing nothing. "The Lord of Surjalana envied the Dragon King, mightiest of the five, who ruled the Great Forest. He believed that title belonged to *him,* and his jealousy poisoned the others. They engaged in a terrible battle, then removed their treasures and returned to the heavens, battered in spirit and heart."

The demon queen turned her face upward, her eyes reflecting the dreams of the stars. "Still, there may come a day when the kingdoms unite once more. When a great ruler of mankind joins them in alliance against evil. Or perhaps it is only my idealistic heart that hopes for such joy." She turned, and they all followed her gaze.

A second bridge arched over the pond to the opposite side of the clearing, where imposing oaks stood like sentries by a stone gate. Beyond it lay another pond like a reflection of this one, in the middle of which stood a young sapling of a tree. Half of the tree reposed in winter, with clouds of snow wreathing its trunk, while the other half basked in spring, with pink-white buds emerging from its virginal branches.

It brought to Xifeng's mind the poem that had frightened Guma:

The moon shines down upon us, beloved

The water a vast and eternal mirror

A voice whispers from every tender branch

Turn your face from the world's apple-blossom fragility

And embrace this boundless night

The queen answered their unspoken question. "There have been no apple trees on the continent for more than a thousand years, save this one . . . the very last."

Gooseflesh rose on Xifeng's skin. According to the old stories, the Dragon King had removed every trace of these trees when he returned to the heavens. "But what does this have to do with the *tengaru* coming to our rescue, Your Majesty? Or with whomever called for our aid?" she asked.

The queen's pointed ears swiveled. "Everything has to do with you." But she explained no further and returned to her bed, head drooping against the blossoms. "You are my guests tonight. There is food, and you may drink of the waters of my pond and know you are safe in your sleep. You shall not be harmed. But you must leave this forest when the sun rises anew." The light of her eyes disappeared as they closed.

A breeze rose up then, swirling Xifeng's long hair around her.

For one breathtaking moment, she thought she could see her own face and that of Guma in the waters of the pond, side by side among the stars. But when she blinked, the images vanished, leaving nothing but a mirror of the sky.

11

A simple, wholesome supper awaited them: nuts, berries, and roots from the forest and flaky, roasted fish from the pond. They ate by lantern light, speaking quietly though the *tengaru* were no longer guarding them. In the tranquil twilight, the clearing seemed to be alive. It seemed its truest self by night, like the whole of the Great Forest.

Hideki picked at the roots with a grimace. "I don't understand why they brought us here. We weren't responsible for what happened."

"They must have their reasons," Shiro said. "But it makes me uneasy, not knowing who called them to our rescue or why."

"The queen said everything had to do with you," Wei told Xifeng.

For once, all of their eyes on her made her uncomfortable. "She was speaking to *all* of us, I'm sure," she said quickly.

Hideki sighed. "As for the five kingdoms of Feng Lu reuniting, that will never happen as long as mankind exists. They won't do it under the banner of one man, at any rate, as they did centuries ago for the Dragon King."

"I wish you hadn't ranted about the treaty," Shiro told him. "It isn't our place to decide the trade stipulations. A bit of jade is a small price to pay for peace, even if it won't last long."

Xifeng leaned forward. "I find it fascinating, the politics of kings."

"What it must be like to be the Emperor." A spark appeared in Wei's eye, and he speared his fish as though he held a sword. "Marching into weaker territory, bribing and threatening to get what you want. Commanding an army to do your bidding where words fail."

"True, but he can't use physical might all the time," Shiro said. "The politics of kings, as Xifeng put it, requires balance. He would not agree to this treaty unless it benefited both parties."

"But mostly him," Hideki added, and the dwarf sighed.

"It must be like using an apothecary's scale," Xifeng said. "Knowing when to add more of this or that. Evening out the two sides so they *seem* equal, though one may hold only dirt and the other gold dust."

Shiro regarded her in surprise. "You're a poet."

"And you're a nobleman." She chuckled, gesturing to his plate. "No one in a poor family would risk dining that slowly."

"I've emptied my plate three times," Wei agreed, and they all laughed.

"My family is high in our king's favor," Shiro admitted. "But I'm the only one in his employ, whereas my brothers lead lives of leisure. When one has the misfortune of being born small among the tall and handsome, one must prove oneself in any way possible. What better choice than politics, the realm of the powerful?"

"You work directly for your king?" Wei asked.

Shiro nodded. "I had to work ten times harder than a regular official to get to the same place. But I got there. I ignored the taunting and focused on winning the respect of my kingdom. It didn't earn me any more approval from my family, but what do I need of that when I have the king's?"

Wei listened with his chin lowered. "But you are noble, and already that sets you far ahead of a poor boy. I don't mean to imply your life has been easy, but your family's relations with the king was your open door."

Hideki regarded him with interest. "Do you wish to be an ambassador yourself?"

"I want to be a fighter. A warrior in the Emperor's army."

"And do his bidding where words fail?" Shiro asked, repeating Wei's earlier statement.

"Swords speak a stronger language when needed. But where is that opportunity for me?"

"Perhaps in this journey we're taking," the dwarf said kindly. "You may find your goal at the end of it, but now, I believe sleep is what we should all find." He grimaced, one hand flying to his shoulder. "It's nothing," he added, seeing their concern. "The scythe nicked me when I stabbed that attacker. I'll wash in the pond first. Those waters must be cool and healing."

"I owe you my life, Ambassador. He would have killed me."

Shiro waved Wei's thanks away. "It was what anyone would have done for a friend." They bowed low to each other.

Xifeng smelled sweet jasmine and bamboo as she lay on her pallet. Wei pulled her closer and draped a blanket over them both, and she fell asleep instantly. But despite how tired and comfortable she was, she woke several times, heart racing from nightmares of a cave in which ink-black serpents glided toward her, their eyes like drops of blood.

The third time she woke, Xifeng sat up. Wei slept like a child, his hands pillowed under his cheek, and Hideki and Shiro slumbered peacefully nearby. The sky was still bright with stars, though low clouds had begun to shroud the moon. She padded down to the pond, savoring the sensation of the soft grass between her toes, and splashed water on her fevered face.

"You do not sleep well." That ancient voice, like leaves of autumn and snow in winter. The *tengaru* queen approached, her body so frail it seemed transparent. In the dark, with her horns and tail less defined, anyone might think her simply a small, old horse. But there was no mistaking the human awareness in those eyes.

"I've been dreaming, that's all."

"That's all? Isn't that everything?" The queen's fathomless gaze took her in. "You interest me. You are divided. I knew it as soon as I saw you."

"Divided?"

"Look at yourself in the water, and perhaps you will understand better."

Slowly, Xifeng bent over her reflection in the pond, her hair spilling over one shoulder. In the moonlight, she could only see the right half of her face. The other half lay in shadow, the eye dark and wild as the night.

"You have two faces. Two beings live within you, struggling for control. One has a heart that thrives in darkness and feeds on the pain of weaker souls. The other longs to stretch a hand to the light, to live and love as others do. Have you never sensed this?"

Xifeng stared into the star-scattered water at her own face: one half bright, the other hidden, unknowable. Sweat bloomed on her forehead as she placed a hand below her heart. The creature was still and silent now, but she knew how it could come alive, writhing within the prison of her body.

"Warriors kill every day." She pictured the bloodshed on the forest path: Shiro stabbing the scythe-wielder and Wei beheading him with one sweep of his arm. "Why are they not divided, as I am? Why is it *my* fate to have this creature? The cards tell me I have a destiny beyond all others, but . . ."

"It is *not* an honor," the queen said sharply, and Xifeng turned to her, startled and chastened. "Your . . . *aunt* has done more harm than good in filling your head with this destiny. No, it is not a lie. You *are* indeed bound for the glory she foresees, if you choose that path. But isn't it better not to know? Isn't it better to wake up each day, living for the present rather than waiting for the future?"

Xifeng released a breath, her shoulders slackening. Though a part of her had doubted Guma, the truth was undeniable from the mouth of the queen. But her overpowering joy was tempered by the painful weight of what such a future would mean for her and Wei. "It is a secret I must continue to carry, then."

The *tengaru* tossed her majestic head. "You will be Empress only if you are willing to take the dark road there. But you are not the only exceptional one, and you are not alone in being favored for greatness. The sooner you understand that, the better your choices will be."

"I was annoyed with Shiro for assuming the attackers had come for him," Xifeng confessed. "You are right to scold me. I told myself I questioned Guma's prophecy, but all this time I wanted her to be right. I want . . . I *need* to be more than what I am."

"You can be," the queen said, her eyes gentle. "You can be, without taking this murky passage set before you. Your Guma wants wealth and power, but that's not why *you* want to be Empress. What is your reason for wanting such a cage?"

"A cage protects. It sets apart what is inside." Xifeng hesitated. "I want to mean something to a great deal of people. I'm tired of being no one. As Empress, I would have the right to choose for myself. Guma could not command me, and Wei would not own me."

"But another man would."

"I would sit on a throne," Xifeng argued. "I would be feared and respected, not weak and powerless like Guma or my mother. I would raise up the ones I love." She imagined her aunt well fed and resting instead of hunching over her sewing, and Wei in a high station in the palace. She could even find a husband for poor little Ning. "I would be Empress for them as much as for myself. My life would have a purpose, and I would do *anything* for that."

The queen's mouth twisted. "How quick you are to throw aside the blessings you already have. But you are young. You will learn and regret, as we all do."

"I don't understand what you mean," Xifeng said, her confidence slipping. "What blessings do you speak of?"

"The truest love and friendship rarely come to those in power." The demon queen bent her head into the pond, and when her horns met the surface, a beautiful pattern of ripples shook the night sky. They skimmed over the pond in the direction of the second bridge, the one leading to the apple tree, whose branches glistened. "That tree is the most valuable treasure on Feng Lu. I have guarded it all these ages on behalf of one for whom it is meant."

"The one destined to unite the kingdoms and bring peace to the continent?" Xifeng's heart thundered as she considered the possibility of *being* that one. Perhaps, as Empress, that was the glorious fate Guma had envisioned for her.

"The waters speak of a pair of great destinies, intertwined. One will lead to Feng Lu's salvation—the other, to its ruin. That tree could be meant for you . . . or for *her*."

Her. One word, filled with so much meaning.

The first meaning: *It may not be for you.* The second meaning:

There is another woman. And the third: *Her destiny may be greater than yours.*

"The Fool," Xifeng said flatly. Her vision blurred, as it had the day she'd seen herself destroying Ning. Every nerve in her body tingled with the sudden powerful desire to burn the tree down, to raise a torch to its branches and watch the flames weep crumbling ashes. One moment, a great relic protected by the *tengaru,* and the next, a mound of embers as fleeting as the seasons of the world. Then, they would see if the Fool—that beautiful, long-lashed, stargazing Fool—would be able to thwart Xifeng and fulfill that greater destiny.

But when her mind cleared, her anger faded as quickly as it had come. As Xifeng envisioned the pink-white blossoms withering away, never having lived, she felt a tear roll down her cheek. "If it is meant for *her,* I hope she finds it."

"Ah." Indescribable grief shaded the corners of the queen's smile. She placed a paw on Xifeng's hand. "I'm afraid life will always be a battle for you, but *that* is the part of you that you must never forget. Let it help you fight that darkness within, and perhaps you shall be the one to save us all."

"I don't know how to fight it," Xifeng whispered, her eyes stinging. "How can I destroy this creature . . . this *monster* when it is inside me, *always* with me, no matter where I go?"

"You must choose." The demon's stare on her was fierce, wild. "You wish to be Empress to have control over your life, but you already do. You have both the poison and the antidote, and you can choose not to give in. But it will be a bitter struggle if *he* has anything to say about it."

A movement caught Xifeng's eye. The water was still rippling on the surface of the pond, and a spot of darkness had formed. It resembled the yawning mouth of a cave, and someone waited for her inside—

someone she sensed had been waiting a long time. She turned away, knowing and fearing who lurked within.

"Who is he, this Serpent God?" she asked, and the trees themselves trembled.

"He means more to your Guma than she will say. Beware, Xifeng, of magic that comes too easily. There is a price for everything, as she learned and you, too, will learn. Some magic requires blood. Other magic requires a piece of your own self and eats away at your soul." The queen tensed her paw, the buds of her talons pressing into Xifeng's skin. "He taught her all she knows, but she has yet to finish paying him."

Xifeng knew, instinctively, that the *tengaru* did not mean money. So what did Guma owe this man? The breeze brushed across the grasses and they seemed to whisper: *you, you, you*.

The pond rippled once more to show Guma, gazing up with a flicker of recognition. Her sad mouth moved to form Xifeng's name, and the veil of water between them trembled.

"You are very like her. There is water in both of you, the element of resourcefulness. You drift toward each other, two streams from the same river." The queen began walking away to her pagoda between the trees. The shadows of the bridge cast dark stripes on her coppery body.

Xifeng rose, her mouth dry. "Please don't go. I don't want to be alone."

The demon turned around, a look of pity on her ancient face. "You are not alone. And all of your questions will be answered in time, but not by me. I will, however, give you one last piece of advice."

"And I will listen."

"Magic and knowledge often cost blood, but blood itself costs something, too. You pay each time you take it from a beating heart. Take care not to pay too much when you do not yet understand the currency. Beauty is not worth your soul."

She knew about the rabbits. Xifeng felt a powerful rush of resentment. What could a demon understand about the power of her face, the only gift the gods had seen fit to give her? But when the queen came close, bringing the scent of the snowy lotus blossoms, Xifeng's irritation dissolved into regret. The tips of the *tengaru*'s horns gently touched her healed cheek.

Up close, it was even clearer how weary the *tengaru*'s eyes were and how feeble her body, like the newly grown branches of the apple tree. The earth and Feng Lu would surely feel such a loss and would never again be the same. "Who will guard this clearing in your absence?" Xifeng asked, surprised by the sadness in her own voice.

"There will be another after me. Do not fear. We must all protect the treasures we are given and fight for them." Her stare pierced the area beneath Xifeng's rebellious heart.

"Thank you, Your Majesty, for your kindness."

"Is it kindness, I wonder? Good night, Xifeng," the demon queen said softly as she retreated to her grove of trees. "And if you return to the Great Forest one day, treat it with respect. My body is meant for the earth soon. We will not meet again."

12

Xifeng slept deeply, but woke the next morning still tired from the queen's riddles and half-truths. Having the ability to destroy what lay within didn't change the fact that she harbored a monster. And no matter where she was or how far she ran, it would still be with her.

She joined the others at the table, which had been replenished with roots, nuts, and sweet red cherries. But Wei and Hideki seemed more concerned about Shiro's shoulder than the food. The ambassador's injury had significantly worsened overnight.

"Gods, the wound is bleeding through your tunic." Ignoring his protests, Hideki pulled the cloth away from Shiro's shoulder, revealing a jagged cut that had turned yellow green.

Xifeng recoiled, despite having dressed the rotting skin on Guma's damaged leg daily.

"It's infected. That scythe was poisoned," Wei said ruefully. "You wouldn't have been wounded if not for me."

"You are all worrying far too much. It was nothing." Shiro yanked the tunic back in place. "You didn't ask me to save you."

"But you saved him all the same, and for that, we both owe you," Xifeng said. "Let me get you some water to clean the wound." She soaked some cloth in the pond, relieved that in daylight, the water did no more than reflect its surroundings.

Shiro sighed with relief when she placed the compress on his skin. "Thank you, my dear. That does feel better. But I'm sure it will heal in time."

They were ready to leave within the hour. Wei and Hideki gathered their sacks while Shiro filled their pouches with fruit and water. Xifeng fashioned a broom from a fallen branch and swept the platform they'd eaten on. However the *tengaru* truly felt about humans, they had treated them with fairness and generosity, and she felt it right to repay them however she could.

Wei came over with flowers the color of the dawn sky: pink tinged with gold and violet, which he had painstakingly woven into garlands. "I made them early this morning. For the queen," he explained, and she felt a rush of affection that he'd had the same impulse.

One of the *tengaru* approached their little camp. "Our queen wishes you a safe journey. You will find the path again beyond the horses. Follow it north to the city."

Xifeng and Wei exchanged glances. "We left the path over a week ago. Has it moved closer, for our convenience?" he asked.

Hideki chuckled, but the *tengaru*'s stare remained icy. "You have something for the queen. I will take it to her." It bent its head so Wei could wind the flowers around its mane.

"Then we are not to see Her Majesty again?" Shiro asked.

"She is tired. But she wishes you well and asks that you remember to respect the forest."

The demon retreated without another word, and Wei helped Xifeng onto the old gray mare. She turned her eyes back to the lake as the men prepared their own horses. Today, the blossoms strung over the pagoda had withered, their creamy petals yellowing in the sunlight, and there was no sign of the demon queen herself. Perhaps she had passed on in the night . . . or perhaps those deep, inscrutable eyes of hers watched them now from her shelter of trees.

"Great lords of the skies," Xifeng whispered, closing her eyes, "take the queen's spirit into your keeping and let her find peace in your eternal halls." They had never cared to respond to any of her prayers before, but she hoped they would now.

She looked again at the water that was so like a mirror, it seemed a piece of the heavens itself, and wondered if she would ever see this place again. A part of her almost yearned to stay.

But then the others mounted their horses and they were back in the Great Forest, on the path winding through the trees, and the clearing vanished like it had only been a beautiful dream.

They reached the Imperial City before nightfall.

The path became a wide cobblestone road, flanked every mile by the Emperor's banners. Xifeng gazed up at the dragon with a forest curled within its talon, remembering the emblem from the concubine's procession three weeks ago. They passed people leading donkeys and pushing wagons full of goods. Soon, a massive stone bridge appeared before them. In the rushing waters below, men loaded small vessels with sacks of charcoal, lumber, and rice for the city dwellers.

Across the moat, Xifeng saw two other identical bridges in the distance.

"I didn't know there were this many people on the earth," she told Hideki, who fell back to allow a large caravan to pass. The men walking beside it stared at his elegant Dagovadian horse and muttered to each other in a foreign tongue.

"There are many opportunities in the city. This is where people dream of a better life. See the men with the crude wooden spears? Likely recruits hoping to join the Emperor's army."

Xifeng noticed a great number of travelers were young women. Several were clearly seamstresses, laden down with bolts of fabric and baskets of supplies. She recognized the cheap silk she and Guma had used. "They must have purchased those from an outside market. I suppose silk is much more expensive in the city."

"I'm sure of it. The taxes are higher closer to the palace, at least in Kamatsu." Hideki watched a girl struggle with four reams of cloth. "Silk is worth a king's ransom back home."

Xifeng nodded. Silk was made only in the Kingdom of the Great Forest; it was against Imperial law to take silkworms outside its borders. Guma used to rant about the preposterous levies they'd had to pay for materials, despite how much profit the kingdom was making.

Other young female travelers carried few possessions, like Xifeng herself. Did they, too, approach the city with a fortune similar to hers? "The Fool," she murmured, scanning their faces, but they were all plain and unremarkable, and soon she grew bored and turned her attention back to the entrance.

A stone wall hundreds of feet high surrounded the city. Soldiers patrolled the towers along the top, above a burnished gold gate carved with images of dragons rampant. The immense doors stood open, flanked by armed guards observing the crowd.

The men with crude weapons clustered around one guard. He seemed to be directing them through the city. Xifeng caught the words *training field* and *tomorrow afternoon,* and knew Hideki had been right after all; they had come to try to secure a place among Emperor Jun's warriors. They looked laughably rural to her, with their twigs that longed to be spears.

She glanced at Wei, who wore an expression of ferocious delight as he studied the Imperial guards' weapons: exquisitely crafted crossbows, iron-tipped arrows, and scabbards worked in the finest bronze. She could easily imagine him in armor, wielding such beautiful and deadly tools. If he went to the training fields, she knew he could outshine those hopeful recruits.

What he might be able to do, if only he were trained, she thought.

The guards allowed them to pass without question when Shiro presented a scroll bearing the stamp of the Kamatsu king. Xifeng noticed them scrutinizing her companions' black steeds. None of them bothered to look at her old horse, and as a result, Xifeng herself. She wished fleetingly she had insisted upon riding one of the Dagovadians.

The road widened into a bustling avenue lined with fruit trees and graceful buildings, and immediately Xifeng felt her eyes and ears being pulled in every direction. She had never seen so many people in one place: men and women, young and old, their hair every shade in between black and brown and their skins gold, russet, and ebony. There were monks, officials, merchants, and seamstresses in silks of every shade, walking and riding and leading horses, oxen, sheep, and camels. They spilled from taverns and inns with sloping roofs, gated monasteries, and warehouses full of heavy crates and furniture.

The smells of roasting garlic, onions, and pepper wafted over from the food carts lining the avenue, and a cluster of stalls sold a hundred varieties of fragrant spices: saffron and cinnamon, cloves and nutmeg, cassia and ginger. A stage in the square featured dancers accompanied by an old man on a barbarian's fiddle. The instrument had twisted silk strings that produced a lilting melody when he drew a stick of horsehair across them.

Xifeng turned to ask Shiro whether they had similar fiddles in Kamatsu and saw that he had developed a sickly pallor. He swayed atop his horse, a fine layer of sweat coating his face.

Hideki steadied him, his face grim. "Hold him up, Wei. I'll make inquiries about a physician." He rode off and returned a few minutes later, breathless. "We're in the market district, quite far from the best physicians in the city, but there is one down the street. There's just one thing. She's a woman."

"You mean she's a healer?" Xifeng asked. In the poor villages surrounding her town, there had been women reputed for their knowledge of herblore. But they had mostly been called to attend difficult births or help get rid of pregnancies. In times of true need, people sought a male physician with great skill and prices to match.

Wei shook his head. "Can't we find someone else? There must be another nearby."

"She's a trained physician and she is the closest, but still . . ." Hideki bit his lip.

Shiro sagged against Wei's arm and Xifeng gave a growl of frustration. The men turned to her in surprise. "She's the best chance we have. Better to see if she can help than stay here and have Shiro sicken even more. Would you risk his life?" Wei's mouth turned down at her forceful manner of speaking, but neither of the men could argue with her logic.

"To the woman physician, then," Hideki agreed.

The tidy building they found stood on a quiet offshoot of the avenue. It had two levels and a sitting area shaded by the curving roof. A tall woman emerged who was older than Xifeng, but not yet middle-aged, with hair so black it looked blue in the shadows.

"Are you Bohai, miss?" Hideki called. "We seek a physician for our wounded friend."

"My family name is Bohai, yes." The woman spoke in a low voice, the kind music would suit well. To Xifeng's surprise, she spoke the common tongue with the same lilting Kamatsu accent as Shiro and Hideki. Hideki looked astonished as well, but made no comment as the woman approached Shiro and studied his face. She was not a beauty; Xifeng assessed that at once. But there was something pleasing about her intelligent eyes, smooth, flat nose, and wide mouth, which turned down as she felt Shiro's forehead.

"This man is deathly ill. Bring him in. You can put your horses in the back."

Hideki leapt off his horse at once and carried Shiro inside, laying him on one of several clean pallets in a chamber off the front room. Xifeng followed, scanning the shelves that held jars of herbs, roots, and powders, each labeled with the neat calligraphy of a learned woman.

The physician looked at Xifeng as if to say something to her, but then she turned to Hideki. "Could you please bring me the jars of peony root and wolfberry? They are in the front room, on the bottom shelf."

Xifeng watched him hurry to retrieve the items, bristling a bit. Did the woman imagine she couldn't read? "Can I do anything to help?" she asked pointedly.

The woman bent her blue-black head over Shiro, inspecting his wound. His eyes were closed, and his chest rose and fell with labored breathing. "Not at the moment, thank you," was the absent reply. She tugged his tunic from his injured shoulder, and Xifeng saw that the injury had grown even worse. The ragged edges had turned an oozing pale green, and the sour-sweet smell that emanated from it made her cover her nose.

Hideki rushed back in with two small jars, followed closely by Wei.

"Is he all right?" Wei asked Xifeng, hand brushing her shoulder.

"I don't know."

Shiro winced and hissed through his teeth, eyes still closed, as the physician pressed a moistened cloth over his wound. She gathered a mortar and pestle, mixing the root, powder, and several other ingredients. She used a scale to measure some of the components, and when the mixture became a white paste, she carefully daubed it on his cut.

"This is an old remedy that will keep the wound clean," she told Hideki, seeming to sense that Shiro's well-being was in his charge. "The peony root will draw out the infection. That should take a few days, and then I'll add a paste to hasten the healing of the skin." She had Shiro's calm, knowledgeable manner of speaking.

"It's a pleasant surprise to have my friend in the care of a countrywoman," the soldier said gratefully. He seemed to have forgotten his reservations about the physician being female.

"I see my accent has given me away." The woman bestowed a brief smile upon him.

"If the healing will take a few days, we ought to find lodgings. Or I suppose *I* should." Hideki glanced at Xifeng and Wei. "I don't wish to keep you two. You've been more than kind to wait with us this long."

"It's the least we can do. We're all friends now," Wei said.

Xifeng hesitated. Reality had begun to sink in now that she was so close to the palace. She needed to find a way in and figure out what to do about Wei. She thought of his envious gaze on the city guards' armor, and of the soldiers' training taking place tomorrow. This delay could buy her time to come up with a solution. "I've never had many friends," she confessed, gazing at Shiro's pale, drawn face. "And I find them precious to me now. I'd like to stay until he heals completely."

Hideki beamed at her. "It's settled. I'll see about finding lodgings."

"As for that," the physician said, wrapping a soft cloth around Shiro's shoulder, "you are all welcome to stay here while your friend heals. I'd be happy to have you."

"You are most generous, miss." Hideki reached into his tunic for a purse, but the physician stopped him.

"I do not seek payment until my charge has healed. And please, call me Akira."

13

Akira offered them lodgings, but it was clear she expected them to earn their keep. She sent Hideki to fetch water from the well and Wei to market to buy items for the evening meal. Again, she had turned to Xifeng first as though to ask her, before changing her mind. A bit insulted, Xifeng went out without being asked and carried in their belongings for the night. When Shiro had fallen asleep, his face relaxed and gaining a bit of color, Akira turned to her.

"Hideki will stay with Shiro tonight. If you'll help me prepare the upstairs room, you and Wei may have that."

Xifeng followed her, noting that the entire house was neat and meticulously clean. The physician did not seem wealthy, but she clearly did well enough never to go hungry. "When did you come here from Kamatsu?"

"My mother came from Kamatsu, but I was born here in the Imperial City. In the palace."

Xifeng gave a start. "You're a noblewoman?"

"Unfortunately not. But my father is a person of some standing at court. You might say he is *the* physician." Akira studied her with an odd expression, like pity mixed with anger. She spoke slowly, as though to a child. "What I mean is that he cares for the Emperor and Empress."

"Yes, thank you. I understood that," Xifeng said, too astonished to be annoyed that the woman thought her stupid. Moments ago, she had wondered how to find a way into the palace, and now she had been presented with a potential key: the daughter of the Imperial physician. "You would rather live alone than with your father in the palace?"

"Who is closer to the Emperor than he who cares for him in illness? A man of such rank would never acknowledge a bastard, however grudgingly he may provide for her." Her eyes cut to Xifeng. "I apologize if that offends you."

Xifeng bit down her irritation as she compared Guma's hovel with this well-kept house. She was a guest under Akira's roof and had to show respect, no matter how she actually felt. "It doesn't offend me at all, since I'm a bastard myself," she said with forced politeness. "Only *my* father never cared to provide for me at all."

The physician had the grace to blush. "I am sorry. I don't mean to complain. I know how fortunate I am to support myself without a husband. And what man would wish to marry me, anyway? I wasn't lucky enough to be born a beauty like you." The corner of her mouth lifted, taking the edge off her bitter tone. "Will you allow me to make amends with some tea?"

Xifeng accepted, satisfied that as poised as she seemed, Akira was not unlike other women Xifeng had known in her town: jealous and quick to judge.

Downstairs, Akira poured tea for her and placed a sweet rice cake on her plate. "I've imagined meeting my father many times, but he can never leave the palace. He is like the nightingale in the old legend, trapped in a gilded cage to sing for the Emperor alone." She studied Xifeng. "Your skin is as pale as the Empress's must be. I hear she and her ladies never step into the sun without a hundred servants to shield them with silk coverings."

"I wore a hat whenever I went outside. My aunt was afraid I would look like a lowly farm girl, tanned from always working outdoors, instead of a lady." Xifeng stroked the rabbit painted on her cup. A drop of tea had dripped onto the image, like blood slipping from its heart.

She felt relieved when Hideki came in and Akira turned her attention to him. "It's an honor to have guests from my mother's country. I expect you and Ambassador Shiro have come from Kamatsu on business." She glanced at Xifeng. "But what is your husband's purpose?"

Once again, the assumption that Xifeng belonged to Wei—that she had no direction of her own. She wondered what they would say if she told them they might be sitting in the presence of the future Empress of Feng Lu. "My aunt wished me to seek my fortune at court . . . as a lady-in-waiting. It is where my fate lies."

Hideki choked on his tea. "I wasn't aware of this. I thought Wei wanted to start a business in the city. Did your Guma tell you whether it is a good or a bad fate?"

"The greatest seer cannot know the end of a person's story. In any case, Wei and I have not yet come to an agreement about this." Xifeng's stomach twisted as she spoke. That was one conversation she wanted more than anything to avoid, but could not.

"The Empress's ladies are not allowed to associate with men. You would be parted from him, perhaps forever," Akira pointed out. The truth stung even more, coming from a stranger.

"Court is a dangerous place," Hideki said grimly. "It's made up of power and those poisoned by it. It's like a sand pit in the desert: you can't see one until it traps you, and then it's too late. You struggle to regain your footing, but you won't go far before sliding to the bottom."

Xifeng's eyes cut to Akira, who nodded sagely, though she probably didn't know much more about court life than Xifeng did. Xifeng struggled not to roll her eyes.

"For every step you take, there are ten others close by, hoping you'll fall so they'll have their chance," Hideki continued. "It's a madness, a desperation to climb to the top even if the slippery walls betray you."

"This is what you think of me." Xifeng set her teacup down, hard. They *dared* question her. "That I'm silly and empty-headed, and my Guma would send me to court unprepared?"

"I've no doubt she wanted a better life for you," he said, disturbed. "But in my country, mothers fought to keep their daughters away from the palace. I've seen what court can do to someone with a good heart. I've seen how Shiro has been treated simply because he is smaller than other men. The courtiers are kinder to their dogs than they are to him."

"Not even the Empress is exempt from their cruelty," Akira added. "She has given three sons to the crown, but longs for a daughter and keeps trying though she's nearly fifty. The gossips say she celebrates every festival with yet another failed pregnancy."

"And if I were the Empress," Xifeng said in a quiet, dangerous voice, "I would teach them the meaning of respect. I would execute anyone who dared speak a word against me. And that includes anyone who dared speak ill of my friends." She glanced at Shiro's motionless form in the other room. He was so kind and gentle, and he had saved Wei's life. Yes, she would take much delight in sentencing his tormenters to a painful, prolonged death.

There was a long, tense silence in which she could hear her own brutal words ringing in her ears. Where had they come from? Had it been the creature within her, once again breathing its evil thoughts from her lips?

"I would be merciful, too, to those who deserved it," she said hastily. "I would raise my friends high and treat my subjects with kindness."

Hideki's face relaxed, though his lips were still thin. "You'd be someone to be reckoned with at court, then."

Wei came in at that moment, pink cheeked and jubilant, and Xifeng rose gladly to meet him. At the physician's request, he brought the food into an adjacent room. He glanced at Xifeng as he stacked his purchases on the shelves. "Is everything all right?"

"I'm fine. Just annoyed with everyone judging me and the things I want. I told them about Guma's hope that I serve in the palace."

Wei's cheer faded. "You didn't need to bring *that* up. Hideki has a dim view of everything to do with the Emperor, including his army. I heard at market they'll be recruiting soldiers on the training fields tomorrow . . ."

Xifeng's heart leapt. "Yes, I know. I thought you could go and . . ."

"But that's an old dream. I'd prefer to stay here in the city with you."

But me, she thought helplessly. *What about what* I *prefer?*

"I passed a smithing district on the way to market. It would be simple to find work there."

"But that's not what you truly want to do," she argued, watching with acute hunger as he hesitated. If only she could make him see he belonged with the army. And if his entry into the Imperial Palace facilitated her own—if it brought him into proximity to high-ranking officers and their wives, who might mention her to the Empress—so much the better.

But Wei shook his head resolutely. "Sword-making is the craft I know, and it makes money. I can take care of you. You won't have to serve at court like that witch wanted after all."

"The *tengaru* queen told me I would end up at the palace one day." Xifeng placed a hand over her heart. "And she told me *this* was real. Something inside me threatens to poison me."

Wei took her face in his hands. "There is nothing evil inside you that your Guma didn't put there. This is what the queen likely meant."

"She told me I can choose not to listen to the creature and somehow it will go away." A tear slid down her cheek. "I could save myself, and more besides. But I'm afraid, Wei. I'm afraid I'm not strong enough and it will consume me."

He wiped her face tenderly with a calloused hand. "You *are* strong enough. You chose to leave Guma and come with me, didn't you? She tried to make you twisted like her, only you can't see it because you love her for some reason."

"Wei . . ."

"Listen to me. She raised you in the way a farmer raises oxen. For a purpose, not love. She never saw what you really are. You need to let go of her, Xifeng, and be free."

"You make it sound so simple."

"It *is* simple. Forget her and her teachings." Wei's fingers hovered over her heart. "Let no one have this but me. I love you as you are. I've tried to tell you for years."

Xifeng closed her eyes, imagining the life he had described to her: a quiet home where they'd raise babies with hearts like his, hearts that loved deeply and faithfully. She could turn her back on Guma and her destiny forever.

But what do I *want?*

Choosing Wei would be choosing obscurity. He would shield her from the world and she would know nothing but the walls of their home. She would wonder every day if their children had somehow inherited the monster within her. She would have Wei forever, but there would be no glory: nothing to work for, no one to admire her, no cause for which to fight. Loving Wei might be the end of her freedom before it had even truly begun.

But loving Guma might be the end of her sanity.

The creature would poison her from inside, and she would weaken more each day until she could no longer resist it. And even if she fled to the corners of the earth, it would be with her, this being of malevolent dark despair, haunting her in her sleep and terrorizing her when she woke. The *tengaru* prophesized that two destinies would shape their world—but which was hers? Would she save herself and Feng Lu, or would she send them to destruction?

According to the *tengaru* queen, Xifeng had both the poison and the antidote. Somehow, she had to hold fast to the latter, whatever it was—she had to resist.

"I'm afraid," she said again.

Wei stroked her hair. "I know. But I'm here, and I always will be."

If only you knew, she wanted to say, but could not.

Instead, she remained silent and let him believe what he said. It was the kindest thing she could do for him.

14

The next morning, Xifeng knelt in Akira's garden, picking flowers for Shiro's room. Heavy clouds veiled the sun and threatened rain, but she lifted her face to the sky, enjoying the smell of an impending storm.

"Gloomy day," Hideki called from where he was feeding the horses. "Will you and Wei still explore the city, as you planned?"

"I hope so. I'd like to see more of it." In fact, she had a very specific destination in mind. She grasped a flower by its stem and wrenched it from the earth, feeling satisfied when it gave way. If Wei refused to grasp his own dream, then she would seize it for him. It pained her to know that helping him might mean losing him—being parted from him forever. *But I love him,* she tried to tell herself, *and if this will make him happy, I must let him go. I'm doing this for Wei.* She ignored the tiny laughing voice that remained unconvinced, that knew the disturbing truth: the path she preferred would always place her own happiness first.

Hideki came over, scuffing his boots in the dirt. "I want to apologize if I insulted you yesterday. It was not my intent," he said awkwardly. "You never mentioned going to court before, and it took me by surprise. I only wished to warn you of the dangers you might face."

Xifeng surveyed the flowers before her. "It's not something Wei and I see eye to eye on, either. But I'd like to honor my aunt's wishes."

He cleared his throat. "A piece of advice, then. I don't know how it is here, but in Kamatsu, the eunuchs had a great deal of power."

"The half men?"

The soldier gave a start. "That's quite an insult."

"That's what my Guma called them," Xifeng recalled. "But she always believed the concubines to be more dangerous. I know eunuchs guard the king's harem and have many responsibilities in the palace. Yet how much power could a personal servant wield?"

"You'd be surprised. Some are highly respected in the royal household and even tutor young princes. Our queen had a favorite in whom she confided. If you go to court, befriend the eunuchs. They may prove useful." He gave her an encouraging nod, and she felt ashamed of her own scornful behavior the day before.

"Would you like to join Wei and me on our walk? I'll bring these to Shiro and we can go." She beamed when he gave his ready consent, and went into the pallet room, where Shiro was sitting up and chatting with Akira. His face brightened when he saw the blossoms.

"You've brought the garden to me. Thank you, my dear."

"It's only fair, since you can't join us outside today," Xifeng replied.

"You'd better take an umbrella," Akira said stiffly, handing her one without a second glance. She adjusted Shiro's pillow, pushing the vase of flowers away as she did so.

"Akira's certainly very attentive," Xifeng remarked to Hideki and

Wei, who were waiting outside. "She seemed almost jealous when I brought Shiro flowers."

"Best not to come between a healer and her charge," Wei said. "Where shall we go?"

"I'd like to see the smithing district you mentioned." She watched him for any sign of awareness, but he cheerfully took the lead, rambling on to Hideki about shields. She suspected the training fields would be near the swordsmiths, and lo and behold, as they passed through the district, men appeared carrying makeshift weapons like the ones she'd seen the day before. "Let's go this way," she called, eager to follow the recruits. "I want to see the public gardens."

Despite the threat of rain, merchants were out in full force, hawking wares beneath small umbrellas to protect their goods. Within moments, the training fields appeared in the midst of a few schools and city offices, taking up an entire section of the district.

Xifeng glanced at Wei. He stopped midsentence, his eyes fixed on the swords, targets, and crossbows. "Is *this* where the Emperor's army trains?" she asked innocently. "Wouldn't they practice in secret on the palace grounds, to hide their tactics?"

"It must be a basic training ground." Despite Hideki's disapproval of the Emperor's army, he seemed as interested as Wei. "It appears they're holding trials for new recruits today."

It was simple work to distinguish between the hopefuls, who stood gawking with their homemade weapons, and the true soldiers, who were all bare chested, shaven headed, and dressed in the same loose red-and-gold pants. Some of the soldiers emptied crates onto the field, revealing spears, swords, and granite boulders, as several men on horseback watched from the perimeter. These mounted warriors wore full armor that appeared wrought with pure gold.

"Is that the captain?" Xifeng asked, eyeing the oldest among them.

Wei shook his head in awe. "Captains don't wear armor that expensive. That must be the General himself, inspecting his junior officers."

The soldiers on the field divided into four groups for demonstrations. One group ran around the edge of the field, arms and legs pumping in perfect time, while another set themselves up on the far end with the boulders, taking turns throwing as far and as fast as they could. A third group used heavy sacks as targets for their spears, and a fourth broke up into pairs for fencing.

Xifeng peeked again at Wei, whose eyes shone as he watched the swordplay. No matter what he said, his dream of being a warrior was more alive than ever. His body tensed with energy, awakened by the music of swords dancing. She felt a tug beneath her heart at his joy. *I'm doing this for you, my love,* she thought, once again ignoring the creature's low, sardonic laugh from deep within.

"Join them," she urged him.

He gave a great shout of a laugh. "You're not serious. Those men have trained for years. They would run me through like a wild boar."

"You'd be as good as any of them," she said staunchly. Wei pressed his lips against her forehead, eyes still on the field.

The running soldiers steadily approached them, skin dewy with sweat. They were of varying heights, many shorter and stockier than Wei, but each was a warrior in his own right. Muscles rippled in their shoulders as they moved, breathing easily despite their speed. They were a mass of force and strength, powerful and relentless, trained to overtake a battlefield in the name of the Emperor. They kept their eyes forward as they ran, intensely focused on the horizon.

Someone giggled nearby, and Xifeng turned to see a flock of girls about Ning's age, watching the warriors with undisguised lust.

"Now *there's* a good reason to enter the army," Wei joked, and she scowled at him.

"We didn't have that back home. Or at least, *I* didn't," Hideki added with a grin.

The officers in gold armor dismounted and paced in front of the prospective recruits, scrutinizing them. Every so often, they would point at one and instruct him to join a group. The youngest officer had an open, friendly face that reminded Xifeng of Ken. Unlike the others, his hair grew long and thick on his head, blending in with the neatly trimmed beard he wore. He stood not twenty feet from them, and Xifeng longed for him to turn and point at Wei.

"He isn't much older than we are," she told Wei. "The Emperor must hold him in high esteem to put him in gold armor."

The older officers had pointed to at least a dozen recruits, but the young man hung back, his head tilted in consideration. *Turn around,* Xifeng thought, chewing on her nails. Spot after spot filled, and still he stood with his back to Wei. How many spaces were left?

"Are you all right?" Hideki asked her, grinning. "You look as nervous as some of those would-be soldiers."

She dropped her hand, but kept her eyes on the young officer. Even the way he crossed his arms reminded her of Ken. He certainly looked kinder and more approachable than his stern elders. The other gold-armored men gathered together, talking in low voices. In a minute, they would retreat and tell those they hadn't selected to go home. Guma's words reverberated through her mind, distant chimes of her old life: *It is for you to take your destiny in your hands.*

Now was her chance.

"I humbly beg your pardon, sir," she said loudly, approaching the youngest officer.

"Xifeng! What are you doing?" Wei demanded, but she ignored him.

The officer turned in surprise. Up close, she saw he couldn't be older than twenty, and again she marveled that the Emperor would appoint a youth to such a high position.

"Yes, what is it?" he asked as his companions watched suspiciously.

Xifeng's heart beat so fast, she thought she might faint, but still she barreled on. "I wondered, sir, if you might have room for one more recruit among your swordsmen." Her blood pounded in her ears as she waited for his response, her head bowed with respect. His boots were of the most beautiful, thick brown material, soft and durable. She thought of the blisters Wei had to endure because of his ill-made shoes.

"You're not offering to be one of my men, are you?" There was a smile in the young officer's voice, and kindness, too.

Xifeng took heart and would have continued speaking, when another man approached. He was in his fifties with a face devoid of humor and spoke to the young officer with a stiff, resentful manner. "Sir, we don't have much time."

"I'm aware of that, Second Commander," the young man replied calmly, then addressed Xifeng again. "Unfortunately, miss, I'm sorry to say all of the positions have been filled."

"You can't mean that, sir," she said, panic rising within her. "My friend . . ."

"There are many hopefuls whenever we recruit. We cannot choose all of them. We can't possibly feed or train that many men." His voice held genuine regret. "I am sorry to disappoint you, but we've selected everyone we want. Perhaps your friend can come back next year."

A year? Xifeng's stomach dropped as she watched him walk away, his armor glinting despite the lack of sun. She had been thoroughly dismissed.

The creature suddenly shifted within her, and then the words on her tongue slipped out before she could stop them. "Would you turn your back on greatness?"

The young man stopped and slowly turned to face her as the other officers stared, shocked into silence by her rudeness. Xifeng pressed her lips together, beads of perspiration forming on her brow. She almost wished the creature would tell her what to say next, but the movement beneath her breastbone had stopped as abruptly as it had begun.

"I beg your pardon, sir," she stammered, her face burning, "but my friend's talent is such that he deserves a chance, and I didn't see you choosing anyone, as the other commanders did. You wear the same armor they do, and I think you ought to have a say in the matter, even if they are superior to you." As soon as she said it, she realized her mistake: the Second Commander had referred to him as *sir*, indicating that he ranked *below* the younger man.

But however she expected the officer to react, it was not by laughing. She kept her head down and felt him studying her as he chuckled. "You think that, do you? Your friend is lucky indeed to have you fighting his battles for him."

"He fights his own battles, sir," she said quickly. "I am merely his messenger."

"Well, then, little messenger, where is he?"

Xifeng turned to Wei, who looked mortified as he and Hideki came forward.

The young man looked them both over. "Enjoying the demonstrations, are you?"

The crease between Wei's brows deepened. "I hope you take no offense at this woman's forward manners. I did not ask her to speak for me." Xifeng hid her annoyance, knowing he would see—sooner or later—that she had been brave enough to steer his life on the right course.

"I'm not offended. I'm glad she spoke on your behalf." The young man's keen eyes moved to Hideki. "You're a soldier. I can tell by your stance. Kamatsu, I suppose, on a mission to our court," he added, without a trace of judgment, and Hideki gave a startled nod. The officer turned back to Wei. "You, on the other hand, are a son of the Great Forest. But if you keep such company, you must indeed be a swordsman as this woman proclaims."

Wei puffed up his chest, though he spoke modestly. "I'm a novice, sir. I was employed by a craftsman and often fenced with customers." He hesitated. "Your men's swords must be of fine quality. But I can hear from the sound that they aren't as sharp as they could be. There's a lower pitch when two blades meet."

The young officer listened with interest as Wei described the best types of animal hide to buff and hone the blade. "Well, as I told your little messenger, our ranks are full. But I admit I'm curious to know whether you fence as well as you craft."

"Better. He has won contests," Xifeng blurted. It was a small lie, as Wei had only ever entered one unofficial competition. Truthfully, it had been more of a drunken display of bravado when young townsmen combined cheap wine with swords, but still, Wei had emerged the victor.

"Wei, why don't you join us on the field and show us what you know?"

Wei's nostrils flared, his hunger palpable. "I have no formal training . . ."

"What's formal training without natural talent?" The man surveyed him once more. "The Emperor's soldiers you see on the field fight under the Red Banner. It is their responsibility to train new recruits for the Green Banner."

Xifeng struggled to recall what Wei had told her about the banners, the divisions of the Emperor's army. Warriors belonging to the upper hereditary banners enlisted based on family name and status; the Red Banner might be one of these prestigious groups. If so, each of the soldiers here belonged to families of the highest rank.

"Sir," the Second Commander interrupted, "it is your decision, of course, but do you think it wise when we have already selected all the swordsmen we need?" Xifeng darted a glance at him, noting how his mouth twisted with displeasure, and wondered again what rank the young man held. It didn't seem possible for him to claim such high status over experienced soldiers.

But the young officer answered him in a calm, decisive tone. "I do." He led Wei onto the field without a second glance. The fencers halted their activity and faced him with respect, then one stepped forward and handed Wei a sword. Within moments, Wei became one of them—running, lunging, and parrying, though he did so with less finesse than they did.

Xifeng couldn't help smiling, knowing how much he longed for this. She felt Hideki's eyes on her and waited for his disapproving comment. But it didn't come.

"That was bold of you," he said. "If Wei impresses him enough, I wouldn't be surprised if he kept him for the army."

She didn't need Hideki's confirmation; she knew in her bones the young officer *would* be impressed. How could he not? Wei would join the Emperor's army, and then she would use his connections to gain entry to court herself. If that somehow failed, she might be able to leverage Shiro's position as ambassador. But then again, he came from Kamatsu, a nation that had only just stopped warring with the Great Forest and had entered into a tentative peace.

Akira, a voice whispered.

Yes, if somehow her plan for Wei failed, she might exploit Akira as a link to the palace. Surely a friend of the Imperial physician would rise high in the royal circles.

There were so many paths, so many open doors—Xifeng had only to be bold, to be alert. And then she and Wei would both be on the inside, their fates intertwined as the cards predicted.

There are no coincidences, Guma always said. *Everything that happens is meant to.*

Xifeng listened for the voice again, but it said no more—nor did the creature move within. It had awoken during her conversation with the officer, when she thought all hope had been lost for Wei. She had roused it . . . or perhaps—thinking of the bold words she'd spoken—*it* had roused *her*. For once, her horror was tempered with curiosity.

Could it be possible that the creature had her interests at heart? If she dared embrace it, would it come and go—would it help her at her will? The idea both intrigued and terrified her.

A warm rain began to fall, lightly at first and then in sheets, and Hideki held the umbrella over their heads. The soldiers didn't seem to notice it at all as they continued training, though the senior officers had also opened umbrellas of their own.

"We should go," Hideki said. "It might be dark by the time they've finished training, and I'm suffering for a drink."

They made their way back down the avenue, passing people who ran by with jackets over their heads. Hideki ducked into one of the teahouses to get his drink, so Xifeng continued on back to Akira's house alone. She shook out the umbrella on the front step and entered.

Shiro and Akira were still talking in the pallet room, as though they hadn't moved since the others left. Shiro was sitting up with a clean bandage on his shoulder and healthy color in his cheeks. So deep in conversation were they that neither of them noticed Xifeng watching from the doorway. The topic seemed innocent enough—they spoke of the merchant ships that sailed between Kamatsu and the mainland—but she was more interested in the way the dwarf leaned toward Akira, and the way the physician's cheeks turned pink as she responded to him.

The woman's earlier jealousy had not been that of a physician for her charge, but another kind entirely.

Xifeng flushed, knowing she was witnessing a private moment, but her feet seemed locked in place. *This is how love begins,* she thought wistfully. The shy meeting of eyes, the exchanged smiles, the tentative brush of hands. A kindling grew in her heart that had nothing to do with the creature within; it was a *want,* a longing as palpable as hunger for food.

She couldn't recall how it had happened with her and Wei. It seemed like he had been there forever, a constant in her life, as permanent as the seasons. And though she loved him, she had always maintained a distance. That was what living up to Guma's fortune meant—guarding herself from falling completely, even when she desperately wanted to. But watching Shiro and Akira made the yearning rise inside her like chilled hands stretching toward a flame.

What would it be like to fall together?

She backed away, feeling cold and alone and hoping they wouldn't see her. But her footsteps broke the spell. Instinctively, Shiro and Akira moved farther apart. The physician excused herself and left the room, eyes still shining, and Xifeng took her place beside Shiro's pallet.

"Akira tells me you plan to enter the palace," he said, folding his hands over his stomach. "I won't warn you off like Hideki has, but I hope you've given it careful consideration. Once inside a king's court, it's very difficult to come back out again."

"You must know that well." The candlelight lit the elegant lines of Shiro's face. He seemed too young, Xifeng thought, to wear the sadness she saw on his features.

"My father was our king's chief adviser. I grew up in the highest circles of the court and married a woman of even greater rank. A daughter of the king."

"Is she the princess you spoke of before, who wore pearls in her hair?"

"That was her. One of many unimportant daughters the king had to marry off. A spare to give away to a useless being." He gestured to himself as he would to a beast and not a man merely small in stature. "He did it to please my father, who was keen to be connected to the royal family and even keener to get rid of me. My wife and I moved to a small house in the country."

Xifeng watched the play of emotions on his handsome face. "What happened?"

"She killed herself. She preferred death to being married to someone like me."

The sorrow and anger in his voice moved her deeply. "You are good and honorable, and you deserve a better family than the one you were given."

Shiro raised his beautiful, sad eyes to hers. "Some of us must rely on friends to see the best within us. That is how we find balance." He made an effort to smile as he changed the subject. "And balance is what you need to succeed at court . . . like that apothecary's scale you so aptly mentioned."

"Balance?"

"The balance between your ambition and your soul. Between being strong and being kind, which some perceive as weakness."

"It must be like a game," Xifeng ventured. "Maintaining relations at court and overseas. Allowing other kings to believe they have power when you hold all the cards."

He tipped his head, observing her. "Do you relish such a life?"

She evaded the question. "I accept whatever the gods bestow upon me, as we all must." Something in his gentle manner made Xifeng want to tell him everything she could not say to Wei. "There are things I hate to admit about myself. I'm not the kind of person I want to be . . . the person my mother must have hoped I'd be."

"We all have our battles to fight, but we can choose to overcome them. I see how much you love Wei, though you try to hide it. Why is that?"

"I'm afraid. My mother loved my father so much, it killed her when he left. Guma wanted to protect me, to avoid my giving someone that much power over me. She wanted me to forge my own path, free of any shackles." *Except the ones she put on me herself.* "Perhaps it would be better for him to take his road and I, mine."

"But you and Wei clearly love each other. Such a love wouldn't be a risk, would it?"

She shuddered. "I might lose him, and what would happen to me then?"

"Perhaps your mother was never happier than when she had your father. Isn't it better to give up a fraction of your freedom to gain tenfold in happiness, even for a short time?"

Though Xifeng's hungry heart lurched at his words, she felt something—like a small, determined hand—tugging it back into place. And when she left to let him rest, Shiro's question haunted her all the way upstairs.

15

Wei joined the soldiers every morning for the rest of the week. On the seventh day of their stay with Akira, he announced that the Commander had requested his presence once more.

"He has a proposition for me," he said casually, though his eyes shone and he hadn't eaten a bite of his porridge. "I'll be meeting the craftsman who makes their weaponry."

Xifeng squeezed his hand, even as her heart sank. A craftsman, after she had fought to win the officers' support of him. "We can all guess what sort of proposition he'll make. But I thought you'd be asked to join the army, at least."

"The other officers overrode the Commander's decision," Wei explained, his face falling a bit. "They say they have too many swordsmen already, but I'll take whatever they give me. I don't want to ask for more and risk losing the offer."

Shiro's eyes widened. "Did you say the *Commander*?"

Wei nodded. "He's young, only my age, but brilliant. Xifeng and

Hideki met him the first day, too. He said I was a natural-born swordmaker."

"But the Commander of the Army is the Emperor's eldest stepson. That's the Crown Prince himself who has taken an interest in you. You didn't know?" Shiro and Akira burst out laughing at the expression on Wei's face.

Xifeng ignored them and sat back in her chair, hard. The Emperor's stepson, the heir to the throne of the Great Forest. That explained his youth but evident superiority over his fellow officers. Her cheeks warmed when she remembered him laughing good-naturedly at her blunder.

"This is a sign from the Dragon Lords themselves," she murmured to Wei, who looked at her with fierce joy. "It's a testament to your hard work."

"Why don't we all go and support Wei?" Hideki asked. "Is Shiro well enough, Akira?"

"Please say yes." Shiro clasped his hands in mock entreaty. "I'm growing fat from sitting around with nothing to do but admire your pretty face."

Akira turned bright red. "I can't go, so I entrust your care to everyone else. If you come home with that wound open again, you'll have to fend for yourself."

"I'll make that smelly paste for him," Wei offered, and they all erupted into laughter.

Later that morning, they found the soldiers already running and fencing on the field. The Crown Prince, as they now knew him, approached when he spotted Wei. He was too soft featured to be handsome, but the pleasure in his greeting brightened his face. They all bowed low to him, and he nodded at each as they were introduced.

"Ambassador Shiro, it's an honor. I look forward to seeing you in the palace," he said, then smiled at Xifeng. "So you've brought your exquisite wife and loyal messenger again, Wei."

"I am Wei's loyal messenger, Your Imperial Highness," Xifeng confirmed.

"But not his wife?" the Crown Prince asked, noting the omission. He raised an eyebrow at Wei, who shifted his feet, and surveyed her with heightened interest.

Xifeng pounced upon his curiosity. A maiden was more appealing than a matron, and she wanted very much to appeal to this stepson of the Emperor. "Not his wife," she agreed, ignoring Hideki's appalled expression. "I traveled with Ambassador Shiro as my chaperone. My aunt was unwell and charged him with the task of protecting my virtue." The men stilled at this blatant lie.

"Forgive my mistake."

"There is no forgiveness needed, Your Highness, except from yourself. I did not know you the first time we met and spoke too boldly."

He made a gracious gesture. "Truth cannot be spoken too boldly. What you said about Wei's talents was true. He has a gift and I am in a position to offer him employment."

The tension eased a bit as Hideki and Shiro murmured their congratulations and Wei bent his head in gratitude, his sharp-featured face so full of emotion that Xifeng longed to take his hand. But she knew he wouldn't thank her for it, not in front of the Commander of the Army. She settled for bowing to the Crown Prince in thanks, though she felt a crackling beneath her heart. This was not what Wei *truly* wanted. He would resign himself to sword-making because it was safe, and it was what he knew and would help him provide for her.

Xifeng summoned her courage. "If I may again speak boldly, Your

Highness, you should know Wei's greatest wish is to join the Emperor's army. Craftsmanship is his trade, one he will happily accept from your generosity. But to be a warrior, a swordsman, is his passion . . . one I hope you'll consider fulfilling." She avoided Wei's eyes, knowing what she would see: displeasure that she'd spoken for him, and suspicion that she'd done so to put off marrying him.

The Crown Prince gazed at her in silence.

"I understand your fellow officers believe the ranks to be full, but I entreat you to make an exception on Wei's behalf. You will not regret it, Your Highness, the way you will regret wasting his true talent." She kept her eyes respectfully on the field over his shoulder, praying she hadn't gone too far, and noticed a group of monks gathering to watch the training. One of them glanced briefly in her direction and she shivered, remembering the monk in the mirror.

"You speak well, Xifeng," the prince said at last. "And speaking on behalf of a friend is to be commended. What you say about Wei's talent is true. I did not know he felt so strongly about joining the army, as he seemed content to accept the role of craftsman." He glanced at Wei, who flushed slightly. "I will grant your request, if that's what he wants. I can persuade the others to recruit him on a trial basis. If he proves himself, then he shall be made a full soldier."

Xifeng forgot all about respect as she looked at the prince full in the face, breath catching in her throat. Had he truly spoken those words?

Wei looked as stunned as though the Commander had offered him his own job. "It is what I want, Y-Your Highness," he stammered.

The Crown Prince smiled. "Then it's settled. Come with me."

Xifeng watched them go, cheeks still aflame at her own daring. It was as though the heavens had suddenly opened. She didn't think she would be surprised, just then, if the gods themselves appeared on the field before her. "Did I persuade a prince to give Wei a better position?" she asked, hands on either side of her hot face. "And did he agree instead of ordering my execution?"

Shiro and Hideki laughed.

"I knew you had spirit, but I didn't know how much," the dwarf said.

"I was wrong when I warned you about court. I think you'll be the one everyone else should watch out for," Hideki added, turning to Shiro. "She hasn't even reached the palace and she's already ordering royalty about."

Xifeng felt clammy with nervous sweat. "It was worth taking a chance. I knew he would have resigned himself to whatever the prince gave him and never asked for more."

"A soldier's salary won't make anyone rich, but there's comfort and security, no matter which banner he'll be placed under. Now you can marry and truly be man and wife." Hideki hummed as he strolled away down the field, tracking Wei's progress like a proud older brother.

Shiro eyed Xifeng solemnly. "Should I assume that what you did just now means you've made up your mind? About the matter we discussed?"

She averted her eyes from the sorrow in his face that was not for her. "I can't trap myself like that. There are things I know about my future . . . things I can't tell Wei. Not yet."

"The future may yet be changed. Consider that before you throw away a certainty for a possibility." Shiro turned and walked after Hideki.

Xifeng twisted her hands together, watching Wei on the field through a film of tears. *I am destined for another,* she imagined telling him. *I can never be yours, for you cannot take me where I seek to go.*

The cards insisted Wei would always be a part of her fate, in spite of the Empress prophecy. Perhaps they had known all along that he would be tied to her through pain and hopelessness, kept forever at arm's length—that he would be her ultimate sacrifice to achieve the destiny they foresaw.

She closed her eyes and wished fervently that she had never met him.

16

The dreaded subject came up that night.

"I'm glad Shiro has healed enough to go to the palace, but Akira didn't seem very happy," Xifeng remarked. "Do you think he'll come back?"

"He will, if he truly wants her." Wei wore an expression she feared, knowing what it meant. "And now I'll tell you what *I* truly want. What I've wanted since I first met you."

"You were nine when we met," she said, smiling, though dread rose in her throat like acid.

"No jokes this time, Xifeng," he said gruffly. "No excuses. I want you to be my wife. I can't ask you in a grand, poetic way. I haven't had a fine education like Shiro. But I've loved you for ten years, and there's no one to stop us now."

She wanted to weep, not because of the tenderness in his eyes, but because she loved him too and could not let herself admit it. If she gave in, if she yielded her heart and her life to his keeping, she would be no better than her mother. And now the *tengaru* queen had confirmed her destiny; she had as good as promised that Wei would be Xifeng's sacrifice. *You are meant for much, much more,* came a whisper from deep within, which did nothing to comfort her.

"You impressed His Highness today," Wei went on. "He said you spoke as well as any lady and you're every bit as beautiful. He wanted to ask you to join the Empress's attendants, since you're still unmarried. He's certain his mother would like you."

Her mouth went dry. She grasped the table edge, for her knees threatened to buckle beneath her. She had dared to seize her fortune and Wei's, and the heavens had rewarded her. "He said that?" she whispered, heart drumming with fierce triumph.

"Yes, but you don't need to do that anymore," he said earnestly. "Why slave for the Empress when you could be the mistress of our home? Every soldier gets a bit of land and a small income. I won't have riches, Xifeng, but I never wanted them. I want you."

She leaned her head against him, knowing he liked her best when she was gentle and quiet, but inside, she felt like screaming. She felt like raking her nails on the walls until her hands bled to make him understand.

"You mean everything to me," she said, and in her voice he could already hear her refusal. He pulled away, his face darkening. "I care more for you than I do for anyone else."

"Then why?" he demanded. "Why do you keep refusing me?"

"I'm not refusing you. I have never refused you."

"You always find a reason to delay. That's the same thing." He backed away from her pleading hands. "If you truly loved me, you would've agreed years ago. So what are you doing? Waiting for someone better to come along? Is that it?" His voice grew louder with each question. He took in her silent, downcast face. "That *is* it. You're saving yourself for someone else."

"Stop it, Wei."

A vein throbbed in his neck. "Who? Who is he?"

Xifeng glanced toward the door. "Please . . ."

But his was an anger that had grown and festered for ten years, and there was no stopping it now. "Tell me, what more can I do to deserve you?" He yanked his arm from her reach. "Maybe you're too busy missing your Guma's beatings to see what's in front of you, so I'll tell you. I'm a good man, Xifeng. I let you have your own way and speak your mind . . ."

"You think I don't know that? That I'm so blind and stupid?"

"Yes, I do!" he shouted, his face bright red. "I offer you the world . . ."

"Yes, the world as *you* see it!"

"I saved you from that evil woman!"

"Only to trap me yourself." She watched him turn away and run a trembling hand over his head. "I was Guma's, and now you want me to be yours. I have my own soul and my own destiny, and I'm tired of belonging to someone else."

The wrath in Wei's eyes made her take a step back. "I know what this is about. This has something to do with her scaring you into thinking you'll lose your mind like your mother did."

Xifeng dug her nails into her palms. He was so close, *too* close to the truth.

"She never thought I deserved you," he said through gritted teeth. "So she made up some story about how you're not destined to be with me, is that right? You're such a child to believe her. The only magic that bitch has, and will ever have, is her foolish lies."

"You've never understood and you never will. Guma decides nothing for me where you're concerned. Do you know how many beatings I've suffered to see you?" She shut her eyes, exhausted. "I can't give you everything without the risk of losing *myself* in the process."

"You're unnatural," Wei breathed, his voice ragged with disbelief. "You'll throw away something you have, for fear of losing it anyway. Do you see what she's done to you? You *are* her creature." He was frightening in his fury and despair, nothing close to the gentle lover she knew. "What if I were to kill her? Is that what I need to do to free you of this obsession? Shall I put my hands around her useless neck and squeeze the life out of her?"

"She has nothing to do with you and me."

"She has *everything* to do with you and me!" he bellowed. He stormed to the doorway, shoulders convulsing. When he spoke again, he was so quiet she could barely hear him. "You think I'll always be there and I'll wait forever. But it's not true, Xifeng. It's not true."

She heard tears in his voice, and it felt like a sword had run her through. "You are why I was brave enough to leave her. You are my reason to live," she pleaded, desperate to believe her own words even if they rang untrue.

He braced one hand against the doorway, speaking in that strange, choked voice. "But not your only reason. You live to fulfill some destiny she saw for you."

Xifeng shut her burning eyes and pictured the card with the handsome warrior holding a bloodstained flower. That card appeared in each of Guma's readings without fail. But how could they be sure of its meaning? And if the sacrifice called for *was* Wei, would Xifeng have to give him up so soon, before she had even reached the palace?

For if this part of her destiny broke away before it was meant to, who was to say the rest of it wouldn't disappear, too? She might be left with a future in which she had nothing at all.

"You are part of my fate," she said, tears choking her voice. "You've always been part of it and always will be. If you go, it will be all wrong,

Wei." She flung her words like a rope to keep him with her, but he was drifting and they could both feel it.

He leaned his head against the wall. "I told the Crown Prince today you would accept his offer. He expects you at the palace tomorrow, to be introduced to his mother."

Xifeng stared at his drooping shoulders and the reddened, curved shell of his ear. "You knew. You knew I wouldn't say yes."

"I knew."

"And you still asked me."

"I'm done. You're free."

His words bled her dry. She sank to her knees, and behind her closed eyes, she saw an endless stretch of meaningless years in which they led separate lives. Years in which she did not occupy his every waking thought, as she did now. He would go on without her and perhaps grow to love someone else, someone unhindered and unafraid to give her whole heart. She believed she understood, in that moment, what her mother had died to escape.

Xifeng felt flames igniting in her breast. She needed him. He was the warrior on the card, and his fate and hers were twin rivers carved into the earth, deep and permanent. She burned with the determination of it. "We will find a way to be together still," she vowed.

"You've got what Guma always wanted now," he said bitterly. "And you'll learn it's more of a prison than marrying me could ever be. You'll be locked away in that *harem* forever."

"I won't believe that. I can't." She went to him, her heart a scorching bonfire of a storm, lightning raging from within her rib cage as she forced him to face her. "It's not the right time for us to marry, but that doesn't mean it never will be." The lie slipped from her lips as easily as venom. She would not lose him. She would not lose her destiny.

He scoffed and would have turned his tear-streaked face away, but she gripped his jaw, fingernails digging into his skin.

"Everything I do will be for you. I helped you get into the army, didn't I? I can do more from within the court. Is that not love enough for you? Why do I need to be your wife to prove you are the one I hope and dream for?"

The words spilled out on their own, ringing with seductive power and promise. She would wrap her coils around him in tender confinement and be not his captive, but his captor. She felt him catching the edges of her fire, no matter how badly he wanted to resist.

He gripped her wrist and pulled her close, fierce eyes meeting her own. "I don't want your hopes and dreams," he said in a voice like a fresh-hewn blade. "I want you to give all of yourself to me. To be as much under my spell as I am under yours."

She would not lose him, she thought as she took his hand and led him to the bed. She wouldn't let him go, no matter how much he wanted from her that she couldn't give. Their bodies fit together like interlaced fingers. And he need never know that to her, he was a mere possession: a cloak on her shoulders, the feathers on her wings. She needed him, but without her, he served no purpose. She would let him believe whatever he wanted.

Later, he lay with his head pillowed on her breast and the tears drying upon his face.

"I will always find a way to be with you," she whispered tenderly. "I will break down the gates of the palace if that's what it takes."

But he didn't reply.

And when Xifeng woke the next morning, she was alone in the bed, and he and all of his belongings had vanished.

17

The Imperial Palace seemed to Xifeng an earthly rendering of the Dragon Lords' home in the heavens. It shimmered through the gates, a colossus of gold roofs, pillars, and courtyards of stone. She stared at it with the strange sensation that it gazed back—recognized her. Her fate lay here, in this vast city of interconnected buildings linked by covered corridors, and in a moment she would enter.

Will I ever come out again?

She squared her shoulders and approached the guards. "The Crown Prince requests my presence," she told them. They stared as though they had never seen anything like her. One of them had an eye that kept twitching suspiciously. "His Highness said to tell you I seek the Little Fisherman." She had no idea what that meant, other than it was some sort of password Wei had left for her. But it seemed to work, for they stepped aside to let her through.

"Find Master Kang in the Sunset Pagoda, at the top of the stairs," the twitching-eye guard said pompously. "His Highness has instructed him to take you to Master Yu and Madam Hong."

Xifeng held her head high. She would not be intimidated by their scornful appraisal or the important-sounding names he had flung at her. At least, she could *appear* not to be intimidated.

She crossed a courtyard of rocks like gray eggs, and a great emptiness rose up to meet her. A meditative, eerie silence reigned here, though guards in fine armor were stationed everywhere. It made her feel more alone than ever, and she felt Wei's absence like a phantom limb.

The ache was so sharp she had to pause for breath, his face swimming before her eyes. He had always been there, a thread of joy in her frayed life, and now he was gone, off to begin the life he'd lead without her. Had she done right to push him onto a different path? If only she'd been brave enough to tell him *he* was far too good for *her*. She was nothing but a selfish coward who could neither love him nor let him go.

She despised herself. But there was nothing to do but live with her choice.

With great effort, Xifeng climbed the sprawling steps to the first level of the palace. The royal family clearly revered nature, for all around her, the stern lines of the walls and pillars were softened by peony gardens, ponds full of brilliant blue-and-orange fish, and little red-roofed pavilions dotting the grass. Lanterns graced every archway and lined each flower bed, and she knew at night, they would shine among the blossoms like stars fallen from the sky.

She passed grave, important-looking men, each with a different cap or symbol embroidered upon his clothing to mark his rank or position. She had no idea who they were supposed to be—only that they all appeared clean, well fed, and well rested.

The Sunset Pagoda lay across the garden. It stood about twenty feet high, its vaulted ceiling supported by nine sturdy pillars, each carved with a blessing or prayer. It faced another pond full of sun-colored fish swimming joyfully against an imaginary current.

As Xifeng came closer, she saw a man standing inside with his back to her. For a moment, she felt an irrational, overpowering fear, for his bald head and the powerful slope of his shoulders reminded her of the monster she'd seen in a bronze mirror, his brown monk's robes fluttering in the wind. But he turned around with such a pleasant face, she went forward without hesitation, feeling foolish.

"You are Master Kang?" she asked.

His smooth, unlined face broke into a toothy smile, his eyes twinkling like pebbles in a stream. "I am indeed." His lilting singsong voice rose above the normal pitch of a man. "And you are the maiden of whom the Crown Prince spoke so well. Xifeng, is it? A queenly name."

From his high voice, Xifeng knew he must be one of the eunuchs Hideki had advised her to befriend. He took a fan from his robes and fluttered it as he studied her, wrists twirling delicately. He looked to be a bit older than her, likely in his midtwenties. She tried to keep her eyes down with respect, but couldn't help glancing at the shining yards of silk he wore, which were the soft hue of a mountain in summer.

"Beautiful, isn't it?" He plucked complacently at his long tunic embroidered with turtles. "Our seamstresses are very good. Though they did assure me this color wouldn't suit me, and see how wrong they were?"

Xifeng hid a smile. She found it hard to imagine him as scheming or powerful, the way Hideki had painted the eunuchs. But Guma had warned that cunning far outweighed physical might in the palace, and Xifeng might well believe it of this man, whose flippant manner did not entirely mask his intelligence.

"You're as beautiful as His Highness said, I'm afraid," the eunuch remarked, continuing his friendly scrutiny. "All the ladies are talking of it, you know. I'm sorry to say you won't be very popular." His giggle shimmered like a dragonfly skimming over the pond.

"I only seek the approval of Her Imperial Majesty." After a beat, she added, "And yours, of course, if you'll grant it to me."

Kang's eyes crinkled. "Oh, yes, you'll win my heart with that flattery, but I'm not popular enough to have influence here. I've been here ten years, and they still haven't forgiven me for being the son of humble fishing folk." He beckoned with his fan, and they began walking around the edge of the pagoda. "Tell me about yourself before I fling you into the nest of female vipers."

"There isn't much to tell." Xifeng briefly described her journey and newfound friends.

"Ambassador Shiro, come at last," Kang repeated, raising an eyebrow. "The Emperor has waited impatiently for him. I hear he carried important documentation."

The eunuch paused, waiting for her to elaborate, but she remained silent. Despite his harmless appearance, Xifeng knew he was likely searching for a way to advance—and it wouldn't be through her, not where Shiro was involved. Not when she had herself to worry about.

"Where are you from?" she asked, changing the subject.

"Oh, a tiny village in the middle of nowhere." He winked. "They aren't fond of people like us rising to their station, though most of them weren't born in a palace, either. That's why you and I will be friends."

Xifeng gave a polite laugh, but privately resolved to keep her own counsel. It had been simple to fall into friendship with sensible, straightforward Shiro and Hideki. But the eunuch, for all his wrist-twirling, might be something else entirely.

They passed a structure housing fruit trees and medicinal gardens smelling of mint, sage, and lemongrass. Each building boasted ornate windows and intricately chiseled doors of fine wood. The price of one, Xifeng felt sure, would be enough to feed her entire town for a full year. In the adjoining courtyard stood another edifice equipped with a stage for palace theatricals, which adjoined the musicians' quarters and the scholars' complex.

"The mathematicians, lawmakers, poets, and other intellectual servants of the Emperor live there," Kang explained.

He led her across a covered bridge offering a view of the Imperial City, with the forest wrapped around it like an emerald serpent. Directly ahead of them stood a stone gate a hundred feet high, over which Xifeng saw a cluster of slanting scarlet roofs.

"The 'city of women,' as we call it," Kang said. "The Emperor's women are guarded like jewels. There are no aboveground entrances to the harem, save the Empress's personal walkway. We can't have naughty men coming in to soil what belongs to the Emperor."

Perhaps Wei *had* been right about it being a prison. *But there is always a way out,* Xifeng reassured herself, pressing her clammy palms against her tunic. The *tengaru* queen had told her she possessed water in her constitution, an element of a most resourceful nature.

Still, she found it hard to be optimistic when they came to a staircase leading directly into the ground.

"This is one of only three entrances," Kang informed her. "A long tunnel links it to its sister passage, which opens somewhere in the Imperial City. The third is the walkway I spoke of. It is the grandest, used only by the Empress and her servants when she attends royal functions in the main palace. All are heavily guarded."

Xifeng could see that for herself. A pair of armed eunuchs flanked the stairs, and another pair opened the barricaded door below for them. Instantly, she and Kang were swallowed up by the darkness. He removed a torch from the wall and held it aloft in the eerie gloom.

The long stone passageway was wide enough for her fingertips to brush each wall. Aside from their footsteps, she heard no sound except for the dripping of water. The air felt moist, stagnant. Every so often, another corridor branched off into blackness on either side.

"I wouldn't wander down any of those. Some of them have caved in and the air isn't always safe, but if you have a torch and it goes out, you'll be warned. Not to fear, as this main passage is perfectly harmless," Kang added when she put a panicked hand on his shoulder.

"I know the Emperor wants to protect the women," Xifeng said shakily. "But why do these tunnels have to run underground?"

"They're easier to protect, I imagine. The earth itself acts as an additional impediment."

The pools of darkness and contorting light gave her a sickening feeling. Would she hear slithering, if she stood still long enough?

At last, they came to another stairway leading up to a heavy door and Kang led the way outside into an exquisite walled garden. Xifeng followed him with relief, staring at the sunny, lush greenery of her surroundings. The willow trees beckoned with their sweet-smelling trunks, and flowers bloomed in every shade. Butterflies danced over the stream, which was crystal clear and wide enough for a rowboat. The compound comprised three magnificent buildings, each several levels high and connected to the others by elaborate walkways and balconies.

The *tengaru* clearing had been magnificent in its natural beauty. But this was a spectacle, a display of wealth only the Imperial family and the world of women within would ever see.

"Come. Master Yu is waiting."

Xifeng followed Kang through a doorway carved with a phoenix rising into the sun. Bamboo mats lined the room they entered, soft, clean, and warm. A lighter wood had been used for the furniture here, and cream-colored lanterns sat on trays of green and gray stones.

A short eunuch in sky-blue robes lifted his head. He had been writing at an elegant oak desk, an ink-dipped brush poised in one hand while the other held back his sleeve. He looked to be in his fifties and wore an expression of annoyance. His eyes, sharp as black glass, took in Xifeng in one sweep.

Kang bowed low to him. "Master Yu, the Empress's chief eunuch," he said, for Xifeng's benefit. "Sir, I have brought the maiden of whom the Crown Prince spoke."

Xifeng inclined her head, sensing the man's disapproving stare on her. She kept her gaze on the table, where his calligraphy stood out dark and swirling against a pristine page. He had been composing a poem; she caught the words *dove* and *twilight of the years*.

"So this is what the Little Fisherman has caught for us," Master Yu said, and Xifeng's eyes flickered upward at the password. "I am surprised by the Crown Prince's choice."

"Surprised? With so much beauty, sir?" Kang asked.

"Beauty is all very well. But it is merely the gleam of the sword," the chief eunuch said. "It is the mind that provides the sharp blade, and without that, well. We have a pretty piece of metal and not a weapon at all."

Xifeng recognized the metaphor—he had stolen it straight from a poem, one she'd had to memorize—but she kept her face blank.

"Step backward," Master Yu ordered, and she did so at once. He circled her like a hawk, the smell of lemongrass and something sour, rank, beneath its sweetness, emanating from his robes. "No," he said, continuing to speak to Kang, "I am surprised the Crown Prince would recommend a girl of such lowly origin to Her Imperial Majesty's circle. Perhaps she may make a good maidservant of some sort? To empty the chamber pots and dust the furniture, and so forth?"

"His Highness did not specify, sir. But you'll find it would be a waste to put Xifeng to such tasks. She is educated."

Master Yu's perfectly plucked eyebrows rose. "Educated? She's dressed like a beggar's daughter. Where did you get your education, *Xifeng*?"

She struggled to keep her face blank. This coddled little man thought himself quite fine, stealing lines of poetry to insert into conversation. As though that would intimidate *her*. She spoke in a polite, neutral tone. "My Guma taught me everything I know, sir. I can read and write, and I know history, a bit of geography, most poetry from the last century, and calligraphy. I sew, embroider, and play the barbarian's fiddle proficiently."

The chief eunuch crossed his arms over his ample chest. "Well, that's something at least. Most of the ladies and concubines come from high-ranking families, and I'm pleased you will not disgrace yourself with total ignorance. What poetry do you know? Recite something for me."

Clearly he was used to people bowing and scraping. But as much as he prided himself on his intelligence, he was stupid enough to underestimate her. Xifeng kept her eyes on his fat feet, which had been squeezed into silk slippers. She knew exactly which poem to recite.

The shining blade has two faces

Of a honed beauty to please the eye

But it is the edges of the sword felt most keenly

For what is the gleam of the sun on bright metal

Without the strength of its sting?

There was a long silence in which she feared she had overplayed her hand. Would he recognize her insult in choosing the poem he had stolen from? He had an ego large enough to throw her out of the city of women entirely. She chewed on her lip as the silence stretched on.

Master Yu uncrossed his arms. "Well, I must say, the Crown Prince's choices are astonishing but usually right, in women and warfare," he said at last. "You are indeed clever to recognize the poem to which I alluded earlier. Your person is pleasing. Your manners are acceptable. What is your opinion, Kang?"

"I rely upon your judgment, sir."

Master Yu turned his attention back to her. "You're fortunate I'm a man of reason. Someone more prejudiced would have turned you away. But when I see potential in a young woman, I must consult with a few trusted others before she can be accepted officially."

The ones who actually make the decisions, Xifeng thought.

"Follow me," he ordered.

She had made it through the first gate of the city of women.

18

Xifeng clasped her damp palms together as she followed Master Yu and Kang into a reception room. Painted lanterns dangled from the ceiling, lit despite the hour, and cast a warm rose-gold light throughout the chamber. Jasmine blossoms floated in bowls of water, and petals sprinkled on the floor emitted a heady fragrance with each step she took.

In the center of the room stood a wooden dais scattered with brocade pillows, on which sat four women sewing. Their eyes immediately shifted to Xifeng.

She wondered which was the Empress, the one she was destined to replace, and her stomach clenched. Here in this splendor and elegance, her fate seemed painfully like a delusion in the face of reality. She was, after all, nothing more than a seamstress in the presence of a descendant of the Dragon King, and no amount of preparation from Guma could have kept her hands from shaking.

"Your Imperial Majesty." Master Yu bowed until his nose nearly touched the floor. "I am honored to bring you the maiden of whom your son spoke."

"Thank you," said a gentle, musical voice. "Come closer, child, and tell us your name."

Xifeng prayed her own voice wouldn't falter. "Your Majesty, my name is Xifeng."

There was a long silence in which she felt the ladies' intense scrutiny. Her cheeks warmed, but she lifted her chin in determination. Why should she be ashamed? According to Kang, some of them came from humble origins, too. It was certainly true of the newest concubine, and she may not even have had Xifeng's education.

There was an intake of breath from one of the women, and without thinking, Xifeng met their eyes.

Two of them were too young to be the Empress: one was about thirty, with pomegranate silk robes and hair like charred wood, and the other was closer to twenty, with a peach-shaped face. Xifeng felt instinctively that the thin, sour one to their right was not Her Majesty. So it was the fourth on whom she focused, and she was rewarded with a smile.

"I am Empress Lihua." The great lady spoke with an elegant inflection, the words crisp and clear.

She looked like everything a queen should be and more. Silver streaks glinted in her hair, and the dangling ornaments she wore caught the light as she moved. She wore robes of a fine brushed silk the color of a sunrise and held herself and her white, white hands with a regal air. Xifeng ached with envy at the sight of her. What was it like to be born to such grace, such innate privilege? Here was yet another woman with a destiny greater than hers.

For that is the way of the world, Guma's voice echoed. *Some are given a rope to the moon, and others claw up the sky.*

Xifeng looked at her soiled fingernails, imagining the dirt was shreds of night sky, ripped down by her fingers as she climbed.

"Tell me, Xifeng, how did you come to meet my son? He seemed taken with you." Beside the Empress, the youngest lady with the peach face stirred restlessly.

"Lift your head when addressing Her Majesty, girl," Master Yu barked.

"The Crown Prince was taken with my friend, not with me, Your Majesty." Xifeng's eyes flickered up to the Empress's face, which wore a look of friendly but intense scrutiny. The woman's odd, engrossed expression seemed to take in her every feature and movement, but it relaxed at Xifeng's words.

"Your humility is admirable. But though my son was taken with your friend, it was you he could not stop talking about."

The peach-faced girl shifted again, her eyes on Xifeng sharp and mistrustful.

"The prince is always correct in his judgments," the Empress added proudly. "He has an eye for potential. That's why they call him by his childhood nickname, the Little Fisherman."

"His Highness is ever discerning and wise," Master Yu interjected smoothly. "This girl lacks refinement and polish, Your Majesty, but time at court should change that. She has an education and knows a bit of poetry."

Xifeng felt, again, the intensity of the Empress's gaze upon her. With one word, this lady of the cultured, honeyed tone could decide the course of her life. *Oh, to have such power.* The world would not deny a thing to such a woman; even the *tengaru* clearing and its mystical tree might be hers for the taking, if she wanted them. The thought prompted a slow stirring deep within Xifeng, and two words floated up like leaves in a still pond: *the Fool* . . .

"How does a girl from a poor family learn poetry?" the sour-faced older woman asked.

"Never mind that, Madam Hong," the Empress responded. "I'd like to hear a poem, Xifeng. Would you please recite one for us?"

Xifeng clasped her hands together, mind racing through the lines Guma had forced her to learn over the years. She thought of the light in the Empress's eyes when speaking of her son, and a homely little piece appeared that had always caught at her motherless heart:

Threads of silk in careworn hands

Become clothes for a wild boy

And tear against the rocks and branches

Only to be mended once more.

"But what care I," the mother sighs, "of toil when spring ends all too soon?"

Master Yu was staring at her with overt displeasure, but the Empress's eyes shone.

"A sweet poem. It's true of all mothers whose children grow up too fast. It seemed my boys were no sooner out of swaddling clothes than they began commanding armies."

"It's a poem all mothers should hear," cooed the woman in pomegranate robes, with a sidelong glance at the peach-faced girl. "What is your opinion, Lady Meng?"

"I am not a mother, as you well know," the girl said in a curt, oddly familiar accent. Xifeng noticed how she tugged at the snagged threads in her sewing with restless vigor.

"Allow me to introduce the two favored consorts of the Emperor." The Empress gestured to the woman in pomegranate. "This is Lady Sun, whose twin daughters you may meet at some point. And this is Lady Meng, who came to us a month ago."

"We are fortunate to have her." Lady Sun's lips curved with sly, feline pleasure. Every word she spoke seemed sugar laced with poison. "Remind me which *little village* you hail from again? His Majesty spoke so feelingly of traveling through it . . . and seeing you."

"You wouldn't know it if I told you," the girl replied, but Lady Sun's smile only widened, unaffected by her rudeness.

Xifeng lifted her eyes, startled. So *this* was the newest concubine, the girl who had ridden through her town in a palanquin. She still spoke in the cadence of the common villagers, which explained why her accent sounded familiar. She *was* very pretty, Xifeng had to admit, with her round, pink cheeks and lips like petals. It was easy to believe she'd caught Emperor Jun's eye out the window of his royal litter. But her eyes were dull and her movements listless; she sewed like someone who would rather be doing anything else, anywhere else in the world.

"This is Madam Hong, my chief lady-in-waiting." Empress Lihua indicated the sour-looking woman. "You will get to know her better, as all of my ladies are under her care and supervision."

Xifeng's heart leapt at the implication that she might stay, but she kept her expression neutral and bowed low to each of the women. When she straightened again, she noticed for the first time a magnificent tapestry on the wall behind the Empress. The piece was woven in shades of fern, emerald, olive, and moss, and she let out a quiet gasp when she saw the scene it depicted: a clearing in the woods, with a pond from which sprouted a flowering tree.

"Do you like it?" Empress Lihua asked, glancing from Xifeng to the tapestry and back. "It was commissioned by my grandfather in honor of our kingdom's five hundredth anniversary."

"It's b-beautiful." Xifeng hated herself for stammering, especially when she saw Lady Sun's smug expression. She made an effort to speak slowly, in measured tones. "It reminds me of a clearing we passed on our journey here. I saw a tree similar to that one."

Lady Sun laughed contemptuously. "There have been no such trees on Feng Lu for a thousand years. Her Majesty hasn't time for your fanciful stories."

But the Empress brushed away her words like fleas. "You needn't trouble yourself to speak for me, Lady Sun, especially on matters of which you have no knowledge."

The concubine stiffened at the Empress's rebuke, though the eyes that returned to Xifeng still wore a predatory gleam.

Empress Lihua leaned forward in her seat. "I'd like to hear your story, Xifeng. Alone," she added. "Kang, stay behind a moment." The others rose at once and departed in a reluctant, colorful parade of silk, Lady Sun leading the way with an air of distaste.

Xifeng felt a drop of sweat slide down her neck as the Empress continued studying her. There was only Kang, and then she would be alone with the Emperor's wife. Her mouth was dry as sand, and she felt hopelessly ill-mannered before the woman's polished elegance. *Breathe,* she told herself. *The whole of your fate hangs upon this meeting.*

"Would you send for tea?" the Empress asked Kang, and the eunuch gave Xifeng an encouraging nod before he scurried off. "He is most efficient, is he not?"

"He has been very kind today." The words sounded insipid even to Xifeng as she spoke. She twisted her hands, searching for something clever to say, but her thoughts slipped like clumsy threads. It had been easy to speak to the Crown Prince. Why did it seem so frightening with the Empress?

"Unfortunately, Master Yu seems to underestimate him."

"Being underestimated can be a blessing in disguise," Xifeng said. "That is to say, it gives us a chance to astonish those who doubt our true worth."

"Well said." The Empress indicated the cushion beside her, which Lady Meng had vacated. Xifeng felt acutely aware of this as she sat, remembering how she had envied that girl in the palanquin only to be sitting in her seat weeks later.

Two servants entered, setting down a plate of sugar-dusted persimmon cakes and two cups containing bulbs of bundled hibiscus leaves. The bundles gently unfurled into blooming orange flowers when the servants poured boiling water over them.

Xifeng took only a small bite of her cake, though she could have happily swallowed it whole. She studied the Empress as the woman dismissed the servants and helped herself.

Her Majesty's face and neck were lily-white, the skin of a wealthy lady who never had to expose herself to the sun. She had wide, trusting eyes, but the lines of weariness around them belied her age. She was the mother of three sons, but she seemed lost and lonely. Akira had said that the Empress was nearing fifty but still longed for a girl child. This was a woman who wore her longing like a cloak against the cold—who understood heartache. Xifeng noticed that the Empress's frame beneath her elegant silks appeared fragile and delicate; with such a frail, narrow body, she did not look nearly strong enough to carry and bear another baby.

Perhaps she'll die in childbirth. Yearning so for a daughter that she would risk her life, Xifeng thought. That could be one way fate would clear the path for a new queen and a younger, healthier woman . . . for Xifeng. Her cheeks burned as hot as the tea when she noticed Empress Lihua staring back at her.

The queen had a laugh like wind moving through the trees. "There's no punishment for looking at me." She brushed a crumb off Xifeng's sleeve absently and Xifeng thrilled at her touch, though she felt embarrassed by her own rough clothing. The Empress had taken a cake, too, but seemed to have no appetite; she neither touched it nor sipped her tea.

"I'm afraid Master Yu spoke the truth, Your Majesty. I lack polish and refinement, for all the education my aunt gave me."

"Your aunt educated you? Where is your mother?"

"I have no mother. She died long ago, and I never knew her." Xifeng could not keep the longing from her voice, and to her surprise, she saw an answering hunger in the woman's eyes. She wished there were still crumbs on her sleeve so the Empress would touch her again. Something in her muted sympathy drew the story from Xifeng, and her family's disgraceful legacy poured out. The Empress listened intently to the story of the journey, her fingers tightening on her teacup at the mention of the assassins.

"But you were saved, you say, by the *tengaru*." Her Majesty's voice held a note of relief, as if something had been confirmed for her. "The demon guardians hold special significance for me. Not many have the privilege of seeing them, let alone staying in their clearing under their protection. I love their queen as one who protects my family's realm, and anyone she chooses to favor is a friend to me."

Xifeng studied the flower in her tea, remembering the garlands Wei had woven for the queen. "She is gone from the earth now."

The Empress made the sign of the Dragon Lords, pressing her fingers to her forehead, lips, and heart as she blinked away tears. "It is a holy place you saw, and one inextricably linked to my family and my future. To have had the honor of seeing that tree will mark you for the rest of your life." She hesitated. "I have a strange feeling you belong here and we were meant to meet."

A chill slithered down Xifeng's arms at the prophetic music of those words, and at the lingering darkness beneath the beauty of the sentiment. "In friendship, I hope, Your Majesty."

"Yes, I hope that, too." The Empress's gaze seemed to bore right into her head.

Xifeng lowered her face, her mind muddled. She had not yet been deemed worthy to approach the apple tree; the *tengaru* queen had said the honor might belong to another—to the Fool. Could the Empress be that woman? If so, Xifeng had to be cautious. She pictured a wall of thorns growing over her heart, keeping her foolish craving at bay.

"Your aunt must love you a great deal." Empress Lihua's expression held only guarded courtesy now. "Not many see the use in educating a girl. Why didn't she come with you?"

"My aunt loves me," Xifeng repeated, trying out the words. They tasted foreign on her tongue. "She wasn't well enough to travel with us."

The Empress's fingers twitched toward Xifeng's hand. "I'm sorry, my dear. I can hear how much you miss her."

This is how I win her, Xifeng realized. *By playing to her need for a daughter . . . and mine for a mother.* She allowed tears to enter her eyes. "There are so many things I've said to her that I regret," she said, and there was truth in the words.

This time, the Empress did not resist. She reached shyly for Xifeng's hand. "You mustn't be hard on yourself. I've never had a daughter, so I feel like a mother to the maidens here and even to Lady Meng, though she is my husband's concubine." She opened and closed her lips a few times, clearly struggling between warring instincts. "I'd like to give you a home here, Xifeng, and be someone you may speak to when you are missing your aunt."

The kindness in her voice dug a small hole in the wall of thorns around Xifeng's heart. But at the same time, she felt a part of herself observing how Empress Lihua's thirst for a daughter weakened her. The woman was a descendant of kings and should have been nothing but strong and willful. How many had been clever enough to exploit this frailty?

Xifeng bent her head, shocked by her own callous thoughts. "Thank you, Your Majesty." This time, the tears that slipped from her eyes were real.

Save me, she thought. *Save me from this long dark road.*

19

Xifeng followed a maidservant back into the garden, her mind an exhilarated jumble. She struggled to keep up with the girl, who walked at a frenetic pace. They passed a sitting area with a fountain, where Lady Sun sat sewing alone. She inclined her head with condescending grace, but the twitch of her mouth implied that she found Xifeng's whole person offensive. Xifeng turned away, her cheeks hot, noting that even the maid wore clothes more presentable than her own.

They passed through exquisite rooms adorned with pillars, paintings, and silken rugs. The luxury seemed like a dream, and Xifeng eagerly wondered what her chamber would be like. When the maid at last led her to an open door, she struggled not to show her disappointment.

The room was small, with plain furnishings: only two low stools and a table with a washbasin. One window illuminated three beds built into three walls, with a simple curtain of undyed linen beside each. The maid gestured to Xifeng's bed, which was closest to the door. Xifeng noticed a folded tunic, a comb with long hair in its teeth, and an empty bone cup.

"With whom am I sharing?"

"Two other maidens." The maid handed Xifeng her sack and a folded pile of clothing with cotton slippers on top. As ordinary as they were, they were finer than anything she had ever owned. "Her Majesty requests that you speak to Madam Hong when you have finished washing."

When she was alone at last, Xifeng collapsed on her bed. The last hour had exhausted her more than the entire journey through the Great Forest. But she had made it to the Imperial Palace. She had impressed the chief eunuch, charmed Empress Lihua, and earned herself a position—exactly as Guma, and fate, intended.

It made her dizzy to think how drastically her life had changed in such a short time.

Her sack of belongings looked strange without Wei's possessions beside it. He would have laughed at her for expecting grander accommodations, and joked about the grim prospect of instructions from sour old Madam Hong.

He would have made this place feel more like home.

From the sack, Xifeng pulled out the bronze box containing her mother's dagger and hairpin. She tucked it beneath her pillow, vowing to find a better hiding place later, and made to put the sack away when she felt something unfamiliar inside.

Frowning, she removed the object and gave a choked cry upon recognizing it: a bundle of incense and a cheap metal holder to burn it in. Even unlit, the thin bamboo sticks emitted a noxious fragrance of black fungus and swamp herbs that took Xifeng right back home to her aunt's secret room.

Guma had known all along about the hidden sack. She knew Xifeng would abandon her and wanted to make sure she couldn't ever forget her.

For a moment, with the scent seeping back into her skin, Xifeng felt as though she had never left Guma behind at all.

Xifeng met Madam Hong on the South Balcony with her face scrubbed, hands washed, and hair pinned into a knot. She wore the clean clothes that had been provided, but she still felt out of place in the luxurious sitting area where the Empress's chief attendant awaited her.

Vines of spring roses shaded the balcony, and sweet azalea looped over the railing. Madam Hong sat at a stone table, gazing off into the distance, her face sallow above her embroidered coral jacket. The whole scene appeared staged as though for a performance.

"Do you know how many girls long to be where you are?" she asked, without looking at Xifeng. "Yet the gods saw fit to throw you in the Crown Prince's path, and thus his mother's."

Master Yu leaned against the railing behind her. "What a lucky girl you are. Sit down."

Xifeng obeyed, wishing Kang were there. His presence would have made this seem less like a standoff, with the eunuch and lady-in-waiting glaring from the other side of the table.

"You are here as a *servant* of the Empress, reporting directly to me and Master Yu," Madam Hong announced. "You will work hard at any task you are given, whether it is arranging flowers, mending clothes, or emptying chamber pots, if the maids can't get to them on time. You will find nothing beneath you, for there *is* nothing beneath you."

"You will be respectful at all times. None of that impertinence and showing off your knowledge to your betters," Master Yu snapped. So he hadn't been too stupid to recognize her poetic insult, after all. "You have no license to speak to or disturb Her Majesty in any way. You will not leave the city of women without permission from us."

"Well, girl?" Madam Hong barked. "Do you understand?"

Xifeng's hands itched to slap the pompous expression off the woman's face. She felt the creature shifting between her ribs and the accompanying spasm of dread. *Please, not now,* she begged. *I can't afford to make enemies so soon.*

"Speak when you're spoken to," Master Yu shouted, startling even Madam Hong. He seemed quite comfortable showing his venom with only the chief lady-in-waiting present.

Xifeng recalled a story she had read about how the elephant and the grassland bird existed together. The bird ate small pests on the elephant's body, thereby sustaining itself, while the elephant benefited by staying clean. She imagined Madam Hong as the wrinkled, ungainly elephant and the eunuch as a bald, bad-tempered bird, and almost laughed out loud.

"I understand, Madam Hong," she said, trying to keep her lips from twitching.

The woman scowled. "The ladies wake before sunrise, wash, comb, and dress. They go to the shrine for an hour of prayer, during which they honor the blessings of the Dragon Lords." She made the sign of respect Empress Lihua had earlier. "Between meals, each works intently on a task given to her. In the evening, they spend an hour reading or practicing calligraphy or music, and then there is another hour of prayer before bed."

"The lanterns you see all around us are not only ornamental, but also measure time," Master Yu said curtly. "They will keep you on task.

We do not tolerate lazy, stupid women in proximity to the Empress."

"What is to be my task?" Xifeng asked as politely as she could manage.

Madam Hong scowled. "You were *not* given permission to speak, girl."

Xifeng willed her hands to stay in her lap. She imagined returning to Akira and having to explain that she'd been thrown out of the palace because she had slapped the Empress's chief attendant. The urge to laugh grew stronger, as did the movement in her rib cage. Before she could stop herself, she said tartly, "My name is Xifeng, not *girl*."

With one smooth flourish, the eunuch leaned over and cracked his folded fan across her shoulder. Xifeng felt stinging warmth where he had hit her and peered at him in amusement. After Guma's imaginative beatings with the cane—including pouring water over her back to intensify the pain—did the fat little man truly imagine he could break her spirit?

"They're all the same when they come here," Master Yu sneered to Madam Hong. "They think because Empress Lihua is kind and welcoming that they are different. *Special.* Arrogant and high-strung, with some notion of rising to the top, like foam on an ocean current."

"That's a beautiful turn of phrase, sir," Xifeng said sweetly, ignoring the pain in her shoulder, and he scanned her face for impudence. Was the imbecile even aware how much of his speeches were stolen from poetry?

A spiteful smile blossomed on Madam Hong's lips. "My dear Yu, wasn't it just this morning that Lady Sun complained about her maidservant? Perhaps we can put *Xifeng* to use there, and have her . . . assist while the lady finds a replacement."

"You always have the most appropriate solution. I'll speak to her tonight, and you, *girl,* will start next week. You'll have to have a bit of training first; we won't send a complete novice to Her Ladyship. Now get out of our sight."

Xifeng rose with a brilliant smile, enjoying their disturbed expressions at the sight of it. "Thank you for your time. When I see the Crown Prince again, I'll let him know what you've done for me." She bowed before their shocked stares. Apparently they had forgotten that the prince had recommended her for the position—not that she would likely see him again, but gods above, that threat had been *fun*. She strolled off as merrily as though they hadn't treated her like dirt. Outward grace at all times, as Guma had taught her, no matter how she boiled inside.

Kang waited for her on the ground level. Despite his customary simper, he surveyed her with quick, clever eyes. "You survived. They haven't broken you like a colt in the stable?"

"It is impossible to break me."

"Good. I knew you had spirit," he said warmly. "Intimidating new girls is how they assert their dominance. The Empress has given them power over us and they never want us to forget."

"Why do you speak so freely of them?" Xifeng asked, arching a brow. "Are you hoping to catch me off my guard and report my careless words to Master Yu?"

Kang's eyes widened. "My dear, no. I speak my mind because I want to be friends . . . *never* to trap you."

Xifeng stared at him, unnerved by the earnestness in his expression. If this was a ploy, he was a very good actor indeed. All of her instincts warned her not to trust him—but then again, an ally could be useful. "I would like to be friends," she said carefully, and his face lit up.

But a roar of laughter from the adjacent building dissolved his cheer. "Eunuchs," he muttered. "They're playing one of their table games again."

"Why aren't you with them?"

"They despise me. They hate the young and ambitious and, above all, the talented," he said matter-of-factly. "They don't know where I come from, but they know where I aspire to go because I have the capacity to do so."

"Where would that be?"

"I would join the Five Tigers, the most powerful eunuchs in the Empress's household. That fool Master Yu is the worst of them. They're getting old, but they must hope to live forever, because they guard their positions jealously. They haven't asked any younger men to join."

Xifeng frowned. "What real power do they have?"

"You'd be surprised. Empress Lihua's father was often away fighting in the wars, and his favorite eunuch, Tao, would rule in his absence. Tao was the one who drafted the treaty about the Unclaimed Lands between Dagovad and the Sacred Grasslands."

"The lands near the Gulf of Talon," Xifeng recited automatically, as she would to Guma after a lesson. "A barbarian horde swept out of the Shadow Sea and populated those lands for a century. The queen of Dagovad and the king of the Grasslands joined forces to muster up an army large enough to roust them out."

Kang grinned. "I should have known you'd already know all about it."

"I don't know much about the treaty," she admitted. "Or the invaders themselves. Guma told me they originated from Kamatsu and the Great Forest many ages ago." She had often wondered about these warriors who spent their lives on the wild sea and were spoken of with such fear and awe. They were called barbarians, disparagingly, though their clever methods of shipbuilding and even their musical instruments had been adopted by the mainlanders. Perhaps, she reflected, they in *their* turn thought of people on the continent as barbarians.

"After they drove the invaders away, as you said, the two kingdoms turned against each other and fought over those lands. Rich soil and a port, you know. People have killed for less. So the eunuch Tao stepped in as an impartial third party on behalf of the old Emperor and drafted a ten-year treaty to split the wealth between them." He paused significantly. "That ten-year treaty ended last winter."

"What happens now?" Xifeng asked, fascinated. "Do they draft a new treaty? Or will one of them claim the land for themselves?"

"The latter, I'm afraid. The queen of Dagovad grows bolder every year, especially now that her elderly husband has died and she has come into her own. She has made enemies of many, including her own sister."

"Her sister?"

"The queen of Kamatsu. They've been enemies since they were girls, and Emperor Jun's treaty with Kamatsu does not sit well with many—Dagovad in particular." Kang pursed his lips. "This eastern conflict will be a problem for Emperor Jun. At least Tao's actions secured peace for a decade, something Dagovad will not forget."

"How intriguing that someone else can rule in the Emperor's place." *But a eunuch is still male,* Xifeng thought. *Would they feel the same about a woman?*

Kang led her away from the building, his knuckles white on the painted fan. "You'll learn that the eunuchs are every bit as powerful and conniving as the ladies. It's all a game."

"Why have you decided to trust me? How can you be certain I won't repeat your comments to Master Yu, for instance?"

"Because that's not who you are."

"But how do you know?" Xifeng persisted. "We've only just met."

"I'm a good judge of people, and perhaps a bit lonely, too." He gestured to their surroundings, his silk sleeve billowing. "This is a place built for secret alliances. Everyone has someone to eavesdrop and whisper with, and I long for a friend of my own. And to be honest, Xifeng . . . if anyone were to make themselves a success at court, my wager would be on *you*."

They paused beneath a wooden archway with letters etched into the base: *Pride, prosperity, perseverance.* "You are so confident in me?" Xifeng asked lightly, running her hands over the last word.

"I sense a ruthlessness in you. An unwillingness to be refused or defeated. Yes, my dear, I want to be your friend, and I want to be there when you make it."

His stark honesty astonished her—but gratified her, too. "You hope to use me," she said, only half jokingly.

The eunuch twinkled at her. "In time, you may come to trust me, too."

"I may," Xifeng hedged, though she felt herself thawing at his kind manner. It wasn't like anyone else was being friendly toward her. Still, something in Kang's playful demeanor made it difficult for her to tell whether he was serious. "Well. If they wish us at the bottom of this pond, weighed down by stones, at least we'll be together."

"Mustn't say such things too loudly. You never know to whom you're giving ideas."

They laughed.

"The concubines aren't above it, either. Lady Sun would claw Lady Meng's eyes out if she could, to secure the Emperor for herself only. There's a whole harem of consorts left over from Empress Lihua's first husband, but thankfully Emperor Jun prefers only the two of them."

"Lady Meng seems so unhappy," Xifeng said. "She came through my town, you know, on her way to the palace, and I envied her good fortune."

"She'd best improve her attitude or she'll be shipped off to a monastery. But I admit it's not a life to which everyone is suited, especially when you are Lady Sun's direct competition." A scowl creased his features. "Lady Sun is His Majesty's favorite because she gave him two daughters *and* a son. Her power is absolute. Now *there's* someone I wouldn't mind seeing at the bottom of a pond."

Xifeng remembered the gilded palanquin she had seen and the pale, listless girl she had met. "I was stupid to be jealous of Lady Meng. I didn't think what it would mean for her."

"No, a concubine's life wouldn't suit you, would it? You'd want to be the first and only in a man's affections, such as that warrior of yours." He laughed at her shock. "I put two and two together when you mentioned that your friend Wei had first attracted the Crown Prince's attention."

Xifeng remained silent, her eyes downturned. Wei was no one's business but her own.

"Oh, come," Kang said kindly. "You don't have to tell me anything. I was only teasing. Let us talk of something else, and we will discuss matters of the heart when we're better friends."

They spent the evening walking the grounds. He showed her the bathhouses and rooms full of thread-bound books, inkstones, and sharp pens ready for writing. The music room was as fully equipped with lutes, drums, and pipes.

"People in my town would laugh at the idea of calling books and music work," Xifeng told him. "How is it some men break their backs farming a dead land, whereas others sit in comfort and ruminate on stars and poetry?"

The eunuch shrugged. "It is as the Dragon Lords will it. You know that."

They chatted comfortably as they explored, and Xifeng felt she had wasted much of her life cloistered in her forsaken town. Almost as soon as she had left, she had made friends, and Kang might one day be another. His wicked sense of humor and sharp tongue suited her perfectly.

"What are you thinking of?" he asked on their way to the evening meal.

"Of friends. I've never had any," she admitted. "The boys wanted . . . other things and the girls avoided me. But I watched their friendships come and go. I saw how much more time and trust it took for women to form bonds, and how easily they could break apart."

"Women are complicated creatures."

She eyed him. "You may be one of the few men with whom I can *truly* be friends. After all, you don't want anything more from me."

Kang gave her an inscrutable smile. "What makes you think that even if I don't wish to sleep with you, I don't want something else?"

With his dry, enigmatic humor, she was hard-pressed to say whether that had been a joke.

20

When Xifeng was young, she had imagined that each day in the Imperial Palace would be special and significant. But she found that time passed just as it had in her town. She had a routine she was expected to follow, one that included plenty of sewing, and she was treated with as much contempt and disapproval as she had known from Guma. The only difference was she slept in a clean, soft bed every night and wore fresh, dry clothes.

Always, she kept her eyes open for signs of the Fool. But she hadn't seen the concubines or the Empress since she had first arrived, and the other women left her alone for the most part.

The morning gong woke her on the first day of her second week. Dandan and Mei, the two girls who shared her chamber, were already up and washing their faces.

"Good morning," Xifeng said, but they only blinked at her in silence. She sighed. It had been like this all last week. "You don't need to be afraid of me, you know."

She ran a brush through her hair, almost missing Ning's endless chatter in the mornings. Perhaps Dandan and Mei had been instructed not to talk to her. Only the gods knew what dire warning Madam Hong might have fed them.

"Hateful old crow," she muttered.

But maybe it was better this way, staying isolated from the others. She needed her wits about her, what with her servitude to Lady Sun looming ahead. She remembered the woman's cruel, catlike smile when she had needled Lady Meng about her lowly origins. If the best punishment Madam Hong and Master Yu could find was for Xifeng to serve this favorite concubine of the Emperor, they had a reason for it, and she had to stay alert.

The building where the Empress and consorts lived connected to a gate in the wall lining the city of women. The Empress occupied the top two levels, and Lady Sun had the entire level underneath. Xifeng found the concubine's quarters sumptuously decorated in brushed satin and scarlet brocade. A eunuch directed her through a labyrinth of curtained recesses and corridors until she came to the immense bathing chamber.

Lady Sun glanced lazily up at her from a gilded tub covering almost the entire room. It had been filled to the brim with searing hot water, which was hidden under a sea of crimson rose petals, their perfume heady in the whorls of steam that rose up to the porcelain-tiled ceiling. Elaborate folding screens did nothing to conceal the woman's nakedness. She didn't bother covering her breasts as she stretched a languorous arm on either side of her.

"Come closer," she cooed. "Don't be bashful, young one. I won't bite you."

Xifeng approached with caution, as she would a tigress. Everything about the scene felt purposefully arranged to increase her discomfort, as with Madam Hong.

Lady Sun's hair had been swept into a beautiful knot that shone alternately jet-black and russet in the light. Her slanting, heavy-lidded eyes took Xifeng in from head to toe. "I must say," she said, slender fingers dangling in the water, "I was pleasantly surprised when Madam Hong suggested you assist me. I was hoping I'd get to know you better. Xifeng, wasn't it?"

Xifeng remained silent, all her nerves on edge. What sort of game was this? She had seen this woman shamelessly taunt another in the presence of the Empress herself. She kept her eyes on the rose petals, which were like a sea of living blood lapping at Lady Sun's alabaster skin.

The concubine arched her back luxuriously, like a wildcat preening. Her heavy breasts bobbed in the water. "Come talk to me," she said, stroking the rim of the tub as though it were a man's bare chest. "Take that stool there and have a persimmon, if you care for them."

Xifeng obeyed, but didn't touch the food: tofu fried in chili sauce, green vegetables in a simmering broth, and the persimmons, fragrant in a bowl of cut glass. She hadn't expected the concubines to eat what she did, but still, the extravagant amount of food surprised her.

"I wasn't alone," Lady Sun drawled, guessing her thoughts. "The Emperor was with me. I give him quite an appetite in the mornings. But I shouldn't speak of such things to an innocent maiden. You *are* a maiden, aren't you? You haven't left some heartsick peasant man behind on that dreary farm, or wherever it was that you came from?"

"No, my lady."

The woman examined her through the slitted eyes of a predator. "I notice you and Kang have become fast friends. Interesting how he kept to himself until you arrived and suddenly he can't stay away. How men do enjoy a beautiful face, even if they can't do anything about it anymore." She gave a throaty laugh. "A word of advice, my dear. Don't trust any of the eunuchs—especially Kang. No one knows where he came from, you see, and you can't be sure of an ending unless you know the beginning. Don't you think?"

The cryptic words were meant to confuse and intimidate, Xifeng knew. It was all part of Lady Sun's little game. "I'm aware I must be cautious with my friendships."

"Are you?" Lady Sun's languid voice filled with delight, as though Xifeng were a monkey that had done something extraordinary. "How clever of you. All the eunuchs are the same, anyhow. They're men without the danger, but they still want a woman to serve them. I wouldn't wish that upon you." She leaned her head against a silk pillow and closed her eyes.

Xifeng watched her with mingled scorn and envy, feeling certain she herself was lovelier. Yet Lady Sun had brought an emperor to his knees. She commanded him the way he commanded armies; she could make him fall at her feet with that supple body and those bewitching eyes.

Guma had taught Xifeng that such women harbored powerful essences, charged with frenetic vitality and potential. She had spoken of them like rabbits—easily captured and killed, their precious lifeblood ready to turn into formidable strength in the drinker's system. And though she had found the speech terrifying, Xifeng couldn't help picturing the glorious, burning heart beneath Lady Sun's ample pearl-white breasts. A twinge of hunger rippled through her.

"You're an advocate of women, my lady," she said quickly, to distract herself.

Lady Sun's eyes opened. "Naturally. You may have noticed *I* am a woman. Your welfare is my own, I assure you. But I must be boring you with my talk. Let me show you how you can help me." Before Xifeng could offer to bring her a robe, she rose from the tub and stood dripping before her, wearing nothing but the rose petals that clung to her skin. Whereas Empress Lihua was thin and frail, the concubine had a healthy, full-figured body. "Come with me." She strolled to a set of doors at the rear of the chamber, leaving a trail of wet footprints behind her.

Xifeng noted the eunuch guards maintained stony expressions, their eyes fixed on the wall, no doubt through long practice. They had probably remained as stationary when the Emperor had been there frolicking in the tub with her.

Lady Sun strolled through the corridors, paying no heed to the flustered maids who stopped in their tracks to bow. An army of them was parading to the bath chamber, probably to clean up the mess of rose petals. "This is who I wanted to introduce you to. Come closer."

Xifeng followed her through a heavily curtained doorway into a room lit by ornate lanterns. There were no windows; instead, a hundred bronze mirrors lined the walls, dimly reflecting the opulent silk floor coverings, the dark rosewood furnishings, and the magnificent carved oak bed that stood in the center of the chamber.

The woman bent to pick something up, admiring her own plump, well-fed form in the mirror as she did so. She turned, and Xifeng saw a scrawny mass of grayish hair quivering against her wet breasts: a hideous little dog. It wore a scrap of carmine silk tied around its neck.

"This is Shenshi, my *second* son." Lady Sun laughed and kissed the top of its scruffy head, eyes on the mirror as she tilted her hips to get the best vantage point of her buttocks. "He was a birthday gift from the Emperor. Isn't he the sweetest thing? Would you like to hold him?"

Xifeng decidedly would *not,* but the woman dumped the animal in her arms anyway. She stood holding the trembling mass as far from herself as possible while Lady Sun preened before the mirrors and ran a hand down her pillowy stomach. The dog smelled like it had been rolling in its own filth. A slick brown stain appeared on Xifeng's sleeve, confirming her suspicion.

"I forgot to mention, Shenshi is a bit ill." Lady Sun draped a robe of transparent tangerine satin around her shoulders and flung herself on the bed, dangling her bare legs off the side as she watched Xifeng. "Your task is to care for him while I find another maid to do so. The one I had . . . didn't suit. You're such a dear to help me." A sly smile crossed her face, one that promised this was only the beginning of the fun.

They both knew there was no one Xifeng could go to—not Madam Hong or Master Yu, who had sent her here, and certainly not the Empress.

No, I'll deal with this myself.

Xifeng looked down at the detestable rodent of a dog. "It's my honor, Lady Sun. I hope to serve you in the manner you deserve."

The concubine's face froze. "You're a treasure," she breathed, and on her lips it was a threat. "You can start by cleaning this room. Shenshi has left a few messes in here, and we can't have the Emperor seeing that when he returns tonight. Find me on the balcony when you're done." She rose, her open robe concealing nothing as she brushed carelessly past Xifeng.

Xifeng dropped the animal, which scurried after its mistress, leaving more foul-smelling streaks in its wake. "A few messes," as Lady Sun put it, turned out to be the dog's droppings and puddles of vomit smeared across the floor. What had she been feeding the stupid thing?

"A bucket of water and some rags," Xifeng snapped to a eunuch outside the door. "Now."

She wished Guma could see her scrubbing the floor like a servant. Would she advise her to fight back or keep her head down? She almost,

almost considered lighting the incense to find out and to feel closer to Guma.

"A brilliant destiny, indeed," she seethed.

As she worked, she imagined a whole series of violent deaths for Lady Sun: boiling alive in the gold tub, which had been filled with cooking oil instead of water, or bleeding out from a shard of one of these mirrors impaled in her perfect white stomach. The vain tart.

Xifeng caught a glimpse of herself in the mirror. It was this perfect face that threatened them all so—those wide bright eyes and full plum lips—and what they saw behind it: the gleam of the blade *and* the lethal sharp edge, together in one. That was what they hated; that was what they sought to stamp out of her. But no matter how much Lady Sun hoped to degrade her, she would not succumb; she would not be defeated or intimidated.

She slithered closer to the mirror, the bronze lanterns casting patterns over her body like scales. A shadow like a bruise hovered over the cheek she had healed with lifeblood.

"Careful not to cut yourself when you play with a sword," she hissed.

Her reflection bared its fangs in a smile of grotesque promise.

Lady Sun sat on her balcony, her robe still wide open and legs propped on the railing. A maid sat beside her, applying something to her face. The horrid beast, Shenshi, curled around her chair and bared yellow teeth at Xifeng when she approached.

"Finished already?" When the woman turned, Xifeng saw the maid had been caking what appeared to be mud on her face. She looked ridiculous, like something that had crawled out of a swamp. Despite the literal dirt on her forehead, she still managed to look contemptuously at the dog shit on Xifeng's clothes. "I'll have to find something more challenging to give you next."

Xifeng smiled gently as she imagined choking her with that mud, spooning thick globs of it down her throat to block the air. She felt a tremulous laugh of pleasure deep inside her.

"Go away," Lady Sun told the maid. "Why don't *you* finish the job, Xifeng?"

"With pleasure." Xifeng picked up the brush the maid had been using and swirled it distastefully in the porcelain bowl. From its smell and texture, it *was* mud.

"A treatment I learned when I first came to the palace," Lady Sun said smugly. "Fresh mud mixed with a few ingredients from the Imperial physician's stores. It smooths and beautifies the skin and keeps me young for His Majesty. You'll understand one day, when you become a wife like me." She laughed, as though she couldn't imagine anyone wanting to marry Xifeng.

"You mean a *concubine,* my lady?" Xifeng slashed the brush across the woman's face. "Empress Lihua is the Emperor's wife."

Lady Sun's mud-caked face stilled. "It is I he visits at night. I have given him three children, whereas she has given him none," she said in a low voice. "Those three sons from her first husband are nearly all grown. What use is she if she can only give him a Crown Prince not of his blood? He has a son of *his* blood, *my* son."

"Yes, my lady. You must be proud the Emperor has chosen to include him in the line of succession. Behind his three stepsons, of course, who are the children of his Empress." She enjoyed the way the woman's mouth twisted in anger. Here was a crack in Lady Sun's seemingly perfect veneer: the knowledge that even as the Emperor's favorite, she—and by extension, her son—would only ever be second to Her Majesty and the princes.

"I *am* proud I have more to offer him than another man's children," said the concubine. "Perhaps one day he'll realize that."

Xifeng placidly continued daubing mud while her mind raced. It was clear Lady Sun wanted His Majesty to put the Empress and Crown Prince aside in favor of her and her son. But how much of it was blind hope? Hideki had said Emperor Jun was a distant cousin of the Empress and had only married into the throne. He owed his crown to his dragon-born wife; putting both her and his heir aside would surely mean a revolt he couldn't afford to risk.

And it occurred suddenly to Xifeng that she shared something with Lady Sun. The concubine, too, wanted what fate had dictated for Xifeng: she wanted to be Empress of Feng Lu. Was Xifeng sitting in the presence of the Fool, the enemy of whom the cards had spoken? It took all of her effort to continue calmly stirring the mud as the creature moved inside her, sharpening her growing panic.

Our list of enemies grows with each passing hour, the voice whispered from within. *They seek our destruction. They would see us cast down.*

Xifeng darted a quick glance at Lady Sun, though it was impossible that she could have heard it speak, too. Still, the concubine was staring right at her, head tilted shrewdly, and Xifeng's hand gave an involuntary jerk. A few drops of mud splattered the table.

Lady Sun encircled her wrist with one hand. She was surprisingly strong for a pampered, spoiled woman. "I know what you're thinking. That because my wealthy father gave me to His Majesty, and because I've only ever lived in luxury, that life has been kind and easy."

"I wouldn't presume to think of you at all, my lady."

"Life is difficult when you're born a woman in this world," the concubine murmured. "You've entered a game you can't win. Men make the rules and we are left to be used by them or claw our way to whatever scraps they've left behind. Do you think my father gave me to the Emperor because he loved me? Did he care when he tore me from my mother's arms? He thrust me into this pit of scorpions to be stung and forgotten."

She released Xifeng's arm and reached for a cloth, wiping the mud off. Slowly, her creamy skin emerged, like a pearl revealed in the dirt.

"But I had this." She touched her face. "This is how a woman plays the game. It makes men weak and forget they make the rules. She becomes the player and they the pawns."

Xifeng swirled the brush in the bowl of mud, listening in spite of herself. There was truth in these words—she recalled the panic she'd felt upon seeing her damaged cheek.

"That is why, my little flower, I must keep you close. To protect you."

Or to make sure I don't snatch your pathetic victory from your fingertips. Stupid woman, confessing her deepest weaknesses. If she chose to underestimate Xifeng's strength, as Master Yu had, she would be making a grave misstep.

"You speak wisely, my lady," Xifeng said, though she raged inside at the powerful essence Guma would say resided in this woman. What a shame it couldn't be put to use by someone who deserved it. She shuddered, but from horror or anticipation, she didn't know.

"Are you cold, young one?" Lady Sun asked, her eyes glinting at the tremor.

Xifeng shook her head. Let the woman believe she was afraid. "Not at all. Is there anything else I might do for you today?"

Challenge issued.

The concubine gave her a slow, feral smile. "Oh, I'm sure I can find something for you."

Challenge accepted.

21

The cool spring thawed into a warm, wet summer, and one morning, Xifeng woke to find sheets of rain cascading down. Today marked one month since she had begun slaving for Lady Sun, though the concubine had promised to find a replacement by now. Clearly, it was to be torture and degradation: cleaning up after her repellent dog, scrubbing her chamber pot, and personally hand-washing her undergarments after her moon's bleeding.

Xifeng swung her feet to the floor. Not showing up would be admitting defeat, and she would not give Lady Sun that satisfaction. If the concubine *was* the Fool, Xifeng had to avoid showing weakness in any form. She needed to stay strong and alert, and formulate her plan of attack. She drew a hand across her cheek, reassuring herself of its perfection, and stood up.

"Good morning," a small voice said, and Xifeng glanced at Dandan and Mei in shock. It was unclear which of them had spoken, for both were red as poppies.

"Good morning," she returned, not daring to say more for fear of spooking them.

"You were laughing in your sleep." Dandan blushed even more.

Xifeng paused. All week, she had dreamed of murdering the concubine in various violent ways and burying her in a cave of serpents. "I'm sorry. I've been having nightmares," she lied.

"It didn't sound like a nightmare," Mei observed.

Xifeng shrugged and turned to see something sticking out from under her pillow. It was the bundle of black incense. Had she clutched it in her sleep? She hurriedly tucked it out of sight, and a piece of her dream returned: that monk she had seen at the trading post, only this time he had been watching her from Lady Sun's room of bronze mirrors. She brushed her fingers over her face again—in the dream, the cut Guma had given her had returned in all of its bloody glory.

She scurried through the rain to morning prayer and then made her way to the banquet hall, where two eunuchs were placing fresh beeswax candles into the lanterns to mark the start of the hour. She found Kang sitting alone, glowering at a table full of merry, gambling eunuchs. Each time one of them rolled a pair of stone dice, they all erupted into groans and cheers.

Kang stabbed at his porridge. "They're having their monthly outing in the Imperial City today. A *select* group of them goes to market to buy silks and spices. I, of course, am never chosen, though I have the best eye among them for silks."

"Don't sit around and wait. Why not ask if you can go?"

"I've asked a hundred times," he protested. "I asked before you came in and they told me I'm a disgrace who stinks of urine."

Xifeng rolled her eyes, knowing he referred to many eunuchs' tendency to wet their beds. It was an unfortunate effect of the procedure they underwent, particularly if they'd had the bad luck to have an inexperienced knifer. "That insult should have been directed at Master Yu," she said without thinking, remembering the chief eunuch's stench, and Kang let out a great roar of laughter. "Don't you *dare* tell anyone I said that."

"Who would I tell? The Empress, who alone doesn't loathe me?"

"I don't know, but I don't wish to annoy him or Madam Hong any further. I'm the only lady they haven't asked to help Her Majesty with festival planning."

The upcoming Festival of the Summer Moon celebrated the first full moon of the season. It marked a momentous occasion in which the Empress and her chosen ladies and eunuchs joined the Emperor in the main palace for a banquet and a moon-viewing party. Xifeng had seen other girls sewing costumes and practicing music for the performance that would follow.

Kang's mouth lifted humorlessly. "Too busy cleaning up Shenshi's shit, are you?"

Xifeng scowled. "I'm supposed to be a lady-in-waiting, not a glorified maidservant. Likely today she'll ask me to clean her balcony with a paintbrush. She's trying to break me, but it won't work."

"She thinks she's the Empress already," the eunuch sneered. "She threatens to leave the Emperor all the time. *Threatens* him. She's forever accusing him of going after her ladies."

"Leave the Emperor? Where on earth would she go?"

"It's something she says whenever she wants more of his attention. He always sends gifts after a tantrum." The gambling eunuchs erupted into laughter and Kang's face darkened. "She had me beaten once with a bamboo cane, you know. Master Yu did it with enthusiasm."

Xifeng winced. "What did you do to her?"

"Do you know what black spice is?" She shook her head. "It comes from a poppy plant grown near the Gulf of Talon and costs more than our lives put together. In small amounts, it's medicine for pain. It relaxes you, gives you the sensation of ultimate well-being. But when smoked in large amounts, it brings . . . *visions*."

Images swirled in Xifeng's mind: a dark room full of smoke, and sticks of jet incense glowing with fire. A chill danced across her skin. "What sort of visions?"

Kang leaned forward. "Some say you can see the future. But I've never been stupid enough to smoke enough for that. And I've never gone snooping around the Imperial physician's cupboards looking for some, yet Lady Sun accused me all the same."

"Why would she do that?"

"She hates me because I don't worship her like the other eunuchs. Lady Sun may be arrogant, but she's not an imbecile. She knows when someone doesn't like her. She hasn't the gift to make people love her, so she takes revenge on them."

"She falsely accused you of stealing and had you beaten . . . for nothing." The concubine repulsed her, but Xifeng couldn't help admiring her gall. She knew how to deal with enemies.

Kang lowered his tunic over one shoulder so she could see the long, raised scars, stark white against his skin. "This was the punishment I received."

Xifeng hissed through her teeth. Her back ached in sympathy as she remembered her own scars from Guma. "Why hasn't anything been done about her?"

"Everyone's scared of how much power she wields over the Emperor. Not even the Empress can control her, as these prove." Kang gestured to his injuries. "And she knows having people beaten will irritate Her Majesty."

The Empress's tired, gentle face appeared in Xifeng's mind. What patience she must have to endure Lady Sun, toying with her husband and grappling for her throne. "I'm sorry for Her Majesty. No wonder she looks so ill. She barely ate a thing the day I met her."

"She's had no appetite for a long time. Was that you I saw outside the door of her apartments yesterday, delivering something?"

"You don't miss a move I make, do you? I made a poultice to help encourage her to eat. It's the kind I used to make for my aunt." Guma had always demanded the poultice during spells of illness. It was a simple, soothing herbal mixture of ginger and crushed rose hips, sewn skillfully into a cotton pouch and placed in one's tea.

But Kang did not tease her about flattering the Empress, as she expected him to. "Her Majesty will appreciate it. The gods know she needs all the strength she can get with a thorn in her side like Lady Sun. But aside from the concubine's children and beauty, she has nothing to keep the Emperor. Soon he'll grow tired of her."

"She's not *that* beautiful," Xifeng seethed.

"She humiliated me, and now she's doing the same to you. I tell you I would gladly see her dead." Kang's eyes gleamed with undisguised malevolence. "Promise you'll be careful. She's gifted when it comes to stirring up trouble for others, and I don't want to see you get hurt."

"I promise," she said, and he patted her arm.

It was a dangerous gamble to despise this favorite concubine of the Emperor, she knew. But if Lady Sun had never been challenged before, it was high time someone taught her a lesson. And who better than Xifeng?

Iron striking iron might create a spark, and a spark might be just what she needed to change her fortunes.

An hour later, Xifeng squatted in the pouring rain, contemplating even more brutal ways in which she would like Lady Sun to expire.

The woman had sweetly ordered her out into the storm to collect mud for her beautifying routine, citing that soil soaked with fresh rain was best for her complexion. She had not given Xifeng anything to cover herself, nor had she provided anything with which to dig. So Xifeng crouched in a corner of the garden, scraping her nails in the dirt and splattering herself as she deposited it into a bucket. But at least it was warm summer rain, and at least she was out in the fresh air, away from the cloying perfume of the concubine's apartments. And there was something soothing about the way the mud squelched in her fingers.

Xifeng stood up and stretched, glancing around the empty garden. She wished the evil wretch Shenshi attended to his bodily needs here, so she might add some of it to the concubine's mud mask. The bucket was full, but she didn't want to return yet. She set it under a table to protect it from the rain and walked over to the wall. There was a slight overhang of stones along the top, which sheltered her somewhat.

She closed her eyes, wondering how long she would be able to hide out here before Lady Sun sent someone to fetch her. Unless the Emperor had come calling, which would no doubt put her well out of the concubine's mind. What kind of man could attach himself to such a cruel, hateful woman? But Lady Sun likely didn't show him that side of herself.

It had been many weeks since Xifeng had arrived at the palace, and still she had never seen Emperor Jun. The closest she'd gotten was when he came to visit the Empress, accompanied by a retinue of simpering eunuchs who shielded him from view with frilly silk screens. Perhaps he was fat, with triple chins and liver spots, and preferred to travel undetected.

Xifeng grinned at the idea of Lady Sun having to feign passion for an aging, overweight Emperor with a loud, smelly belch. But, of course, if her own destiny were to come true, it would soon be *Xifeng* having to pretend.

Yes, it was time to find out what the illustrious Emperor Jun was like.

But before she had time to finish the thought, her feet began to sink. Slowly at first, and then faster and faster, as though the soaking earth were swallowing her. She screamed, gripped by panic as she sank into a muddy hole chest-high, her arms desperately flailing for purchase.

"Help!" she cried, but there was no one to hear her.

Her frantic fingers seized a clump of grass as her legs dangled into nothingness. She couldn't die . . . not here, not now. Not such a pathetic death, with all she had done and all she had left to do. She gritted her teeth and pulled with all her strength.

But her hands slipped, and she screamed again as her body sank through the ground.

She landed in a heap on a hard stone floor, groaning. The sound of the rain was muffled down here, like someone had shut a window, and a few drops splattered onto her face from the muddy hole above. Xifeng pulled herself up, wincing at the sting in her leg, though nothing felt broken.

The light illuminated a stone passageway, similar to the one she and Kang had traveled through a month ago. But this one seemed more crudely made, with only a dirt ceiling and a few stones placed halfheartedly on the walls.

Somehow, she had ended up back in the tunnels below the city of women. This must be one of the passages Kang had warned her about, the dangerous old ones that might cave in or contain poisonous air. She glanced warily at the dirt ceiling, hoping the rest of it wouldn't collapse on her because of the rain.

"Hello?" she called, hoping a eunuch guard would respond, but there was only silence. How far was she from the main passageway? The winding passage led into blackness on both sides. The familiar anxiety crept over her—that sickening feeling of being enclosed by the earth—and she took a few deep breaths. Kang had told her three exits led out of the city of women, and she was bound to find one before long.

She had fallen straight down against the wall. She didn't know where the passage on the right might lead, but the left would likely take her back to the entrance she had come through on her first day. She limped in that direction, wishing she had a torch.

If the air in this tunnel was deadly, it might be a long time before they found her body.

Xifeng continued calling out as she walked, hoping a eunuch would hear her. The passage branched and she continued down the tunnel she thought might lead her back to the entrance. Was it her imagination, or did the ground slope downward as she walked? Beneath her thin cotton shoes, the stones were warm and slick with moisture. The air became thick and heavy, drawing beads of perspiration on her forehead and upper lip. A primal, earthy smell emanated from somewhere below.

Suddenly, her foot stepped into nothingness. She cried out and dug her nails into the dirt wall. But further observation revealed not a hole, but a set of stone steps winding down into the darkness. She stared in disbelief. Who would build such a thing in this place?

Her rational mind told her to turn back and take the other tunnel, but another voice spoke within. It reminded her of how she'd felt when Guma read her cards, or when she had talked to the *tengaru* queen, or when Wei had told her the Crown Prince wanted her in the palace. It was a feeling of destiny come full circle, of *belonging* to this place in some strange way.

Xifeng, the voice crooned. The creature stirred beneath her heart, caressing her rib cage.

Something waited for her below, and she wanted—*needed*—to find out what it was.

She hugged the wall as she descended, trying not to slip. The darkness seemed to recede, or perhaps her eyes had grown used to it. A dozen more steps, and the warmth and the dripping sound intensified. Abruptly, she reached the bottom and found a flat stone floor leading to a vast emptiness that stretched out before her.

Xifeng stood in a cavernous space with walls of rough, unhewn stone. Shimmering rays of light crept through holes in the rock ceiling dozens of feet above her, illuminating the edge where the floor ended and the water began—a slow stream swirling in the depths, steaming and billowing gusts of hot air around her. Along one wall, a sheet of the scalding water poured from a crevice in the ceiling. Her breath came in short, ragged gasps when she realized she could see her own reflection in the waterfall as clearly as if it had been still water . . . or a mirror.

"A hot spring," she murmured in disbelief, the hairs rising on her arms and neck. "What sorcery is this?"

She had half dismissed these natural wonders as fables, for how could water be naturally hot? The rivers and swamps near her town had always been cool even in summer. But the stories she'd read claimed some waters ran deep into the bowels of the earth, where the Dragon Lords had once stoked the fires from which all mankind had sprung. It had been a privilege of kings and queens to bathe in such water.

The springs did not lie calmly as the Imperial ponds did, far above. They did not shine or trickle as the streams in the Great Forest had done. This water *gurgled.* It *belched.* It shoved along fissures and fractures in the rock, forcing its way along with a ferocity she had to admire. It bubbled in a glorious ugliness that was almost beauty.

There was a small outcropping of boulders alongside the waterfall, which Xifeng climbed gingerly. It was like a balcony overlooking the rest of the cavern. *My own private court,* she thought. Some of the water had collected on the boulders, forming a sizable, quiet pool protected from the barreling stream. She dipped a few fingers in. The water was hot, but not unpleasant—it felt comforting against her rough skin. Boldly, she stuck her whole hand in, fluttering her fingers in the silken water and enjoying the serenity of this secret, forgotten place.

Xifeng sat on the boulder, watching the springs roar, her unease melting away. A thick coating of dust lined the floor, with no footsteps other than her own. It looked as though no one had been here in years . . . perhaps centuries.

The stairs meant someone had known about these springs once. One of the Empress's ancestors had likely bathed here long ago, and it had been abandoned or become inaccessible.

Xifeng liked the idea of a place where no one could find her—a hidden sanctuary, tucked away just for her. She peeled off her rain-soaked clothes and laid them on a boulder to dry, enjoying the hot air on her skin. She dipped her feet into the pool and searched with her toes for the shallow bottom, then immersed her entire body, gasping at the heat. She had already grown used to the thick, sour smell of the water, and splashed some of it on her face and hair.

"My own gilded tub," she told the darkness.

The pockets of light seemed to twinkle at her, and her skin prickled with the awareness she had felt in the *tengaru* clearing. This was an ancient place of rooted memory—a cavern etched in stone while kingdoms rose and fell and gods created the world above. The water vibrated with a deep undercurrent of magic, and she thought if she allowed it to, it might pierce her body and enter her lifeblood.

She stepped out of the pool naked and faced the waterfall, echoing Lady Sun's gesture as she ran a hand over her smooth, bare stomach. The steam licked at her skin as she stared deep into the glassy mirror of water, certain there was nothing in the world lovelier than what she saw within. That face like a flower in the first flush of spring, and the curve of those breasts and hips like the outline of a priceless marble vase.

Nothing, not even Lady Sun at the height of her seductive power, could rival it.

Fairest, the voice within her whispered.

Xifeng tilted her face, a pale moon in the evening of the water. She felt like a goddess in the shimmering light. She was a poem come to life, and each vein was a lyric.

She had been so wrong to doubt her destiny, to assume the cards were mistaken. This struggle, this difficult beginning, was only a trial to test her strength and her mettle as Empress.

Fairest of all.

"You have nothing to fear," she murmured. Though she herself spoke the words, they came from another place, another world. The swirling of the steam was like the slithering within her. "You have only to hear me and to do as I ask."

Trust me. I will help you, my child, the voice said, and it was so like Guma's that Xifeng cried out in love and longing, hands outstretched for a face in the dark.

Her aunt was here, and she would help her. She would not beat her anymore, but love her as a mother should. Together, they would vanquish their enemies. Xifeng wished she had the bundle of incense hidden in her bed, so its fumes could mingle with the steam and she might see Guma before her once more.

A sound came at the edge of hearing. Xifeng turned her head quickly and the movement broke the spell.

Once again she was alone, and there was no one and nothing in the darkness.

22

"Why are you so sleepy today?" Madam Hong snapped.

Xifeng wiped her watering eyes. "I'm sorry. I've been having nightmares . . ."

"Well, work faster or I'll give you something else to have nightmares about." The woman turned to scold another girl nearby.

Today, Xifeng was on cleaning duty with a dozen maidservants, scrubbing Lady Sun's lacquered wood floors. She dipped her rag in a bucket of water, splashing a few drops on her face to help her stay awake. Madam Hong had rushed them through the morning prayers and meal to clean the concubine's apartments from top to bottom.

Xifeng stifled another yawn. She hadn't slept a full night since finding the hot springs a week ago. She kept dreaming about the mirror-water and the creature's whisper: *fairest.* In some of the dreams, Guma came to her, bleeding from a wound in her chest. In others, a man too tall to be human rose from the water and spoke to her, but when she awoke the next morning, she could never remember what he had said.

"Stupid, useless thing!" Madam Hong shouted at another girl.

Xifeng scrubbed harder, not wanting to be the woman's next victim. Her mind wandered back to the hot springs as she worked. It had been difficult finding a way out of the tunnel. She had scraped her hands climbing up slippery rocks to the main passageway, and she'd had to lie to the guards about being on an errand for Lady Sun so they would let her back into the city of women, but it had been worth it. She would do it again in a heartbeat, just to see that image of herself—beautiful, queenly, and invincible—in the strange mirror-water.

I took action once, for Wei, she thought. *Now I must do so again for myself.*

Boldly putting herself before the Crown Prince had gotten her access to the palace. This time, she needed to do the same with Emperor Jun.

It was time to meet her destiny.

"You don't look like a servant," a maid whispered, eyeing her with suspicion when Madam Hong's back was turned. "Are you new?"

"You could say that." Xifeng didn't offer any more information. No one, least of all an ugly maidservant, needed to know she was here on a mission. Lady Sun hadn't summoned her today, so she'd made sure to volunteer for scrubbing duty in order to be in the apartments.

Madam Hong clapped her hands for attention. "Stop your work. Take your buckets and go. Hurry." She darted a glance at the lanterns, which burned low. The maidservants scurried to obey, and she turned in time to see Xifeng pick up a tray of persimmons and walk toward the concubine's inner chambers. "Where do you think you're going?"

"Lady Sun is hungry," Xifeng lied, holding up the tray she'd stolen from the kitchens, and left without another word.

A eunuch snapped to attention in the corridor when he heard her footsteps, relaxing when he saw her. "She's sulking in her bedchamber," he said, not bothering to hide his delight. "She's warming up for another argument with the Emperor. You'd best come back another time."

"I'll leave this with her and be on my way."

She had no desire to see the concubine in a temper. She just needed a place to hide while she waited for the Emperor to arrive. All week, she'd been asking subtle questions here and there about when His Majesty would visit the concubine. A few well-placed queries had informed her that today was the anniversary of Lady Sun's arrival at court, and the Emperor would be coming to dine with her; all of the cleaning had been for his benefit.

She passed a procession of frazzled maids bustling in and out of the bedchamber where Lady Sun wailed loudly. It sounded like she was breaking things, too, from the shattering that punctured the air every few moments.

"You are all useless!" the concubine shouted, her voice growing louder with each word as though she were pursuing the fleeing maids.

Xifeng deposited the tray on the floor and dashed down the corridor, ducking into a random doorway just as Lady Sun emerged, screeching for the eunuchs' help. No doubt His Majesty's visit would be short today. Xifeng would wait until he was leaving and put herself before him. She had to cross his path, see his face and hear his voice.

She needed to glimpse her future.

The very idea made her palms dampen, and Wei's face appeared in her mind. *He's happy where he is,* she told herself determinedly. And when she became Empress, she would again be able to see him whenever she wanted; their fates would still be entwined as the cards predicted. She would be able to do anything she wished.

Xifeng studied her surroundings. The room she had entered didn't seem to belong in these apartments. It was elegant in a sparse, simple way, with a few paintings and a heavy rug that muffled her footsteps. But what attracted her was the mahogany table in the center of the room. It held a magnificent map of the continent and its surrounding islands, painted on a sheet of paper so large she wondered at the tree from which it had come.

There had been a few maps in the volumes at home, but this was Feng Lu as she had never seen it. The artist had sketched the trees of the Great Forest with such exquisite detail, she could almost hear them rustling in some unfelt breeze. A red pin marked the Imperial Palace, from which she retraced her journey through the city and back into the forest.

According to this map, she had traveled the distance of her two hands placed palm to fingertip. She marveled at the immensity of the world in which they lived. Truly, they were nothing more than mere specks in a landscape of mountains and grasslands, oceans and rivers.

What might it be like, to be Empress of all these lands? She ran her fingers across the sea, imagining the waves stirring beneath her touch. Her heart soared.

"Do you like it?" a voice asked, and she jumped and spun around.

A man sat in the corner, his face partially hidden from view by an ivory folding screen. He was neither young nor old and wore a simple tunic of dark blue. He reminded her of painted mountains she had seen in books: sharp and jagged, with a bleak beauty honed by wind and struggle. He rose and came closer, observing her as intently as she did him. He seemed familiar somehow, like someone she had once known, though she was certain they'd never met. He could not be a eunuch, with that starkly masculine face and rich, dark voice. Nor was he a prince, for she had met the eldest, the Crown Prince, and this man seemed older than he was.

"I've never seen a more beautiful map," Xifeng said cautiously.

He approached her with confident dignity. His chin was upturned and the lines in his face were hard, strong, as though he were used to giving orders that were obeyed without question.

All at once, it struck her: this was the man for whom she had been waiting—the Emperor of all Feng Lu. It could only be him—what man, aside from a eunuch, would be allowed in the women's quarters? And she had never seen anyone with a more commanding presence. He walked as though he owned not only the palace, but the entire world.

He must have come in, unseen, from a different entrance.

It took all of her willpower not to falter or collapse to her knees before him.

Why should I bow? He is my equal. A slow hum of approval whispered from the dark depths beneath her heart.

Still, she felt conscious of her plain hair and clothing. "I'm sorry, sir." She spoke in the respectful tone she would have used for a minister or high-ranking eunuch. "I didn't realize the room was already occupied."

He had a twinkle of humor she never would have expected from a ruthless invader of foreign lands. "I suspect you came in here for the same reason I did." He tilted his head toward the corridor, where Lady Sun was still shrieking.

Xifeng kept her face blank and watched the Emperor lean over the map, forearms braced against the edge. He was shorter than Wei and not as broad, with a lithe elegance better suited to rooms like this than to a training field. In short—nothing like what she had expected. She forced herself to remain calm, to curb the mixture of confusion and eagerness and recognition boiling inside her.

"It's a birthday gift for the Empress. The eunuchs hid it here so she wouldn't find it."

"It's an impressive gift, and one I think will be appreciated," she responded.

How could this man with the quiet, thoughtful air possibly be the iron-willed ruler of Feng Lu? And yet it was certainly him. He was Empress Lihua's second husband, Xifeng knew, but still she had expected someone stern, rotund, and in his sixties. This man had to be about thirty, Lady Sun's age, and carried himself not with the swagger of a soldier, but with quiet thought and intelligence.

He was more like a bird, she decided, with his sharp, clear-cut features. But whereas Wei was hawk-like, wild and savage, Emperor Jun was more like a falcon, practiced, polished, and precise. *Still a bird of prey.* She averted her gaze when his keen, narrow eyes returned to her.

"You don't speak like a maidservant. Who are you, then?" She told him, and his laugh was a bright, merry sound. "I wish you luck in your new position. So you think this is an appropriate present for Her Majesty?"

"It's not my place to say, sir, if the gift is already meant for her."

"Are you sure you're new to the palace? You speak as guardedly as one who has lived her whole life at court."

"It would be a marvelous gift for any lady, but particularly one who reigns above all others." She glanced at his hands on the map. His fingernails were immaculate, the thumb lingering off the coast of Kamatsu. Wei's had always been dirty and covered with cuts and bruises, the hands of a working man.

Emperor Jun's eyes crinkled. "Most ladies would disagree with you. Women like Lady Sun, for instance, prefer silks and jewels."

Xifeng bit her tongue to keep from saying something about the concubine she might regret later. "This is a much more romantic gesture."

"Why?"

"Any woman of means might expect silks and jewels, but how many can say she has been given the world?"

His face broke into such a delighted smile, she couldn't help returning it. "A lady-in-waiting with a way with words. I thought such a thing couldn't exist," he teased. "You know, that chief eunuch fancies himself a poet. You should speak to him. Perhaps he'll mentor you."

If he's not busy stealing from poems himself, she thought, but saw he was still teasing. He must have known about Master Yu, too. It was almost too easy to forget she was speaking to the Emperor himself, not to a friend. "I'm afraid he'd find me a bit beneath him, sir."

"Nonsense." He turned back to the map, tapping a section above the Great Forest at the continent's northernmost tip. "Do you see this mountain range here?"

"The Mountains of Enlightenment. The shrine of the Dragon Lords lies there."

"Very good," he said, as though praising a pupil. "And a hundred monasteries besides. There's an envoy leaving the palace this winter to go there. They make an offering of loyalty to the gods once every nine years. The last time they did that, I had just come to the palace. Just a poor distant relative of the Empress . . . certainly nothing to her or her first husband, Tai. They were first cousins of the purest blood, directly descended from the Dragon King himself."

Xifeng glanced at him, and the feeling of familiarity intensified. Perhaps it was the bitter edge she heard in his voice, that others should be born to such greatness; he was, after all, a bit of an outsider like herself.

He's my destiny, she realized. *He seems familiar because our names are written together in the cards.*

"Any offering to the shrine is an offering to the Empress, her children, and their godly blood," he continued.

"The shrine must be empty, isn't it?"

"Of the gods' treasures, yes." His face returned to its calm neutrality as he traced his thumb across the painted peaks. "The lords removed their heirlooms when their alliance dissolved. Some say they brought the relics back to the heavens, whereas others think they left them hidden on Earth."

"What is your opinion?"

Emperor Jun arched his eyebrows. "That they're still here, for the taking."

"For the taking?" she repeated. "By whom?"

"The scholars still speak of that fabled peace of Feng Lu, when the shrine was full. They say peace will return one day when the treasures are restored. Pretty thought, isn't it?"

The *tengaru* queen's ageless eyes materialized in Xifeng's mind. *That tree could be meant for you . . . or for her.* Was it only a pretty thought if the demon guardians believed it enough to have protected the Dragon King's apple tree for all the ages of the world?

"Apart from the relics, the shrine isn't empty," the Emperor went on. "Envoys from every kingdom on the continent bring food and jewels and precious metals as tokens of worship."

"I'd like to see it with my own eyes," Xifeng said wistfully. "Will you go with them?"

He shook his head. "The palace officials will. Ministers and scholars, with soldiers from the Imperial Army to escort them. They'll bring our Ambassador Liao, of course, and a visiting one from Kamatsu . . ."

"Shiro?" Xifeng asked eagerly, and he stared at her in astonishment. "He was one of my companions on the way here, as was his friend Hideki. He was my guardian and chaperone, in fact," she added, remembering the story she had told the Crown Prince.

"They're both doing well and will be part of the envoy," he said heartily. "I would have brought them today if I'd known that . . ." He stopped, his eyes on the doorway.

Lady Sun stood watching them, her whole body trembling. "Why," she said in a dangerously quiet voice, "are you not on your knees, girl?"

"There's no need for that. Xifeng and I are good friends now."

Lady Sun's eyes on him burned like black embers. "*Friends*?" Lady Sun whispered, and Xifeng despised herself for stepping backward at the hatred in the woman's eyes. "I don't think you understand, Your Majesty, that this impertinent girl is nothing but a maid in my service . . ."

"Lady-in-waiting," the Emperor corrected her, the corner of his mouth lifting at Xifeng.

She longed to smile back, but dropped to her knees instead. "A thousand apologies, Your Majesty. I did not recognize you," she lied.

"Of course she did." Lady Sun still spoke in that low voice like a storm about to break. "She knew exactly who you were the whole time. She's been asking questions about us, trying to find out when you'd be here with me!"

There are ears all over this palace, Kang had warned, *and many of them listen on her behalf.*

Xifeng raised her head. The stark, wind-chiseled peaks of Emperor Jun's face held amusement, not surprise. Had he known all the time that she was aware of his identity? She lowered her nose to the floor again, cheeks warming. *Well, what of it? Let him know fate has come calling.*

"Insolent girl!" Lady Sun shrieked. She flew at Xifeng, slapping the side of her head with all of her strength. The force of it sent Xifeng down, her ear ringing and stars dancing before her eyes, embarrassment forgotten. "How dare you stand before His Majesty like an *equal*!"

Xifeng covered her face as the woman continued to hit her, reaching into her tunic to pinch the tender skin on her arms and neck. The concubine drew back and kicked her, sending flares of fire into her ribs, and Xifeng choked on a sob as memories of Guma flooded back. The screaming pain, the warmth of blood rushing to the injured area. But there had always been a lesson in every beating, and this was nothing but senseless, jealous violence.

"Stop this!" The Emperor grabbed at the irate woman, but in this storm, he was mere thunder to the fury of her lightning.

She pried herself from his grasp and fell upon Xifeng once more.

Every muscle in Xifeng's body tensed to retaliate. She was beyond caring that the Emperor stood witness. She would grab Lady Sun's ankle and pull her down to crack her head against the table. But it was a gamble, for when she uncovered her face to do so, she felt the nails of the concubine's hand rake down her right cheek. Five trails of fire burned from her eye to her jaw as the skin shredded, and Xifeng screamed, dripping blood onto the priceless rug.

Two eunuch guards rushed in and dragged Lady Sun away, but Xifeng hardly registered their presence. The room spun as she touched her ruined face, the fingers coming away bloody. Her heart roared like a funeral drum. Someone spoke to her, helped her up, but she heard only an unintelligible rumble. There were eyes, so many eyes on her. She tucked the side of her face against her shoulder, sick and ashamed, and felt the floor tilting beneath her.

The eunuch who had helped her up shook her. "Get ahold of yourself, girl," he hissed.

Lady Sun stood weeping in the Emperor's arms a few feet away, clutching at his tunic. "She said she didn't know me," he was telling her in a voice as frigid as the northern winds. "There was no need to abuse her like that."

"I don't care about *her,*" the concubine moaned. "Why were you hiding from me, my love? I didn't mean to get angry about the map. I only want all of your presents to be for me. There is no one I love above you . . ."

He shushed her, his face twisted in anger and embarrassment. His eyes met Xifeng's, and she instinctively hid the injured side of her face beneath a curtain of hair. "Are you all right?"

"Answer His Majesty," the eunuch snapped at her, but Emperor Jun shook his head.

"She's in shock. Take her away and have someone clean her face."

The room continued spinning as the eunuch led Xifeng out. Behind them, she heard the Emperor say wearily, "You forget your place," and Lady Sun pleading, "My place is by your side, but if you wish, I'll go to a monastery and never return. I'll go away. I'll leave you for good!"

Xifeng turned back to see Emperor Jun burying his face in the concubine's neck. It was clear from the way they came together that this was a private, regular routine.

A crowd of maids and eunuchs clustered around Xifeng in the corridor. She stared at them in a daze, listening to them murmur and cluck their tongues at the blood on her face and clothing. Someone handed her a wet cloth and she took it gratefully, her hand shaking as she covered the unsightliness of her cheek. A maid asked if she was all right and she tried to reply, but the words stuck in her throat like food that couldn't be swallowed.

The others stood whispering, their horror and delight doing nothing to ease Xifeng's still-pounding heart or her dizziness.

"She flew at her like a cat . . . ruined that girl's face . . ."

"Did you hear she threatened to leave him again?"

"He'll grow tired of these games, mark my words . . ."

Xifeng summoned all of her strength and pushed through them, running out of the concubine's apartments and into the rain. She stopped to empty her stomach into a flower bush, choking on her bile, still hearing the sound of her skin splitting beneath Lady Sun's nails. There was blood, so much blood drying on her fingers and her clothes. She sank to her hands and knees, crawling through the downpour to the stream. Raindrops marred the surface, but it was enough to see the mess of ripped skin and blood on her face.

She tipped her head to the sky, opened her mouth, and let out a savage scream, devastating in its despair. Not even in Guma's most terrible fits of temper had she *ever* destroyed Xifeng's face this way. She pressed her damaged cheek into the dirt, body heaving with sobs. The cool mud against her burning skin calmed her a bit. The ground stopped tilting and her heart slowed.

Cry not, for your tears are no more than rain upon your enemy's face.

It was a line from a poem she had once been forced to memorize. If only Guma had known how Xifeng would need that advice. What would she say if she were here?

Lady Sun thinks she's playing a game with no opponent. She trusts the Emperor will never put her aside for someone younger, brighter, more beautiful.

That was what Guma would tell her. And it was true—that was a king's privilege in a man's world. If the concubine didn't understand that, she was dangerously overplaying her hand.

Hideki had compared the court to a sand pit. Xifeng imagined Lady Sun clawing for the edge, her greedy grip only pushing it farther away, the soft sand tumbling down the sides to the bottom. Somehow, there would be a way to make sure she fell straight down.

And Xifeng would be there when she did.

23

The eunuchs burst into her chamber late that night. Xifeng blinked as they stood over her bed with a glaring lantern. "Search her and all of her things," Master Yu commanded.

"What's the meaning of this?" Xifeng sputtered, slapping their hands away. She leaned on her pillow, hoping they wouldn't reach beneath it and find her mother's treasures. But they didn't need to, for one of the eunuchs pawing through her clothing on the chair gave a shout of triumph.

"You said it was a gold ornament, Master Yu?" he asked smugly. From the tunic she'd worn all day, he had pulled an exquisite gold hair comb in the shape of a crescent moon.

"That's it," Master Yu said. "Take her."

Dandan and Mei sat up in their beds, their eyes round as the eunuchs grasped Xifeng none too gently and propelled her toward the door.

"Let me go! I haven't done anything!" she shouted.

Master Yu slapped her soundly across the face, and a stabbing pain shot across the still-raw, ruined half. "Don't you dare speak to me, you vile little peasant," he spat. "You need to learn some manners." He led them out into the courtyard. Several ladies-in-waiting and eunuchs trailed after in their nightclothes, drowsy eyes growing alert at the sign of trouble.

Though it had stopped raining, the ground was still wet. The eunuchs pushed Xifeng down, the damp stone tiles scraping her bare legs. The moon shone upon the long, evil-looking whip Master Yu held in his hand. She struggled, but the eunuchs tightened their grip, and she searched desperately for a friendly face. She only saw a lovely, moon-pale face that made her cheek sting again, this time in memory: Lady Sun, staring placidly back at her.

The destruction of Xifeng's beauty had not been enough. She must have had someone—Dandan or Mei?—plant the comb on Xifeng while she was sleeping. Xifeng's head swiveled left and right, but Kang was not there. She had not a single friend to save her from this humiliation.

"Strip her," Master Yu ordered, and the eunuchs tore her tunic from her. She knelt, naked and hopeless, hugging her thin arms across her breasts as they pushed her face into the ground. Every muscle in her body shook as she closed her eyes in despair at Guma's betrayal, at the spirits of magic who had lied to her and made false promises to bring her to this torture.

She gave one last, hopeless wrench in the eunuchs' grasp. They each gripped a shoulder and stretched her back bare for the whip.

"One hundred stripes ought to do it, Master Yu," Lady Sun commanded.

The eunuch's reply held a note of shock. "One hundred, my lady? I assumed . . ."

"You dare to question me? One hundred."

I'm going to die tonight, Xifeng thought. She would be nothing but a puddle of blood and shredded skin on the cobblestones. She squeezed her eyes shut, fiery tears rolling down her cheek. *Help me,* she begged the creature, her only ally, *please help me*.

Master Yu stepped behind her. She heard his whip dragging behind him and the swish of his arm as he raised it, bringing it down with tremendous force.

Searing, fire-hot pain lashed across her tender skin. Xifeng had thought she'd known pain, *true* pain, but Guma's cane had been nothing compared with this. She screamed and squeezed her eyes shut, struggling with all of her strength against the eunuchs forcibly holding her in place. The whip whistled as it moved up in the air again, then sliced into her body. The world spun around her as she shook from the excruciating agony of it.

How ironic that she would die tonight in such a cruel, familiar manner.

The whip cracked again, a sharp, blistering sound as it rose into the air to descend upon her yet again. Xifeng braced herself for the blow, hoping this one would make her lose consciousness. She could already feel the stripe of heat before it was even etched into her skin . . .

But it did not come. The eunuchs loosened their grip, enough for her to turn her head around in astonishment.

Kang stood there, his eyes burning with black wrath, one hand gripping the tail of the whip. Behind him was Empress Lihua, her face white with anger.

"One hundred lashes would be enough to kill a grown man many times over, let alone a girl, don't you think?" Her Majesty said contemptuously. "What has she done to warrant this?"

Lady Sun squared her shoulders, her eyes defiant. "She stole a comb in the presence of not only myself, but the Emperor as well. I wanted to teach her a lesson."

"By killing her? It's difficult to educate a corpse." The Empress glared at the eunuchs. "Put the tunic back on her at once and summon Bohai to my apartments. All of you return to your beds." There was a flurry of bowing as the onlookers hurried away.

"I have the right to exercise authority upon any in my service!" Even Master Yu drew back at the overt hatred in Lady Sun's voice.

"Xifeng is not in your service, but in mine. Remember that before you murder all of my women." The Empress turned her scathing glare upon the chief eunuch and Madam Hong. "I'm told you assigned Xifeng to work as Lady Sun's personal maid. I trust with over two hundred servants at our disposal, you can find someone more appropriate to clean after her animals than a lady-in-waiting recommended by the Crown Prince." She was magnificent in her disapproval, in the tilt of her chin and the flash of her eye.

A daughter of dragons, Xifeng thought as Kang helped her stand up. She leaned against him, still shaking from the pain as he slipped her tunic over her head. She hissed through her teeth when the cotton snagged on her fresh wounds.

The Empress's fiery gaze turned on her. "Did you steal the comb, Xifeng?"

"I did not, Your Majesty," she said, her voice ragged. "I have no purpose for it."

A smile tugged at the Empress's thin lips. "You wouldn't have worn it longer than five minutes without a scene." She glanced at Lady Sun, who reddened. "Master Yu, Madam Hong, we'll discuss this in the morning. Xifeng, come with me, please." She turned, the gold phoenix embroidered on her robe shimmering as though aflame.

"I'll wait for you outside the door," Kang promised. He helped her climb the stairs to the uppermost level of the building. Along with the stripes of heat on her back, she could still feel the eunuchs' grasp on her arms, which would be purple with bruises by morning.

On the walkway, she saw Lady Sun still watching her. Xifeng clenched her jaw. One day soon, she vowed, it would be the concubine's turn to cower before her in pain and fear—and Xifeng would enjoy every minute of it.

The Empress led her into a chamber lit by white lanterns. Whereas Lady Sun's apartments were showy and overstuffed, the Empress's were simple, with tasteful furnishings and nature blooming on every surface. It was the home of a woman with nothing to prove. A table of creamy, light wood held an exquisite miniature tree standing no more than a foot high. Its branches were tiny clouds of evergreen bursting with little white blossoms, their hearts apple-red.

"The tree of a thousand lanterns," the Empress said, noticing her interest. "A gift from the palace gardener."

"It's lovely," Xifeng said. "Thank you, Your Majesty, for saving me tonight."

"Kang is the one who deserves your thanks. He caused a considerable commotion to notify me."

Xifeng hadn't considered how many layers of guards the eunuch had to get through to reach the Empress. If he hadn't succeeded, if he hadn't brought Her Majesty in time . . . She shut her eyes, feeling a rush of horror mixed with gratitude.

Empress Lihua regarded her with bright, youthful eyes in a face marked with sorrow. "I see the whip wouldn't have been the first to touch you today." Her fingers hovered over the cheek Lady Sun had damaged. "What have you done to make her hate you so?"

Xifeng ducked her head. "It seems one doesn't have to do much, Your Majesty."

"I don't often deem it worthwhile to interfere with Lady Sun's doings. My husband's consorts are given much freedom, but occasionally I find it necessary to remind them that they need *my* approval, as well." A muscle worked in her jaw as she turned to the miniature tree.

Xifeng pressed a hand over the vicious scratches, recalling how the Emperor had wearily embraced Lady Sun. "It can't be easy for you, sharing him with them."

"It's not for me to choose or complain. My husband is the Emperor, and I must put his needs before mine. I am first in his heart and his home, and there's nothing more I can ask." But her face wore an expression of resigned patience, one she must have had to learn. She hesitated before laying a gentle hand on Xifeng's arm. "Don't let Lady Sun's mistreatment make you sad, my dear. She behaves that way to anyone she sees as a rival."

"I won't forgive her for this," Xifeng whispered, longing to lay her head in the Empress's lap and be soothed. "She's ruined my face."

"Wounds heal in time."

"But they also scar." She closed her eyes, another wave of dizzy panic threatening to overcome her. "I wish I knew what my Guma would advise. I don't think it wrong that I came to the palace . . . to you. But I feel I'm not where I ought to be."

Careful not to drink your own poison, the creature hissed as her words poured out. *You may win the Empress by playing the daughter, but remember she is not your mother.*

Footsteps sounded from the doorway. Xifeng's eyes flew open as one of the guards approached. "The Imperial physician, Your Majesty."

"Show him in." The Empress raised an eyebrow at Xifeng. "This is another reason I suspect you are favored by the gods. Tonight, I have been without my usual sleeping tonic, and the physician brings it now. If I had taken it as I do every evening, no power on earth could have awakened me."

Xifeng shuddered, as a man in his sixties entered the room. Despite the late hour, he wore formal blue silk printed with gold circles and a cap marking his rank. He was short and stout, with bright black eyes and an impressive silver beard that fell in a long, straight point. This, then, was Bohai. He had nothing of his daughter, Akira, in him until he smiled, and then Xifeng was struck by the resemblance in the way his cheeks drew back and his eyes shone.

She flushed under the physician's keen eyes. Perhaps he pitied her—such a beautiful girl, her face so unfortunately marred.

"Your Majesty, I've brought your tonic."

The Empress lifted a hand. "Tend to Xifeng first, please. Her need is greater than mine."

Xifeng tugged her hair over her disfigured cheek, thanking the gods she'd had the foresight to heal the other one. The physician opened a black case, revealing bottles and metal instruments.

"Turn your back and bend at the waist, please," the physician instructed her, tutting at the bloodstains on her tunic. "With permission?"

Empress Lihua placed a calming hand on Xifeng's shoulder as Bohai lifted her tunic. There was a sharp, burning sting as he washed her wounds, then applied a cool solution to her torn skin. "This is a salve to help heal the injury. Try to sleep on your side for a week."

Xifeng nodded wearily. The movement shifted the hair on her face, and Bohai's quick eyes saw the scratches on her cheek.

"Let me give you something for your . . ."

"Hideous disfigurement?" she whispered.

Bohai and the Empress exchanged glances. "It's not as bad as you think, and you are not the first young woman I've treated for this." His manner was so kind, Xifeng pushed aside her hair and her pride. "I can give you something for the pain, but there may be faint scars."

Xifeng gasped. "Permanent scars?"

"If they are, you'll hardly be able to see them," Bohai assured her, but the room seemed to tilt and spin once more. She bent her head, heartsick at the damage Lady Sun had caused and ashamed of the way Bohai and the Empress regarded her with pity. She barely heard his instructions as he pressed a small tin into her hand.

"Thank you," she murmured as the physician turned to Empress Lihua.

"I apologize for not having this ready sooner, Your Majesty. I've had to formulate a new draught that would not be harmful." His gaze flickered to the Empress's abdomen.

Xifeng struggled to hide her surprise—she hadn't noticed the woman's slightly rounded belly beneath the patterned silks she wore. "My congratulations, Your Majesty," she said, to which the Empress smiled as she waved away Bohai's apology.

"You've made me the same tonic for fifteen years, since the birth of my youngest," she told the physician. "Of course you need time to adjust the prescription. It's a blessing I've carried this baby long enough to need a new formula."

"I replaced the black fungus with licorice, ginseng, and crushed longanberries," Bohai said. "It should be as effective in helping you sleep. How have you been feeling this week?"

"I ate a bit more than usual today. But I've had an ache here." The Empress laid a wan, trembling hand on her belly. "I haven't felt the baby moving or kicking as much. Has she been lost?"

"With your permission, Your Majesty." Bohai placed his own experienced hands on her belly, pressing here and there. His face was thoughtful as his fingers moved over the material of her robe. "Have you had any bleeding?"

"Not a drop."

"Has the pain been very sharp?"

The Empress shook her head.

"The baby has not been lost."

Empress Lihua closed her eyes and exhaled very slowly. She held out a hand to Xifeng, who took it, thrilling at her touch. "Then it's nothing to be concerned about?"

"We should always be concerned about symptoms, Your Majesty. But not overly so." Bohai gave her the gentle smile he shared with Akira. Xifeng stared, amazed a father could have his daughter's smile and never know it. "You must continue to eat. The baby's strength depends upon it. And if the ache returns, send your lady for me. I'd rather come and tell you a symptom is not worrisome than not be told and have it be serious." He bid them good night and left.

"Are you all right?" the Empress asked Xifeng when they were alone. "Don't fret, my dear. A few scars will not change how beautiful you are."

Xifeng shook her head in misery. The Empress didn't understand; none of them did. With one swipe of her claws, Lady Sun had ruined everything. She had ensured the Emperor would not look at Xifeng again. Surely the destiny written in her stars would now change, now that His Majesty had seen the blood and scratches that ravaged her beauty. He would not want a marked, flawed woman for his queen.

"All this because I spoke to the Emperor. Without knowing him," she added quickly. "I didn't mean to show disrespect. I didn't know I should have been kneeling at his feet."

An unseen enemy lurks . . . the Fool.

Lady Sun had done everything Xifeng expected the Fool to do. But there were two players in this game, and she would not sit back and wail and weep. She had come to the palace to seize her fate with both hands. All she needed now was to show the concubine she had made an enemy of the worst possible person. She had to strike before Lady Sun made her next move.

A tremor ran through her hand. The wound from Guma had vanished, and these would as well if she could find some lifeblood. It would be simple to find something small and weak in the gardens. But to take yet another life for her own benefit . . . She could not. She *must* not. Xifeng pictured the *tengaru* queen's fathomless eyes when she had delivered her warning.

"Lady Sun would be jealous of the Emperor's horse if she could." Empress Lihua rose and paced the room, brow furrowed as she made the sign of the Dragon Lords. "I won't leave you at her mercy. Starting tomorrow, I'd like you to serve in my household alone. I will inform Madam Hong and she will find a suitable occupation for you."

Xifeng gripped the table, all thoughts of the *tengaru*'s disapproval gone. "Truly, Your Majesty? You would bestow such an honor upon me?"

Empress Lihua's lips didn't quite form a smile. "There is something about you, Xifeng. You belong here, but to what end, I know not. Perhaps you've come to save me." She gestured to an object beside the tree of a thousand lanterns: the poultice Xifeng had made for her. "My appetite has improved greatly. But let's not hurt Bohai's feelings, for he has tried longer than you have. All I know is that if you were my child, I wouldn't let that woman within an inch of you."

Xifeng's heart lifted and soared. She knelt until her forehead met the floor, her eyes prickling with emotion even as gooseflesh rose on her skin. Everything was happening as it should, but all so fast she scarcely had time to draw breath. In one day, she had met the Emperor, and now she would be close to his wife—the woman whose place she would take.

The Empress extended her hand, and Xifeng took it, trembling. Thinking of the future, of what was meant to be, was no better than wishing for this woman's death. "I don't deserve such kindness from you, Your Majesty," she whispered.

If only you knew . . .

Empress Lihua tucked a strand of hair behind Xifeng's ear, and it felt so natural that her tears sprang anew. In this abrupt hunger, she thought she knew what it might be like to be a daughter, and what kind of mother the Empress might be to a girl.

"Perhaps now you will find yourself on a better path," the older woman said. "Sleep now, my dear, and come back to me tomorrow."

But as grateful and overjoyed as she felt, Xifeng's heart sank as she left the royal apartments. The Empress thought she was merely showing kindness to a lonely, friendless girl, but she had unwittingly embraced her fate. There could only be one ending to this story, one woman who could sit upon the throne of Feng Lu.

And it would not be Empress Lihua.

24

Kang was waiting by the pond when Xifeng left to collect her possessions and move them to her new chamber in Her Majesty's apartments.

"I'm to serve in the Empress's household. Starting tomorrow," she said, still stunned.

He gave a laugh of genuine delight. "Didn't I say you would find success here? How do you feel about being plucked away from danger?"

"Tigers can still climb trees." Xifeng's heart sank again as she touched her cheek. "How can I succeed in Her Majesty's household like this? Bohai gave me a salve for the pain, but he warned there might be scars." The very word made her physically ill.

Kang tilted his head. "You'll be under much more scrutiny as one of the Empress's ladies," he agreed. "But at least now you're under her protection. I do wonder whether our gentle Empress is gathering you closer because you're Lady Sun's enemy."

"You think the Empress is plotting against Lady Sun? It seems beneath her." She wondered if the concubine were watching them from her darkened windows. Her chest tightened when they passed the place where she'd knelt at the mercy of Master Yu's whip. "Those hundred lashes weren't for any comb, real or imagined."

The eunuch growled. "She's depraved. I'd like to snap that alabaster neck in two."

"How many stripes did you get?"

He looked her in the eyes. "Ten."

For merely speaking to Emperor Jun, the concubine would have given Xifeng *ten times* Kang's punishment. Lady Sun had saved the most violent, horrific punishment for her, and who else would resort to such measures but the Fool?

Xifeng gritted her teeth. "She will pay for what she's done to us. There has to be a way."

Everyone despised Lady Sun, from the Empress down to the lowliest maids. The woman hung by a thread, but by the most important one at court: the Emperor. That was the thread Xifeng had to rip from the tapestry.

Xifeng closed her eyes, imagining a winking from within her ribs. The creature had made her feel such powerful anger before. She almost, *almost* longed for that fury again, for this time it seemed more than justified. What dark visions would it give her? An alligator trap whose teeth widened for the concubine's limbs? A torch to singe the flesh from her bones?

Her eyes flew open in horror at herself, her delight fading. "Thank you, my friend," she told Kang. "You saved my life tonight."

"Then you truly believe I am your friend now? You trust that I will protect you?"

"And I will protect *you,* if I can," she promised.

When Xifeng returned to bed at last, her sleep was filled with poison smoke, steel-tipped daggers, and the forgotten springs, locked in time, waiting for someone worthy. Waiting for her.

She felt the creature dreaming inside her, pressed against her impenetrable heart, its head a vault of toxic reveries. And when she woke in the inky blue darkness, hours still before the first rays of morning, she knew she needed to speak to Guma. She needed to see her, if only in a vision, and to hear her advice.

At the very least, she needed to try.

She rose, collecting the incense, an unlit lantern, and a few sulfur matchsticks in her sack. After consideration, she included her mother's jeweled dagger and amber hairpin—they would be safer hidden underground—and crept out into the night. The Empress's rooms were guarded night and day, but her ladies-in-waiting shared a separate entrance to their own chambers, to ease their coming and going to the shrine and bathhouses without disturbing Her Majesty's rest.

Xifeng retraced her steps to the garden with ease, undetected. She struck a matchstick against the wall, applying the flame to her lantern. It illuminated thick grasses heavy with rain, almost obscuring the hole in the ground and the stone floor some twenty feet below. The palace gardeners never bothered pruning this corner, as Empress Lihua preferred a touch of nature in the otherwise meticulous landscape, and the hole had been left undisturbed. Xifeng hadn't noticed before how irregular the stones in the wall were, some jutting out enough that she might be able to climb back out of the tunnel with the help of the surrounding shrubs. It would have to do, or she would be forced to climb up to the main passageway again and think of another excuse for getting past the tunnel guards.

She jumped into the hole with her sack and lantern hugged to her body. With each step she took toward the hot springs, the creature grew more awake inside her. She felt a movement like fangs emerging, but through the fear she felt comfort, too, in something familiar.

The lantern light gave the cavern an ancient air, an aura of mysticism, and Xifeng felt at once she had done right to come. If she could find answers anywhere, it would be here.

She approached the strange waterfall, still unnerved by how clearly she could see her reflection in the sheets of fast-moving water. Striking another matchstick, she lit the incense. Within seconds, the powerful scent snaked into her nostrils. It was almost like being back in Guma's sanctuary, with the door shut and all the world's secrets laid bare.

Xifeng knelt beside the gurgling water and closed her eyes, letting the smoke surround her. She had once hated this thick, cloying fragrance, but when it mingled with the steam of the water, it became something alluring, irresistible. She gave herself up to it, taking it in.

Fairest, said the voice within, and she opened her eyes.

Though she was on her knees, her reflection in the waterfall was standing, strong and proud with shoulders flung back. On her imperious head, above the black silk-spill of her hair, she wore a pointed crown of sharp, lethal steel. All around her, the shapes of men huddled in surrender, and her eyes glittered in a face white as the moon, white as snow, gleaming like a blossom in the tree of a thousand lanterns. Over her chest, where the creature nestled, was the outline of a phoenix with a tail licked by fire—the symbol of the Empress of Feng Lu.

Fairest of all.

A breeze blew from some unseen crevice, pushing away the threads of incense, and for one moment Xifeng felt overpoweringly afraid. Where was she? *Who* was she? And then the plumes of smoke overtook her once more and dashed her terror and confusion away.

"Guma," she commanded, her eyes on her crowned reflection. It transformed into an unsettlingly familiar image: a sea of grass crashing against a cave and a slithering, too-tall man, facing a girl who looked like Guma. He flicked the cards of fortune at her and she caught them in delight, turning them into other objects: a snakeskin, a jeweled dagger, a gilded book of poetry.

The man held out his hand—for the objects or for something else—and the girl ran away. The image changed to show a nobleman bending over the hand of a pretty girl while young Guma watched in a rage of jealousy. Xifeng watched in bewilderment as Guma returned to the cave, her hands outstretched, imploring.

The waterfall shifted back to the crowned Xifeng, with a figure at her feet resembling Lady Sun. In her chest, the woman's heart glowed like the moon, or a precious red apple.

"Is she the Fool?" Xifeng called, pulse thundering.

Instantly, the vision shifted into the card: a youth gazing at the stars, one step away from brutal death.

Memories swirled in her mind: lying awake at night, too hungry to sleep; Guma hunching over her embroidery; Wei turning away from the shoes he needed but could not afford. And then: Xifeng herself, crouching, skin weeping beneath the cracking whip, Lady Sun flushed with triumph. Everything she had endured to get here. All of the suffering and hope and pain.

"I have not come this far to fail," she said through gritted teeth, balling her hands into fists. This could be confirmation from the spirits of magic . . . They could be telling her that Lady Sun was the enemy who would vanquish her.

There is only one way to make certain, the voice rasped.

A glint of light caught her eye in the blanket of fog around her. She saw the dagger that had belonged to her mother: hilt and sheath of burnished bronze, inlaid with kingfisher feathers and slivers of deep green jade. In the mirror-water, the dagger's painfully sharp tip hovered inches above Lady Sun's heart.

Be the blade and the edge together, the light and the dark. You have two faces, Xifeng.

She felt sick to her stomach, the way she had when Guma had thrust the first squirrel into her hands years ago. "This is a woman," she protested, utterly repulsed, but the memory of the rabbits returned. Her first kill away from Guma. How their slippery hearts had scorched her throat, how the hot metallic tang of blood had given way to a roar of satisfaction that shook her whole being. The hunger came back, primal and potent, nearly overcoming her disgust.

Another breeze dispelled the smoke and she backed away from the dagger's deadly shine. "Blood has a price. It is not worth my soul." She spoke the *tengaru* queen's words with all the conviction she could muster.

The billowing, purple-black smoke expanded and wrapped its gossamer arms around her. It reminded her of the Empress's silvery robe. Destroying Lady Sun wouldn't only be revenge for herself and Kang, but also a favor, a gesture of loyalty to Empress Lihua, who might come to love her like a mother.

Xifeng panicked. If Guma truly was there, she may have heard that thought. But there was no betrayed reproach in the humming that grew louder in her ears. The smoke turned into a thousand forked tongues before her eyes, emerging from fanged mouths.

You know what to do. It's only a matter of choosing to do it. It's her death . . . or yours.

"There *has* to be another way," she cried into the darkness. "I will find another way."

There is only one choice.

"No!"

Falling, crying, screaming, she pushed through the tongues of smoke and stumbled toward the incense. She flung the burning sticks into the springs and ran in terror back to her bed, safe above in the city of women. But when she fell at last into an exhausted, dreamless slumber, a voice still lingered at the edge of her consciousness . . . *There is only one choice.*

And even after she awoke, it remained in the deepest shadows of her mind.

25

The ordeal of her first month having passed, Xifeng found herself in a better situation among Empress Lihua's ladies-in-waiting. The other women—whose names she did not know, as they all insisted she call them Madam—were too old to harbor resentment toward her. They taught her to perform their duties: arranging flowers, ensuring the smooth running of the household, and stitching emblems on Her Majesty's ceremonial robes. This last task occupied most of their time, with the Festival of the Summer Moon days away.

"Your embroidery is beautiful," one of the ladies told her as they sat working on the balcony. "That rabbit looks real enough to jump out of the fabric."

Xifeng glanced up, taking care to keep her cheek concealed. It had healed well, thanks to Bohai's salve, but she felt certain everyone pitied her and talked about it when she wasn't there. "I've had practice." She smoothed the ocean-blue festival skirt on which she was stitching lucky rabbits in silver thread. "It was difficult to satisfy my aunt. Her needlework is superb."

"It must be, if yours is of such quality," the woman said, and Xifeng returned her smile.

"The Empress has a different outfit for all seven days," a rosy-cheeked lady told Xifeng. "Three for the prayer days, one for the moon-viewing party, and three for the carnival days, which are my favorite. It's a tradition Emperor Jun bestows upon the city. The markets expand, and people come to buy and sell, eat, and drink. The Imperial Army even gives a demonstration."

Xifeng stopped sewing. "The Imperial Army? Do all of the soldiers attend?"

"Of course. His Majesty wants a large spectacle. There's music and parades, and the Emperor and Empress award prizes to the best performers."

The ladies continued discussing the carnival, but Xifeng didn't hear a word. She picked at a snagged thread, her heart lifting as she thought of Wei. They hadn't seen each other for eight weeks, and she was ashamed she had to work to remember details: the way he laced his fingers through hers, his teasing laughter, and the slow, warm smile he saved just for her.

"We're to accompany the Empress to the gates of the main palace," said a woman with steel-gray hair. "Wait until you see the dragon dance."

"We won't be there long if Madam Hong has anything to say about it," grumbled the rosy-cheeked lady. Xifeng watched her companions hush her and giggle like schoolgirls, amused that even these senior ladies hated Madam Hong. "I can't wait to see what Lady Sun will wear. She'll probably strap her son to her back as her costume, to remind the Emperor."

"And squeal like a pig about how she deserves the Empress's apartments," another woman added, grinning. "Like that tart could ever grace these walls."

Xifeng's needle slipped, and she winced as it stabbed her thumb.

She hadn't seen the concubine in weeks, but still the unspeakable hunger haunted her. She pushed it deep down and focused instead on her anger. *The Fool, the Fool, the Fool.* Lady Sun was the enemy, and no other; she would stop at nothing to destroy Xifeng. Had she succeeded in having Xifeng whipped to death, her path to the throne would now hold one fewer obstacle. If the game was kill or be killed, she would strike again and Xifeng's hesitation would cost her.

But unlike the concubine, Xifeng would not shed blood again if she could help it. The creature might whisper as many evil thoughts as it liked, but she would hold fast to the *tengaru* queen's words. Violence wasn't the only means by which to deal with Lady Sun.

"The way she speaks to Her Majesty," one woman growled, yanking her needle as though she were pulling the concubine's hair. "If I were the Emperor, I wouldn't let her treat my wife that way. But men are all the same: they think not with their brains but with . . ."

"Watch your mouth," the gray-haired lady scolded her.

"It's true. He's the only reason she can do and say whatever she wants."

Xifeng kept her eyes down, listening intently. It seemed Emperor Jun would forgive almost anything where his lover was concerned. If she wanted to discredit Lady Sun, it would have to be a public spectacle . . . an embarrassment. Everyone at court despised the woman, even her own informants. Xifeng imagined them pointing and whispering as Lady Sun stood red faced and humiliated, and the Emperor livid . . .

"Hush, all of you," the rosy woman hissed. "Look who's here."

Lady Meng approached them, clutching needlework in her thin hands. "I thought I might join you," she said awkwardly.

Xifeng noticed the young concubine still spoke with the messy, slurring accent of the village commoners, which Guma had beaten furiously out of Xifeng. It grated her ear after months of hearing the cultured, educated tones of the court ladies. Once again, she found herself feeling sorry for the girl she had envied, with whom she would have gladly traded places once.

The girl sat down with a shy, diffident air. She was younger than Lady Sun, with a lovelier face, but one had only to observe the way she carried herself to know the difference in their positions at court. Her health, too, did not seem as robust as Lady Sun's; the girl had a slight, delicate frame and narrow hips and shoulders like the Empress. Whereas Lady Sun was a tiger waiting to pounce, Lady Meng was a doe among predators.

"We're glad to have you, Lady Meng," the rosy lady said. "I was about to tell the fable of the moon tree. Xifeng doesn't know the story behind the Moon Festival."

The concubine's vague eyes turned to Xifeng and sharpened. "Oh, yes," she said slowly, as though struggling to search for words. "You're the maid the Crown Prince brought to court."

"I'm one of Her Majesty's attendants, my lady," Xifeng said after a pause, wondering whether Emperor Jun regretted taking such an odd, awkward girl for his concubine, despite her beauty. Lady Meng continued staring fixedly at her as the rosy woman began her story.

"Once there was a rabbit who was attacked by a dog. It lay near death with its leg broken. A boy found it and brought it home to his mother, and together they nursed it back to health and shared what food they had with it, though they were poor. The rabbit soon healed, and when the boy set it free again in the field, it dropped nine seeds into his lap. He gave them to his mother to plant in her garden, and that night, a beautiful tree sprouted from the earth, its branches growing nine white fruits that glowed like the moon."

Xifeng put down her needle to listen and noticed Lady Meng doing the same.

"The boy and his mother were overjoyed, thinking the fruit would be delicious. But when they opened them, they found not sweet nectar, but gold, silver, and jewels, more than enough to make them wealthy for the rest of their lives. Their neighbor saw their good fortune and decided to earn it for himself. So he went into the fields and broke the leg of the first rabbit he found."

"Imbecile," said the steel-haired woman, and they all laughed.

"This rabbit gave him nine seeds, too, after he nursed it back to health. But the tree that grew for him was much taller and bore only one enormous fruit. When he cut it open, an old man jumped out and told him to follow. Together, they climbed the tree all day, and when night fell at last, he saw that the old man had taken him to the moon. There, they found another tree in which jewels grew like fruit. 'If you can cut this tree down,' the old man said, giving him an ax, 'everything on it will be yours.' But as it turned out, the tree was enchanted and couldn't be cut down, and the greedy man spent eternity in vain. So you see, the lesson of the fable is to . . ."

"Never break a rabbit's foot," the other woman interrupted, prompting more laughter.

"Why didn't the man climb the tree and retrieve the jewels?" Lady Meng asked plaintively. "He could have gotten himself the same reward as the boy and his mother."

There was a silence, and then the storyteller said, "There were no branches, I suppose."

"But he had all eternity to figure it out. He could have made a rope ladder or something."

Xifeng saw the women exchange amused glances, even the ones who had accompanied Lady Meng. The girl had completely missed the point of the story.

The rosy woman cleared her throat and rose. "I'm going to fetch some water. I'm a bit parched from all of this storytelling."

"I'll come with you," Xifeng offered. "I've run out of silver thread."

As they walked, the woman whispered to Xifeng about Lady Meng. "I pity her. She hates it here and the Emperor knows it. They say she's desperately lonely and has turned to wine for solace. She talks to herself and wanders at night when she ought to be sleeping."

Xifeng remained silent, not wanting to engage in gossip.

"The Emperor never spends the night with her and I think our friend Lady Sun had a hand in that." The woman shook her head. "His Majesty will likely send the poor girl to a monastery soon. He'd do it faster if he knew how she felt about the Crown Prince. Oh, it's common knowledge," she added, seeing Xifeng's surprise. "His Highness was kind to Lady Meng when she first arrived, lonely and homesick, and she took a shine to him. She prefers the Emperor's stepson to the Emperor himself, but the prince is too careful to . . . oh!"

She cried out as they turned the corner and came face-to-face with none other than the Crown Prince himself, leaving his mother's apartments with a retinue of eunuch guards. He looked the same but for the elaborate robes he now wore and the slight pallor of illness. His raised eyebrows showed he'd heard the woman's last words. She wrung her hands, flustered, and Xifeng congratulated herself on not having joined in the gossip.

"You're the lady I was hoping to see," the Crown Prince told Xifeng.

"I asked my mother where I might find you." He glanced pointedly at the lady-in-waiting, who scurried away in mortification, and chuckled. He turned his gaze on the guards, who stepped back twelve paces to give him privacy. "I'm glad to see you making friends, and you look better than ever. I'll have a good report to bring back to Wei."

"Please tell me how he is." She might have felt shame at the longing in her voice if she hadn't been so eager, but the prince stroked his thin beard indulgently.

"He's learning more quickly than I anticipated and has made it his mission to improve all of the swords in our service. He works hard, but he seems forlorn, and I think I know why."

She lowered her eyes, her face warming. Wei missed her, too.

"He heard I was visiting my mother today and begged me to give you a message," His Highness told her with a grin. "I'm as bad as any of these gossips; I can never resist a love story. Take this and hide it well. I don't wish to bring trouble to you, and neither does Wei." He shifted so that the guards couldn't see him hand her a thin scroll, and Xifeng gratefully tucked it away, warming to the young prince. She understood why Lady Meng had been drawn in by his kindness, if the gossip were true.

"How can I ever repay you, Your Highness? You gave Wei and me our positions at the palace, and now you've made me happy again." He waved away her thanks, his pallor a bit more pronounced. "But are you well?"

"I haven't been sleeping much." He ran a hand over his weary face. "Bohai has come every day this week, pinching and prodding and feeding me bits of herbs. I hope to be well enough to lead the Imperial Army on the first carnival day. My stepfather likes a big production."

"Will Wei be in the procession?"

The prince leaned against the railing. "He might. Will you be watching?"

"That depends on Her Majesty."

"I'll speak to her," he promised. "You shouldn't miss a minute of your first Moon Festival. I wouldn't know much about it, though. My brothers and I were always expected to work."

"Are the other princes in the Imperial Army as well?"

"My middle brother commands the Silver Banner. He ran away to fight rebels and expand our territories when he was seventeen. He's been gone two years. Sometimes I fear I'll never see him again. The conflicts in the east grow more tiresome, but it is Dagovad at the helm of the dispute. My brother's men are only there to help." He rubbed the worried lines on his forehead, then gave her an apologetic smile. "I'm sure this is more information than you wanted to know."

"Why does the Great Forest serve the interests of Dagovad?" Xifeng asked, and he looked surprised, but not displeased.

"Dagovad breeds the finest horses on the continent. Our cavalry relies on their mounts and their queen's good favor, and she knows it, too." The prince sighed again. "As for my youngest brother, he should be learning from me, but is always ill and abed. So there is only ever me, ready to do my duty. I tell you a throne is a greater imposition than it is a gift."

Xifeng watched him pick absentmindedly at the railing. She had never imagined a prince not wanting a kingdom. "What would you do instead, if you could?"

The Crown Prince allowed himself a small smile. "Go adventuring with my brother in unknown lands. Make sure he doesn't do anything foolish." He looked down at his folded hands. "I was twelve when my father lay on his deathbed, mortally wounded in war. His marriage to my mother had been happy, though they were first cousins matched for political reasons."

An image of Empress Lihua's face appeared in Xifeng's mind, younger but no less careworn. "Your stepfather is a cousin as well, isn't he?"

"A very distant relative. Still, he shares our blood, and his boldness and intelligence made an immediate impression on my father. I was too young to assume the throne then, and my father was forced to choose a successor or risk leaving behind a vulnerable kingdom with no regent. So Jun was crowned Emperor and my mother became his Empress consort. And according to Imperial law, any sons she had with him—the living Emperor—would displace my brothers and me in the line of succession. My father was content with this."

"But why, when another man's sons would be closer to the throne than his?"

The Crown Prince gave another humorless smile. "My mother is fragile and no longer young. My youngest brother's birth almost killed her. Bohai assured my father in private that she would likely never carry another child to term, despite her hope for a girl. And here I am, still the Crown Prince."

But if fate comes to pass—if Lihua dies and I become the Empress—I might give the Emperor a son. The thought made Xifeng feel unsteady on her feet—that with one move, she might secure her position and displace three royal princes. But somehow, as she watched him fix his eyes dreamily on the forest beyond the wall, she didn't think the Crown Prince would mind. She could never tie herself to a man with so little drive, so little ambition.

"Sometimes I have these strange dreams . . . dreams in which I never take the throne after all. In which I'm not destined to rule," the prince murmured. "For me, they are not nightmares but fantasies." His words raised the hairs on her neck. He glanced at her ruefully. "My mother mustn't know any of this."

"I will not say anything, Your Highness." Xifeng felt a twinge of sympathy for the Empress. No wonder she longed for a girl; a princess would stay with her in the city of women instead of fighting in wars far away or becoming wrapped up in kingly duties.

"I know she's lonely. The Emperor dotes on her, but he's often . . . distracted." The prince peered at a woman in the gardens below: Lady Meng, who had left her sewing and was walking in odd, looping circles. She looked up at them, clearly keeping watch. "I suppose we should be thankful he only has two favored concubines and not two dozen, as my father had."

Here is my opportunity, Xifeng thought. "I hope I won't offend you, Your Highness, but you and your mother have done so much for me, and I feel compelled to speak frankly. I've noticed one of the concubines taking a great deal of liberty with your mother." The Crown Prince's eyes turned back to her, at once keen, alert. "I've come to love and respect the Empress. I have no mother of my own," she added softly, "and I look upon Her Majesty as someone from whom I may seek advice and affection. She saved me from the whip, after all."

"I assume you speak of Lady Sun," the prince said sharply.

Xifeng related the whipping incident to him, sparing no detail in the way Lady Sun had addressed Her Majesty. "But it doesn't matter what she's done to me. I care about her impudence to your mother . . . and dare I say, downright hatred. She considers herself quite the Empress already." She watched the prince from the corner of her eye.

A nerve twitched in his jaw. "My stepfather will never put my mother aside."

"Of course not, Your Highness. But I worry Lady Sun may be desperate enough to bring about other circumstances." She lowered her voice and the prince bent his ear closer—once the little fisherman, now the fish on the end of her line. "Her attendants bring ingredients from Bohai's cupboards every week. She collects them in great amounts."

Satisfaction rippled through her as his eyes widened. He could check this fact if he wished; he would learn it was true, though he didn't need to know the ingredients were for Lady Sun's beauty rituals. He would hear the story of Kang's senseless punishment, and connect that incident with Lady Sun to the black spice stolen from Bohai. Xifeng hadn't told a single lie. All she had to do was plant the seed and let him grow it in the manner he wished.

"Xifeng, I charge you with the care of my mother," the prince said grimly. "I can't always be here. Be my eyes and ears while I think of what to do. Send a eunuch if you need me."

"Gladly, Your Highness." She saw Lady Meng still watching them with an unblinking stare; perhaps they had been talking for too long. "I must return. I am forever grateful to you and pray for your health."

The Crown Prince inclined his head. "Until the festival, then. Goodbye."

Xifeng crossed the walkway in the opposite direction, unwilling to return to her sewing and the ladies' chatter. She ducked into an alcove outside the eunuchs' quarters to wait for Kang, burning to read Wei's message.

The familiar, untidy scrawl brought tears to her eyes. He had written only a few lines:

I love you and I think of you every day. I wish I could run away with you again.

There was no promise to meet, no hint at a reunion. Just simple words from a heart she didn't deserve. He didn't expect to see her again.

"Xifeng? Are you all right?" Kang appeared on the walkway as she wiped her face, and the kind sympathy in his eyes made her tears flow faster. Xifeng clung to his hand, longing to pour her heart out about her destiny and what it might cost her. But not even Wei had understood. She couldn't—*wouldn't*—risk the only friendship she had at court.

"Someone cares for me and I can't return his feelings. He needs a better woman who isn't a coward and can love him as he deserves." She tucked the scroll into her robes, against her aching heart. "My Guma told me he wasn't for me. I've never been able to forget that."

"You can't blame yourself if it's what she taught you." The eunuch wiped her tears with a large, gentle hand. "She wanted only the best for you. We must listen to those who raised us. Duty to our elders is the greatest responsibility we have."

An overwhelming sense of relief flooded her. "You understand, then. He didn't know how I could keep Guma's teachings in my heart and still care for him, too."

Kang tilted his head like a benevolent bird. "This is the soldier friend, Wei, you speak of? What if the two of you were to meet?"

A sensation like feathers fluttered in her chest. "That's impossible. I can't be alone with a man. Madam Hong would throw me out on my ear, and the Empress . . . she's given me a home and protected me from Lady Sun. She cares about me." Her Majesty's words ran through her mind like cool water: *If you were my child, I wouldn't let that woman within an inch of you.*

"I know she's easy to love," Kang said slowly, "but have a care, my darling. She's not like us. She doesn't have to keep her promises, and she likes to make daughters of all the maidens. It doesn't last, and it isn't real."

"You're implying the Empress has false feelings?"

He patted her hand. "I just don't want you to be hurt if she gives birth to a true daughter. Anyway," he added, before she could question him further, "I have a plot boiling in this head of mine. I fear I'm something of a romantic. I want to help you and Wei meet."

"Stop it," Xifeng told him, though she couldn't help the urgent longing to see Wei. He, too, was part of her destiny, after all—that faithful, dependable boy who had always been her moral compass, who had always only seen the good in her. If anyone could keep the creature's dark whisperings at bay, it would be him . . . But she pushed the hope from her heart. "I'd never forgive myself if you were whipped again for my sake."

"You needn't fear on my behalf, and I won't make you do anything you don't wish to. But there are ways." He rubbed his palms together in delight, and Xifeng found it difficult to maintain her scowl. "And if the Crown Prince is sympathetic, as you say, we can use that to our advantage."

"What do you know?"

Kang gave her the naughty smile of a child stealing sweets. "I know the tunnels better than Master Yu thinks. Getting lost in the passageways all those years of running errands might prove useful after all."

Xifeng hesitated. She couldn't deny the desire to be in Wei's arms again, in spite of all the risks they would take. "I'll consider it, my friend. Thank you."

He walked her back to the balcony. "I'll have a plan for you . . . if you need it," he said, mincing away with a roguish wink.

She pressed her hands against the scroll, and despite her doubts and misgivings, she wondered if her fortune might at last be changing for the better.

26

On the eve of the first festival day, Xifeng went to the Empress's apartments to deliver her sewing before supper. Earlier, she had helped carry Her Majesty's ceremonial clothing to the palace laundresses, who steamed each piece above boiling pots of fragrant lemon-mint water.

As she walked, she admired the festival decorations: pink paper blossoms adorning the railings, bright silks draped over doorways, and chrysanthemums in overflowing pots. At the Empress's command, the eunuchs had brought out even more lanterns to hang on the trees surrounding the palace, so it seemed the Great Forest itself would partake in the festivities.

Xifeng entered the royal apartments, and her mouth went dry when she saw Empress Lihua slumped over the table. The woman's face was ashen as two maids fluttered about in distress, fanning her.

"Your Majesty," Xifeng gasped, wondering if something had happened to the baby. She glared at the maids. "Stop scurrying about like that. If you haven't anything better to do, put away these clothes. Bring cool water and a cloth." She enjoyed the way they cowered as she snatched the fan and waved it over the Empress's fevered face.

"Don't worry," the Empress said faintly. "I'm often this way after a visit from Lady Sun."

Xifeng's fingers tightened on the fan. "What did she want?"

"Much of the same. Things to increase her importance: my ladies-in-waiting, part of my living quarters, and my place at the Emperor's side during the festival."

As though His Majesty had put his wife aside already. Wrath and a powerful craving squeezed Xifeng's gut.

"She accused me of pretending to be pregnant so I could keep my husband's favor." A tear slid down the Empress's face. Her distress curled fingers around Xifeng's heart. "I know I shouldn't let her upset me, but to spread such malicious gossip about my child . . ."

"Don't listen to her evil words, Your Majesty. She is remorseless and wicked, and a time will come when her deeds turn against her."

"I've lost so many babies, born too soon. She knows it and hopes to turn the Emperor against me." The Empress closed her eyes, and Xifeng wondered if Lady Sun was the only cause of her sickly pallor. "Will you sit with me a while? It is such a comfort to know you're here."

Her words dissolved every thought of Kang and his warnings. There was only this moment, here and now, as Xifeng took the Empress's icy hand in both of hers. "I won't leave you," she vowed, her heart singing inside her.

"I should be thankful when the gods have given me so much," the Empress said in a voice full of endless sadness. "I was my parents' only child, and they did not deem me fit to rule, as few other women in my line have been. But they gave me a strong, good husband. It seems I lost myself when I lost him." She closed her eyes in grief. "People only see what I wear, what I eat, and the servants that surround me. They don't know I'd gladly trade places with a peasant, the only wife and mother to her husband and children. Do you think me ungrateful?"

Xifeng squeezed her hand in mute pity, though she couldn't help noting the irony. She had refused that life when Wei offered it to her—a life for which the Empress of Feng Lu longed. "We can't choose what we are given," she said gently. "But your child will be fortunate to have you for a mother." She imagined a roly-poly baby, deeply loved and wanted, and felt a stab of jealousy that faded when the Empress patted her cheek.

"Do you think so?"

"I never knew my mother, but I imagine she might have been like you."

The Empress's eyes shone. "And I imagine if I have a daughter, she might be like you."

Underneath the overwhelming rush of joy, Xifeng recoiled. She rose and began to fan the Empress to hide her shock as a mocking voice echoed from within her ribs.

She wouldn't say that if she knew what you truly are. She wouldn't say that if she knew her end is your beginning.

A maid reappeared with water and a cloth, and Xifeng rose, grateful for the distraction. She dabbed at the Empress's forehead, trying to quell the knot of dread in her chest. Up close, Her Majesty's ill health was even more apparent and pronounced; her skin, tinged with gray, was thin and fragile, like parchment. She noticed a constellation of white hairs at the woman's temples, like a crown, and longed to stoop and kiss them and smooth the lines of worry from her face as a daughter would. Not once had she ever imagined doing so with Guma. *Her end is your beginning.* Guma had never told her how it might come to be, supplanting the Emperor's wife.

The knot above her rib cage throbbed again, painfully, and she gasped for breath.

"Are you all right, Xifeng?"

The Empress's eyes stared up at her—eyes that had to close before her own could open to the throne of Feng Lu.

"It's a bit warm. Let me open a window for you." Xifeng crossed the room and slid open a bamboo panel, gulping in the fresh air. Had Guma meant for her to be a killer? To end the life of this good, gentle woman, whose only crime was being born to the crown meant for Xifeng?

Behind her, Empress Lihua rose. "I must rest for my journey. Tomorrow, I make my pilgrimage to my private shrine in the forest."

The image of the *tengaru* clearing came to Xifeng's mind, unbidden, and she remembered the tapestry in the reception hall. "Will you be going far?"

"To a quiet lake a day's ride from here. I'm in need of time to pray and reflect, and receive guidance." She turned to the miniature tree, lost in thought.

Xifeng watched her with an odd, unsettled feeling, wondering if the Empress's private shrine lay with the demon guardians. Surely the *tengaru* would not deny her entrance to the apple tree; surely she was worthy where Xifeng was not. But that, then, might make her the Fool—the woman whose fate could not coexist with Xifeng's.

Don't be silly, she chided herself. The Empress had only ever been gentle and kind; she had raised Xifeng closer to her destiny, whereas Lady Sun sought to push her down.

"Are you fit to travel, Your Majesty?" she asked, worried. "Won't it be dangerous to go on horseback in your condition?"

"The guards will carry me in a litter. The baby and I will be quite safe." Her face shone like sunlight. "You needn't worry about me, my dear. And I hope you'll join me for the moon-viewing party. I'd like you to be part of my retinue for the carnival days as well."

"I would be honored, Your Majesty."

The Empress came close and touched her face. "It was lonely for me before you came," she said softly. "I'm glad you're here to care for me."

Xifeng's lips quivered as she left the royal apartments.

If only she knew.

After three long days of worship, a charge of excitement filled the Empress's apartments on the day of the moon-viewing party. The ladies washed in basins of rosewater and helped each other dress. Xifeng combed her hair until it shone like a moonlit river, sweeping it into a thick knot pinned with a white jasmine flower. When she donned the simple gold silk Her Majesty's women would wear, the other ladies stopped what they were doing to admire her.

"How beautiful you are," one of them said grudgingly.

Xifeng dipped her head, as though she wasn't fully aware of the power she would always have over others. She had made every effort to ensure all eyes would be on her tonight, to show Lady Sun she was no shrinking flower. She would bloom where she was planted and let her roots close around the throats of her enemies.

The ladies assembled in the royal bedchamber to dress the Empress.

"You seem rested and refreshed, Your Majesty," Madam Hong told her.

Empress Lihua looked like she had spent the past three days sleeping. Her eyes were brighter, her skin appeared more vibrant, and she greeted her women with complete peace as they set about preparing her for the banquet.

Madam Hong took the responsibility of brushing the Empress's thin hair and wrapping it around an elaborate wooden headdress. Two ladies fussed over her hair ornaments while another dusted her face with a silken rice powder and painted her lips with vermilion paste.

Because of her junior position, Xifeng stood to one side, approaching only to hand the ladies whatever they needed, but Empress Lihua caught her eye a few times and smiled.

"Bring me the clothes," Madam Hong told her brusquely.

Xifeng handed her a tunic of deep blue-gray silk, which rippled like rainwater and had silver frog clasp buttons down the front. The collar was embedded with tiny pearls of jade, so priceless and delicate that Madam Hong hadn't trusted anyone but herself to work on it. The skirt was of a darker gray like a winter sky, embroidered with clouds in azure thread. The ladies had been hard at work on the other pieces in the royal ensemble all week, expanding the clothing to fit the Empress's growing, four-months-pregnant belly.

The sky at last began to darken, and eunuchs filed into the royal apartments to light the lanterns. Empress Lihua led them through an entrance Xifeng had never seen, with the fourteen ladies following her in pairs and flanked by a guard of thirty eunuchs. The heavy oaken doors opened onto a splendid walkway, which led into the main palace itself.

Xifeng felt as though her eyes didn't have time to take it all in. They passed pillars of imported marble, crystalline fountains, corridors draped in red-and-gold silk, and basins spilling fragrant flowers from the palace gardens. After two months of seclusion with women, Xifeng found the sight of so many men startling and pleasing. They looked to be of every lofty rank: palace officials, ministers, scholars, foreign officers, and nobility.

But the banquet hall was the most magnificent sight of all. It seemed large enough to fit the Imperial City within its gold-veined marble walls. Artfully placed bronze mirrors reflected the lamplight and the masses of courtiers dressed in their finest silks and brocades. The savory-sweet aroma of steaming rice, herb-roasted meat, and exotic spices blanketed the whole room.

"Her Imperial Majesty, the Empress of Feng Lu," a eunuch announced at the door as Empress Lihua approached the dais where her husband awaited her.

The Emperor wore dark blue-gray robes to match hers, the simplicity of his attire suiting his austere handsomeness. He led his wife to a high table they would share with the Crown Prince and a sickly-looking boy Xifeng supposed was the youngest prince.

Xifeng noticed Lady Meng still had a place next to Lady Sun, as a favored concubine—though that might change any day now, what with the rumors swirling that His Majesty would soon tire of her indifference toward him. The girl stared at her plate with empty eyes while Lady Sun dandled a boy of about five in her lap. This, then, was the "prince" she had boasted about giving the Emperor. Xifeng noticed she hadn't bothered to bring her daughters.

A gong sounded, and four court musicians began playing a soft melody on four different instruments: a flute, a barbarian's fiddle, a pipe-harp, and a stringed, oblong object Xifeng learned was a zither. An army of servants appeared with enormous bowls and platters. The Imperial cook himself carved a massive wild boar before the Emperor while all around the hall, his attendants served fish, glazed duck, and quail to the eunuchs, ladies, and assembled guests.

Xifeng sighed at the taste of the tender, juicy meat flavored with summer onions and garlic. The vegetables were equally delicious: crunchy, vibrant greens slathered in a ginger soy sauce and sweet potatoes roasted with sugar and chili powder.

"It's nice to see a lady with a healthy appetite," one of the eunuchs said approvingly.

"How could anyone resist such delicacies?" She peered around at the other ladies pecking at their meals like birds. Of the two concubines, only Lady Sun was eating her fill. For her part, Xifeng ate until every morsel had disappeared from her plate.

She looked up to see Emperor Jun, of all people, smiling at her. His eyes held the spark of humor she recalled from their first meeting. She was struck again by his familiarity, like he was someone she had known a long time ago, and her heart gave an uneven beat. Beside her husband, Empress Lihua glanced at her.

"Stand up and bow when His Majesty acknowledges you, girl," Madam Hong hissed.

Xifeng obeyed. When she looked up again, the Emperor nodded to someone: a small, handsome man with elegant features. The ambassador to Kamatsu approached, beaming at her.

"Shiro, my dear friend." She drank in the sight of him. "I told His Majesty you and I traveled together. How kind of him to remember."

Shiro surveyed her affectionately. "I was surprised when he mentioned you. You look lovely as ever and right at home. I always knew you'd do well at court despite Hideki's ominous warnings." He gestured across the room to the soldier, who lifted a cup of wine to them.

"It seems more like home than my town ever did. But that's not to say it has been easy." She glanced at the Emperor, who was still watching them.

"You've certainly won the Emperor's approval. He insisted I come speak to you tonight."

"He seems a kind man," Xifeng said, but he did not respond. "How have you fared? Do you miss home?"

"Hideki would have a ship ready tomorrow if I desired it. But I'm happy to remain here for the full year, with good reason. Akira and I were married a week ago."

"Congratulations." She blinked, feeling a pang of envy as he drew his shoulders back, his eyes bright. How simple it was for others to love and live life—how perfectly easy. "I wish you both much joy. Why isn't she here with you?"

"She was too busy to come, though I'm sure she would have liked to have seen you."

"I've spoken to her father," Xifeng told him. "I wonder if they'll ever meet."

"Not if my wife has anything to say about it." She felt another twinge at the way he lingered proudly over *my wife*. "He chose not to have her in his life, so she's happy to lead hers without him. Oh, I saw Wei the other day."

Her heart jumped. "How is he?"

"Very well. He was practicing for the procession. Perhaps you'll see him if you go."

She didn't miss the pity in his eyes. Even Shiro thought they would never meet again. "His Majesty mentioned you'll join the envoy to the mountains. How far is the journey?"

"Two weeks there and two weeks back, but Hideki and I don't mind. I couldn't pass up this chance to go." He toyed with the hem of his sleeve. "I haven't had the easiest life, as you know. It was prayer that saved me, and I want to thank the gods for my good fortune."

"I'm happy for you," she said softly, and meant it, though the old lingering resentment—that the gods never seemed to hear *her*—returned.

"Did you enjoy the prayer days? I thought you might, since the readings are like poetry and tell the history of the gods."

"I did. But I've always wanted to know why we include the Lord of Surjalana in our prayers when he was the one who broke the alliance. I always assumed things might be contentious for him once they all returned to the heavens again."

The dwarf gave a conspiratorial smile and lowered his voice. "Some court scholars say he never returned to the heavens, but remained here on Earth. They say he hid himself so well, no one could ever find him again." He glanced at the others, but they were all busy talking and eating. "That's a revolutionary theory even among the scholars, so keep it to yourself. I know Empress Lihua is extremely devout and would take a dim view of it."

Chills snaked down Xifeng's spine. "But why would he remain here?"

Shiro shrugged. "Some say he was beyond saving after mankind poisoned him with jealousy against the Dragon King. I've heard some speculate he burrowed underground, lured by the human concept of ultimate power."

"Underground? Why?"

"To build himself a hellish army with which to overtake the continent one day, kingdom by kingdom." He rolled his eyes, to show her what he thought of that idea. "It seems a bit outlandish, but the theorists argue that is the reasoning behind our wars and conflicts. They say his continued presence here has spoiled any hope for peace and unity."

"It sounds like something Hideki would come up with." They laughed at his expense.

"He is rather dramatic," Shiro agreed, grinning. "I should go back and save those around him from his company. It was a delight, my dear. Perhaps I'll see you during the carnival."

They bowed to each other, and she watched him go with a bone-deep sadness for the simpler time when they had all traveled together. But her melancholy did not last long, for the gong sounded again to signal the end of the banquet.

A smile crossed Xifeng's face. She had a feeling another spectacle was about to begin.

27

The Emperor and Empress led the way outside, followed by the princes, concubines, and court. The terrace faced the western edge of the Great Forest, where a calm, wide river ran from beneath the palace into the trees. The sun had long since set, but the air was still warm, and streaks of peach lingered in the sky between the dark blue fingers of night. Servants wove in and out of the crowd, serving sweet rice wine in delicate bone cups.

Xifeng lifted her face to the full moon, which stood out clear and bright in the heavens. Someone moved beside her in a rustle of heavy brocade, smelling of fir and sandalwood, and she knew who it was before he had even spoken.

"Last year," said the Emperor of Feng Lu, "it was so cloudy we couldn't see the stars."

She bowed low, murmuring, "Your Majesty."

Though every face around them was turned to the skies, she sensed their acute awareness of the Emperor . . . and on her, trailing in his wake like a toy boat on the sea. He was not much taller than Xifeng, but he had the grandest presence of anyone she'd ever met. He seemed to fill the terrace merely by *being,* another moon on the earth itself.

"I couldn't have asked for a more perfect evening. It's a very good sign."

"A good sign, Your Majesty?"

"Of a new beginning." He gave her a boyish smile, and she could see the stars reflected in his eyes. It was his close-cut beard that made him seem older, she decided; he was youthful in all other aspects. Over his shoulder, she caught a glimpse of the only person who dared to blatantly watch them: Lady Sun, with her little boy in her arms. Xifeng noticed with satisfaction that the Crown Prince stood close by, his sharp gaze on the concubine.

She gave His Majesty her brightest smile. "The ladies told me the fable of the moon tree."

"There it is. That movement you see is the greedy man chopping away at the trunk." He pretended to point at a spot on the moon, and they both laughed. They watched a dozen eunuchs cross over to the riverbank, holding tiny boats of rice paper and bamboo. "Each of those boats holds a drop of beeswax," Emperor Jun explained. "The eunuchs will light them on fire and send them down the river in the moonlight's path to honor this auspicious phase."

"A pretty tradition." She turned her eyes from the boats, which sparkled like fireflies, to him. "Thank you, Your Majesty, for allowing Ambassador Shiro to speak to me at the banquet."

"Shiro's a good man." The Emperor folded his arms, and the shining lengths of blue-gray silk caught the light. "I don't need to see eye to eye with him to realize that. He's an advocate of peace in every circumstance, even when force is required."

"Is that a bad thing?"

He was silent for a long moment. "A king and a diplomat both care about their people. The difference is the king has to make the hard decisions, even when lives are at risk." A steely glint surfaced in his eyes. "Peace often comes at the cost of war."

"You speak of the conflicts in the east?"

Emperor Jun raised his eyebrows. "Yes, I do. What do you know about that?"

"Only that it afflicts Dagovad and that the Great Forest is aiding their queen, thus remaining in her good graces."

The corners of his mouth turned slowly upward. "How do you know of such things?"

"I listen to the eunuchs talk at mealtimes."

He let out a great laugh that sent more than one glance in their direction, including Empress Lihua's. Xifeng felt oddly proud and happy to have pleased him, considering he was a person she didn't know at all well. But that, she supposed, was a king's power.

"Will a new treaty be drawn to settle the dispute over the Unclaimed Lands?" she asked, and he had opened his mouth to respond when a great shattering sound echoed over the whole terrace. A woman cried out, and the music and chatter silenced immediately.

Xifeng spun to see a tray of bone cups scattered across the stones, wine having splashed all over the guests, including the Empress in her priceless silks. The Crown Prince stood in front of his mother with his hand still raised, and it took Xifeng a moment to realize he had knocked the tray of wine right out of the servant's hands. His face was red with anger as he looked down at Lady Sun, who stood close enough for him to strike her. For a moment, with his chest heaving and his hand in the air, Xifeng believed he would.

"What is the meaning of this?" Emperor Jun demanded, stalking furiously toward the Crown Prince. "What have you done?"

"What have *I* done?" the prince repeated, eyes glittering with hatred. "I have protected my mother, Your Majesty, as is my duty." The crowd murmured at the sword-sharp edge of his voice, which was not lost on the Emperor.

"By your tone, I see you're implying I was not doing mine." Emperor Jun spoke calmly, and though he moved toward his wife, he looked at his concubine. "What has Lady Sun done to you that you should waste this good wine?"

"It isn't good wine when it has been poisoned," the Crown Prince said, prompting gasps from the crowd. "I saw her standing near my mother's cup. I saw her raise her sleeve."

"Your Majesty," Lady Sun sputtered, her face stark white. For the first time since Xifeng had known her, she seemed at a loss for words, and Xifeng reveled in her discomfort. Her little boy stood clinging to her robes with wide eyes. "I would never . . . The Crown Prince . . ."

"I have it on good authority that you have been gathering poisons from the Imperial physician's stores. I don't blame Bohai, as he has loved and served my mother well all his life," the prince said icily. "Forgive me, Your Majesty, for causing this scene, but I will not stand idly by when this woman seeks to supplant my mother as Empress."

Xifeng clasped her hands together with delight, though to anyone else, it would seem a gesture of deep concern. She fixed her gaze on Lady Sun's face; she wanted to remember the concubine's expression of shock and humiliation for a long time to come.

"When my mother's wine came," the Crown Prince continued, his voice shaking with fury, "I noticed that this woman made certain to stand nearby and hover over it. The gods only know what she has put into the Empress's cup."

"You lie!" Lady Sun hissed, turning desperately to the Emperor. "He lies. I would never dare poison her. Believe me, my love, please . . ."

Empress Lihua stiffened at the term of endearment addressed to her husband.

But Emperor Jun ignored them both, focusing his attention on his eldest stepson. From her vantage point, Xifeng could only see his profile, but it was enough to see that the man with the jovial manner had disappeared. In his place stood a king of cold and ruthless anger. "Where is your proof?" he asked, and though he spoke quietly, his voice rang out through the crowd. "If I have her searched and I don't find evidence of poison, what will that tell me about you, my son?"

The Crown Prince, to his credit, did not quake. He lifted his chin and looked his stepfather directly in the eyes. "It will tell you I at least sought to protect what is yours."

Several of the ladies-in-waiting covered their mouths, horrified and fascinated, while the eunuchs fluttered their fans faster. Kang stood among them, his simper gone for once.

Emperor Jun came closer. "No. It will tell me you dared to criticize me. Speak against Lady Sun and you speak against me. You accuse her of treason, of the darkest deed against a sovereign, but she represents me. I chose her, you see."

Xifeng's stomach dropped at the triumph on Lady Sun's face.

"I did not intend disrespect to Your Majesty," said the prince with a flicker of unease, as though he were starting to doubt himself.

"And yet you accused my concubine before all the court without a shred of evidence. You might have spoken to me confidentially."

The Emperor tilted his head, surveying the younger man. He took a menacing step closer, then another. "Your brash behavior tells me a different story. It tells me you think little enough of me to insult me before my family and all my court."

Xifeng watched them, jaw tensed. The prince had laid bare Lady Sun's deepest aspiration, the truth everyone else already knew, and still the Emperor would protect her. He would take the concubine's side without attempting to see his stepson's reasoning, without considering that his wife's life might have indeed been in danger.

Xifeng's plan had failed. Hopelessly.

"We will discuss this further in private, as we should have done from the start." The Emperor clapped his hands for the music to begin once more, but it was several long moments before the courtiers began moving and whispering among themselves again.

Lady Sun, smiling now, pushed her little boy toward the Emperor. "My love . . ."

But His Majesty ignored her, his face stony. "Search her," he said in a low voice to the guards, and the concubine's jaw dropped as he stormed back inside the palace.

Xifeng knew the search would come up empty, but still the words were music to her ears, evidence of a crack in the bond between Emperor Jun and his most cherished concubine.

Lady Sun gasped. "Your Majesty!" she called after his retreating back. She glared at the Crown Prince just in time to see him look at Xifeng. Her eyes moved from him to Xifeng and back, and realization dawned on her features as the guards escorted her through the doors.

To Xifeng's surprise, the festive air returned as soon as the Emperor and Lady Sun had gone. The guests continued to sip wine and mingle as though nothing had happened. Xifeng wished she too could escape, to reflect in private, but she didn't want to raise suspicion.

It wasn't long before Kang materialized beside her. "Well, that was certainly interesting."

"The Emperor knows the prince spoke the truth," Xifeng said, some of the bitterness in her mouth receding. "Lady Sun *hates* the Empress and would take her place tomorrow if she could. He was only putting on a show for the court to protect his dignity." Still, it didn't sit well that His Majesty—the man destined for *her*—had defended the Fool. She watched the prince speak a few words to his mother, then retreat back inside.

"What a delight it was to see Lady Sun whimper and cower so. I wonder who had the ingenious idea to suggest poison to the prince," he whispered, his voice rippling with glee, but Xifeng didn't respond. "Lady Meng is staring at you again."

The younger concubine stood near the space the prince had vacated, watching Xifeng with undisguised intensity. Xifeng gazed back, her emotions warring between pity and disdain. "She's just a sad, strange girl who needs something to cling to."

"Speaking of something to cling to," Kang continued in a whisper, "I've delivered a message to Wei on your behalf."

Her eyes locked with his, the Emperor and Lady Sun vanishing from her mind. "How could you take such a risk? Do you want us both killed?"

"Have a little faith in me, Xifeng. Do you think I'd do anything to endanger you?" He seemed so ruffled that she apologized. "He expects you in the main palace gardens tomorrow night, outside the entrance I took you through on your first day."

Xifeng pressed her damp hands against her sides. "Tomorrow night?"

"Yes, but you can tell me if that's inconvenient for you," he said stiffly.

"I'm sorry, Kang. I don't mean to be ungrateful. I just don't want anything to happen to you because of me." She turned back to the river without really seeing it. She and Wei had been apart for two months, ever since their horrible argument at Akira's house. Had his feelings for her changed in all that time . . . and did she want them to?

"You worry too much about me. As long as you come unseen, after the Empress's household has gone to sleep, there isn't a soul who has to know besides us." Kang's eyes danced at her as he returned to his usual good humor. "I'm on guard duty at that entrance for three nights with Chou, who has a weakness for rice wine. He'll be asleep within the first few sips."

"Why does Master Yu allow him to be on guard duty, then?" Xifeng asked, appalled.

"The useless prune doesn't know anything about it. Our challenge is how to get you past the guards in the city of women." Kang chewed on his lower lip. "I have a few ideas . . ."

Xifeng's veins hummed with anticipation as she envisioned the hole in the garden. If she could climb the stones jutting out from the wall on her way back, as she had last time, she wouldn't need to confront the guards at all. "Don't worry about that. If you can promise to have Chou asleep, I can get there."

The eunuch beamed. "For heaven's sake, don't let anyone see you."

"I'll have an excuse ready in case anyone does."

A soft, lilting melody came from where the court musicians had set up on the terrace. The riverbank was now aglow with the light emanating from the flame-lit boats.

"Thank you, my friend," Xifeng said quietly. "I will not forget how you've helped me."

They watched in silence as the bamboo boats began drifting away on the river. Soon the water was filled with dozens of twinkling lights floating along until at last, one by one, they vanished into the trees.

28

The following night, Xifeng waited an hour after the Empress and her ladies had gone to bed. She tossed and turned and ran her fingers over her near-invisible scar, alternately burning with impatience and feeling cold with worry that Wei would find her changed . . . and not for the better. She didn't know whether she could hide the shameful thoughts poisoning her mind lately.

"They're not your thoughts, they're Guma's," he might say.

But would that argument work now that Xifeng was on her own, far away from her aunt? Would it excuse her cruel hunger for Lady Sun's suffering? Or her muddled feelings for the Empress's husband, a man so out of reach, and yet . . .

Xifeng covered her eyes and let out a slow sigh. The search for poison on the concubine's person had of course turned up nothing, but still the Emperor had pardoned the Crown Prince. And aside from the fact that Lady Sun hadn't left her apartments all day—no doubt sulking and embarrassed—it seemed things had gone back to normal. Still,

Xifeng had her doubts, remembering His Majesty's fury. She suspected he wouldn't let the prince off so easily. She wouldn't have, in his place.

There was no sound but the snoring of the others as she slipped on a robe and ducked out of the ladies-in-waiting's entrance. She took care to stay in the shadows of the building, avoiding the sentries stationed outside Her Majesty's apartments.

The night was as clear and lovely as the last. Moonlight shone on the tunnel entrance, where she could make out the outlines of two guards. She crept into the darkness and slipped through the hole in the garden. Though the thick, warm air of the springs called to her, she found her way through the tunnels to the main passageway.

Kang peered into the darkness, his face anxious in the torchlight.

"It's me," she whispered.

His shoulders sagged with relief. "I feared Chou had awakened from his drunken stupor. I can give you one hour, but please be back by then."

Impulsively, Xifeng kissed his cheek and he reddened with pleasure.

"Be happy," he said as he shut the door gently behind her.

Her earlier worries faded as she stepped back into the evening's embrace. The lush palace garden soothed her with its arching willow trees, frogs and crickets singing in the reeds of the pond, and the perfume of night-blooming jasmine. The warren of buildings that made up the main palace loomed nearby, and she dared not call out for fear of guards. But no sooner had she reached the shadow of a tree than she felt arms around her and heard Wei's soft, joyous laugh.

"It's you," she said, in half bliss and half disbelief.

"It's me." He pressed a smile into her hair.

She clung to him like a drowning woman as he kissed her, his mouth tasting of salt and metal. How could she have forgotten this fire racing through her veins, charging her entire body like a lightning storm? His burning lips moved to her neck, tasting her like he had been starving for weeks, and he gripped her waist as though fearing a stray breeze would take her from him.

Heavy footsteps rang out across the walkways of the nearest building. She tugged at his hand and they raced across the grass.

"You're beautiful," he breathed, and she could no more stop the smile on her face than she could the moon shining in the sky. They ran deep into the refuge of the gardens, a jungle of trees, tangled vines, and heavy-headed flowers shielding them from view. A pagoda stood close to the edge of the pond. It was not entirely concealed, for there were pillars instead of walls.

"There?" Wei asked. "But someone might walk past and see us . . ."

Xifeng's only answer was to grin and pull him toward it, and he followed without protest.

He lifted her in his arms and pressed her against one of the pillars. There was a low bench he had to sidestep, and she enjoyed the image of someone prim and proper sitting there in the afternoon, only to have her and Wei make ferocious love there in the evening. She locked her arms and legs around him, closing her eyes as he crushed his mouth against hers. The skin of her back felt raw as it scraped against the pillar. Tomorrow, there would be bruises, and none of the Empress's well-bred ladies would guess it as she sat among them, sewing demurely.

Voices rang out on the palace walkway, and Wei stilled, burying his face into her shoulder. She noticed him shaking uncontrollably as the garden grew quiet once more, and when she realized he was laughing, she had to bite her tongue to keep from joining in.

He lowered her to the ground, his arms still around her. They leaned against the pillar, foreheads pressed together, his slowing breath warming her face. Xifeng couldn't believe she had ever forgotten the freckle beneath his eye or the faint scar along his smiling mouth.

"You kept your promise," he said. "You said we'd find a way to meet. But how?"

"I have a eunuch friend."

He shook his head. "You always find a way to get what you want."

She pulled him even closer to her. "I wish I could take you back to my chamber."

"With the Empress only a few rooms away?" He gave her such a funny look that she kissed him, her heart swelling. He shucked his robe, spreading it on the floor and drawing her down beside him. They lay wrapped in each other, staring at the intricate carvings on the roof. "I can't take you back to where I sleep, either. I share a room with five other soldiers."

She traced the lines of his face with her fingertips, and he caught her thumb with a kiss. For the first time since entering the palace, she almost felt like herself again, with Wei beside her. *Almost, but not completely.* She shifted and a sliver of moonlight crept over her tunic, just over where the creature slept—or listened in silence. "You haven't changed at all," she told Wei, to take her mind from it. "You're just as I like to think of you. Still that same boy from our village."

He pressed his lips between her ear and her neck, and she shivered. "You seem different to me. You've always been beautiful, of course, but . . ." He held her away a bit, scanning her face, and some of her dread returned. Could he see, in the dim light, the dark thoughts soiling her mind? Did he know, just by looking at her, what she had allowed the creature to suggest to her, as Lady Sun's heart glowed in her chest in the mirror-water?

"I'm well fed now." She snuggled back against him to hide from his discerning gaze. "Three square meals a day will do that to a woman."

He ran his fingers tenderly along her new curves. "That must be it. I wish . . ."

"What? Tell me." But even as she urged him, she feared what he might say . . . what he might again ask of her. She saw in his eyes that he too was remembering their fight.

"I wish we could be like this always."

Relieved, she nestled in his arms as he talked about his life in the army, about training and the weapons he'd learned to use: chariots and catapults, crossbows and siege ladders. She closed her eyes, enjoying the familiar rise and fall of his chest. In that moment, she thought she might not have hurt him if he'd asked her to marry him again. She might have said yes and let him sweep her away from kings and destinies and scheming concubines—away from what she both feared and yearned to do to protect herself and him, too.

"What has life been like for you?" he asked, and it was a long moment before Xifeng knew how to answer. She couldn't hide her emotion when she told him about the concubines. Wei went rigid when she spoke of the hundred lashes Lady Sun had ordered for her.

"Even I've heard much of her," he said. "They say she considers herself invincible and quite the Empress. You must be careful not to anger her further."

Too late, she thought, remembering the realization in Lady Sun's eyes when the guards had taken her away to be searched. Still, she said forcefully, "She ought to be careful of *me*. She stirred up trouble first, and Guma always said what one brings about will return." She immediately regretted mentioning her aunt as Wei sat up.

"Lady Sun has given the Emperor a son, the first and only of his blood. The child is in the line of succession behind the three princes.

Whether or not she truly is untouchable, that fact gives her a great deal of power." He frowned at her. "What has that Guma of yours advised you to do? I hope she wasn't so unwise as to encourage you to plot against a consort."

Xifeng gave a growl of frustration. "You always assume I'm some flighty, stupid creature of my aunt's, and not a separate, thinking being of my own."

"She was the one who wanted you to come to court . . . but to accomplish what, exactly?" he persisted.

She sat up and drew her robe more tightly around her shoulders. They were close, too close to the truth, and if Wei probed further, he would find the answer she'd tried so hard to hide from him. "Have you ever considered that *I* wanted to come here? That I am capable of making my own decisions? After all this time," she said bitterly, "you still believe I'm naïve and helpless." He tried to put his arms around her, but she pulled away. "If we're going to fight every time we're together, we shouldn't meet anymore."

"Don't say that, Xifeng," he begged. "I'm sorry. I only want you to be free of her. She has a hold on you I can't understand."

"She's my *aunt*. She's my family. You're determined to hate her until the end." It both touched and irritated her, his insistence on blaming Guma for every bad thought she had and every choice she made. But he had a point. Through the haze of incense, the waterfall had shown visions of Guma's past that complicated the stories she'd told Xifeng. There were too many mysteries, too many unanswered questions. "Everything I do is my own choice. For *us*."

He kissed her shoulder. "I don't mean to upset you. Our time is so short, so precious. Please don't be angry with me."

"I'm not. But I want you to have faith in me." She relented, holding his trusting face in her hands. He was still a boy, after all, who would rather imagine the light even when darkness stared him in the eyes.

It was as the Emperor had said: some sought peace without understanding its costs. Thinking of Emperor Jun's charming humor and calm voice while in Wei's arms was so unsettling, Xifeng hid her face in his chest. *I am destined for another,* she wanted to tell him, *and he is the reason I can't give you my whole heart.*

"I wish I could walk you back. I don't want to leave you just yet."

He pulled back and looked at her wistfully, as though she were already gone. "The soldiers would want to know where you came from."

"I'll see you again soon. My friend will help us."

"Do you promise?"

She answered him with her lips. They stood and held on to each other, breaking apart reluctantly when footsteps sounded once more on the palace walkway.

And then it was back through the fragrant tangle of the Imperial gardens, the moon still shining overhead as she kissed Wei goodbye and faithful Kang opened the door for her.

29

"If I have to see one more performance or parade, I'll leave the palace and join a monastery." Kang flopped melodramatically onto the bench, fanning himself. "Is the festival over yet?"

Xifeng laughed. "I don't mind the spectacle, but I'm only a simple peasant girl who could never have imagined such things. Didn't you feel like a god looking down at the people?"

For the past three mornings, as part of the Empress's retinue, they had joined the Imperial couple on the balcony jutting out over the palace gates, overlooking the city. The crowds had cheered to see them, and it had been magical, just for a moment, to imagine the raucous applause had been for *her*.

It had been her first taste of what it might be like to be Empress.

"I suppose you're right," Kang conceded. "I must be tired from the performance. Thank the gods Their Majesties seemed to enjoy it. We've only been rehearsing an entire year." He had taken part in a dramatic stage play the night before, put on by the eunuchs each festival.

"Your acting was my favorite part of this week."

He wagged a finger at her. "I told you, flattery will win my heart every time."

She grinned, enjoying the evening breeze that blew strands of her hair across her face.

Seeing the city come alive had a way of putting one in a brilliant mood. That morning, the performers had worn costumes representing each kingdom, accompanied by men beating enormous drums that had to be pulled on chariots. Acrobats had flipped and twirled through the air as the dragon dance began: five serpents of silk, metal, and glass, each as long as a city block, concealing twenty dancers who shook the shimmering coils in time to the thundering drumbeat.

"If we could go into the city tonight, I'm sure *that* would be your favorite part." Kang scowled at a group of dignified eunuchs who walked by without acknowledging him. "Normally, each district closes at sundown, but the Emperor extends curfew on the last night of the festival. I'm told the marketplace and food stalls are a sight to behold."

"I can't go, but you can."

"Not without permission from *them*." He glared at the eunuchs' retreating backs. "Anyway, if they let me out, they probably won't let me back in. To amuse themselves."

"Have they been treating you worse than usual?"

"It's nothing I can't handle. The more you and I are seen together, the more they isolate themselves from me to curry Lady Sun's favor. They're afraid of her. And they won't have anything to do with anyone who challenges them or might hurt their prestige. But I will *never* turn my back on you, my one true friend."

Xifeng gripped his hand warmly. "Nor I you, sweet Kang. I'm forever indebted to you. The least I can do is speak to the Empress on your behalf. I'm sure she'll help us."

"You're that certain of her good favor?"

"Trust me. Let me do this for you, as thanks for all you've done for me."

But Xifeng couldn't speak to Her Majesty that night, as the household was in a flurry of preparation for the final banquet. And they'd had another invitation besides: the Emperor had requested that his wife be present in the reception hall before supper. The ladies took special care in dressing and flocked after the Empress in her resplendent red-and-gold silks.

The princes and concubines were already waiting when they arrived. Xifeng recognized the gold, crescent-shaped comb Lady Sun wore as the one she'd been accused of stealing. The woman's resentful eyes found her at once, and her hand tightened on the shoulder of her little boy. Her gaze promised revenge for the humiliation brought upon her, and though Xifeng's pulse picked up, she kept her expression neutral.

Emperor Jun swept in and embraced his wife, sparing no glance for her ladies, and Xifeng felt something strangely like disappointment. "I've come to give you your birthday present, my dear one. I commissioned it five years ago and the artist has delivered it at last."

The Empress's eyes sparkled at him. "You are the most generous of men, husband."

One wall of the room had been covered with a heavy cloth. On His Majesty's command, four eunuchs tugged it down to reveal the map of Feng Lu that had been hidden in Lady Sun's apartments, and a murmur of appreciation arose.

Lady Sun glowered at the top of her child's head, her hand like a claw on his shoulder. For someone who had triumphed and had been defended by the Emperor himself, she seemed sullen, subdued. Xifeng noticed His Majesty didn't look once at the concubine. It made her wonder why, of all places in the palace, the Emperor had chosen to hide the gift in Lady Sun's quarters for so long. It seemed cruel, like he was taunting her. Xifeng turned her eyes to the Emperor just in time to see him look away from her, and her heart gave an odd little lurch.

"It's a splendid gift," the Empress was saying, "and I will treasure it always, my love."

The Emperor caressed her cheek, and immediately Lady Sun pushed her child toward the map. The boy stared up at it with round, intelligent eyes, and asked a question in his childish babble. Xifeng made out the words *sea monsters* and couldn't help chuckling with the others.

"Do you see how clever your son is, Your Majesty?" Lady Sun asked loudly. "Already he knows where the kingdom of Kamatsu lies."

Everyone exchanged uncomfortable glances and the Crown Prince raised his eyebrows. Xifeng noticed he had positioned himself squarely between his mother and Lady Sun.

She's not so different from Lady Meng after all, Xifeng realized as the concubine looked pleadingly at His Majesty. All of her talk about playing the game of men had been nothing more than a cover for her fear and desperation.

"I've been assured this is a fitting gift for you," the Emperor told his wife, as though no one had spoken. "It suits you better than jewels, as a woman of thought and intelligence."

Red faced and without a word, Lady Sun seized her child and began to leave without permission. It was clear to all that she had somehow displeased the Emperor in private.

Xifeng kept her eyes down, satisfied that her plan had at least led to this small victory.

The Emperor continued speaking to his wife, pointedly ignoring Lady Sun's departure. "The Crown Prince himself agreed with me, and one of your ladies as well. Xifeng, I believe, is her name."

She froze as the Emperor's eyes found her in the crowd. Everyone in the room turned to her, even Lady Sun, who stopped in her tracks, her face drained of color.

"Come forward, if you please."

The room was still as Xifeng obeyed. She caught a glimpse of Lady Meng muttering to someone and Master Yu's lips turning downward in disgust as she bowed to the Imperial couple. When she straightened, the Empress was staring at her like she had never truly seen her before.

Her Majesty's jaw worked, and beneath her silken sleeves, her clasped hands were white. "I wasn't aware you knew of my birthday gift, Xifeng. How . . . kind of you to keep it a surprise."

Her voice was gentle as ever, but Xifeng flinched inwardly as though she had shouted. She had spoken to the Emperor only twice, and they had never said or done anything remotely close to betraying the Empress, but still her gut twisted beneath the older woman's stare. It was so different from the way she'd looked when she had thanked Xifeng for caring about her.

Her end is your beginning . . .

"Xifeng happened upon the map in the course of her duties," the Emperor said carelessly. "I echo her poetic words to you, my dear one. For your birthday, I give you the world."

"She is quite the poet." The Empress still wore her strange, disconcerted expression. "She recited a beautiful verse about motherhood when we first met."

Xifeng flushed as she met Emperor Jun's gaze. There was interest in those handsome eyes, and not a small degree of confidence. Clearly, he thought her certain to fall if he pursued her; he believed he had as good as won her already. She bristled at his arrogant presumption that she was like a maid he could tumble after eyeing her once. *I am not one of them.*

She would not be another plaything to frolic with in a tub of rose petals, only to be flung aside when he got tired of her. She would be his Empress, his equal, and nothing less. She steeled herself against those eyes, which regarded her with even more interest.

"Would you do us the honor of reciting another verse for the Empress's birthday?"

She took a deep breath and focused only on the Empress. "It would be *my* honor."

The Empress's eyes softened a bit.

Perhaps because it was the celebration of the full moon, Xifeng found herself reciting the lines she had found in Guma's mysterious volume of poetry:

The moon shines down upon us, beloved

The water a vast and eternal mirror

A voice whispers from every tender branch

Turn your face from the world's apple-blossom fragility

And embrace this boundless night

The Emperor and Empress led the room in polite applause. Xifeng retreated among the ladies, exhaling when the attention turned from her once more. But she felt their awareness still, especially Lady Sun, who stood watching her for a long moment before leaving at last.

All through the celebratory birthday banquet and the musical performance that followed, Xifeng's skin prickled with foreboding. She noted the Emperor and Lady Sun were both absent.

"She's exploding at His Majesty in private again," Kang informed her. "All the eunuchs are talking of it. She's been screaming in her apartments, threatening to leave him."

Xifeng waved her hand dismissively. "That's nothing new."

"She accused him of ignoring their son to chase after a 'farm girl's skirts.' Be on your guard. She's angrier and more desperate than anyone has ever seen her, and *you* are her target."

And in spite of herself, Xifeng felt gooseflesh emerging on her arms. The concubine would take her revenge, and Xifeng could either wait . . . or take action first.

30

The next morning, a eunuch approached their table and interrupted their meal. He looked vaguely familiar to Xifeng. "Lady Sun wishes to see you in her apartments," he told her.

Xifeng exchanged glances with Kang. *That* was where she knew him from—he was one of the guards stationed in the concubine's living quarters. "What could she possibly want with me?" she asked, arching a brow calmly though her pulse picked up.

"She and Lady Meng wish to speak to you."

Lady Meng? Xifeng hadn't known they were friends. In fact, it seemed illogical. In spite of her wariness, Xifeng felt curious. "I'll go as long as Kang accompanies me."

"Lady Sun wishes him to wait outside the door."

Kang gave the other eunuch a contemptuous once-over. "I serve Madam Xifeng, and I will go where it pleases her."

Instead of arguing, the eunuch bowed and turned to lead them out of the hall.

"See how powerful you've become?" Kang whispered as they followed him. "Everyone knows of the Emperor and Empress's regard for you, and they respect me by association."

"You did right to befriend me," she said, only partly joking. "But it's all right. I want to enter alone, to show Lady Sun I'm not intimidated by her."

She clasped her hands tightly as they climbed up to the concubine's apartments. Lady Meng was harmless, but whatever Lady Sun had planned would be cruel and destructive—of that Xifeng felt certain. She had to be prepared for anything.

Lady Sun was lounging in her main room, draped over a nest of red and gold brocade pillows, while Lady Meng paced restlessly and froze like a rabbit when Xifeng came in. Xifeng didn't bother to bow, but she bit her tongue. She had been invited for a reason, and she would not say anything they might use against her. Lady Sun examined her fingernails, content to let her wait, but Lady Meng was not so patient. The gossips said she was desperate, and from the frantic gleam of her eyes, Xifeng might well believe it.

"How long have you and the Crown Prince been lovers?" she snarled. Her slurring rural accent intensified with her anger. "Don't play the innocent with me. I saw him give you a love letter."

Caught off guard, Xifeng struggled to hide her astonishment. She glanced at Lady Sun, who continued studying her nails with a little smile. "The message was not from His Highness, and it was certainly not a love letter."

"I don't believe you." Lady Meng looked so pale, she seemed about to faint. "I want to see it with my own eyes."

"It was a private note and I have disposed of it." The memory of Wei's words disappearing into smoke still stung, but Xifeng thanked the gods she'd had the foresight to burn them. "I swear to you, my lady, the Crown Prince was only delivering my friend's message to me."

The young concubine leapt at Xifeng, standing so close, their noses nearly touched.

"What friend of *yours* could ask favors of His Highness?" Lady Meng demanded, and on her breath Xifeng smelled strong rice wine.

"Ambassador Shiro of Kamatsu." Xifeng did not pull away, though she would have gladly done so at the girl's sour breath. "He was my guardian on my journey through the Great Forest and wished to assess my well-being. He cannot visit me here, as you know."

Behind them, Lady Sun laughed quietly.

"Ask anyone. His Highness has no interest in me, my lady," Xifeng said as gently as she could. She pitied the poor girl, with her thick village accent and her steadfast unhappiness. "Ask the Crown Prince himself. He was merely doing the ambassador and me a kindness."

The concubine gaped at her, face shaded with doubt. "Then why was he staring at you during the Moon Festival?"

"If you remember, he was upset with someone he believed wished his mother harm." Xifeng locked eyes with Lady Sun. "I imagine he was looking off into space, wondering what sort of *monster* would want to hurt her."

Lady Meng chewed on her lower lip, turning to the older concubine. "You lied to me. You told me you had read the prince's love letter to her. You said he wanted to run away with her!"

"You are so quick to believe everything you hear, aren't you?" Lady Sun draped an arm over the back of her chair. "So silly, so empty-headed. But you do have your uses."

"You promised to help me. You said you'd find a way for me to meet the prince in secret."

Xifeng regarded the girl's crestfallen face, vexed and yet darkly amused by Lady Sun's catty, underhanded dealings. The woman had not only used this girl as an informant, but also exploited her secret love and tormented her for pure pleasure.

"In time, my dear," Lady Sun said patronizingly. "We must not rush matters of the heart. Besides, I am not the one who would slip into the Crown Prince's bed at the first chance." She angled a sly glance at Xifeng, lips curving upward.

Lady Meng rocked back and forth on her heels, her eyes wet, frantic. Surely, Xifeng thought, she had been driven to despair; surely her hopeless situation had brought it upon her.

"She lies, as you said yourself," Xifeng told Lady Meng in a gentle voice. "I would never do such a thing, not when the prince isn't mine to take. Believe me." But the girl only stared back, hopeless tears streaming down her face, and then fled without another word.

"Since when do you care about men who aren't yours to take?" Lady Sun lazily arched an eyebrow. "Noble of you, being kind to that little lunatic. I did promise to influence the Emperor to help her win the Crown Prince. But she never thought that through, did she? She belongs to His Majesty, so why would he help her win another man's love? You and I should be thankful we're cleverer than that."

Xifeng bristled at the use of the word *we*. She had nothing in common with this conniving woman. "Tell me what you want. If you're hoping to plant something on me and have me whipped, I'm afraid you already tried that."

"Oh, no, my beautiful one. I have other plans for you. And for Wei, too." A feline grin crossed her face at Xifeng's shock. "You think that drunken idiot Meng is my only informant? I've known for some time now that Wei isn't so much your friend as your lover. It won't take more than a twitch of my finger to exile you both to whatever hovel you came from."

A steady hum sounded in Xifeng's ears.

The concubine continued smiling, but her eyes were burning metal. Whatever hatred she had felt, making Xifeng clean up after her dog, had gone far beyond that. "You're new here, so I'll tell you. Unmarried girls in the city of women are *never* to associate with men without permission. It makes my head spin to think how quickly your precious Empress will throw you into the streets when she finds out."

The hum grew louder in Xifeng's ears, pulsating to the speeding rhythm of her heart.

"You're a good liar." The concubine put her head to one side, shining waves of hair tumbling over her shoulder. "I commend you for that. I enjoyed your little story about the dwarf being your guardian. Imagine that tiny man protecting anyone from *anything*." She tipped her long, elegant throat back and laughed.

The blood rushed to Xifeng's face. "Do *not* speak about my friends. You have no right."

Lady Sun's eyes widened as though an idea had occurred to her. "You know, Wei is quite handsome. Didn't I tell you I met him the other day?" she asked, twirling her hair around her slim fingers. "He looked at me like I was a delicacy he'd very much like to try. But he had to restrain himself, as the Emperor was with me. It wouldn't do to covet something belonging to His Majesty, now, would it?"

The hum intensified. Flashes of red sparked into Xifeng's vision—the beginning of that familiar anger, slow burning and steady. *It's a lie,* she told herself, struggling to stay calm. *She's trying to make me jealous of her the way she is of me.* But she could easily imagine Lady Sun flickering her tilting eyes at Wei—imagine her escaping His Majesty and pulling Wei into the gardens where he'd been with Xifeng . . .

"I'm sure the Empress would love to know what you've been up to with that gallant soldier." The concubine's playful tone hardened. "You didn't think you could play the daughter always, did you? If by some miracle she carries that parasite to birth and it's a princess, she won't even remember you exist."

Kang had given her the same warning, but from Lady Sun, it was a flaming arrow aimed at her heart. Xifeng reeled at the harsh truth in her statement, the splinters of the woman's hatred embedding themselves under her skin.

"You may be clever," Lady Sun said softly. "You may know how to win them over, including the Emperor, who can't seem to see you're nothing but a little drudge. But I've given my life to them. I've given them a prince. They'll remember that when tomorrow comes."

Xifeng wanted to cut the smug, knowing expression right off her face. "Tomorrow?"

"You and your lover will be thrown out of the gates. Your time at court has come to an end."

It was Xifeng's turn to laugh. "I'm sure that's what you hope . . ."

"Oh, it's more than a hope." The concubine rose and crossed her arms, the yards of peony satin catching the light. "I've written to the General, you see. My eunuch left to deliver the letter just minutes ago. Wei will be dismissed for consorting with a lady-in-waiting, and the Empress will denounce *you*."

Xifeng's stomach dropped. "You can't prove anything."

"My dear girl, you underestimate me. I know *everything*. When you went to see him, what you said, what you *did*. My eyes and ears are everywhere. Soon, the General will know . . . and Their Majesties will too. Don't worry," Lady Sun added. "My letter was very . . . *poetic*."

The anger built and turned to ice, and Xifeng shivered as though someone had upturned a bucket of water over her. The sensation tingled down from her head to her toes, freezing her blood. This woman—the *Fool*—had succeeded in her mission to single-handedly destroy Xifeng's destiny. She had outwitted, outmaneuvered Xifeng at every turn.

Wei would lose his position, and Xifeng would never see the Empress again, never hear her gentle words or earn her loving smile. And the Emperor, with his warm, handsome eyes and the unspoken promise within them, would never be hers. The Fool had won.

The taut strings of her fury had been strummed, and there was no stopping her anger now. Images flashed before Xifeng's eyes: Kang and his raised white scars, Empress Lihua weeping over her belly, Master Yu lifting the whip. She pictured Wei, with his brutal beauty and savage pride, turned away from court. Both of them, exiled in shame to return home to Guma's wrath.

She saw it so clearly, it was almost like it had happened: the point of her dagger biting into the concubine's chest, her moon-white skin vomiting a crimson river. It spilled down her breasts as her heart was laid bare, ready for the taking. Xifeng wrapped her lips around the muscle, slippery with gore, and the woman's essence filled her like air. Lady Sun's lifeblood was as intoxicating as wine, heady and powerful, and Xifeng felt herself stand taller—she saw the eyes of the Emperor's court on her, adoring and worshipful . . .

Lady Sun suddenly fell backward in one swift movement, tripping over the leg of the chair in her hurry to get away from Xifeng. Her sneer had vanished, and in its place was horror at whatever she had seen on Xifeng's face. "Wh-what are you?" she choked out.

The beautiful vision of the concubine's heartless corpse had disappeared, but Xifeng didn't mind. "What's the matter, my lady?" she asked softly, relishing the tang of the woman's fear. It was almost as delicious as slick heart muscle, sliding down her throat smooth as silk. She took a step forward, taunting her, burning with exhilaration as the concubine pressed herself against a mother-of-pearl folding screen, shoulders shaking.

"Stay where you are," Lady Sun cried. "Don't come any closer."

Xifeng pressed her fists beneath her breast, where the creature slithered and basked. It fed on the woman's terror and grew stronger. *She is nothing, and you are everything*. And then it opened Xifeng's mouth and poured its voice from her throat. "Do not threaten me, girl," she rasped in a harsh, guttural voice. "You don't know who you're dealing with."

Lady Sun fell to her knees, her confident, seductive demeanor forgotten. "What are you?" she repeated.

"I am the moon and the darkness around it," Xifeng hissed in that ancient, ageless voice. "I am the wind and the rain and the ceaseless sea. I am time itself, and yours is running out." Her chest felt like it would explode from the sheer immensity of her power. She never knew it could feel like this, the creature's shifting like a mother's touch.

This woman and her petty lies were nothing more than beetles she would crush beneath her feet. Everything would come to pass as she had hoped—as *they* had planned.

Lady Sun fixed her eyes on Xifeng's face and screamed and screamed, clawing at the folding screen. It toppled and collapsed to the floor with a crash.

The door flew open and eunuch guards appeared, bringing a rush of wind with them. Xifeng came back to herself, feeling the tension release like trapped air. She let out a great gasp as she clutched her raw, aching throat. Everything was still—the guards, the room, the creature in her chest. Lady Sun sobbed and curled up against the wall.

"She's not human," the woman howled. "She's not normal! Get her out this instant."

Two of them grasped Xifeng's arms and steered her out like a limp rag doll. She felt weak and bone tired, as though the open air were leaching away the strength she had experienced. Several of Lady Sun's maids, who had been scrubbing the railing, turned to stare as she leaned heavily against the wall, closing her eyes against the light of the lantern dangling nearby. She couldn't go anywhere without seeing those wretched lanterns.

Kang was by her side, patting her dazed face. "What happened? What's wrong?"

But she could not find it in herself to answer him. Away from her visions of might and power, reality came back to her in a devastating rush. She might frighten the wits out of Lady Sun, but it still didn't change the fact that the General would receive the woman's letter. Even now, he could be reading it and preparing to throw Wei out of the gates.

Wei's dream had come to an end . . . and so had hers.

It was over. It was done. She had let the Fool defeat her.

Xifeng raised her head and let out a scream of fury, ignoring Kang and the maids as they all fell back in fright. What would Guma say if she knew how Xifeng had failed? She pictured Lady Sun sitting on a throne and the Emperor placing a crown on her head.

Xifeng's crown. Xifeng's throne. They belonged to her; the cards had promised.

You know what to do, the creature had told her. *There is only one choice.*

In the hot springs, the mirror-water had shown Lady Sun's heart glittering in her chest. But Xifeng had turned away in horror, believing it to be too cruel and herself too weak. Perhaps she had been wrong. Perhaps it had been the perfect solution all along. If Lady Sun lived, it would mean the Fool had triumphed.

Xifeng clenched her fists. She had let this go much too far.

31

The wounds came back.

Xifeng had climbed into bed to wait for the Empress's household to fall silent. She hadn't meant to fall asleep, but she woke with both of her cheeks burning. It felt as though Guma had just struck her with the cane, as though Lady Sun's nails had raked across her jaw moments ago. Blood soaked her pillow, and she stumbled out of bed, one hand over her face as she shakily lit a candle. The cuts and gashes were hot trails against her palm. She screamed, nearly fainting at the mutilated face that stared back at her in the mirror from a mess of shredded skin.

"What's wrong with you?" demanded the lady-in-waiting who shared her chamber. "Do you know how late it is?"

"My face," Xifeng sobbed, her bloody hands trembling so hard her whole body shook. "How could it be?"

Lifeblood had a permanent healing effect. Guma had taught her that, promised her that. The scars had never, *never* returned before.

"Why?" she moaned as blood dampened her tunic. "Why am I being punished like this?"

Rough hands grabbed her shoulders as the woman turned her. "There is nothing on your face," she said in a flat voice.

Xifeng tugged at her tunic and thrust out her hand. "Look at the blood!"

But the woman looked, instead, into her eyes. "You've had a bad dream, child," she told her slowly. "Go back to sleep now and you'll feel better in the morning."

Xifeng stared at her in disbelief, then glanced down at her clean palm and clothing. Her face in the mirror was as smooth and unblemished as it had always been, but her eyes were wild.

"How could it be?" she repeated in a whisper.

She had felt the hot blood on her hand and touched the edges of the gaping wounds. She had seen the injuries with her own eyes.

The woman returned to bed, grunting, and Xifeng went to her own, embarrassed.

Her pillow was covered with blood.

"What is it now?" the woman snapped, hearing Xifeng's choked scream.

"N-nothing. I'm sorry to have woken you." She stared at the dark red smears, her heart pounding so fast she thought she might collapse. She sat on the edge of the bed farthest away from the pillow, breathing in and out slowly for a full minute before turning her eyes back to it. The white cotton was now as clean as if it had been freshly laundered.

Xifeng bit her knuckles to keep from crying out again, finding relief in the sharp edges of her teeth. That had been no dream—the bloodstains had been real, as had the torn flesh on her face. A vicious cut where Guma's cane had bitten into her cheek, and five trails of ripped skin where Lady Sun's fingers had scratched her. What could this mean?

She burned with the need to see Guma: her aunt would know what this meant; she would know how to deal with Lady Sun. Then, perhaps Xifeng would find a way to intercept and destroy the concubine's letter. Surely the General had been too preoccupied to read it; the Empress's ladies had been buzzing with news that the Emperor and Crown Prince were at odds again, this time over a military matter that had called for an emergency council. A wild hope lodged itself in her breast.

Eyeing the pristine pillow the way she would a snake, Xifeng muttered some excuse about her moon's bleeding—though the lady-in-waiting was already snoring—and fled the royal apartments.

The tunnel felt different when she slipped into it from the gardens—charged and alive, like she had unwittingly entered the veins of some predatory animal. The slimy stone wall seemed to pulse as she trailed her fingers along it, though it might have been her own thundering heartbeat. She touched her smooth face again, cursing the day she had met Lady Sun. Her bare feet pattered a rhythm on the dirt floor: *she must die, she must die . . .*

There would be no going back if she harmed the woman. She would never again be the girl who had yearned and struggled, the girl Wei adored. She let her intention run through her mind, over and over, until she almost believed it, too: she would give up that former self to protect him, to save his dream. If that wasn't love, she didn't know what was.

And so, for love, she descended into the hot springs.

The minute Xifeng lit the lanterns and stood before her makeshift altar, with the incense and the dagger, she sensed she was not alone. There was a familiar presence here—she heard her name being whispered in the shadows, and a sound like a gentle tapping of fingers.

"Guma?" She strained her ears and caught a faint reply beneath the bubbling of the water. But it was too quiet, too low, and with a growl of frustration, she bent to light the incense, closing her eyes as the thick black fumes emerged. Still, a thin veil separated her from Guma.

The tapping came again. Xifeng froze as a thick, skulking body darted from the shadows. It approached, and she nearly laughed with relief when she saw the rat, its beady eyes flashing in the light. It paused beside her, fearless, and she could almost hear its blood drumming in her ears.

To imbibe another's lifeblood is to strengthen your own.

Would it be enough to help her see Guma? Before she had even finished the thought, Xifeng's fingers had snatched the rat, quick as lightning. She broke its neck cleanly, so it would feel no pain, and wondered why she had ever hesitated to kill. After all, the animals would live forever through her, in the strengthening of her vitality and magic.

She laid the dead rat on the ground, by the edge of the water, and sliced it open with the dagger. Dark splatters shone on her fingers as the warm fur gave way to her prodding, revealing a lump hot as the springs themselves. She placed the heart on her tongue and swallowed it whole. The rich, metallic taste scorched her throat as it went down, and she shuddered as her nerves tingled with delight and newfound strength.

"Xifeng."

Startled, she knocked the rat's corpse into the water. She faced Guma, seeing her as though she truly stood there, the increased magic in her veins enhancing the vision.

"I knew you were here." She reached out, but her fingers slipped right through Guma's shadowy form. Nothing but air, of course. Her aunt looked older than she remembered, and thin and worn, her head barely reaching Xifeng's chin. Had she truly been capable of beating the life out of her?

Guma surveyed her, too, with pride. "You look as I hoped you would." She listened with a dark expression as Xifeng told her of the phantom wounds.

"It was no dream. I felt the injuries with my own fingers and there was blood on my pillow." Xifeng touched her chest, where the creature listened. "Am I losing my mind?"

The older woman did not answer right away. "There are consequences for everything we do. You know that," she said at last, with a slow, sad smile. "You've come seeking answers. I've wanted to tell you the truth for years, and it seems the time is now. You are fulfilling what I wanted for you and more. You've learned well."

Approval, after all this time. A thousand questions sat on the tip of Xifeng's tongue, but her aunt held up a filmy hand to silence her.

"We don't have much time, for this sort of magic will not last long. Listen well. I know the visions you've seen." She turned away and the very air seemed pregnant with tension, with things left unsaid for far too long. "When I was your age, a handsome young nobleman named Long came to town. Our family fell in love with him. Our parents, because he was the means to a better life; my sister Mingzhu, because of his gentle way with her; and me."

Xifeng turned to the waterfall, where her reflection stood small and alone.

"I was plain and awkward. I never had your or Mingzhu's ability to win a man's heart with my face," Guma said bitterly. "But I had something else. You see, I used to play by the river as a girl. I found a black snake there once and followed it to a cave, where . . . it became a man. He told me I had the makings of a great wielder of magic and taught me all I know about poisons and poetry. He gave me books of poems and my first deck of cards. He taught me the dark magic of lifeblood, which he had shared with no one else. Only me."

"The Serpent God."

"He told me to call him that." Her aunt grimaced. "He forced me to keep our meetings secret and took payment here and there for our lessons over the years. Things he said I wouldn't value: My ability to read music. Memories of my childhood. My sense of direction. My vision in the dark. Things I was willing to give if it meant I could be special like Mingzhu."

"He took all of these things and you never questioned him?"

"Not at first. I was young and desperate to make something of myself. Over time, I began to suspect things were not as they should be, but still I felt a duty to him, and a desire to be more—much more—than what I was."

Xifeng gave a slow nod. She understood that desire well.

"He cared for me like a father. He was the only one who saw me as anything." Guma's shoulders drooped with every word. "So I worked hard to please him. I progressed so well that he promised me one great wish. Anything I wanted. I should have known the wish wouldn't be free, either. Something else would be taken, and this time, it would be something I'd notice."

"You wished for Long to fall in love with you?" Xifeng asked, though she was terrified of the answer and what it might mean . . . what it might change.

Guma's body faded with each passing minute, but her grimace was clear. "My parents wanted him to marry Mingzhu badly enough that they bribed the matchmaker and astrologer to favor the union. So I knew it was time. But what I wished for was one night with Long, to convince him he should be with me. I still had my pride. I would not have him unless I had earned him myself."

She clenched her jaw. "That night was the worst of my life. The whole time, he believed I was Mingzhu. He came to me in the dark, drunk with passion, believing I was my sister. Afterward, he screamed when he realized it was me. And we both saw what had become of my leg. Rivers of blood. Unimaginable pain. It came on suddenly, as soon as Long found me out and our night together was over. The payment was due, you see."

Despite the heat of the springs, Xifeng felt ice in her veins. "The Serpent God injured you as payment for granting your wish."

Guma stared into the waterfall that did not reflect her. "Long left in terror, convinced my parents had used black magic to entangle him with their daughters. Mingzhu's mind had never been strong—a vein of madness runs through our family—and grief destroyed her."

"A vein of madness?" Xifeng repeated. "You told me *magic* runs through our family."

"Are they not the same, I wonder? My parents never recouped the fortune they'd wasted trying to attract him into marrying her. They died, one after the other, followed by my sister. Your *aunt,* Mingzhu."

Xifeng felt faint as she stared into the face of this woman . . . her mother. "I spent my childhood yearning for you, and you were there the whole time." The *tengaru* queen had known. *You drift toward each other,* she had said, *two streams from the same river.*

"I wrote to Long's parents when my baby was born. They told me he had died and never to contact them again. They didn't want anything to do with me or their granddaughter." Guma shook her head. "But there was someone else who could help me, who had done this to me so I might depend on him. He called me back to him, insisting he had given me my gifts and talents out of the goodness of his heart. But those gifts and talents now allowed me to see exactly what he was: an evil spirit using me for reasons I didn't understand. He told me his secret."

The Lord of Surjalana, a voice whispered inside Xifeng.

It was one of the many names of the jealous god who had ruled the desert and coveted the Dragon King's wealth and might. Xifeng remembered Shiro telling her a theory in which this god, seduced by power, never returned to the heavens at all.

"The Serpent God is the Lord of Surjalana." Xifeng shivered. "All those nightmares you had . . . All of those times you came running home to lock the doors and windows . . ."

"I would rather have starved and watched my baby die than crawl back to that cave, to that *being* who had destroyed my life." Guma's eyes met hers. "I burned everything he gave me. Every book of poetry, every gift . . . even the deck of cards. I bought a new deck myself, though it cost me dearly. I wanted nothing more to do with him, now that I had a child to protect."

Xifeng felt a lump in her throat, as though the rat's heart had lodged itself there.

"I promised myself you would be better than I was," her mother told her, eyes blazing. "When I read your fate in the cards, I *knew* you would be, though I was afraid at first. If I pushed you toward your destiny, might you encounter *him* on your path? But then I asked myself: where is the safest place on earth for my daughter? Where will she be mightiest, most powerful, and under the rule of no one but herself? Ah. As Empress of Feng Lu, protected by the Great Forest. Just as the cards predicted. A woman of unimaginable strength, with an army at her back."

"But you served him for so long. He controlled you," Xifeng argued. "How do you know he isn't controlling you now?"

"He can't. He isn't. I took precautions . . . I denounced him . . ."

"How could you have agreed to give him all of those things without knowing the costs? Without knowing what you were paying for?"

"Aren't you doing the same thing?" Guma countered. "You are following your destiny without knowing the costs. You are willing to pay in other people's lives to get there. Do not dare pass judgment on me, daughter, without first accepting your own actions."

"No," Xifeng whispered. "It's not the same."

Her mother's fading mouth twisted. "Do you see now what I've tried to teach you? Love is weakness. You open yourself up to choices you'd never make if your heart were your own." She moved closer, desperate. "I was ashamed. I didn't want you to be like me. I'd rather have you hate me as your aunt than pity me as your mother. And I was so afraid *he* would find you."

A dark, terrible anger settled into Xifeng's bones. "You pushed my destiny on me to get me away from him. You knew I would leave you to pursue it."

Guma's sad face was a wisp of smoke now. "I wanted a better life for you."

"How do you know you aren't connected to him still?" Xifeng enjoyed watching her flinch at the cruel words. She flung them like daggers, wanting Guma to hurt as much as she did. "How do you know he hasn't been speaking to you through those cards? Through this incense?"

"I know I've done things you can never forgive. But I did them for you, and my time is almost over now. Protect yourself, child. Rid yourself of the Fool, whoever she may be." Her mother's eyes flickered to the invisible wounds on her face. "Until you do, you will never be safe, and you will be reminded of it again and again. It is a consequence, like everything else."

"This was a reminder?" Xifeng touched the pristine skin of her face, which had been shredded only moments ago. *A vein of madness runs through our family.*

"I want you to know . . . I wanted the world for you."

"This destiny you saw for me could be what *he* wants," Xifeng shouted as her mother faded out of view. She hoped Guma was still listening, hoped the pain of this revelation would make all those years of brutality and abuse worthwhile. Maybe, at last, they would be even. "How do you know he isn't in my very bones, and his eyes aren't looking back at you?"

The creature inside her roared with this truth. The realization twisted Guma's disappearing face: the Serpent God had taken his final payment, after all.

He had taken Xifeng.

She felt him burst free, and though her mother was gone—though Xifeng stood alone—the strange waterfall now reflected a being too tall to be human, once a darkness twisted within and now joyously released. Exhilaration tingled in her nerves as she watched herself beside him, tall, imposing, as treacherously beautiful as an immortal.

My shadowed goddess. My dark queen. My fairest, he said. *Guma was only a means to an end. You are my prize.*

She licked blood from the corner of her mouth, still ravenous for more. In the reflection, the man ran long, thin fingers down her neck, and she closed her eyes as though she could feel it.

The moon shines down upon us, beloved . . .

"Our deal is different from what she had with you," she told him, still smarting from Guma's accusation. "I know my ending. I understand my destiny. I'm different from her."

Fairest. The water a vast and eternal mirror . . .

Another image appeared in the mirror-water: Lady Sun, waiting alone in the tunnel. Lady Sun, descending the stairs to the hot springs as if in a trance.

"She's here? But how . . . ?"

My servant has brought her to you, my queen, the man told her in the creature's voice reborn. *She is a threat to us, and you will end her.*

"Turn your face from the world's apple-blossom fragility," she recited softly, dutifully, "and embrace this boundless night."

But though she had waited for this moment—though she knew she would destroy Lady Sun for good—hearing her desire spoken aloud made Xifeng dizzy. Her reflection in the mirror-water looked pale and afraid. One by one, the oozing wounds reappeared on her face, a thousand times worse than she remembered . . . spreading across her perfect skin until she could not recognize herself. She was a horrible leper beside the image of Lady Sun's luminous beauty.

Which of you looks like a queen? the man's whisper taunted her.

Xifeng imagined the concubine's heart pounding, her blood pure and rich beneath her flawless skin, and she felt faint with hunger. She could taste the woman's lifeblood on her tongue, feel the slippery muscle of her young, fresh heart gliding against her teeth.

"Rid yourself of the Fool, whoever she may be," she echoed Guma's words.

Would she accept the Serpent God's help in destroying Lady Sun, even knowing what he had done to Guma? It dawned on Xifeng that she had run out of other options. But she was *not* Guma. She would not accept the same fate. The cards promised her victory as Empress . . . the great destiny surely protected her from enduring Guma's defeat.

She had harbored the Serpent God's spirit within her for a decade, she had struggled with the dark side of her own self, and now he would reward her. In the swirling darkness, the god waited for her to choose.

So Xifeng chose.

She picked up the dagger and lay in wait by the stairs like a vengeful goddess of the old world. She slithered into the shadows, listening to the concubine's footsteps. The dark god's servant, whoever it was, had as good as handed Xifeng her prize. She gave a quiet, chilling laugh that did not seem to have come from her. Nothing seemed to be hers tonight—not her voice, not her words, not the slender fingers braced on the blade. Perhaps that was best. Perhaps she preferred to feel disembodied, watching from above as this new Xifeng prowled and hunted.

Lady Sun appeared, the smell of fear pungent in the air around her. There was a moment, before the woman reached the bottom step, when Xifeng's hunger intensified with such strength she wanted to scream from it, from this need for the concubine's blood to trickle down inside her and fill the empty places in her dark, dark soul.

Just as it had the first time Guma had made her kill, Xifeng could hear a piece of her old self pleading: *Let me go. Don't make me do this.* Her limbs shuddered with her silent prayer for mercy, for her own salvation, but she heard nothing in return except the thundering of her own heart.

"Save me," Xifeng uttered aloud, one last time, before she let the darkness take her. She knew nothing now but her uncontrollable hunger.

Lady Sun entered the cavernous space without seeing the Serpent God, who now stood beside a hulking figure robed in black, a hood concealing all but two glittering eyes. His servant.

"Hello?" Lady Sun called in a thin, high voice. Her figure on the steps was soft and appealing, the kind a man like Wei or the Emperor would want to protect. Such loveliness might even distract them from

Xifeng, but she told herself soon there would be no one who could turn his eyes from her. The darkness whispered its approval.

Lady Sun's shadow flickered across the damp, archaic stone as she stood transfixed before the waterfall. Did she look as beautiful as Xifeng in the mirror-water? Did she see in its ripples an image forever held in the depths of perfection? If only, Xifeng thought, they could remain that way forever.

And she realized, as she leapt shrieking from the shadows . . . *she* could.

All it cost was blood magic, Xifeng mused, staring into the concubine's terrified face as she plunged the dagger into her chest. The woman collapsed, her cry stifled in her throat, eyes gazing at Xifeng with pitiful innocence.

Even in death, she was a liar.

Xifeng watched her die, thinking of the girl she herself had been. A girl who longed to love as others did, who had prayed to the gods for guidance—and had at last been answered by one. She stood alone in the mirror-water as Lady Sun stopped moving. "I was born a woman into this world," she said, echoing the concubine's words. "And I will play the game, but I won't lose."

The dark god's servant stepped forward, his robes smelling of dank, forgotten soil. He held out two enormous, cruel hands, on which rested a scroll, still sealed. There was something familiar in the way he bowed his head and backed away respectfully when she accepted it. She broke open the seal and unrolled the edges to find the letter Lady Sun had written to the General, detailing Xifeng's romance with Wei.

"I am saved," she whispered. "You stole it back before he learned the truth."

The servant bowed again, then bent his massive bulk over Lady

Sun's motionless form. There was a cracking sound as he tore into her ribs with his massive bare hands, and Xifeng watched dispassionately as blood burst out, so dark it was almost black, staining the ground a brilliant cherry. He moved aside, clearing her path to the prize.

There is nothing I won't do for you, the Serpent God told her. *There is no door now that will remain closed to you. The world is yours.*

A roar of triumph ripped through Xifeng's body. *This* was her destiny. *This* was the fate the cards had seen: unimaginable power and beauty at the cost of lesser women's lives. The throne of Feng Lu lay just beyond, ready and willing to be taken. She knelt beside the dead concubine and dug the dagger into her chest, feeling the tip catch slightly. And then there it was, Lady Sun's heart—perfect, and glistening in the dim light. The hot metallic smell mingled with the incense in an intoxicating blend as Xifeng brought it to her lips.

In the waterfall, the Serpent God watched her take a bite.

The power that plunged through her made her cry out loud. She bit again and again, savoring her invincibility. The woman's essence was stronger than wine, headier than incense. Her limbs shook from the magnificence of it. Never in the deepest throes of passion with Wei had she ever felt so alive, so physically charged. She tipped her head back, gasping as the blood gushed down her throat. Lady Sun swam in her veins, alluring and seductive, everything that could win an Emperor. But Xifeng would know how to keep him.

Eternal beauty for such a small price. A life for a life of beauty, forevermore.

Never again would the wounds haunt her.

Xifeng did not stop until the heart was gone. The cavern hummed with energy, vibrating with the power within her. Hands and lips drenched in blood, she dragged the hollowed body to the water and slipped it in, watching it land beside the rat she had killed. The concubine lay faceup, her hair streaming around her face like the petals of a flower. In the water, her skin shone pure white and her lips were as red as the blood that still oozed from her gaping chest.

In time, that beauty would fade. It was inside Xifeng now, dancing through her veins. She had given Lady Sun a gift, really, by ensuring the woman would continue to live through her, by harnessing her power. And there were so many other hearts that might do the same—so many other enemies who would not be wasted by death, who would instead contribute their essence to the night that had begun inside her.

And there was no going back now; there were no second thoughts.

The world was hers.

32

Guilt. Self-hatred. Fear.

Whatever Xifeng might have felt afterward, it was none of those. Instead, she woke and faced the day with a light heart. She and Wei were safe, Kang was avenged, and the Empress would no longer be tormented. Lady Sun was gone and the danger she posed had ended.

"Everyone's saying she finally left him as she threatened to do for years." Kang sat beside her at the morning meal, eating with more vigor than usual. "She didn't even bother to take her precious son."

Xifeng thought of the little boy gazing up at the map, babbling about sea monsters, and forced herself to harden her heart. "What will happen to her children if she doesn't turn up?"

The eunuch shrugged. "They'll go back to her family, I suppose."

The banquet hall seemed even noisier and more crowded this morning. Xifeng watched ladies-in-waiting gossiping, maidservants scurrying, and eunuchs tossing dice in the corner of the room. A woman's life had ended, but everyone else's would continue—including her own.

Not a shade of suspicion touched her. No one truly knew what had happened aside from herself, the Serpent God, and his servant, who seemed unlikely to talk. She wondered who he was, this slave of the dark god. From his build, he could have been a soldier or a guard. A man sworn to protect the Emperor by day . . . and do the god's bidding by night.

"Everyone is saying His Majesty questioned all the guards and eunuchs in the city of women, and dismissed many of them," Xifeng said.

"He got angry because they all gave conflicting accounts of whether they'd seen Lady Sun in the tunnels, or outside her apartments at all. I was questioned, but even Master Yu vouched for me," Kang added cheerfully. "I'm famous for my snoring, you know, and I'm told I provided remarkable music the night Lady Sun left."

From then on, Xifeng felt different. She felt the concubine's essence in the way she greeted each day, her feet like bronze claws ready to seize the world. Her skin glowed and her hair hung blacker than ever, and neither the ladies nor the eunuchs could take their eyes from her. The wounds returned every so often and her cheeks burned as though they'd been scraped raw. But she reminded herself that the injuries weren't real, and then the blood would vanish and her face would return to its usual perfection.

Now, when she spoke, even the highest-ranking women stopped to listen, drawn in by her voice, beauty, and newfound power. She pitied their ignorance. They were so jealous, so eager to explain away her sudden popularity. She was something fresh for His Majesty, they whispered, and she would be nothing again once he got tired of her.

They didn't know her secret lay within each and every one of their hearts; they didn't know the magic of Lady Sun's heart now coursed through her veins, placing each and every one of them under her spell.

And they could never imagine Xifeng was here to stay, or that she had just cleared away the last remaining obstacle in her path.

Well . . . not quite the *last*.

Autumn came, bringing fiery touches of red and gold to the gardens, and Xifeng sensed that she had completely slipped out of the Empress's favor. Her Majesty no longer sought her out, and chose other ladies to accompany her to the Boat Festival. Xifeng sorely felt the absence of her motherly care, and resented it, too. She had, after all, done the Empress a great favor by destroying Lady Sun.

"Her Majesty knows the Emperor's affections for Lady Sun were souring," Kang told her. "Still, she must be thoroughly pleased to be without a rival for the first time."

"And everyone knows Lady Meng's days at court are numbered," Xifeng added. The eunuchs were placing bets on whether His Majesty would send her back to her village or to a monastery to live out the rest of her days.

"It seems, my dear, it is *you* to whom Their Majesties' eyes have turned."

"I doubt that. The Emperor hasn't sent a single message or come to the city of women for weeks." It stung to say it, no matter how true. Yet if he wanted to see Xifeng, wouldn't he have sent word? Or come on the pretext of visiting his wife? "The Empress can't possibly view me as a rival. And even if she does, she thought of me as a daughter once. She should give me a chance to explain, instead of jumping to conclusions."

"Queens may jump to conclusions as much as they like. Heads have rolled because of it."

"Would she do that?" Xifeng asked.

"What, behead you?" He shrugged. "She let Lady Sun live, didn't she?"

But as the days grew shorter, Xifeng began to doubt. She woke most nights with a sweat-soaked pillow, drenched in fearful visions of Lady Sun returning from her watery grave. Sometimes, her ghost whispered gleefully in the Empress's ear, as though they were conspiring, and the Empress would give Xifeng the concubine's feline smile. Lady Sun had died . . . but had the Fool? Perhaps Xifeng had guessed wrong. Perhaps she had allowed the *true* Fool to persist. She had defeated Lady Sun, but was she truly any closer to sitting on the throne?

She spent her nights in painful uncertainty and her days in loneliness, sewing in solitude, as the Empress called every other lady-in-waiting except Xifeng to attend her.

So when Xifeng was at last summoned to the royal bedchamber one morning, she obeyed in surprise. Her Majesty was sitting up in bed with an older woman beside her on a stool, bent and gray in the simple cotton clothes of a servant.

"Xifeng, come in," Empress Lihua said warmly, as though nothing could or had ever soured between them. She seemed in high spirits, but her pale, wan face—already drawn with ill health—was beginning to show the weariness of pregnancy. "You're in time to hear the story. I tell it to the baby every day, and when she is born, her nursemaid Ama here can help tell it."

"She, Your Majesty?"

The Empress tapped her rounded stomach. "It will be a girl. I hear her speaking to me. She says she is what I have waited for . . . what we all have waited for. And I, in turn, tell her who she is. I tell her of the

Dragon Lords who created our world, and of the Dragon King whose blood runs through her veins."

Xifeng imagined the child curled inside the Empress's belly, tiny heart pumping the most precious lifeblood on Feng Lu. But lifeblood was easily taken.

"And I tell her the story of the two lovers in the Great Forest. Do you know it?"

"My . . . aunt rarely told me stories." Xifeng's voice shook, unable to say the word *mother*. Weeks ago, Empress Lihua might have responded to the longing in her voice. But now her eyes and her heart were wholly fixed on the unborn child in her belly.

"A long time ago," Her Majesty said in a dreamy voice, "when dragons walked the earth, there lived a queen who loved her daughter more than all the jewels of her court. She gave her everything her heart desired and asked for one thing in return: that the princess marry the man chosen for her. But the princess had already given her heart to a poor musician. He had a voice like a bird and taught her to love the song of the trees sheltering the palace. Though he begged the princess to reconsider, for his was a life of hardship, she vowed to be his wife.

"They made a plan: he would hide in the forest and leave behind a trail of lanterns. Some of them would be draped with red cloth, and it was these she should follow to join him. But before she could do so, her intended discovered their romance and followed his rival into the trees. He killed him with a single stroke of his sword, before the musician could drape any of the lanterns, and the blood splattered one."

Xifeng hadn't realized she had leaned forward to better hear until she saw Ama, the old nursemaid, watching her. The woman's face broke into a smile Xifeng did not return.

"The princess was led to believe her lover had abandoned her,"

Empress Lihua continued, "and that his neglecting to leave behind any red lanterns was his way of telling her not to run away with him. So she married her intended as the queen wished, but grew sad and silent. She ordered all of the lanterns in the forest to be lit and spent her days walking among them.

"One day, she came upon a single red lantern she hadn't seen before. Her heart rejoiced, knowing her lover had wanted her with him after all. On a nearby branch sat a drab brown bird chirping the song the musician had written for her. The bird shed tears of blood and indicated that the princess should drink them, but she refused.

"Three times she came to hear it sing, and the familiar tune it trilled made her grow more certain that the bird was her lover returned. She told the queen, who urged her to drink the tears, knowing how unhappy she was. The princess understood then that her mother had relented at last, and bid her farewell. She returned to the forest and drank the bird's blood tears, and in doing so, turned her arms into wings and her hair into feathers. She flew to her lover on the branch by the red lantern, and it is said they still live there today, joined in eternal love."

Every nerve in Xifeng's body felt charged and on edge. It was only a silly tale, but something about the lanterns in the forest resonated—warned her to be aware.

She closed her eyes and saw vivid images behind her lids: scented spirals of incense; a pool of silent, heartless women; a card depicting a girl in disguise, her foot hovering over the edge of a cliff. And lanterns, one thousand lanterns blazing in the forest, just out of reach. But what they meant and had to do with her, she couldn't guess. It was a secret she felt she ought to know.

Empress Lihua dismissed the nursemaid. "I'd like you to stay and talk awhile with me, Xifeng, as you used to."

"I would be honored, Your Majesty."

"Bohai says I will deliver a strong child. A true miracle. He is as surprised as I am," the woman said. A gentle, satisfied smile softened her features, as though she had proven the physician wrong. "The baby will come in the early days of winter, when the envoy leaves for the mountains. Perhaps I'll be able to see them off and ask them to pray for the princess's health."

"I will do the same." But Xifeng heard the hollowness in her own promise. She had no more use for gods who ignored and neglected her. Only one had answered her prayers, and it was *she* he cared for—not some spoiled sapling of a brat who hadn't even been born.

The Empress gave a slow nod, looking at Xifeng as though she saw a stranger. She picked up an ornate cup, holding it with both hands as she sipped. "I loathe the taste of Bohai's new medicine, but he'll never know. It would be like insulting a meal in front of the cook."

Xifeng felt a gnawing emptiness as she watched the Empress take another sip. It was as though Her Majesty had vacated a hole in her heart and nothing could fill it again.

There are consequences for everything we do, Guma had said. Even—and maybe especially—for the way the Emperor had looked at Xifeng on the night of his wife's birthday.

The Empress's thoughts seemed to run the same course, as she lowered her cup with shaking hands. "His Majesty is taken with you," she said directly. "Lady Sun's departure hasn't upset him as much as I assumed it would, and he has praised you in my hearing more than once."

"He is kind and gracious to remember me."

"You're a memorable woman. Worthy of any man's notice, even that of the Emperor. And you are nineteen, quite old enough. Do you wish to marry?"

In her eyes, Xifeng saw she knew, or at least *suspected,* that Xifeng had something to do with Lady Sun. She clearly believed Xifeng would take the woman's place; maybe she even hoped for it, so she could keep her close as she had Lady Sun for years.

"I'd like to marry, if the right man wanted me. But I want to be a wife, as you are. Lady Sun had wealth and comfort, but not a marriage—a partnership, a joining of equals." Xifeng thought of Lady Meng, too, trapped in a promise to one man while longing for another.

"And this is what you believe you deserve?"

"I do."

For the first time since Xifeng had entered the room, the Empress *truly* looked at her, without fixing her mind on herself or her baby. "A queen's marriage is not as secure as you think. Her husband can put her aside at any time if he is displeased in the slightest. And there is always someone waiting at the door, ready to pounce when that should happen." The Empress lowered her eyes to her belly. "The *tengaru* have told me for years of an enemy on my doorstep. A masked usurper. This person, they told me, would seek to end my line in fire and darkness. To work on behalf of an ancient feud."

Xifeng's hands were clasped so tightly, the knuckles turned white. Guma's cards had warned her about the Fool, and it seemed the *tengaru* had warned the Empress about Xifeng. This would seem to make Empress Lihua the Fool beyond the shadow of doubt.

The Fool. She recalled a high-pitched whistling, a wicked scythe splitting a man in half, Shiro stabbing an attacker to save Wei's life—and presumably hers as well. Perhaps Her Majesty had taken the *tengaru*'s threat seriously. Perhaps she had sought to nip her enemy in the bud with a band of masked killers. Xifeng's breath came in short, painful bursts, remembering how she had once longed for this woman to be her mother. This woman who may have tried to end her before they'd ever met.

"You're pale," Empress Lihua said flatly.

"I'm fine, Your Majesty." Xifeng forced herself to remain calm as the Empress studied her, as though searching for something objectionable in her manner or dress. It seemed not even Her Majesty was above the jealousy and desperation that had plagued Lady Sun. She, too, was part of this game in which women could only hope to survive by keeping each other down.

"Let us return to our previous subject. You would be welcome to remain in my service, if you chose not to wed." The Empress paused. "For me, it was inevitable. I was my parents' only child. Daughters can rule in their own right if their parents deem them worthy, but mine thought me too gentle to be anything more than a consort. Perhaps they were right."

Weak, in other words. Xifeng relished the scorn she felt. It made it easier to accept that she had lost all hope of ever winning this woman's love.

"But even if I'd had the choice, I would have chosen to marry anyway. There is something sacred in the binding of two lives, in the love a couple joined in such a manner may bring to this world."

Xifeng pushed away the image of Wei's face. "Love does not always come with marriage, Your Majesty. Marriage may strengthen a woman, but love weakens her. She has more to lose."

"But in weakness, you find your strength. It takes no small amount of courage to open yourself up," the Empress said gently. "You leave pieces of yourself in the ones you love. Is that not the greatest power, to endure in that way?"

"I don't know," Xifeng said in a low voice. "I may never know."

Something of the mother returned to Empress Lihua's face, though she did not take Xifeng's hand as she would have before. "I've been drawn to you since you came because I felt you truly cared about me. You needed me like I needed you, and no one at court has ever made me feel that way. They all want something *from* me—not *me,* myself. We two have been honest with each other as best we could."

And in her voice was a farewell that confirmed where Xifeng stood. There was now a distance between them that could never be bridged.

The Empress pointed to a beautiful bronze chest in the corner of the room. "There is something in there that belongs to you. Open it."

Xifeng obeyed, curious when she found a pouch tied shut with gold cord. She gasped at the riches inside: a gold-and-ivory hairpin shaped like a flowering tree, a necklace of interlocking jewels that shone like drops of blood, brooches inlaid with mother-of-pearl, and a scroll in the Imperial colors with Emperor Jun's crimson seal, unbroken.

"Those are gifts from His Majesty. To you." The Empress fixed her eyes on the wall. "They've arrived regularly for months, but I asked the eunuchs to bring them to me. I hope you'll forgive me, and I hope you understand why. But my conscience can no longer bear it."

In spite of herself, Xifeng's eyes stung at the pain in the woman's voice. She blinked as she replaced the items in the pouch, fingers lingering on the Emperor's seal. The girl she used to be, the one who might have understood that slipping, jealous fear, seemed a distant memory. That girl was gone, and the Empress knew it, too.

It was why she was saying goodbye.

Empress Lihua turned her attention back to her belly as though it were the only thing that could comfort her.

33

The scroll asked for the honor of a private audience with her. Asked, and not commanded. Xifeng accepted, pleased the Emperor would approach her from a position of respect. She pulled her hair into a plain knot, adorned with only the ivory-and-gold pin he had given her, and wore the simple gold silk under a fur-lined tunic, as the winter days had grown colder.

"Did you see how the other ladies stared at us?" she asked Kang, who escorted her across the Empress's walkway into the main palace.

"Can you blame them? You are the vision of a queen." The eunuch gave a sarcastic bow to the women peering at them from the Empress's windows. The ladies scowled and retreated behind the opaque screens.

It felt strange and natural all at once to use Empress Lihua's entrance, to see eunuchs greeting her courteously where they had once ignored her. Strange and natural to walk down gilded halls in silk and ivory with a loyal servant by her side, to have whispers and admiration follow in her wake.

"The noble families already know you," Kang murmured. "They're wondering whether they ought to spurn you or court your favor."

"If they're clever, they will choose well," Xifeng said haughtily, and he grinned at her. "I'm going to ask the Emperor for something. Master Yu has fallen from favor since Lady Sun left court. He won't be leader of the Five Tigers for long. I will ask that you take his place."

Kang looked at her with fierce pride and bent low from the waist as if she were already Empress. He was still bowing when she swept through the doors of the Emperor's apartments.

A pair of heavy brocade curtains sheltered the main room. The guards hurried to part them for her, wiping away smirks. No doubt they expected to hear interesting noises from behind the drapes in a moment, assuming she was like all the others. Easily used, easily discarded. That was their mistake, and if Emperor Jun thought the same, that was his mistake as well.

She made that clear with her modest clothing, the brisk manner in which she strode into the room, and the restrained bow she gave. There would be no fluttering of her eyelashes, no coquettish tilt of the neck. She looked the Emperor of Feng Lu in the eye like an equal.

His Majesty swept a hand toward one of the ornate chairs. "Thank you for joining me, Madam Xifeng. Please sit." His formal tone perfectly matched her manner. *Perceptive man,* she thought as she sat down. And then a gleam came into his eyes, and she knew he had seen his gold-and-ivory pin in her hair. "I've ordered tea for us," he added.

He sat down several chairs away, meticulously adjusting each fold of his simple dark blue robe. He appeared as he had when they had first met: too masculine to be a eunuch, too well kept to be less than a nobleman, and too young and unassuming to fit her idea of Emperor Jun.

Xifeng suddenly realized he was staring back at her, but did not break her gaze. She only lowered her eyes for her betters, and such a concept no longer applied to His Majesty.

"Are you a painter?" he asked, the corner of his mouth quirking.

"I beg your pardon, Your Majesty?"

"You study me as though you're about to take my likeness. I thought you might be an artist as well as a poet." His face softened to show he had taken no offense. "Come. Paint me a picture that shows me what you think of me."

Xifeng eyed him warily. "I'm not a painter."

"I mean with your words, of course." His eyes twinkled. "You can clearly think for yourself, and you don't bow and scrape like all of my wife's other women. Go on."

"I envisioned Emperor Jun as quite a different man."

"Tread softly now." His grin widened. "Remember I have an entire army at my beck and call, so take care I compare favorably to what you imagined."

She couldn't help smiling back. "I pictured a large, balding man with an impressive beard, who smelled of duck fat and wore a perpetual scowl."

"Duck fat?" He gave a great laugh like rolling thunder.

Xifeng watched him shake his head, still smiling from ear to ear, and marveled that this was a king who invaded other lands in cold blood. He held Feng Lu in the palm of one hand and with the other, beckoned lesser men to help him keep it. Yet even with all the wars he waged and the kingdoms he intimidated, he could be as merry as if he hadn't a care in the world.

He recovered from his mirth. "Tell me what you see, then. What do you make of me now? Can you tell me what sort of man I am simply by my appearance and surroundings?"

She cocked her head at him. "Is this a game, Your Majesty?"

"I like games. Don't you?" Though his voice remained cheerful, he had stopped smiling, and his features became granite once more. But she preferred him this way—it seemed his truer self, and his charming, jovial manner was too disarming for her taste.

Xifeng observed him again with care. He still reminded her of a bird of prey, sleek and silvery, a perfect blend of sinew and feathers. He had a high, open forehead and a soft mouth, but the craggy peaks of his nose and jaw belied the truth of his temperament.

"And don't worry about the army," he added, a glint of amusement appearing in his eyes. "I won't dispatch them on you. I want the truth."

"You expect the world to run on your command. Once your orders are given, they should be followed without question."

"That could be said of any king."

"You live your life with precision, but you have a soul touched by art and beauty."

Emperor Jun followed her gaze to a collection of pipes on an adjacent table, too precious to be handled by servants. He had laid them out so the end of each lined up in mathematical precision with the others. Beside them were volumes and scrolls of poetry, as neatly stacked. The whole room proved her assumption correct: he was more of a scholar than a warrior.

He wore an unreadable expression. "Continue."

"A ruler has little time for kindness. He does not give without expecting something in return. He can't afford to." *And he does not have meetings with no purpose.* She knew this private audience was a chance for him to assess her, and she needed to impress him with her sharpness—without cutting herself. "You consult the Empress in all matters. You want her to feel like she's a part of your decision-making, no matter how trivial the issue."

"Trivial?"

"Your Majesty signed a treaty with Kamatsu earlier this year, which has made other rulers uneasy. The queen of Dagovad, for instance, who supplies your army with fine horses in exchange for your support in the conflicts over eastern territories. She and her sister, the queen of Kamatsu, have not seen eye to eye for a very long time."

The corners of his mouth turned up, as they had at the moon-viewing party. "How did you come by this *trivial* information? Were you listening to the eunuchs again?"

She did not dignify that with a response. "The queen won't dare enter into war with us. She knows she'll be grossly outnumbered, but still we can't afford to make an enemy of her."

"Her people breed the finest stallions on the continent." The Emperor stroked his close-cut beard. "But to counter the first argument, she could rally the nomadic peoples with those horses as incentive. She is still capable of raising a formidable army."

"Either way, we cannot antagonize her or renege on the treaty with Kamatsu. Both options would ignite war and end trade agreements for goods too precious to lose. What we need is a gesture to show Dagovad we value their friendship. That we respect the queen, but our relations with other kingdoms are not her concern."

Emperor Jun looked amused at the use of *we* and *our,* as she knew he would be.

"Hence the festival in the queen's honor, and the envoy to her kingdom in the spring with gifts of spices and lumber." Xifeng raised an eyebrow. "This is a solution Your Majesty and your councilors must have agreed upon in minutes. But still you took the trouble to ask the Empress, knowing she would only tell you what you had already thought of. Maintaining relations is a game of strategy, and you are a master."

His eyes sparkled at her, and she released a quiet breath.

The tea came, brought in by a plain, snub-nosed maidservant. She stumbled in, seeming thrilled and terrified to be in the presence of the Emperor. She kept glancing at him, her face alight with worship and excitement, but he had eyes only for Xifeng.

When the maid left, he moved to the chair beside hers and insisted on pouring her tea. He handed her the delicate porcelain cup, his fingers brushing hers.

"Now, shall I tell you what I surmise about you?" He studied her the way she had him. His liquid eyes seemed to leave a trail of warm ink on every inch of skin they touched, but she managed to keep her composure.

"Your Majesty must do whatever pleases you."

"I see a proud woman, self-aware and unafraid. A little reserved, perhaps. They tell me you came from poverty, but you speak to me like an equal."

Xifeng caught the familiar scent of fir and sandalwood when he leaned forward, as though she sat within reach of a forest and not a man.

"You were meant for greater things and you know it. You understand, as I do, that wealth and family mean nothing if a person is not willing to prove his full worth." Emperor Jun set down his untouched cup, still watching her. "I'm an observant man, Xifeng. People assume that because I'm young and sit on a throne, I don't see the little things. The way a scholar looks at me and wonders whether I know or care that his family is one meal away from starvation. Or the way my ministers whisper behind my back when they think my orders are too harsh. But the hard decisions make us great. They make us who we are."

He was close enough to touch, to run his fingers along the tender skin of her arm. His shrewd eyes scanned her face, steel hidden behind velvet darkness, but he did not flinch from what he saw there.

And then his eyes crinkled at the corners, and she saw again the handsome man with the spark of humor she'd met over a map. "I have humble origins, too. I was a mere nobleman from the Sacred Grasslands, possessing only a drop or two of the royal blood that runs pure through my wife's veins," he said. "My father sent me to court to find a career as a minister, but I had my sights set higher than that. I exceeded his expectations, wouldn't you say?"

Xifeng couldn't help returning his smile. They were as alike as two pieces cut from the same cloth—cotton aspiring to be silk. "You won the old Emperor's affections."

"Enough to be named successor by him before his death, in title and in marriage to his wife. But I wouldn't have reached so high if I hadn't believed in myself. I knew I was worthy, despite my lower blood." He looked intently at her. "I felt in my bones that I was destined to rule this kingdom. I was destined to have three stepsons, none of whom want the crown, not even the heir. Do you believe in destiny?"

"It rules my life," she said truthfully. "I believe our lives have already been decided, and it is our purpose to make the choices that lead us to that fate."

He was sober now, gazing at her. She felt an urge to run her fingers along his cheekbone. She had never been with anyone but Wei, nor had she wanted any other. But she could easily imagine the taste of this man's mouth and the power and possessiveness with which he might kiss her. She wondered if he was thinking about how she would taste, too, as he dragged his gaze from her lips back to her eyes.

"Do you want to know the truth?" he murmured. "I don't feel like I belong, even after all these years. My blood has been tainted with that of lesser men. I'm not a pure descendant of the Dragon King or a faithful worshipper of the gods."

Xifeng lowered her eyes, searching for the right response as though it might turn up in some dusty corner of her heart. But it didn't come to her. It had died that night in the hot springs, when she had given herself to the darkness, and only emptiness lay in its place now.

"My family has never been devout," she said. "My aunt . . . my *mother* only ever prayed when she wanted something. And I never felt like the Dragon Lords could hear me, however hard I tried to find my better self through prayer."

"I, too, am trying to walk that path as we speak. I'm sending an envoy to the mountains in a month, but I still don't know what I'm asking for. Peace and plenty? The means to make the people believe I am as pious as my wife?"

"I know what Her Majesty would ask for," Xifeng said softly.

"And in doing so, she would forget to ask for her own health. This mania for a girl child has ruled her since the early days of our marriage. But I too prayed for a princess, for her sake."

"As is your role as a lover and a husband."

The Emperor turned his beautiful eyes to his tea. "A husband, yes, but a lover no more. There was never any . . . fire between us, like the kind you read about in the old poems."

Xifeng recognized her own yearning in his gaze. Their hands were a mere breath apart, and she could feel the heat, the vitality of his skin.

But a gong sounded in the corridor, and the Emperor stirred. "I'm afraid I must let you go. Thank you for your company, Xifeng. I've greatly enjoyed our conversation." Slowly, his hand lifted and touched the gold-and-ivory pin in her hair. The pin moved against her scalp, sending electrifying tingles down her neck as though she had felt his skin on hers instead.

She found, to her surprise, that she had to bite down her disappointment as she rose. It felt strange to be leaving his side. "Thank you, Your Majesty. It has been an honor."

When she passed through the heavy curtains, the heat of his eyes still branding her skin, she felt like she had left a piece of her own soul behind.

But one day soon, she would return to retrieve it.

34

Over the next few weeks, the Emperor summoned Xifeng to his side almost every day. Wei had tried to hide her and keep her to himself, but Jun took every opportunity to showcase her to others. Seeing her interest in foreign policy, he began bringing her with him to various meetings and councils, which she enjoyed as much as he'd expected.

On one occasion, she listened—with barely contained amusement—as a pack of pompous dignitaries bickered about whether they ought to lower taxes on silks exported overseas.

"These are cheap silks to make. The silkworms are fed a poisonous plant that forces them to produce more. It's cruel, but economical," one minister said. "We ought to keep the taxes high and take advantage of the profit."

"But lowering taxes will increase demand overseas," another councilor argued. "It's only a ruse, of course, so we may increase the price of the silks themselves . . ."

"People won't fall for it. And we'll still lose money."

"Then we'll raise taxes on the silks here at home to make up for any lost profit!"

Xifeng couldn't keep back her snort of derision. She felt all twenty men in the room turn to her in shock, but Emperor Jun nodded at her to speak, the corners of his mouth quirking. She had a feeling he had brought her here for a performance. Well, she would give him one.

"This argument is absurd," she said throatily, enjoying the way their faces stiffened. "The only thing you should be doing is *raising* taxes on foreign export. If you lower them anywhere, you lower them here at home."

"Your Majesty," said the councilor, as though Xifeng hadn't spoken, "do you deem it wise to have an *outsider* at our discussion? I hate to question you . . ."

"Then don't." Jun's eyes remained on Xifeng.

"I beg pardon, Sire?" the man sputtered.

"Then don't question me," the Emperor snapped, "and let her say what she wants to say. Go on, Madam Xifeng."

She folded her hands demurely in her lap. "I may seem an outsider to you, gentlemen, but I am intimately connected to the silk trade. I was a seamstress," she said, speaking more loudly to drown out their hum of disgust, "and I grew up working on silk. It's a slippery material and requires great skill to stitch. My point being: our own people know our own silk best. We know how to work with it and make it appear expensive and attractive."

The councilor had the nerve to roll his eyes at her. His name was Yee, she recalled, narrowing her eyes as she committed his appearance to memory. He would be dealt with later.

"What decision would you make?" Jun lowered his chin, regarding her as he would one of his ministers. There was no playfulness in his manner now, only respectful attention, and Xifeng saw the other men's scorn sobering to match.

"Make silks affordable to our tailors and seamstresses. Strengthen our economy by giving work to the poor. If they can afford more material, they will bring in a greater income."

Murmurs rose up around the table, some dismissive, others reluctantly agreeing.

Minister Yee snorted. "This is a soft-hearted woman's idea of politics . . ."

"And then," Xifeng continued, lacing her fingers together, "force them to contribute a large percentage of that greater income to our treasury, as farmers do. They will end up making what they always have, despite working more, and we reap the benefits."

The room went silent.

Emperor Jun stroked his beard.

"As for the overseas merchants, *double* the taxes. If people can afford exported silks, they can afford to pay the levy. They'll have no choice." Xifeng calmly took in their stunned expressions. "We hold the monopoly on silk. It is the Emperor's law that no silkworms leave the borders of our kingdom. If they don't buy from us, they don't have silk at all."

Jun's elbow rested on the arm of her chair, his hand so close she could feel its warmth.

"You say you were once poor yourself," remarked one of the elderly dignitaries, scanning her face. "Would you so quickly condemn others of your station to harder work for the same pay? That's a cold scheme."

Xifeng gave him a gentle smile. "Warmth has never filled the coffers, Minister. Royal or otherwise."

As the room erupted into murmurs and arguments, Jun's fingers found hers beneath the table, his thumb stroking her racing pulse.

From that day on, he never attended a council without her. That was the first change.

The final and complete loss of Empress Lihua's affection was the second. And as the days grew darker and snow dusted the ground, Xifeng noticed other signs of change, too.

For one, the woman who shared her bedchamber left abruptly one day, removing all of her possessions so Xifeng could have the room to herself. For another, high-ranking eunuchs who had never deigned to speak to her began to show respect and invite her to their little parties.

"No, thank you," she always said graciously. "I have a prior obligation with Kang." And they would know whom she trusted: the only eunuch who had been her friend before she'd gained favor with His Majesty.

"You put them in their place so beautifully," Kang teased her one day.

"It's an acquired skill. One you should learn, now that you have such influence." Emperor Jun had readily granted her request to elevate Kang's position according to his rising importance.

They strolled through the frost-covered gardens in time to see the Imperial physician striding across the Empress's walkway once again.

"Bohai has been here every day this week," Kang observed. "I wonder if all is well."

Empress Lihua rarely left her bed these days, but when she did, she moved slowly and cradled her belly with tender care, so as not to jostle the baby. *Foolish,* Xifeng thought, *for when the child comes, the world will hurt her anyway.* Unless she was born strong enough to resist the pain, like Xifeng.

"I hope for her sake it's a girl. It's nothing to me, of course," Kang said quickly. "It just seems a shame to suffer so for only a boy."

"*Only* a boy. Do you know how many women would kill for *only* a boy?" Xifeng watched Bohai disappear into the royal apartments. "A boy means safety, security, and respect for the queen who bears him."

A daughter would be wasted on the Empress, who was too soft and gentle and knew nothing of the struggle to survive. She would teach a girl useless things like the names of the flowers and the fables of the stars, or how to love the light of the lanterns. All of that power and influence she could wield as the mother of three royal sons, and she chose to use none of it.

"Anyone would be content in her position. She's fulfilled her duty by providing heirs, and now that her sons are grown, she could focus on herself and on making the Emperor happy. He would never have to turn to another woman." She paused, realizing the irony in her words. She had hated Lady Sun, once, for turning the Emperor's head and hurting Empress Lihua. And now Xifeng walked the same thin line. *No,* she told herself. *Not quite the same.*

"How is His Majesty? I see his gifts have only grown more expensive."

Xifeng glanced sideways at him. "Yesterday, it was a barbarian's fiddle, one of only two made from a pine tree that grows in the Mountains of Enlightenment. The day before, it was a tin of flower tea from the Summer Isles he thought I'd enjoy."

Despite the chill air, the eunuch fluttered his fan in delight. "Don't forget that beautiful silk robe and those glass flowers. And, of course, your freedom." It had pleased him to no end that Xifeng, like the Empress and concubines, could now leave the city of women whenever she wished as long as she brought her eunuchs for protection. "But what about that friend of yours?"

"What about him?" Xifeng snapped.

She woke each morning with the reality of Wei, no matter how hard she tried to steel herself against the pain. She had loved him and she had forsaken him. He had fulfilled his usefulness to her and it was time to let him go. Jun was her future, not some childhood lover who could no more take her to her fate than he could to the stars. But as frequently as she reminded herself of this, it still hurt that she hadn't heard from Wei in months. Her budding romance with the Emperor was common knowledge by now, and Wei had to know as everyone else did.

She took Kang's arm. "I'm sorry. I didn't mean to speak so sharply."

"Never apologize to me. You are above that. I only mentioned him because a message arrived from him today." He pulled a scroll from his sleeve and handed it to her.

Xifeng accepted it with mingled dread and relief and read the short message: *Meet me in the gardens tonight.* There were no words of love—only one terse sentence.

"How he must despise me," she murmured, thinking of the last time they had been together in those gardens. "You don't blame me like he does, do you?"

"For seeking a better future for yourself?" The eunuch shook his head. "It may be best not to go tonight or to see him anymore, Xifeng. You are too high above him now."

"This was his greatest fear," she said quietly. "He wanted to hide and protect me."

"Then you know you've made the right choice. There is only opportunity, and those too afraid to grasp it for themselves. Don't let them weigh down your wings."

Hideki had once described the Imperial Court as a sand pit. Xifeng supposed it was still an apt description, but what he hadn't known was that climbing the pit was simple. All one had to do was let the spikes emerge . . . allow long, lethal thorns to burst from the skin. One had to stab into others and climb over them, slick with blood, because the sun shone at the top, and that was all that mattered in this sick and lonely life.

Xifeng tucked the scroll into her own robes. Kang was right; she was out of Wei's reach now. Still, she couldn't help longing to see him, and she decided to go, to assure herself he was well and happy. It was what she owed to a childhood friend; that was all.

They walked past the half-frozen pond and Xifeng caught sight of her reflection warming the chilly waters with shades of black and ruby. She paused to admire herself.

"Not even you are immune to your own charms."

Xifeng smiled archly at him. "If my beauty is my greatest weapon, vanity is the shield that protects me."

Kang simpered and raised both hands, showing he passed no judgment, and she turned back to her reflection. Looking as she did, no man would resist her or choose another to love. She would not fail where Guma and Mingzhu had. They had let Long slip away with their self-pity and frail spirit, and even Empress Lihua had tolerated her husband having other "wives."

"I will never tolerate a concubine," she told her exquisite reflection. "My husband might please himself however he chooses, but I will be the only wife and consort, queen above all."

She knew her own worth. She would seize her destiny with all the strength and spirit within her, and bend them all to her will: every man kneeling and every woman overshadowed.

Xifeng lifted her face to the sun, its warmth like a promise on her skin.

35

Xifeng wrapped her fur-lined, plum silk robe tightly around herself as she strode through the tunnels with Kang and three other eunuchs in tow. In the musty passage, she detected the heat of the hot springs and felt a tug of longing. Perhaps she ought to try conjuring Guma once more. Despite the harsh words they'd exchanged, Xifeng had tried to reach her several times since that night, longing for her advice. She had even sent money and a few of Jun's gifts to the village at great expense. But no matter how much incense she used or how many presents she delivered, there was no response from Guma.

Later, she told herself.

First, she had to find out why Wei wanted to meet tonight.

The eunuchs waited by the entrance as she entered the palace gardens, sweeping her eyes from side to side for Wei's familiar form. Although she understood why his message had been terse and simple, without words of love, the hurt lodged itself in her throat. She didn't deserve him; she never had, and now he must know it, too.

"I'm here."

She turned to see Wei regarding her from the shadows. He stepped out to meet her, but kept his arms behind his back instead of holding them out to her as he did before. They stood apart like performers in a tragic play.

"I'm glad to see you." She moved closer and lifted her hand to his face, but he flinched and turned away. "What's wrong? Why did you want to meet?"

He rubbed a hand over his head, his eyes on the ground. "The General has ordered me to accompany the Emperor's envoy in a week."

She watched him pace, his shoulders taut with tension. His breath emerged on the air in puffs of angry smoke, and he looked anywhere, anywhere but at her. "I'm happy for you, Wei. He must value you a great deal to include you on such an important mission."

"He said he'd make me a captain if I came back."

Xifeng paused. "*If* you came back? Shiro told me you would all return in a month."

"No."

She gave a short laugh of frustration. "Then how long until you return?"

Wei looked at her at last, and she saw he had been crying. It made him seem smaller, younger, and the laughter died on her lips. "I'm not coming back."

She swallowed around the lump in her throat. "You can't mean that."

"They say the Empress is failing. She won't make it through this birth. And with her gone, you can have *him* and these visits you've been paying to his bed will become respectable."

His flat, defeated voice frightened her. This was not like the fight they'd had at Akira's, when she had sensed him drifting away—this felt like he was already on the opposite shore, turning his back on her. She wanted him to rage and scream, drive his fist into a tree, threaten to rip Jun apart. *That* was the Wei she knew. *That* was the Wei who would fight the gods in the heavens if it meant he could have her.

Part of her felt grateful . . . relieved. At last, they both knew the truth. There was no lie left between them, no misunderstanding. They would set each other free. She would be Jun's Empress, and Wei would lead some life far, far away, safe from her reach.

And yet another part of her clung to the memory of his love, to the knowledge that he had once been the only star in her dark sky. And if that light should go out . . . she would truly have nothing left of the person she had once been.

She spoke in a low, desperate voice. "I have *never* once gone to the Emperor's bed. What do you take me for, another one of his whores? You should know me better than that."

He spun so quickly, they were face-to-face before she'd had a chance to inhale. "Do I?" he snarled. "Do I know you at all, Xifeng? Tell me where Lady Sun is. No one has seen her in the whole of the Imperial City, no monastery, no teahouse, no inn. Did she vanish into the Great Forest alone and on foot, late at night? After a life of pampering, she just decided to run headfirst into the wilderness without her precious son?"

"What exactly are you accusing me of?" she demanded, her face inches from his.

"All I know is you're different. You've changed."

Xifeng scoffed. "This again!"

"You've changed into *her*!" Wei roared. "She's been inside you all this time, egging you on, taunting you to hurt others. You think I don't know why you wouldn't love me? Because that snake has been poisoning you this whole time. You have no creature inside you but Guma."

In his eyes she saw agony, breathtaking in its hopelessness. It would always be there now, no matter what she said or did, and knowing that made her heart ache and ache. She wrapped her arms around him and he shook with emotion, but did not move away. "I do what I must to secure my position, so I can help you when you need it." She almost believed it herself. "Whatever happens, wherever I go, do you doubt I wouldn't use my influence to elevate you as well?"

"But where do *we* figure into your plans, you and I? Do you truly think of me at all, when that head of yours is plotting and scheming? Can you imagine a future in which we could be together? Because I can't. Not anymore."

"I love you, Wei. I love you as much as I can . . ."

He shook his head. "It's not enough."

She clutched the front of his tunic. "I love you as much as I will ever love anyone."

"You can't have everything, Xifeng. You can't have him and still have me, too. He doesn't share and neither do I." For the first time, he pushed her away gently. "You were never mine, but you'll be his. And I won't stand by and watch you tie your life to another man. Not even if it's the Emperor. Not even if it's me you think it'll help."

She was in free fall, flailing through the air for something, anything, to keep from crashing to the ground. He meant what he said; he always did. He would ride away from her forever, after all they'd been through. She knew it was time to let him go, but now, faced with the reality of it, she thought it might be the death of her if she did.

Her whole body shuddered with panic. Perhaps Guma had been mistaken. Perhaps they had thought about this all wrong. Xifeng had been so intent on becoming Empress, she had forgotten the warrior card that promised Wei's fate was tied to hers. How could he be the sacrifice, yet also inextricably linked to her forever? If he went away, if that part of her destiny changed . . . what else would? Would her fate still come to light?

Wei watched her struggle, shaking his head slowly at her silence. "What did you imagine, Xifeng? That you'd be safe and warm with him and I'd linger on, watching you from afar and writing you lovesick notes? How cruel and selfish you are. How vain."

She put a hand on either side of his anguished face. "You know me better than anyone in this world," she pleaded. "You know me better than even Guma and you still love me. I will never find anyone like you again in my whole life. I can't let you go, Wei. You belong with me."

"You say this to me," he whispered, "but do you believe it? When the time comes, will you even remember? How long before you forget me?"

"I would never forget you."

Tears slipped, one after the other, onto his unyielding face. "But you wouldn't choose me, either. I've been a fool, setting my heart on something I could never have. I would have given you anything, done anything if only you had loved me." Her hands were still on his face, and he placed his over them. "We've played this game long enough, my love. Let it end." He removed her hands gently and walked away, his breath a ghost of fog on the air.

Every muscle in Xifeng's body was tensed to run after him, to fall at his feet, to beg. He had always been a constant in her life. However much she'd hurt him, Wei had always been there—he would always come back. So she resisted the urge to go to him. Any second now, he would turn around and take her in his arms again. Any second now, he would come back and tell her he hadn't meant anything he'd said.

Any second now, she told herself as his back disappeared into the wintry night.

She waited in the frosted silence.

But he did not come back.

36

The morning of the envoy's departure dawned bright. Xifeng blinked against the sunlight reflecting off the snow, watching the soldiers mount their horses. Empress Lihua was not present, having passed a difficult night, and neither was her husband, who was preoccupied with military matters. Xifeng was glad for it, so she could focus the whole of her attention on Wei.

He stood securing his belongings to his horse, his jaw set and his eyes determinedly averted from her. And though he was still there, she felt his loss as keenly as if she'd been scraped raw from the inside. While she had been flirting and sipping tea with Jun, Wei had been suffering, gathering the courage to say what he had to. The memory of the tears streaming down his face threatened to break her. Though it still angered her, she felt the truth of everything he had said—that she was cruel and selfish and vain—in her very blood and marrow.

Shiro approached, pulling his horse alongside the railing where she stood. "I'm off to the mountains," he said with forced cheer. "Pray for our safe return."

Xifeng tried to remember her manners. "How is Akira?"

"She's going to have a child," Shiro said with a half smile, and Xifeng felt another stab of pain. Love and life came so easily to everyone else. If she had married Wei, she might be expecting his child now, too, and he wouldn't be leaving her. "Only a few months more, but it's been hard for her. She hasn't been well. I hate to go, but I have no choice in the matter."

"His Majesty won't let you stay with your pregnant wife?"

The dwarf gave her that half smile again. "We don't all have your influence with him."

Xifeng had the grace to blush. "I'll send someone to visit Akira every week while you're gone. She will be cared for, I promise."

"And you?" he asked gently. "Will you be cared for?"

She blinked away tears. "Not in the way I'm used to. Not anymore."

He waited, but Xifeng couldn't go on. She knew if she kept talking, she would cry, and she couldn't do that to Wei. What could she say, anyway? *I loved him and I threw happiness away with both hands.*

But in his quiet way, Shiro seemed to know what she couldn't express. He touched her hand, and the comforting warmth of his fingers gave her some illusion of solace. "Goodbye, my dear," he said kindly, and when he turned away, she met Wei's eyes for one blinding moment. She thought she would collapse under the finality of that gaze.

The envoy turned and left the palace gates, and with them rode the man who had deserved her heart more than anyone. She imagined them returning with one fewer rider—imagined watching for Wei's familiar form, but not seeing him. Never seeing him again.

She clenched a fist against her mouth, willing him to turn his head.

My heart is yours, she would tell him with only her eyes, so he would see, so he would understand how difficult it had been for her, too. *My heart has always been yours.*

But he faced forward until they disappeared. And she knew the boy who had loved her, who had woven wildflowers in her long inky hair, had gone from her forever.

Lady Sun lived on.

She certainly *looked* like she did. Something in the water of the hot springs had ensured the preservation of her body, which was as fresh as the day Xifeng had put it there three months ago. Her face was pale and peaceful in its halo of charred-wood hair, like she had simply fallen asleep in the water, her lips parted slightly as though awaiting a kiss.

Xifeng half expected her to open her eyes any moment. She found herself returning to the cavern again and again to see if the woman would finally awaken. She roused herself from sleep in a cold sweat most mornings, imagining it had happened overnight and Lady Sun's body would be gone the next time she came, off to tell the truth of what had happened the night she vanished.

"I'm not surprised you've chosen to haunt me this way," she told the concubine. "It's a common theme in my life, you know."

There was the pain of Wei's desertion, always lurking in the back of her mind. There was her own elusive destiny, which seemed more tenuous every day instead of becoming clearer. Empress Lihua might be ill and weak, but she still lived. The one most likely to be Xifeng's greatest threat—the queen favored by the *tengaru,* the Fool—still lived.

And there was Guma's continued silence, despite how hard Xifeng tried to reach her. The dwindling supply of incense and growing pile of dead rats in the water were proof of that, but no amount of lifeblood seemed to push aside that veil between them again. She had allowed herself to contemplate, just once, the possibility of finding another human heart, but the risks were too great. Besides, Lady Sun had been a threat and had deserved her fate, but Xifeng couldn't justify finding someone innocent to use.

What had happened to her mother? Had Guma died in that rundown house, alone with only Ning, the hired girl, to help her? Alone and forsaken, as Xifeng herself was.

Not alone, the whisper came. *Never alone.*

But she did not wish to speak to the Serpent God just now, with his knowing eyes, so she rose and left her sanctuary. She passed through the entrance into the city of women, tugging her fur cap around her ears. It had been another gift from Jun, who was too preoccupied these days to meet her more than once a week.

News had come from afar that mercenaries had captured the Empress's second son on another continent. The Crown Prince insisted on going himself to lead the negotiations for his brother's life, and it took all of the Emperor's power to keep him at home. The youngest prince was deathly ill, and if the Crown Prince should go, Jun would risk losing all three of his heirs.

"How joyful you must be," Xifeng murmured, imagining Lady Sun listening from her watery grave. "If all of Lihua's sons die, yours is next in the line of succession." Unless, of course, a fourth legitimate heir were born—provided Empress Lihua delivered her child safely.

Night had fallen in the frozen garden and Xifeng had missed supper, but she decided to have a servant bring a meal to her chamber. Maybe Kang would join her. He had grown more popular since attaining his higher position, but he would gladly leave the gambling and gossip of the other eunuchs to keep her company, if she wished.

She spied two of Bohai's assistants on the walkway to the Empress's apartments. One of them was the well-trained young man Bohai had agreed to send into the Imperial City once a week at Xifeng's request, to attend to Akira. It amused Xifeng that in doing so, the physician was unknowingly caring for his own daughter.

Back in her chamber, Xifeng shook the snow from her cap and cloak. "You there," she called to the guard, "bring some more candles to light my room."

But the figure that moved from the shadows was not a eunuch. It held a long kitchen knife in its hand, the blade gleaming in the dim light, and she hardly knew what had happened until the tip of it had stabbed her once, twice, three times.

She was prone on the floor before she felt a burning sensation and the warm gush of blood. A blinding, tearing pain roared in her chest and shoulder, and then the world went black.

37

When Xifeng returned to consciousness, she found herself in bed, her robe lowered over one heavily bandaged shoulder. A bloodstain flowered through the cotton wrappings, and an anxious lady-in-waiting hovered over her. Two eunuchs talking quietly in the corner approached when they saw her eyes flutter open.

"How are you, my lady?" one of them asked. "Bohai gave you something for the pain before he left to attend to Her Majesty."

Xifeng sat up, testing her shoulder. Whatever Bohai had given her had worked, for she felt no sharp pain—only a dull ache that throbbed every time she moved her arm. "I'm all right." She swung her feet to the floor, seeing blood-soaked cloths piled on the table. "Where is Kang? And did they find my attacker?"

"Kang was coming to see you," the eunuch explained. "He saw her attacking you and shouted for help, then ran after her. It's been almost an hour and they still haven't returned."

Every muscle in her body went rigid at the feminine pronoun. "Who was it? Who did such a poor job of trying to kill me?"

The eunuchs exchanged glances. "Lady Meng. She was drunk and barefoot in the snow and I don't believe it will take long to find her. She's as . . . troubled as everyone says. We heard her screaming something as she ran," he added, flushing. "I don't recall what it was."

Xifeng rolled her eyes. "Tell me."

"S-she said you weren't satisfied with just the Crown Prince, so you had to make yourself His Majesty's new . . . whore. And she said you had poisoned him against her and influenced him to get rid of her."

"She gives me entirely too much credit. I need to find Kang. Alone." Xifeng tugged on a thick robe and slippers, ignoring their protests as she stormed back out into the frigid night.

Another inch of snow had fallen, showing clear tracks: one larger and heavier, and the other smaller and barefoot. They led to the underground passageway, where no guards stood, and Xifeng felt a stab of foreboding as she descended.

She knew where they had gone . . . as improbable as it seemed, for she had never told a soul about the hot springs.

The lanterns were all lit in the cavern, illuminating the scene: Kang with his back to Xifeng, standing over the body of Lady Meng. He gripped a knife in one hand, and when Xifeng came closer, she saw the woman had died from multiple stab wounds. Her chest had been torn open and bloomed like a flower, the jagged petals of her ribs reaching for an impossible sun.

The springs bubbled and roared as she gasped out, "Kang?"

A monster turned around.

There was no sign of her friend in his face. He wore a feral, predatory expression, and his smile was an obscene blood-red slash. The lidless eyes had no whites; they were two black holes glistening in the darkness. He was the monk from the encampment, from her dreams, from the nightmarish bronze mirror at the trade market. She had once thought Guma might have sent him to follow her—how wrong she had been, for no human could possibly control this creature.

Xifeng stood her ground, though her palms moistened and her heart thundered, making the wound in her shoulder sting. "You," she uttered. "You've been with me all this time?"

The monster stared back without blinking. "I am your slave, dark queen. Your steward and confidante," he said in Kang's voice, and indicated Lady Meng's corpse. "And now I am your huntsman as well. Don't you remember the last time you saw me?"

A figure robed and hooded, eyes glittering as he tore viciously into Lady Sun's ribs . . .

"You're the Serpent God's servant," she gasped, and his ghastly mouth spread wider.

He held his arms out and his long sleeves billowed like banners of war. "This is my true form. My harmless, bumbling human appearance requires me to expend magical energy. I take the trouble to do so in the palace, but I want you to know . . . I want you to see me as I am."

She took a tentative step forward and the monk-creature placed the concubine's knife on the ground. He backed away courteously so she could examine the body. In death, Lady Meng's once pretty face resembled a drained, contorted melon. Kang had stabbed her through the chest a dozen times, and the deep blue silk she wore was black from the blood that had gushed out.

It seemed like years ago that Xifeng had bemoaned her fate in the village while Lady Meng rode past in a palanquin.

"I saw her with that knife and I knew she had come for you. I was too late to stop her." He sank to his knees. "Forgive me, my queen, and accept her heart as my gift of apology."

Xifeng closed her eyes. The girl's lifeless face felt too much like a different version of her own future. Back in her town, she had longed to be Lady Meng. If that silly wish had been granted, she too might have been a concubine; she too might have been overpowered by desperation, by the tie to a man who neither loved nor valued her. By her hopeless longing for another and her sheer, breathtaking worthlessness.

But now Xifeng held the Emperor in the palm of her hand, and Lady Meng was dead. *How generous is fate,* she thought. *And how cruel.*

She bent to close the girl's eyes, and underneath her pity grew the drumbeat of a relentless hunger, humming in her veins. "Tell me everything," she commanded Kang.

"I was born to a poor village fisherman not far from your town," he said softly. "When I was twelve, the black snake lured me to the cave as he had done with your mother. He transformed into a man and promised me wealth and power beyond my dreams. He invited me to join him and his priests."

Kang spoke of a cave that was merely the mouth and throat of an entire world that had sprung up beneath the ground. There were dank woodlands, a serpentine jungle pungent with the breath of toxic flowers, an ocean that burned hotter than fire, and dagger-sharp mountains stabbing into the dark. This labyrinthine world housed the Serpent God's demonic monastery.

"It is a sordid reflection of the heavens," Kang whispered reverently. "The opposite of all that is goodness and light, balancing the whole universe. When I turned fifteen, he unleashed me from this dark world to establish myself in the Empress's service and wait here for you. I pretended to be weak. I allowed Lady Sun to have me beaten so everyone could see how harmless, how silly poor, fat Kang was." His mouth cracked in a humorless grin.

Xifeng looked into his bottomless eyes. "I saw you at the encampment and the market."

"When the time came, he gave me the task of protecting you and ensuring your entry into court. The Serpent God knows you have great enemies. Someone outside of the palace wanted so much to destroy you, they would have killed all in your party if given the chance."

Xifeng's blood froze. "The assassins who attacked us in the forest and killed two of Shiro's men. Then they *were* sent for me. But by whom? I thought Empress Lihua . . ."

"It was not her, but a threat far greater than any found on this earth. That is all I know. The Serpent God sent me to summon the *tengaru,* to stave off the impending violence in their forest—and rescue you. I had to get you to the palace alive."

That was why the *tengaru* had treated their group with fear and distrust. "The demons sensed something odd, something wrong about you. And therefore, me."

Kang sneered. "Those mules boast about their magic when in truth, they would bow to the Serpent God in a second if he bothered to challenge them." His nostrils flared. "There is an army in that world below the earth, my queen, a dark legion of men and beasts he created. In the sunlight, they appear as black snakes, spiraling in the depths. And they are at your command."

The words raised the hairs on her arms and neck. "An army . . . at *my* command?"

The monk-creature's mouth was an abyss of sharp teeth and scarlet tongue. "You are the consort chosen by His Dark Majesty. He saw you in the sands of time and the winds of fortune. Always, he sensed your presence," he said. "The great queen who would help him overtake the continent that should have been his from the beginning. His mark is on every kingdom, mountain, and ocean. The arrogant lordling who called himself the Dragon King could never have dreamed the lowly Lord of Surjalana would be so worthy of that title. And the Lord of Surjalana, the Serpent God, in turn, dreamed of a queen worthy of ruling alongside him."

Xifeng felt this truth wrap around her like an embrace.

Hunger throbbed in her veins, and her tongue emerged from her mouth, licking the salt of her lips like it was the sweetest lifeblood. Deep in the remote corners of her mind, the apple tree appeared. How far it seemed from her now, how removed. Perhaps it had never been meant for her after all; perhaps she didn't want it to be. She had been chosen for something far, far greater.

"He found the witch who would be your mother and orchestrated your birth. He gave her the incense of snakeskin and black spice, and he left her the book of poetry to remind her what she owed him." As Kang spoke, images flashed before Xifeng's eyes: a woman screaming on blood-splattered grass, begging for death as a baby clawed its way out. "When she transmitted his teachings to you, she passed his spirit on as well, without knowing. And you allowed him to manifest his powers and thoughts within you."

"But she denounced him. She burned what he had given her and turned her back on him."

The monk-creature laughed softly. "She imagined herself to be free, the silly woman. But her soul became his the first time she adopted his teachings. It wouldn't matter if she threw the cards of fortune into the deepest ocean. Once he takes hold, he never lets go."

Xifeng exhaled. "It's true, then. I told Guma he might be controlling her . . . controlling *me* and my destiny all along."

"But *you* made the choices to get there. *You* did what it took to get yourself to the palace, to defeat your enemies, to put yourself before Emperor Jun. Your own two feet walked that dark road, as the Serpent God hoped they would." Kang took a step closer, his dead eyes glimmering. "He is your father, your lover, your true king, and the maker of your fate. He loves you as no one ever has or ever will. Every heart you take, every drop of lifeblood you drink, brings you closer to him. The darkness you felt inside was his protection. He will be with you always and forever."

"What would he have me do?"

The monster lowered himself beside Xifeng, his icy fingers running down her cheek. "Take your place as supreme Empress over all of Feng Lu. Strengthen yourself with the hearts of lesser beings and allow him to speak and act through you. And in return, you will have the whole of his power at your disposal," Kang murmured. "There is only one true god, and it is him. You will gain control of the continent and deploy your army, and together the two of you will finish the work he started. *This* is your destiny. This is what your clumsy mother tried to engineer, believing it to be her own wish."

Xifeng opened her eyes to see Guma's face floating in the mirror-water.

A savage smile tore across Kang's face. "She has been most useful to His Dark Majesty. But now her time is over and you must think of her no more. She has served her purpose."

"What do you mean?"

The vision in the mirror-water changed to show, of all people, Wei. He galloped on his black steed like a creature of the dark world, bent forward through the Great Forest on his way to Guma. In his hands, he clasped a moon-steel sword and a bloody chrysanthemum—the warrior the cards of fortune had shown her, whose destiny was tied to hers.

"I used him to gain your trust," Kang said. "I arranged for you to meet him so you could see me as your friend. And now he will fulfill *his* purpose. He still loves you, the honorable fool he is. He thinks he can save you, and that your salvation will come with Guma's end. He thinks you'll be free at last." His lidless eyes stared into hers, and his next words were shards piercing her flesh. "He left the envoy to kill your mother."

"No," Xifeng cried, hot panic rising in her like bile, and it became a scream. "No!"

The monster's hand came down on her shoulder like a vise. "There is nothing we can do for her, and nothing more we need her for," he said soothingly. "Her time has ended."

Guma, who had fed and clothed her, given her all she could, and taught her all she knew. *That* was what a mother did for her children—she made them strong and prepared them for the hardship and brutality of life. Guma had endured pain and fear, but she had still raised Xifeng. *I wanted the world for you.* The soft, tender mother Xifeng had imagined in Mingzhu and Lihua had been a childish illusion. She'd had a real mother, and she had abandoned her.

"Why?" she sobbed. "Why must I suffer like this? Why must I always be the one to lose and to struggle with the darkness?"

The emptiness inside her roared. She had deserted Guma, and now she would never hear her say, at last, that she loved Xifeng. Wei had taken that from her, that hot-blooded warrior who had loved her so deeply. Once her lover, and now her mortal enemy.

"Wei," she breathed, and it was a curse. She raked her fingers in the dirt, imagining shredding his beautiful golden skin into ribbons of flesh. The warrior on the card had held a bloodstained flower . . . but whose blood was it?

Kang knelt before her with the concubine's knife in his hands. "Being chosen by the Serpent God and facing this darkness makes you special," he said in a low voice. "It sets you apart. Why would you want to be like everyone else?"

Behind him, in the waterfall, she saw her own beautiful face. Slowly, it mutated into something horrid: the fresh youth became a pockmarked, wrinkled visage ravaged by the cruelty of time. She trembled as the ruthless mirror-water stripped her of her beauty. Wei would not have loved her without it, she felt certain. Lihua would not have been drawn to her, and Jun would not have pursued her.

Your beauty is all you are, and all you have, Guma had once told her. *Your only weapon.*

"You have a choice." Kang's words sounded hauntingly familiar.

Once before, Xifeng had chosen to accept the Serpent God's assistance. She had let him help her destroy Lady Sun. This time, he was asking something of *her*—something that would ultimately help her as much as it did him.

She could refuse him. She could return to her town in poverty and obscurity. She could grow old and ugly alone while the concubines' bodies remained beautiful forever, locked in time in the springs. And everything she had been through—including Wei's loss and Guma's death—would have been for nothing.

Or Xifeng could accept him and fulfill the destiny even Guma had not fully understood. She could remain forever young and beautiful, a powerful Empress and the Serpent God's consort, living on the hearts of her enemies. She could surrender what was left of the light others had seen in her—the light Wei had taken with him when he left her. She could give up her old self to the darkness, completely, with both hands open.

Do not resist me, echoed the voice she knew so well.

Once again, she had a choice to make. So Xifeng chose.

"I have no intention of resisting you," she said.

"Why would you want to be like everyone else?" Kang repeated.

And she agreed with him. She agreed in the way her fingers closed on the blade, in the way she used it to dig into Lady Meng's chest, and in the way she closed her lips around the blistering heat of the concubine's heart. She was special, with every bite, every stream of blood spurting from her ravenous mouth. She was a monster, a bride of the darkness, and she rose to face her destiny as though it were the blood-red sunrise of a new day.

38

Xifeng returned to the royal apartments to hear screaming from Empress Lihua's bedchamber. Maidservants and ladies-in-waiting rushed in and out with pale faces, their eyes wide with fear. The Imperial physician stood in the corridor barking orders to his assistants, who raced past without a second glance.

"Is it happening? Is the child coming?" she asked one of the ladies.

"No," was the grim reply. "Her Majesty has been poisoned."

Kang appeared beside her in his human form. Though his face was as round and friendly as ever, Xifeng knew she would always see those lidless eyes and that gash of a mouth whenever she looked at him now. Despite Lihua's piercing screams, he wore an impassive expression that didn't completely hide a flicker of satisfaction.

Lady Sun and Lady Meng had each paid the ultimate price. And now Kang's next victim—and, by default, Xifeng's—would be the Empress, a woman who had once treated her like a daughter.

But what sorrow and revulsion she felt faded quickly. Lihua was the Fool and had to be eliminated, no matter the cost. No one with a destiny like Xifeng's could afford to care or love, not when it came to protecting what was rightfully hers. *Love is weakness.* How right Guma had been.

"Did you do this?" she whispered to Kang.

"I told you Lady Sun once accused me of stealing black spice. She gave me the idea, really. I went back to Bohai's stores and took some later, though I *certainly* did not let a concubine catch me," he added, chuckling.

Xifeng gave a slow nod. Smoked in great quantities, black spice would cause a prolonged, deathlike sleep, but when taken directly through the mouth—as Lihua had—it became a potent toxin. Kang had been slowly poisoning Her Majesty for a year or more, likely in minuscule, undetectable amounts. Xifeng thought of all the times she had noted Empress Lihua's pallor, her shaking hands, her lack of appetite. Over many months, bit by bit, the substance had built up in her body and her symptoms had worsened . . . into this.

Another scream ripped through the air. Xifeng encountered a devastating scene when she and Kang entered the royal bedchamber. Empress Lihua had been restrained to her bed with sheets and blankets. Telltale red scratches covered her arms and legs, clearly made by her own fingernails. Blood splattered her sheets, which the maidservants were trying to change while avoiding the Empress's foaming, gnashing mouth.

She looked as Xifeng had never seen her. This was not the gentle, soft-hearted woman who had confessed her desire for a daughter. This was a wild, untamed animal, with blazing eyes like those of the *tengaru.* The huge, swollen belly on her frail body looked obscene and unnatural, and it shook with the rest of her when she spotted Xifeng.

"Murderess!" the Empress shrieked. "You poisoned me. You . . . poisoned me!"

In her frenzy, one of the sheets tore, releasing her wrist. She immediately used the fingers of her free hand to scratch at her thighs and knees, leaving scarlet tears in their wake. Two eunuchs leapt into action with a new sheet, apologizing to her as they re-bound her wrist.

Bohai stood nearby, perspiration beading his forehead as he crushed leaves into powder. "You must be calm, Your Majesty," he pleaded. "I'm making something to help you sleep."

The Empress strained and struggled, her eyes feverish. "It was her, it was her, it was her."

"Xifeng could not possibly have done what Her Majesty suggests," Kang said in a low, urgent voice to Bohai and Madam Hong. "The Empress is always surrounded by guards for her protection, and Xifeng is always with her own guards, including myself."

The physician nodded apologetically. "Her Majesty is too ill to know what she's saying." He tipped the medicine into the woman's mouth as a eunuch held her head. Within minutes, the Empress stopped thrashing and lay still. Her head lolled to one side and at last, it was quiet. "Change the bedclothes now and get me some cloth to dress her wounds," Bohai told the maids, wiping his forehead, then turned to Xifeng again. "How's that shoulder of yours?"

Xifeng had forgotten her own injury. "It's fine. What happened to the Empress?"

"I don't know," the physician muttered. "I make her medicine myself every day. I haven't let another soul touch it, and every morsel of food she eats is tasted by a servant first."

"Are you certain she's being poisoned?" Madam Hong asked, wringing her hands.

Bohai nodded, distressed. "She shows indications of long-term poisoning. The dosage has been increased slowly, gradually. Clever to do it in such a way that I wouldn't recognize the signs until too late."

"How terrible," Kang murmured. "I recall the Crown Prince accusing Lady Sun of poisoning the Empress, before she left. Could there be truth in his claim?"

Xifeng nodded in approval. "Perhaps we know at last why she abandoned court. She is far from the reach of the Emperor's justice by now." *As far as death, in fact.*

The physician's lips thinned. "Lady Sun or no, this has been going on for months . . . perhaps years. There is an imbalance of the elements in Her Majesty's constitution. The tone of her skin, the vomiting, the seizures and confusion." He sighed and turned to Kang. "Did you find Lady Meng?"

"I'm sorry to say she drowned herself, sir. I found her body half frozen in the pond. Unfortunately the face has been . . ." The eunuch glanced at Xifeng and Madam Hong in a show of fearing for their delicate sensibilities. "She seems to have lost control of her drinking. She damaged herself with the knife in her frenzy, but I knew it was her from her clothing."

Xifeng wondered whom he had killed to dress up as Lady Meng. Some unsuspecting maid, perhaps, who happened to be in the wrong place at the wrong time. More lives to cover up the lives they'd already taken. More deaths to pull over their innocence like a shroud.

Bohai sighed heavily. "I'll inspect her later, when I've finished here. The Emperor will have to be notified as soon as he awakens."

"I'll see a message is sent to him immediately," Kang promised.

"You need to get some rest," Bohai told Xifeng. "You've had quite an ordeal tonight."

If only he knew the true ordeal, she thought as she left the room obediently.

If only he knew the Xifeng to whom he had just spoken was a different being from the one whose shoulder he had bound.

39

The Emperor came as soon as he could to see Xifeng. He dismissed the eunuchs and took her into his arms carefully, to avoid jostling her shoulder. His embrace felt strange and familiar all at once—the sensation of arms around her that did not belong to Wei, of warm hands on her back that were not his. And when he pulled away, she was momentarily surprised to look up into a face that was not Wei's.

He scanned her face and swore as his anxious gaze returned to her wounded shoulder. "What you must have endured. Thank the gods she did nothing worse."

"I am sorry for her," Xifeng said, and meant it. Her final act of kindness to Lady Meng had been to close her staring eyes, shielding her from her last glimpse of the callous world.

Jun dropped his arms, seeming to realize how close they were, and stepped back respectfully. "Bohai told me what the Empress said to you in her feverish state. I apologize for her unjust accusations."

"It isn't your fault."

"Isn't it?" He turned to the window, where snow fell steadily from an ice-gray sky. "Sometimes I wonder if I corrupt these women merely by being myself. I've lost two concubines, and now I may lose my wife as well. There must be something about me that poisons them." He gave a heavy sigh. "My youngest stepson is ill and dying, and now I have sent my heir, the Crown Prince, to *his* death."

"His Highness insisted on going to lead the negiotations for his brother's life," Xifeng said gently. "He told me himself how much he worried about the second prince fighting overseas. He will not rest until he brings him home alive."

"He won't succeed."

"But he was very adamant at the council that . . ."

"He won't succeed," Jun repeated. There was a long silence before he spoke again. "A letter came months ago. His brother has been killed by the mercenaries who captured him. They are sending his head to me as proof of his death."

Xifeng stared at his rigid back, at the shape of his bowed head.

"I kept this to myself. I let the whole court believe otherwise, including the Crown Prince, because I knew he'd insist on going if he thought his brother was still alive. And now he sails into enemy territory to save someone who is already dead." The knuckles of Jun's tightly clasped hands turned white. "Tell me, Xifeng. Did I do wrong? Will you turn against me, knowing I've as good as killed my heir?"

She did not speak, but placed a hand on his warm back. His shoulders rose and fell with the slow, shuddering breath he released.

"He never wanted the throne. He never said as much in my hearing, but we all knew it." Jun shook his head. "It wasn't until he publicly condemned Lady Sun at the Moon Festival that I wondered whether he had changed his mind. I knew he hated her for disrespecting his mother. But I suspected it was also a personal attack on me. Perhaps he had decided he *did* want to be Emperor after all, and sought to discredit and eventually exile me."

"And so he had to be destroyed." Lady Sun's dead face swam behind her closed lids. Xifeng understood him completely—oh, how she understood him.

"I have an old, sick wife and two stepsons who are dead or dying. In time, if Lihua did not recover, I could choose a young Empress to give me sons of my blood and secure the throne. The Crown Prince was the only thing left standing in my way."

Xifeng came close and put her arms around him, resting her cheek against his back. She might never truly love this man and he might never truly love her, but they needed each other, two ruthless souls driven by fate. "You told me once the hard decisions make us great," she said softly. "I would not forsake you for doing what you had to do. And you have saved the Crown Prince from his fate, for he never wanted to be Emperor."

He unclasped his hands and placed them over hers.

"Sometimes it is necessary to do questionable deeds to achieve what the heavens ordain," Xifeng said, thinking of all she herself had done. "But in our losses, we may gain ourselves. We take what is ours and find solace in the quiet places between death and destruction."

Jun turned, took her face between his hands, and kissed her. There was no passion in his embrace, such as she had felt with Wei. But his lips held a promise, as his gifts had. Xifeng took them for what they were worth—payment for the services she would deliver as his wife. It was business, a fair trade: he would give her a throne, and she would elevate his kingdom with her beauty and cunning. Their kiss sealed the pact.

The Emperor ran his thumb over her cheek. "You must have your own household and apartments, for your protection. The eunuchs will arrange the level below for your use."

The level below.

He hadn't even bothered to mention Lady Sun's name, and she approved.

The concubines and Empress Lihua were in the past, and Xifeng was his future.

40

The Empress went into labor on the day of the envoy's return. The first gong had struck for the morning meal, which everyone in the royal apartments ignored in their frenzy. Several eunuchs went to notify His Majesty, and the midwives set to work. They sent the ladies-in-waiting away, keeping only a few maidservants to bring boiling water and clean cloths.

Xifeng preferred to be away, anyhow. She bundled herself in furs and strolled on the walkway outside her apartments, where an army of eunuchs and craftsmen were still working. She had commanded them to destroy everything inside, especially the gilded tub, and bring in new furnishings. The Emperor had given her leave to commission whatever she liked, regardless of expense, and she wanted to erase every sign that Lady Sun had ever lived there.

She twisted her hands as she walked, instead of tucking them inside her robe. She couldn't understand her own anxiety. It was a clear, wintry day, the first time the sun had shown its face in a week. Her apartments would be finished soon. And Emperor Jun wanted her by his side at tomorrow night's banquet, as though she were already his wife.

"A beautiful day," she said out loud, but the words did not relieve her strange agitation.

There was something portentous about the lucid skies, the birdsong, and the smell of flowers on the air, though spring was but a half-forgotten memory in these depths of winter.

Guma had always said decisions came with responsibility. Every choice, no matter how small, had a consequence. The air held a certain resonance, such as she had felt when she had heard Lihua tell the story of the thousand lanterns for the first time. It was a feeling that something bigger than herself had taken hold. It felt like she had pushed a bale of hay down a hill, and no matter how she chased after it now, there would be no stopping it. She had made her choices and the consequences had begun, though she knew not what they might be.

Kang appeared in a robe of somber brown, befitting the monk-creature she knew him to be. "The envoy has been sighted at the gates of the Imperial City. Shall I accompany you?"

"Of course," she said lightly. She had grown used to the idea of his clever, unassuming disguise. Didn't she have one herself, in a way? She summoned two other eunuchs to trail after her as she strode across the Empress's walkway to the main palace.

"Are you all right?" Kang asked.

The unease she felt throbbed like an old injury, and she wondered if it had anything to do with her still-healing shoulder. "I'm perfectly well," she said, but by the time they reached the palace balcony and saw men and horses streaming through the gates, Xifeng could no longer deny that part of her anxiety had to do with the envoy.

Until this moment, she had not known she still harbored hope that

Wei would return. Perhaps it was fear, too, and an understanding that they could never go back to the way they were, now that he had taken her mother from her.

She watched soldiers dismount and talk and laugh, glad to be home after a long month away. She saw Hideki on his black Dagovadian horse, with Shiro behind him. She returned their greeting, but kept her eyes on the gate, scanning each face that entered. She waited, holding her breath, but there was no Wei. A chill entered her bones that had nothing to do with the winter air, and she thought she knew, at last, what true love felt like. Like the snapping jaws of an alligator trap, like a knife biting into the center of her heart. Like losing all of her lifeblood at once.

He had made real his threat. He had left her forever.

Shiro and Hideki approached and bowed to her, and she struggled to bestow a gracious smile upon them. "I'm delighted to see you both back safely," she said.

"I enjoyed the journey," Hideki said heartily. "But Shiro was impatient to get back."

Xifeng looked into Shiro's wide, questioning eyes. "Akira is doing well, my friend," she reassured him. "I sent Bohai's assistant to her twice every week. He gave her a tonic to help improve her appetite, and she's been sleeping better, too."

"Thank you, Xifeng," he said hoarsely. "If you'll excuse me, I will go to her now."

"You have my permission," she said, pleased, and he left at once.

Hideki's beard quivered. "I have something for you from Wei." He reached into the folds of his clothing and drew out an object wrapped in cotton. "He traveled with us midway through the Great Forest, then went west. He said he was going to seek peace."

Peace in my mother's death. Xifeng accepted the object, hating herself for hoping Guma's murderer would return. The cloth fell away to reveal a flat polished stone, rounded like the cap of a mushroom. It was the color of a mushroom, too, but when she regarded it more closely, she saw flecks of blue and gold and purple. It was beautiful as a fallen star.

Hideki watched her with eyes full of pity. "He found it in the ruins of a monastery and asked me to bring it back to you, to remember him by. I believe he means to become a monk."

She looked bitterly at the stone. "Wei, a monk? I can't imagine any place more unusual for him." The silence, the prayer, the plain meals. But he had always longed for simplicity, hadn't he? She had been the one who wanted more.

"There is something else. He sent this through a messenger later, when the envoy came back through the woods." And even before Hideki gave them to her, Xifeng knew what they would be: nineteen rectangles of fine gold wood, tied up in rough cloth, their etchings as familiar to her as the ridges of her own hands.

She closed her eyes and swayed as she gripped Guma's cards of fortune.

A barren field, a dying horse, a man with a knife in his back.

Hideki said her name, and his voice came from far away.

A lotus opening to the moon, a vindictive warrior, an Empress with her hair unbound.

"Xifeng?" Hideki repeated anxiously.

And a girl in disguise, with her eyes on the stars and vengeance in her heart . . .

"Guma would never have given up these cards if she were alive." Xifeng held the deck to her heart. Yet another person lost to her. Yet another who would not return.

Hideki fiddled with the hilt of his sword, shifting his weight from one foot to the other. "I'm sorry. Sometimes the ones we love leave us . . ."

". . . and sometimes we leave them," Xifeng interrupted, tucking the items into her robes. She didn't want to hear his platitudes of stale comfort, no matter how well meaning. Wei and Guma were gone, and that was that. "Do you still plan to return to Kamatsu in the spring?"

The soldier looked grateful for the change of subject. "I do. We have been too long away from home, and my heart yearns for the open sea. Shiro hopes to persuade Akira to raise the child there, and the seas will be calmer in the spring for a woman and a baby."

The image of them all sailing away together made Xifeng feel utterly alone. One happy family, and the final link to the girl she had been and would never be again. "We must have a banquet for you," she promised, with forced cheer. "You will be our guests of honor."

But even after they said goodbye and the eunuchs led her back to the city of women, the restlessness lingered. She took her needlework outside onto the balcony, hoping the glacial air would help her concentrate, but the unseasonable birdsong was so distracting, she gave up. She spent the afternoon pacing in the gardens instead, Wei's stone and Guma's cards weighing her down with every step.

That evening, Kang steered her to the banquet hall with gentle determination. "You must eat something. I haven't seen you take a meal all day."

"I'm not hungry," she returned, when a loud, crashing sound silenced the entire hall.

It was the banging of every gong in the city of women, a joyful, rhythmic beat they could hear echoing from the main palace as well. The clamor repeated five times in a pattern of five, and then there was quiet. Everyone seemed to be waiting. But minutes later, there was still nothing but silence, and activity and conversation resumed.

"A princess has been born," Kang murmured. "We would have heard fireworks if it had been a prince. Her Majesty must be beside herself with joy."

Xifeng remained silent as emotions warred within her. Underneath her resentment, she felt an unreasonable joy for Empress Lihua, who had wanted this child so desperately, and also despair, knowing how little time mother and daughter might have together. Xifeng had not touched a drop of poison, but the choice she had made—and the darkness to which she had bound her soul—might as well have been lacing the Empress's tonic herself.

A life for a life. The loss of Guma, for the loss of the Empress.

Mothers and their love, so easily gone.

One of the other ladies-in-waiting appeared at her elbow. "We're being summoned to Her Majesty's apartments, to pay respects to the Empress and her daughter."

"So she lingers on," Xifeng whispered. The Empress had not yet died of the poison or childbirth.

But when Xifeng saw her, she thought, *She might as well have*. The woman's face was drained of any beauty she had possessed. Though it was stark white against her silk pillows, she wore an expression of pure bliss. She held a small, moving bundle that emitted a tiny wail. The covers on the bed were clean; servants moved quietly around with rumpled sheets in their arms.

Madam Hong lit sticks of clove incense and handed one to each lady kneeling before Her Majesty. She led the group in a brief prayer for the health and good fortune of the princess, and though the Empress smiled, her eyes never left the child in her arms.

"Blessings and congratulations upon Your Majesty and Her Highness," they murmured.

Empress Lihua spoke in a fragile voice barely above a whisper. "Thank you for your good wishes. I feel as though I've woken from a dream and found myself in the heavens." She smiled again, and Xifeng realized she was wrong. Lihua's beauty had not vanished. Her loveliness was still there, but in paler, quieter colors, a smoke-gray autumn in place of a summer long gone. "I am the mother of a daughter I have wished for endlessly. We've been apart for all my life, dearest one, but now you've made my existence complete. The gods are good."

Gently, the Empress shifted so they could see the new princess of Feng Lu. Beyond the edge of the blanket, Xifeng saw a pale, round face with chubby cheeks and eyes pinched shut above tiny red lips. The tips of a few precious fingers emerged from the blanket, cunningly formed, and a shock of night-dark hair lay flat against her wrinkled forehead.

"This is Jade." Empress Lihua beamed down at her daughter. "White Jade, because she is so perfect and precious to me. How her skin glows like the winter snow."

"She is beautiful, Your Majesty," Madam Hong said, and for the first time, Xifeng heard emotion in her hoarse, cross voice. "A princess royal in every way."

The eunuch at the door announced Emperor Jun, who strode into the room. Though his handsome face was careworn, his eyes were bright as he bent over his wife and child. He spoke some quiet words to Lihua, running a finger over the baby's feather-smooth cheek.

For a moment, Xifeng imagined herself in the Empress's place, but instead holding a tiny son, a royal prince of her bloodline. She had never imagined being a mother before—babies seemed too helpless, too needy—and yet she could see herself in that bed with Jun grinning down at her, his *wife,* his *Empress.* Her child would be the trueborn, legitimate son of his blood that he longed for. He would insist on staying with them all day, no matter what pressing business he had at hand, and not lose interest as he did now. He had already turned away from Lihua and Jade after a final caress.

"Continue to bring me news of Her Majesty's health," he commanded a eunuch, who flung himself upon the ground, and left the room.

The Empress seemed blissfully unaware of his indifference or of the ladies-in-waiting flocking out of the room. Xifeng watched her with her daughter for a moment longer, drawn to the way they seemed to breathe together. Her heart tugged with the old ache, the longing for that kind of pure, wholehearted love that need not be hidden and asked for nothing in return. Princess Jade had done nothing—she had merely been born, and already she had a powerful father and a mother who would die for her. She had Lihua's love and Lihua's royal blood, and Xifeng would never have that, no matter how many hearts she took.

All the things I've had to do to get here, she thought, with a sudden maddening hatred. She had lied and lost, cheated and killed, and this tiny, helpless weakling had simply been born a princess.

Lihua lifted her head abruptly, seeming to hear her thoughts. Her serene face was jarringly different from that of the screaming woman who had accused her of poison. "Xifeng, I'd like to speak to you a moment. I was very ill last week. I didn't know what I was saying."

"Your Majesty does not need to apologize . . ."

"I am not apologizing," the Empress said with a small smile. "I've felt for some time that you don't regard me as you once did." Her eyes ran over Xifeng's face, then quickly returned to her baby, as though cleansing her gaze with the tiny form. "But I hope whatever you hold against me will not be transferred to my Jade. I'm aware His Majesty will likely choose you for his wife when I am dead."

Xifeng started, shocked by her bluntness.

"You are surprised. You assume because I am gentle and delicate that I am also silly and spineless, and do not notice everything around me. My parents made the same mistake. Yes, Xifeng, I know the Emperor is serious about you. He would have tired of you long ago if you had merely wanted to go to his bed."

Xifeng remained silent, watching her stroke the baby's small, perfect fingers.

"It was a difficult birth," Empress Lihua said. "I am not long for this world, nor do I ask for your promise to love my daughter. But I can hope you will be good to her."

Yes, you can hope. What use would Xifeng have for a dead queen's useless daughter once she gave birth to her own sons?

The Empress regarded her once more. For that brief moment, Xifeng saw that what she had mistaken for weakness might have been a quiet strength instead. "I will always be with Jade, watching over her," Lihua said quietly. "If the gods see fit to grant it, I will know whose hearts hold good intentions and I will steer her from evil."

It was a threat, and Xifeng took it as such. She did not bow as she swept from the room, but the Empress could hardly care now. Jun was too far gone, too enamored with Xifeng to ever look at his wife again—but Lihua had her daughter, and that was all that mattered to her. She had already turned back to Jade's tiny face as though she could see the clouds of the heavens there.

"A long time ago, when dragons walked the earth," Xifeng heard her say to the baby, "there lived a queen who loved her daughter more than all the jewels of her court . . ."

Outside, a magnificent dark blue sky had swept over the world.

The thousand stars that danced across its face glittered as though in celebration, but Xifeng kept her head down, so she wouldn't have to see what she could not have.

41

Empress Lihua lingered on for two years.

Two years in which she became a ghost of a queen, living a faded life behind the closed doors of her bedchamber. She received only her daughter, the nursemaid, and Bohai, who never discovered how she had been poisoned, but determined that the metal of her cup had leached out most of the toxin given to her. It bought her precious time with Jade, during which the baby grew into a healthy, happy-hearted girl who adored her mother and seemed to understand every word said to her. She spent each evening with the Empress, hearing the story of the princess and the lover who had hung one thousand lanterns in the forest to light her way to him.

Xifeng was too preoccupied to care much about either of them. She spent her days at Emperor Jun's side, attending court functions as his unofficial consort. The youngest prince had died of his illness, and the Crown Prince had not been heard from in over a year. The need for Xifeng to provide a new heir grew more pressing with each day, but still the Emperor did not hasten their marriage. He was an unfeeling scoundrel whenever it suited him, but he insisted upon honoring Lihua as Empress for as long as she lived, and would take no other until her death. Perhaps he feared the Dragon Lords' wrath.

Xifeng told herself to be content, knowing it would not be long. The Empress was no longer a threat to her, and Jun barely cared about his daughter. She was happy to let them rot away together in that chamber of death. She had not been in Lihua's heart all these long years, so she didn't bother keeping Lihua in hers.

So it was that in the spring of Jade's third year, when the Empress slipped quietly away to join her forefathers in the Dragon Lords' heavenly palace, she and Xifeng had not exchanged a word since the princess's birth. Xifeng had been at a banquet and unable to say goodbye, though she almost wished she'd had the chance. There was something unfinished about not saying farewell, like a door left open in the chill night.

She abandoned her bed late that evening, unable to sleep. She passed chrysanthemums, lanterns, and flowing cloths on every surface, pearl-white to mourn Lihua's passing. Sticks of incense lay against each door, emitting strands of smoke that smelled of anise, cloves, and cinnamon to help bid her spirit farewell on her journey to the skies. White jasmine perfumed the air, too, for they had been Lihua's favorite flowers. Their scent made Xifeng almost believe she might turn around and see the Empress as she had once been, gentle and elegant. The rightful queen.

No, she corrected herself, for there was only one rightful queen now.

In the shrine, she lit a candle in Lihua's honor and placed it on the altar, bowing her head.

"Forgive me," she whispered, "for once I was like a daughter to you."

She imagined the Empress's spirit watching and listening on its ascent to the heavens.

On her way back, she paused by the railing over the gardens. In the afternoons, it was common now to see Ama, the old nursemaid, hobbling there after a little girl with eyes like the stars themselves. Jade, a princess. Motherless, as Xifeng was, and now the Emperor's only living child at court.

That will change, Xifeng vowed.

The girl and her nursemaid would be sent away at the first opportunity. A poor village somewhere, to teach her humility, or perhaps a monastery. It didn't matter, as long as the memory of her faded in both Xifeng and Jun's minds. The Emperor would agree with whatever Xifeng decided for the girl. Jade belonged to the past, and she would be forgotten as soon as Xifeng gave Jun his legitimate sons. Princes of the blood, robust and healthy boys a thousand times more valuable than one worthless princess.

In one year's time, when the period of mourning was fully over, the enthroning ceremony would be held in the heart of the palace.

In one year's time, Xifeng would be crowned Empress of Feng Lu.

Xifeng found the Emperor already dressed and waiting for her when she came to his chamber. He looked magnificent in robes of red and gold, the Imperial headdress adorning his proud head. The servants respectfully stepped back ten paces to allow him and Xifeng privacy.

She had dressed tonight with greater care than usual, which meant she had been preparing for the banquet since the early morning hours. It was the Festival of the Summer Moon, the first celebration at which she was not a lady-in-waiting, but the Empress-to-be. She had chosen a silk as red as fire, with exquisite gold embroidery at the wrapped collar, hem, and sleeves.

His eyes caressed her face. "You are the image of a true queen."

"Your Majesty." Xifeng bowed, fully aware of how her silks caught the light, giving the impression of flames curling around her body. Her women had agreed it was a stunning effect, especially with the Empress's emblem worked in metallic gold thread on her back: a phoenix rising to the heavens, its tail burning a trail of brushed satin flames down the train of her skirt.

Jun touched the gold-and-ivory pin she wore in her hair. "I remember this. It was one of my first gifts to you. It suits you, but then a beauty like yours can wear anything."

She beamed at him. She knew how striking she was, with frost-white flowers blossoming in her hair, their simplicity suiting the gold dust dotted on her eyes and on the center of her blood-red lips. There was no need to pretend modesty, and Jun knew it well. He too was full of youth, beauty, and vitality—they were two sides of the same coin.

The Emperor lifted her chin. "I am proud to have you by my side."

"I am proud to be here," she said, taking his hand in both of hers. "I am yours to command. Your happiness is the chief pursuit of my life."

"And yours, mine." His thumb stroked her fingers, light as a nightingale's wing, and she felt a tingle at the base of her spine. She still kept up the guise of a virtuous maiden, but she knew he would be a skilled lover when the time came. His fingers tightened around hers and his face sobered as he added, "Before we go, I'd like to speak to you about my daughter."

Xifeng blinked. It had been almost a year since the girl and her nursemaid had left court and Jun had never brought her up in Xifeng's presence before. "Of course. What would you like to discuss?"

He perched on the edge of the table, still holding her hand. "Ama, the nursemaid, has sent word to say the princess is happy and thriving in the monastery, though she misses being in the forest. She is her mother's daughter, after all."

"Naturally."

He cleared his throat. "She is her mother's daughter and I must honor Lihua's dying wish for her. She was adamant that Jade be added to the line of succession. I saw no reason to argue."

Something seized up inside Xifeng like a clenched fist.

"There have been female regents in the past," Jun continued. "My ministers tell me royal daughters have never been pronounced heirs before the age of twenty. This gave their parents time to determine their ability to rule. So this is a special case, as Jade is not yet three."

It was a bold, daring request, and for a moment Xifeng was rendered speechless by Lihua's audacity. *In weakness, you find your strength,* the former Empress had once said. Even on her deathbed, slowly withering away from the effects of Kang's poison, she had rallied her spirits to secure the throne for her beloved child—the last of the line of trueborn Dragon Kings.

"I know this displeases you, my love, but let me remind and assure you that our own children will take precedence. They will be the sons of my living Empress, after all," Jun said, his eyes searching her face anxiously. "We are young and healthy, and I've no doubt you will give me many heirs of my blood. This little wish of Lihua's will have no bearing on us at all."

He spoke as though the death of the Crown Prince was already a certainty. Xifeng supposed it might seem callous to anyone else, but she brought his fingers to her lips, touched by his confidence. He, too, had every certainty she would secure her position immediately, and she knew the worship in his eyes would grow stronger once she did.

Emperor Jun was like other men, after all, so sure of his superiority he didn't realize how easy it would be for her to control him. To plant *her* son on the throne and make use of the Serpent God's power, ensuring her bloodline would control the kingdom forever.

"Well, then," she said, glancing at him through her lashes, "I look forward to the day I may present you with a prince."

She held her head high as they strode to the banquet hall, hand in hand. The court rose and bowed as one. A young eunuch dropped to his knees with elaborate flourishes of his hands.

"Their Majesties, the Emperor and Empress of Feng Lu!" he announced.

Xifeng heard a few gasps and murmurs, for the mourning period for Lihua was still ongoing. But Jun did not seem bothered by the young eunuch's error as he led her to their table.

The Empress of Feng Lu. The words seemed to echo as she walked, making sure to meet courtiers in the eye with her shoulders held back. She tipped her head as though it already wore a heavy crown, enjoying the flurry of admiration as she strode beside the Emperor, her ladies trailing after her like geese around an imperious swan. Her hair like night, her skin like dawn. One glance from her eyes made gazes drop instantly in respect.

Servants swarmed out in a great rush to serve the meal, and after that, there was music and dancing from some of the ladies-in-waiting.

A familiar form approached their table: Shiro, handsome as ever, though his hair held a few touches of gray and his face was more care-worn than Xifeng remembered it. He held the hand of a little boy about Jade's age, with a bright, intelligent look to him. The child's eyes clearly came from his mother, Akira, but he had inherited his father's diminutive height and short limbs. He would be handsome like Shiro, and also a dwarf.

The former ambassador to Kamatsu bowed to Jun and Xifeng. "Your Majesty, Madam Xifeng. May I present my son, Koichi." He whispered to the child, who fixed his appealing eyes on the Emperor and bent formally at the waist.

Jun looked delighted. "A splendid child, Shiro. Will he come to me?"

The boy stared wide-eyed at the Emperor's open arms. Upon encouragement from his father, he toddled forward on his plump little legs and allowed Jun to place him upon his knee. He darted a timid glance at Xifeng.

"This is the Empress, little one," the Emperor told him, and Shiro raised his eyebrows but said nothing. "You think her lovely, don't you? You can't take your eyes from her, and neither can any other man in this room."

Xifeng gave a soft laugh of thanks, but she felt disconcerted under the child's unwavering stare. Yes, he most certainly shared his eyes with his mother—they even held the relentless judgment Xifeng remembered in Akira's. She sipped her sweet rice wine to hide her discomfort. When she turned back, Koichi had already warmed up to Jun and held out a small wooden toy.

"There, we're friends already." The Emperor was the image of a doting father as he accepted the toy, making sounds as he pushed it across the tabletop for the boy's amusement.

"A glimpse into your future, perhaps," Shiro said to Xifeng, who smiled graciously.

"How are you, my friend? You look well."

"Not as well as you do. You'll be one of those beautiful women who never seem to age," he said gallantly, though his eyes held no joy. "I'm well enough. Blessed to have my boy, though I never imagined I'd have to raise him alone."

Xifeng touched his hand in sympathy. "I lit a candle for Akira in the shrine yesterday. Has it truly been two years since she passed away?"

"It seems an age." Shiro sighed. "Is it silly of me to stay instead of bringing my son home to Kamatsu? Hideki writes often, urging me to return. Our king is displeased with me for resigning. But I have nothing there. My family has never cared about me and I feel closer to Akira here." He watched Jun lift a giggling Koichi into the air. "I'd like my boy to be close to his mother."

"Then it is not silly. You must do what your heart feels is right. And you have a home and a good position here among His Majesty's ministers."

"And you? Does your heart feel this is right?" He lifted an open hand, indicating the opulent court, the banquet tables groaning under the weight of food, and the music and dancing.

Xifeng watched as Koichi ran the little wooden toy along the Emperor's sleeve. "I once feared I had no heart left," she said quietly. "But I hear it speaking to me from time to time, and I believe this is what it wants. A place where I belong."

Shiro's keen eyes observed her for a moment, and he looked as if he wanted to say something else. But his small son ran to him, throwing his arms around his father's neck, and Shiro grinned instead. "Thank you for your indulgence with my rowdy boy, Your Majesty."

"You're a lucky man, Shiro." Jun glanced sideways at Xifeng. "And so am I."

The former ambassador inclined his head before returning to his table, still carrying his son. Xifeng watched him go, feeling both comforted and self-conscious in his presence. What must he think of her, to have so quickly attached herself to another man when Wei had loved her all his life?

But that is the privilege of an Empress, she decided. *I can do as I like, and nothing anyone else thinks truly matters.*

All evening, every person who approached to bow to the Emperor acknowledged Xifeng as his Empress. Not a single one mentioned or seemed to remember Lihua, and as triumphant as she felt, Xifeng couldn't help feeling regret for the woman she had once esteemed. She thought daily of Lihua's promise to always watch over Jade and steer her from evil.

But she can't be unhappy about where I sent the girl, she thought. The monastery was on the southern edge of the Great Forest, close to Serpents' Bay. Surely Lihua would have approved of the beauty and splendor of the location, so suitable for the devout.

And it was the way of the world, was it not? The old dragon died to make way for the new, and the sun set to rise again on another day. Lihua's time had passed, and a brilliant dawn had begun at the court of the Emperor, a dawn as glorious as the cards had promised.

All Xifeng had left to do was wait for the night to pass.

42

The ladies-in-waiting woke her before sunrise on a warm spring morning. Xifeng followed them into the bath chamber, where the servants had filled her porcelain tub with fresh water from the Great Forest, heated until piping hot. The steam rose in translucent swirls, making her smile as she thought of another bath she would have tonight in the hot springs, when all the court believed her to be fast asleep in His Majesty's arms.

She stepped into the tub, relishing the heat of the water. Her women poured lotions and tonics over her skin: attar of night-blooming desert roses from Surjalana, lily-water pressed from a thousand white virgin blooms, and creamy milks to smooth her skin. It was a ceremonial bath intended to wash away her impurities and fully immerse her in the waters of her kingdom. Xifeng emerged, dripping and bright pink from the scalding water, thinking her body certainly felt cleansed. As for impurities . . . well, that remained to be seen.

She sat comfortably in a gilded chair while her ladies powdered her skin with fragrant rose-gold dust, making her gleam in the light like an ancient goddess. They attended to her hands, placing long, lethal-looking nail guards of pure gold on each finger, and pinned her inky hair into an elaborate display. She chose a dozen priceless ornaments to complete her ensemble: combs of glinting gold, fresh yellow flowers twisted around jeweled hairpins, forest-green jade brooches, and a few pieces of enameled ivory, which had been in Lihua's family for generations.

Her wardrobe was equally resplendent: the finest woven silks in every shade of crimson and saffron, rich hues befitting the most powerful woman on the continent. The materials draped beautifully over her body and trailed after her in a shimmering wake, ensuring no lady-in-waiting would be able to walk closer than ten feet behind her.

Today, Xifeng would walk alone.

Kang and two court officials came when she was fully dressed. They led her and her cluster of ladies and eunuchs across the Empress's walkway to the center of the Imperial Palace. Her hair ornaments made a lovely, bell-like sound as she moved, the swishing of her silks like a river flowing to its destination. The procession arrived at the gates of the throne room, from which Xifeng could hear a low hush of voices.

One of the officials handed her a stick of sandalwood with a flame on one end. Pots of fragrant incense had been laid in a long line, starting from the door and leading all the way to the throne that would be hers. Beside each pot was a relic or likeness of one of the Dragon Lords. Xifeng bowed to each one, murmuring a short prayer she had learned in the weeks leading up to this ceremony, then lit the incense. This took some time, as there were dozens of pots lining the luscious crimson carpet that stretched deep inside the throne room.

Emperor Jun awaited her there, sitting on the larger of two gold thrones that shimmered in the sunlight. Xifeng finished lighting the last of the incense and handed the stick back to a court official. She lifted the hem of her robes and carefully ascended three of the nine steps leading up to the thrones, kneeling on the scarlet pillow. She lowered her forehead to the step above hers, hearing the Emperor's gold robes rustle as he rose from his seat. The entire court fell silent as he intoned a solemn prayer to the Dragon Lords.

"We swear to serve you by the rising of the sun, by the gleaming of the moon. We are your children and your heart, and you are our life-blood and the very air we breathe," Jun said gravely, ending the prayer. "In your wisdom and magnificence, we hold faith."

"In your wisdom and magnificence, we hold faith," the court murmured.

Xifeng rose, and an official moved the pillow up three steps, at which she knelt once more. This time, the Emperor's chief adviser recited a prayer. When he had finished his oration, Xifeng ascended to the top of the platform, where she knelt directly in front of the Emperor.

"I give Feng Lu and the Kingdom of the Great Forest an Empress who will serve with all she has." He lifted the elaborate crown that rested on the throne beside his. It consisted of a thick ring of pure gold, with five jagged points topped with priceless jewels. "I give Feng Lu and the Kingdom of the Great Forest a queen who is a daughter of the trees and the wind." The weight of the gold touched her head, then rested heavily upon it. "Rise, my Empress, and rule at my side."

The eunuchs, ministers, and courtiers sang in a low chant as she rose, and one of the officials murmured a fervent prayer as he and several others scattered jasmine buds over her.

The Emperor and Empress each knelt and bowed nine times to the thrones.

Xifeng caught Jun's eye as they both rose once more, and saw the corner of his mouth lift. They sat side by side upon the golden thrones as the court continued chanting and the official continued praying.

The ceremony lasted for hours more, with music and speeches and a procession given by the noble children of the court. But Xifeng felt as if she could have sat on that throne at the Emperor's side forever. She felt the weight of the crown upon her head and the cool gold of the throne beneath her, and as she surveyed the court around them, she felt a lightness in her, a certainty that she had never belonged anywhere more.

At last, at last, the wind seemed to sing in the trees outside.

The court moved to the banquet hall for the great meal. After all of the solemn prayers and speeches, the mood was much lighter, more joyous.

Xifeng felt that when people bowed and made respectful speeches to her that they might have actually meant them. She smiled at Jun, who grinned broadly back at her, and she could have cried for the girl she had once been.

That girl had feared, above all, a life of imprisonment in Guma's dreary town, a life in which the fortune of the cards had gone to waste. That girl had once crossed the Great Forest and met a *tengaru* queen who had seen her as more than she was. That girl had once loved a poor boy as much as she could love anyone, and dreamed of a life in the sun somewhere far away.

Now she wore the crown of the Imperial Empress upon her brow.

Now she slipped her hand into the hand of the most powerful man on the continent.

Now she watched as the court ate and drank, danced and sang, in her honor. Hers alone.

The Emperor's last remaining stepson had been sent to his death in a faraway land. The Emperor's daughter had been exiled to lead an existence for which Xifeng cared nothing. And as for the two favored concubines, she had destroyed them both. Jun had sent away every last concubine belonging to Lihua's first husband and vowed never to take another, for there was nothing he wouldn't do for his beautiful new Empress.

She reigned supreme, and there was no one, absolutely no one, left to challenge her.

Was it any wonder that after the festivities, Xifeng retired to the Emperor's chambers with a heart as light as she had ever known? Jun waited for her in the vast, magnificent room lit by a hundred red candles, on the mammoth bed draped with fresh peonies. She enjoyed his eyes on her in these moments before, taking her time in letting down her hair and pulling each rich ornament from it, like jewels adrift from a black river. She ran her fingers through the strands, humming as she slipped on a robe the color of desert sand, so fine it was almost transparent. In the full-length bronze mirror, her soft, bare body looked like a gold-and-peach fruit wrapped delicately in a webbed skin.

On her way to Jun, she paused at the windows to enjoy the sight of the forest kingdom—*her* forest kingdom. Her first night as the Empress of all these lands, as the mistress of every twig, leaf, and branch, and every singing stream and cave and mountain.

But it was not the cool, clean night air of an early spring that greeted her. It was not the whispering treetops of a peaceful dark wood settling into sleep. It was not a placid midnight sky dusted over with the stars, the eyes of the heavens.

It was not just those.

For the Great Forest was ablaze with a strange and fearsome light.

In the courtyard below, she heard the hum of people rushing outside to look at the trees. They pointed and shouted to each other at the mystical, extraordinary sight, their voices filled with confusion and awe as they swiveled their heads.

Xifeng held a hand to her heart as she stared, and the lanterns seemed to stare back at her: one thousand glittering, dazzling white lanterns that had somehow found themselves hanging in the trees of the Great Forest. They clung to the topmost branches, too high for any human to ever climb, and swung joyfully in the breeze, their light reflecting infinitely off the leaves, turning each tree into an enormous lantern in its own right.

And she knew, as surely as if Empress Lihua's spirit had appeared before her and spoken to her, that these were the thousand lanterns that vowed to a lonely princess that love and justice still awaited her. These were the thousand lanterns hung by one whose love endured even in death, in loss, and in defeat, whose unwavering devotion would lead the way. These were the thousand lanterns of a mere fable, a story told by a sad-eyed queen whose time to die had come.

The lanterns glowed in Xifeng's eyes, and they shone in all their ominous beauty.

ACKNOWLEDGMENTS

However often I dreamed of this moment, there were times I honestly never thought I'd get here. As the saying goes, "it takes a village," and it's thanks to a great number of people that I kept going.

First and foremost, I want to extend love and gratitude to my family, especially my mom, Mai, to whom this book is dedicated. Her support these past few years has meant everything to me and her generosity and encouragement helped this book finally get written. Thank you for being the kind of mother whose love inspires an entire book series. To Jon and Justin, my favorite brothers and personal cheerleaders: thanks for the laughs and for always believing in me! I love you guys!

Lots of people brag about their agents, but I don't think it's exaggerating at all to say that Tamar Rydzinski is a rock star. Two years ago, she saw something in me that no one else did. It's because of her that my dream came true, and I trust, respect, and admire her with all my heart and soul. Thanks for fighting for me, Tamar, and being my advocate and friend through every struggle and triumph! Thank you also to Laura Dail, everyone at LDLA (especially the fabulous interns who read my book), and my film agents, Jon Cassir and Sarah Luciano at CAA.

This book would not exist in its current form without Brian Geffen, my wise and brilliant editor, who loved and understood Xifeng from the very first. His sharp eye and unflinching honesty made my story what it is today, and his kindness and patience helped smooth the rocky transition to authorhood. I'm proud to call you my editor, Brian, and also my friend! And thank you to the wonderful folks at Philomel Books and Penguin Young Readers for their hard work and support, especially Michael Green, my Publisher; Laurel Robinson and Janet Rosenberg, my copyeditors; Jennifer Chung, my interior book designer; Lindsey Andrews, my cover designer; and Jacey, my cover artist.

I've been blessed with the most wonderful group of writer friends: Marisa Hopkins, who has been there for me since day one and whose cheer and gorgeous artwork keep me going; Melody Marshall, my dear Frodo, with whom I would gladly climb Mount Doom again and again; Erin Fletcher, whose optimism and friendship I cherish; Dianne Salerni, a true-blue mentor I can count on for sound advice; and Lola Alessi, whose talent and beautiful spirit brighten my darkest days. I love you all very dearly.

Thank you to Brenda Drake and the Pitch Wars community, who inspire me to pay it forward every chance I get. Brenda's contests not only brought Tamar into my life, but also two important friends and mentors: Stephanie Garber and N. K. Traver, who nurtured me from baby writer to full-fledged author with pep talks, wise counsel, and shoulders to cry on. Steph and Nat, we've been through a lot together, but you always believed this day would come for me. You are my heroes.

Much love to everyone in the blogging community, who are too many to name but no less dear to me. In particular, thanks to my earliest critique partners, Sierra Godfrey and Don Hammons, for giving me the push I needed to begin.

If the writing community were Hogwarts, the Kidlit Authors of Color group would be Gryffindor House, hands down. They are the most courageous people I know and fight the good fight every single day, educating others about diversity in publishing. A special shout-out to Tara Sim, Heidi Heilig, Angie Thomas, Kaye M., Claribel Ortega, Shveta Thakrar, Meredith Ireland, Cindy Pon, Lori Lee, S. Jae-Jones, and Catrina Lim, who are women I want to be like when I grow up.

Endless gratitude to: Emily X. R. Pan, Wendy Xu, and Eileen Lee for looking over my Chinese name pronuniciations, Alice Fanchiang for her beta read and her wonderful friendship over the years, and C. B. Lee and Riley Redgate, my thoughtful and astute sensitivity readers. They all did a marvelous job helping me unveil the world of Feng Lu in a careful, culturally respectful manner.

Thanks also go to: my Ireland Writer Tours friends, especially the inimitable Susan Spann, who gave me the idea for the last scene in the book; the folks on Twitter who keep me afloat every day with their kindness, particularly Erin Bay, Akshaya Raman, Janella Angeles, Kat Cho, and Patrice Caldwell; and my beloved Lucky 13s, including Heather Kaczynski, Austin Gilkeson, Mara Fitzgerald, Jess Rubinkowski, Rebecca Caprara, Kati Gardner, Jordan Villegas, and Kevin van Whye.

Hugs and thanks to all of the saintly people who listened to me rant and vent along the way. They are too many to name, but notably include: Nancy Bruckman, who supplied me with ARCs, publishing expertise, and positivity; Alegria and Matt Cohen, who never forget to ask how my writing is going; Patrick Long, for the advice and support you gave me during our lunch dates on the quad; Johanne Osias Bernard, Will Bernard, and Megan Benjaa, who rooted for me all the way and wholeheartedly embraced my stories; and Theresa "TC" Baker, who has been my friend since the third grade, for reading and loving my previous manuscripts.

To my Wattpad readers, who cheered me on and never doubted I would one day have a book on the shelves: I treasure all of your comments and cannot wait to meet you guys someday soon!

Last, to all young writers, especially those who don't have the support they need: you are magic, you are the future. Never let anyone stop you from dreaming big. This world craves your stories.

Julie C. Dao is the critically acclaimed author of many books from Disney, Macmillan, Penguin Random House, and more. Her novels have earned starred reviews from Booklist, School Library Journal and Publishers Weekly and won recognition from the Junior Library Guild and the American Library Association. A proud Vietnamese-American who was born in upstate New York, she now lives in New England.